I0583367
CLASH
OF
CLAWS
ELIZABETH DEAR

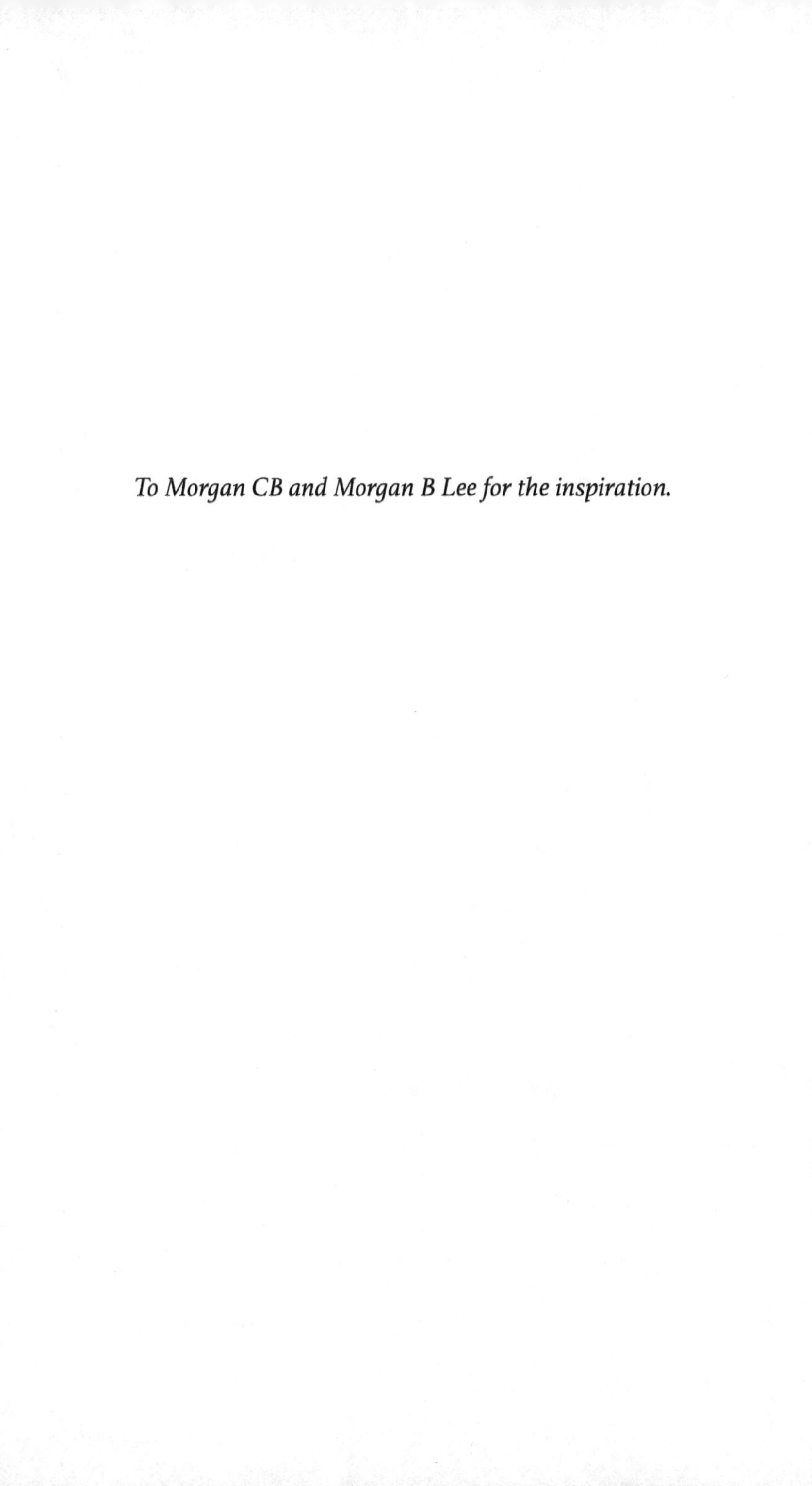

To Morgan CB and Morgan B Lee for the inspiration.

SYNOPSIS

In the world of the shifter elite, a safe female is one without power. For me, that means hide or die.

When wraiths invade my neighborhood and shit goes sideways, becoming a Guardian might be the only way to earn myself—and my beast—protection.

The elite training program begins at the local shifter college, so I pack up my swords and my brother, and off to school I go.

It's no surprise that Guardian training is sexist as hell. But I didn't expect to be trapped inside the campus walls, battling magical simulations rather than joining the real forces as they wage war on the monsters outside.

For me, the stakes are higher than bragging rights and points on the leaderboard.

I won't be distracted, especially not by the pull I feel to the most powerful quad of males in the program.

Heath Blackwell, the dominant Alpha wolf and quad leader;

Wyatt Gale, the cocky playboy bear shifter;

Aiden Blackwell, the uptight jaguar who's also my professor;

And **Elijah Harrow**, the terrifying yet entrancing basilisk.

I'll fight this infuriating attraction because I know the score. Powerful quads want a central bond, and that will never be my future.

Become a Guardian. Stay alive. Nothing else matters.

This is a paranormal romance set at a supernatural college in present-day USA. It is a "why choose" romance, which means our heroine will have multiple love interests and will get her happily ever after with ALL of them by the end of the series. This is book 1 of 3, and it will end in a cliffhanger. It is intended for readers aged 18+ and contains foul language and spicy scenes. Detailed content warnings can be found in the Author's Note. Happy reading!

A NOTE FROM THE AUTHOR

Hey there! Thanks so much for picking up this book and giving it a go. If you're an ED vet, the vibes should be familiar—badass girl, academy, brother, strong family, healthy mix of action plot and spice, slow burn. If you're new to me, hi and welcome! I know that you have a bottomless buffet of choices as to what to read, so thank you for giving me a chance.

A few content notes below, and then we can dive into Avery's adventures.

This is a shifter romance set in the modern world that has some fantasy vibes. There are swords, magic, and monsters, but there are also cars, cell phones, and the internet. Our setting is a supernatural college, and all our main characters are in their early twenties.

This is also a "why choose" romance, which means our heroine will have multiple love interests (four to be exact) and she will not have to choose between them. Our heroes have deep brotherly platonic love for one another and are only romantically involved with the heroine.

There is quite a bit of fantasy violence in this series and

what I might consider a mild horror element. There are themes of bullying and shifter-style hazing, but not from the love interests. Also, our heroine is very tough, so she's pretty hard to bully.

There are several main characters with parental death in their backstory, and there is brief mention of infertility issues affecting a certain segment of society at large.

Also, there's a snake. He's a friendly guy, but I understand if that's really not your thing.

This series is intended to be a trilogy, so each book will end on a cliffhanger until our HEA at the end of the third book.

There are detailed and spicy love scenes, including group scenes later in the series. Our characters also enjoy a swear word. This series is intended for adults 18+ only.

Thank you for coming on this journey with me, and I hope you enjoy the ride.

- Elizabeth

1

AVERY

"Your beast was seen."

I looked up from where I was scratching away some dried blood that lingered on my thigh. Dad leaned against the heavy door of my hospital room, his broad shoulders hardly fitting within the frame. He wore a look of concerned resignation as he raked a hand through his thick brown hair, the room's harsh fluorescent lights illuminating the tired lines of his face.

"I'm not surprised," I said. "It was a loud and conspicuous fight. Who was it?"

"The Martins. They were walking their dog down the street from where Ian found you."

Damn it. I blew out a breath, slumping where I sat cross-legged on top of the itchy bed covers. My leg, which had been nearly shredded to pieces earlier in the night, had healed almost completely, with only jagged pink scars marring my skin. Those would disappear in a week or two, hopefully.

Since I was no longer on the brink of death, I'd been

allowed out of my hospital gown and wore a baggy sweat-shirt and pajama shorts. The needle of my IV drip was still buried in my hand. I'd fought an extremely surly nurse to have that removed and lost.

"And you think *they* might cause us trouble?" I asked.

The Martins were middle-aged, soft-spoken, and had seemed kind in the few interactions I'd had with them. Mr. Martin was a minor shifter of some kind, and I assumed his wife was latent, as most females were. Not the type to stick their noses in the business of Primes.

"I don't know," Dad replied. "But Daniel Martin has a well-connected brother who lives up in the Hills. You're a rarity, and it's not hard to imagine that he might mention what he saw. Who knows where that information could go within the shifter community and what might be done with it."

"You're being paranoid," I replied with a dismissive wave. "And it's not like I had any other choice. I *had* to shift."

My beast half, who was sleepy and quiet as I healed, gave a little growl of pride. She didn't get to come out often, but we'd held our own against some shitty odds tonight.

He swallowed roughly. "I know, honey. We're lucky Ian arrived when he did."

Ian, my younger brother by thirteen months, sat in the single plastic chair next to my bed. His katana was in his lap, and he was also babysitting my two wakizashi blades. He'd tucked them neatly into their sheaths, which were attached to the vinyl harness I wore like a backpack when I was out on patrol. They hung over the arm of his chair, a little too far out of my reach for my comfort.

Ian hadn't moved from that spot since I'd been brought in, apparently, and he glared at me, his usual devil-may-care smile nowhere to be seen. "Yes, it was indeed lucky for me to stumble upon my sister, shifted into her beast and bleeding all over the street, as she fought two wraiths, *alone*, that were definitely a Ripper and probably a fucking Giant."

I'd had to shift because that Giant had destroyed my leg. I'd needed to heal, and quickly. I'd managed to tear up the wraiths, first with my blades and then with my claws, just enough that they'd weakened by the time Ian arrived. He was able to get his blade through both of their necks with what little help I'd had left to give.

"I'm sorry," I told him. "We'd cleared the block, and we hadn't seen anything besides swarmers all night." I looked at Dad. "What the hell were wraiths like that doing all the way down here in the city?"

"I have no idea," he replied. "Joseph and Kai ran the entire block again after we moved you, but they didn't find anything else."

My stomach swooped at that news. My other dads were deadly with their blades, but if they had run into more wraiths of the caliber that'd attacked me, they'd have been in quite the pinch without Rand—the dad that was currently scowling at me from the doorway—on hand to throw his beast into the fight.

Kai's cougar was vicious, but he wasn't very large, and Joseph shifted into a fox, which was no good in a fight with most wraiths. Rand's beast was a mighty Alpha wolf and a true Prime on the power scale, but he'd been occupied carrying me five blocks to the only small inpatient facility in the city that was run and staffed by shifters.

Or so they'd told me. I'd passed right out after Ian had cleaved the last monster's head off.

"Did those two bastards kill anyone before they found me?" I asked.

Dad nodded, his face grim. "Two. No one we know. They're in the small morgue in the basement."

How moondamned terrible. It wasn't the first time—and it wouldn't be the last—that the wraiths managed to kill those of us who lived here in the city, away from the shifter communities, but my family and a few others had been doing our best to keep the casualties to a minimum.

No one else was going to do it, since the Guardians couldn't be bothered to patrol this close to the city.

"And we'll find out over the next few days if they managed to get to any humans," Dad added. "There were a few revelers out and about."

What a disaster this night had been. Ian and I had easily eliminated a small horde of swarmers that'd made their way into our neighborhood, and my dads had cleared another batch of them, along with a weak Ripper. It'd been quiet after that, so I'd just skipped off down the block to see if I could catch the kebab cart before it closed at midnight.

Then everything had gone completely to shit.

But I'd survived, and the fallout of my beast battling wraiths out in the open wasn't anything we couldn't handle. I sat up a little straighter in bed and pasted on my best confident face. "Dad, it will be okay. I know you think the same thing could happen to me that happened to Mom—"

"I don't think, Avery. I *know*."

"—but we'll be careful. Plus, things are evolving. There are more and more females with a beast soul in every generation. It's not so uncommon anymore. Only regressive weirdos think we're an abomination."

His face hardened, and the Alpha wolf appeared in his stare. "It is not the fact that you *can* shift that is the problem. It is *what* you shift into that is the problem, and you know that. I will not gamble with your life. Your mother was targeted and killed because of what she was, and we will not lose you the way we did her."

A knock sounded at the door, saving me from having to formulate a response to the reminder of the worst thing that'd ever happened to us. Dad opened it, and Kai slipped into the room, looking tired. He had on the same dark thermal shirt that we all wore when we were patrolling in the cold weather, and it was torn where something with rather large claws had swiped at his side. His katana was still strapped to his back, and his black hair stuck out in several directions.

"Hey, you're awake," he said softly, padding over to me and dropping a kiss on the top of my head. "You scared the shit out of us, Ave."

"I didn't do it on purpose," I grumbled.

He swept a quick glance over my leg. Satisfied I was not currently at death's door, he squeezed Ian's shoulder before perching in the windowsill. The view of the street outside, shrouded in darkness except for the dim yellow glow of the streetlamps, framed his tall, languid form. There was no moonlight tonight, which was why we'd all been on watch in the first place.

Kai quirked a dark brow at Rand, who was back to holding up the door. "Did you convince her?"

"Working on it."

I felt as resigned as Dad looked. I knew what was coming. It was something my parents had brought up several times before, but I'd always refused.

My family was here. The *need* was here. I didn't want to leave them.

"It's time, Avery," Dad said with finality. "If you enroll at

Proteus College, you'll be away from here if someone comes looking for you, safe behind the wards of the school and blending in with thousands of other shifter students."

"But Dad—"

"And, more importantly, if you enter the Guardian training program and prove what an asset you could be to the wraith defense efforts, you'll be better protected there than we can make you here. The Guardians are a powerful, independent force, and they watch out for their own. The powers that be will see you as useful and necessary despite what you are."

Kai nodded. "Even if tonight hadn't happened, Ave, you can't live your life this way forever. Hiding. Never being able to let your beast run in the woods with the rest of us. Always looking over your shoulder. Risking your life if you face a wraith or any other powerful opponent that forces a shift, but also risking your life if you *don't* shift. Your mom was careful, but we all got too comfortable. Too complacent. We will not let that happen again."

The air in the room grew heavy with the weight of their worry, the wounds left by their loss that would never fully heal. Tears welled in my eyes, and I rubbed them away.

Having a real college experience did appeal to me, at least a little bit, but I had mixed feelings about the Guardians. We needed them, and joining their ranks was supposedly one of the highest honors a shifter could achieve. They were highly respected and paid a very generous salary, but that was because they did one of the most dangerous jobs in existence.

A job my family did several days a month for no pay because the Guardians, like our society at large, didn't bother with those who chose to live outside the shifter communities.

I turned to my brother. "What do you think?" I asked softly.

He looked as tired as everyone else, but a smile finally crept back onto his face. "I think it's time for a change in scenery. I'm going with you."

Joy bloomed in my chest. "Really?"

He rolled his eyes. "Obviously."

"You really think the school will let us enroll this late in the game?" I asked Dad.

He shrugged a giant shoulder. "Joseph knows one of the faculty there from back in his apothecary training days, and she can get your applications onto the right desk quickly. When we fill out Avery's, we will heavily imply that I'm her biological father."

We actually didn't know which of my dads was my biological father, and I liked it that way. Ian and I both looked like our mom, with our cornflower-blue eyes and our hair that was so ashy-blond that it almost appeared silver. But not only was Ian's beast a fox, he also had a solid secondary affinity for apothecary magic, so we could all guess that Joseph was his bio dad.

I wrinkled my nose. "You're dangling me as bait for a Prime quad."

"I can't help it if they assume you're a latent female from a Prime shifter line," he said with another shrug. "And they will fast-track you right into the school because of it, even midyear, which is what we need. We'll ensure Ian's acceptance is part of the deal."

Kai shot me an imploring look from his window perch. "And maybe be open to the whole bonding thing, Ave. There's no better way to have someone constantly watching your back than bonding with a power quad, especially if they are also highly trained Guardians."

I scowled. "I will not whore myself out to a bunch of assholes who can't even be bothered to do their jobs well enough so that shit like this"—I gestured wildly at my healing leg—"doesn't happen on the doorsteps of Fulton City."

My dads exchanged a look, but before they could start on me, the door opened again. Joseph appeared, his long golden hair in its usual disheveled knot. He had a gash on his forehead, but at least his clothes were still intact.

He came straight for me and enveloped me in a tight hug as Dad closed the door behind him.

"Don't do that to us again, honey," he whispered. "The doctor said you lost a lot of blood."

"I'm sorry," I said. I didn't know why I kept apologizing to my family members like anything that'd happened tonight was my fault, but I *was* sorry for scaring them. "I'm all better now, though. See?"

He released me, and I made a show of flexing my leg for him.

He didn't seem impressed. "You still look pale. The doctor says you can come home, but no wraith altercations for the rest of this lunar cycle. If we see any action on the streets tomorrow night, the four of us will handle it. Got it?"

I pouted. "Fine. It sounds like Ian and I have to get packed for *college*, anyhow."

"Oh good, you agreed to go," he replied, his big green eyes filling with pride and also maybe relief. "We'll miss you both, but this is for the best. You and your brother need to have a real adolescence, and *you*, Avery, need to be able to do so in the safest possible environment."

I wasn't so sure I'd be that much safer behind the warded walls of Proteus College or that the fabled Guardian training program would even accept me, much less protect me from the threats my fathers were convinced were lurking around every corner, but if this was what I needed to do to allow my family to sleep at night, then I'd start packing tomorrow.

A laugh cracked in the back of my dry throat. "Merry Christmas to me, I guess."

2

AVERY

The drive from our home on the outskirts of Fulton City up to the foothills of the Blue Cliff Mountains, the location of Proteus College, was only about ninety minutes. As one of the few shifter-exclusive institutions of higher learning in the country and home of the Southeast Region's Guardian training program, it was the crown jewel that sat atop the conglomeration of shifter communities that made their home in Northern Georgia.

Ian and I had stuffed my ten-year-old RAV4 full of our crap and were driving straight up I-77—the backbone of that mass of shifter towns and little cities. These communities stretched seventy-five miles along the interstate, from the outer edges of Fulton City—the major metropolis in the area, populated almost exclusively by humans—all the way up to the mountains. Beyond the borders of the shifter towns, both to the east and to the west, lay miles and miles of dense forest, usually owned by the nearest town, where the beasts could be let out to roam in relative privacy.

The further away from the city you drove, the higher the concentration of both shifters and wealth in each town until you reached the sweeping gated communities and pristine little cities known collectively as the Hills. This was where the wealthiest and most powerful shifter families had settled just to the south of the mountains and the college.

We stopped at a coffee shop in a quaint downtown in the Hills. It was a gloomy winter day, but that didn't detract from the colorful shopfronts, clean streets, and meticulous landscaping. It could've been any small town in the country —until you spotted the names of the stores. Hermes, Gucci, Prada, Tiffany, and other things I couldn't even pronounce.

"Can you imagine living here?" Ian asked.

"It would certainly be a different kind of life," I replied, sipping the cold iced coffee I held in my even colder hands. "I bet they don't have wraith swarms running down the streets three days a month. There are probably a dozen Guardian posts surrounding the Hills, and I bet they have the top-of-the-line wards around the borders of their gated communities."

"Yeah." He sighed, casting a wistful look around the street, and then he grinned at me. "I still prefer our life."

"Me too."

Our parents had lived in a little mountain town in Colorado for years, but they'd packed us up and left after our mom died. I was three years old at the time, and Ian was only two, so neither of us remembered life before that. Only shifters who didn't want to mix much with others would choose to live where we did, so close to a densely populated urban area, and it suited us just fine. Our little neighborhood had everything we needed, and Ian and I had grown up going to school with human kids and the occasional fellow shifter.

But with that quiet separation from shifter communities, especially those with wealth, came the added danger.

Wraiths were drawn to shifters much more than humans, but they could spawn anywhere. The Guardians didn't patrol areas of low shifter concentration, especially in big cities, which meant we'd been on our own.

We climbed into my car and pulled back onto the highway. We were scheduled for a meeting with our assigned guidance counselor later this afternoon, and the spring semester started tomorrow.

"Nice of Dad to let us have one last hurrah before we left," Ian said. "It was lucky school starts so late in January, so we were able to be home for the New Moon this cycle."

It'd certainly been quieter this time around, and I'd threatened to stab anyone who tried to keep me home or fussed over my leg, which was still a little sore, yes, but totally functional.

"It's not like we can't hop in the car and drive back to help sometimes," I added. My chest tightened at the thought of my dads having to defend our neighborhood without Ian and me. They were perfectly capable, but still. Things had been getting worse lately, as evidenced by my getting tangled up with a Giant *in the city*. "Maybe if we get Dad to admit it's looking like it'll be a bad one, they'll ask for our help."

Ian snorted. "Sure, keep dreaming, Aves. They want you tucked behind those top-notch wards and bonded to a Prime quad as soon as possible, as delusional as that idea may be. They aren't going to call us home."

"I am not going to bond with a quad," I replied through gritted teeth. "Has everyone forgotten that I am not, in fact, a latent female? It'll be pretty damn obvious that's the case after I kill a few things in Guardian training. Dad says all those power quads still think a beast soul in their central bond interferes with their ability to share power and settle their animals and all that nonsense."

"You never know," he sang with a shit-eating grin. "Mom had no such issues as a central bond. There might be some more forward-thinking quads running around. Not everyone is scared off by a female with a beast."

"Whatever," I grumbled. Time for a subject change. "Did you get to say goodbye to *Ricardo* before we left? Or are we back to Bryan these days?"

He laughed. "I said goodbye to both of them. Several times. Very thoroughly."

"Of course you did, you slut."

He tutted. "Green doesn't look good on you, Aves. Just because you haven't gotten laid since Tad went off to teach rock climbing in Colorado...."

I scowled. "That ran its course, and you know it."

"I do. He was pretty, but you were going to be so bored if that dragged on any longer."

That about summed it up. My gym situationship last year had been a brief but enjoyable distraction, and I couldn't say I'd been broken up when it ended.

It was simpler to date humans, who had no clue we were anything *other*. Humans weren't sizing up your genetics, or judging your beast or your secondary affinities to determine whether you were *bond* material. Shifter men—powerful Primes in particular—had been conditioned to look for specific things in their mates, and I was not those things.

We settled into comfortable silence for the last thirty minutes of the drive, both of us bopping to Ian's K-pop playlist. We exited the highway, leaving the Hills behind, and climbed our way up a winding road toward the front gates of Proteus College. The midafternoon sun had finally broken through the clouds, and it shone down on the radiant blue mountains that rose in the distance. A redbrick wall stretched as far as we could see on either side of the school's imposing iron gate.

"What is that?" I asked, slowing the car as we approached the gate. A band of shiny metal as wide as my hand ran the entire length of the exterior wall, set just below the top edge. I could just make out the delicate etching of runes on its surface. "Holy shit, do you think that's pure silver?"

"Probably," Ian drawled. "You don't get the highest-grade wards without the best magic conductor money can buy."

The cost to run a band of silver around the entire perimeter of the campus would be *astronomical*, not to mention the fact that anyone with shifter blood would have to wear special gloves to handle it. Lucrative hazard pay was always involved, too—silver was poisonous to us.

"How the other half lives is starting to sink in," I muttered. Our parents did plenty well for themselves, but we were solidly middle-class. We certainly weren't lining our fence with pure silver. Our ward runes had been etched into the concrete sidewalk with Kai's drill. "Dad's sure they agreed to a generous financial aid package?"

"Yes, settle down. Try to act like a fertile latent ready to pop out Prime shifter boys when you get in there."

"Shut up."

I parked the car next to the little hut that housed the gate guard and rolled down my window.

The guard briefly glanced at us before turning back to his computer screen and holding out a hand. "IDs."

The guard was a shifter—we could all scent each other's rich, earthy pheromones—but that was all we'd be able to discern unless he shifted in front of us or volunteered the information. He could be latent, a powerful Prime, or anything in between.

After confirming we were on whatever list we needed to be on to be allowed to enter the campus, he pressed a button inside his hut, and the gate slowly creaked open.

We drove up the entrance road, lined on both sides by a thick forest of oaks, maples, and other stately trees. A historical gothic building, its bricks a rusty red color where they were visible through creeping ivy, greeted us as we emerged from the thicket. Smaller academic buildings in the same architectural style flanked its sides. Lush lawns, tall trees, and manicured bushes abounded. A few students and faculty traversed the sidewalks, most bundled in thick coats. Two small wolves darted across the front lawn and disappeared around the side of the building, followed closely by a hyena.

I blinked. "That will take some getting used to."

"No kidding."

I parked in the large lot in front of the main building. Ian and I sat quietly for a few moments, taking in what would be our new home for the next few years.

"I don't think this is going to be easy," I said in a low voice. "At all."

He reached over to squeeze my hand where it rested on my mostly healed leg. "No, it won't be. But it's time to spread your paws, Aves. I'm so excited I get to be here with you to see it."

That brought a smile to my face. He was right—no matter what this place threw at us, we'd tackle it together.

3

AVERY

Our guidance counselor, Mrs. Foley, studied us over the rims of her glasses. She looked to be in her fifties, but shifters aged a bit slower than humans, so she could've been pushing seventy, for all I knew. She was thin but fit, and she'd twisted her long gray hair into a claw clip on the back of her head. She wore a casual sweater, and her forced smile told us she wasn't thrilled to be dealing with new students in her office on a Sunday afternoon.

Two file folders lay open in front of her. "Avery Baxter?" she asked, glancing at me. When I nodded, she went back to my file. "Twenty-one years old. Enough credits from the Fulton City Community College to enter our school as a second-semester junior. So, right on time, I suppose."

I was lucky all those credits had even transferred.

She looked at Ian. "So that makes you Ian Baxter, twenty years old, with enough community college credits to enter as a second-semester sophomore."

He gave her a little salute.

"However," she went on, pursing her lips, "you are both

lacking in the magical side of your education, which means you will be required to take our entry-level Lunar Magic 101 class. Every student at Proteus College must take it during their freshman year, and luckily for you both, there are a few seats left in this semester's course."

Ian and I exchanged a look, and he shrugged.

"I also recommend grabbing the last few open seats in Shifter History and Culture," she went on. "It is also required, but it can be taken at any time before graduation."

It was obvious this lady thought Ian's and my educational background, given we had attended only human schools, meant we were sorry excuses for shifters and woefully behind the rest of the student body. The truth was that plenty of shifter kids got a human education. There just weren't that many shifter-exclusive schools in the country, and they were almost always expensive and private.

"That's fine with us," I said. "I assume we can take non-magical classes here, as well?"

She waved a hand. "Of course. This is a comprehensive college education, and most of us go on to have careers that don't involve the use of magic. We send just as many students off to medical school and law school as we do to the Guardians or rune apprenticeships."

Until now, I hadn't had particularly strong feelings about what I wanted to do with my life. I took college courses, worked part-time at a fitness center, and occasionally killed things in the streets at night. I'd been taking it one day at a time, but the events of last month had made the decision for me.

My dads thought I needed to prove myself as a Guardian to truly be safe, so that was what I was going to do.

"In that case," Ian said. "I still need to take O-Chem, if there's room this semester."

Mrs. Foley's fingers flew over her keyboard. "We can do that, but it conflicts with Shifter History and Culture. I suppose you can just take that in the fall." She punched a few keys, then she raised a brow at him. "Do you have a secondary affinity for apothecary magic?"

He shrugged. "I'm decent."

He was underselling. Our dad, Joseph, a pharmacist by day, was excellent with apothecary magic and had taught Ian everything he knew.

Mrs. Foley hummed and typed some more. "Then let's get you in our Apothecary 101 class and its evening lab. Pharmacy or Chemistry track?"

"Pharmacy."

"Excellent." She typed some more. "We just need one more course for a full twelve hours for you."

"I'll be joining Guardian training," he said, sounding very matter-of-fact.

She stopped typing and raised a brow at him. "I am not sure they'll allow that. Guardian training is very competitive, and only the top of the freshman leaderboard is allowed into the second year."

He shot me a confused look, which I returned with a shrug.

"I'd still like to try my hand at it," Ian replied, smiling and oozing charm. "I'm quite adept with my katana."

She softened—slightly. "Do you have a beast?"

"A fox."

She considered that. "I suppose that will be okay. We do have all manner of ordinary-level shifters in the Support Squadron classes."

Of course. Only Primes got to be true Guardians.

Ian's smile grew. "Perfect. Then I think my schedule is set."

She didn't look totally convinced, but she moved on. "Now, Miss Baxter," she said, her scrutinizing stare now pointed at me, "what are your non-magical interests?"

I shrugged. "I like the Humanities."

She checked my file. "You do have enough credits to get you into an upper-level Humanities course." She returned to the computer and typed some more. "How does Folklore and Literature sound?"

"Sounds great."

"Wonderful. Now, we just need three more credit hours for you—"

"I will also be joining Guardian training."

Her fingers froze over the keys. "I'm sorry?"

"Put me down for Guardian training, please. Same as my brother."

She stared at me. "There are no females in the Guardians."

Not particularly surprising. Very few females could shift at all. "Why not?" I asked anyway.

She swiveled away from her computer and removed her reading glasses. She looked me over like she was wondering where I'd stashed all the audacity. I didn't necessarily stand out from other females with shifter blood. I was five foot ten, and I had the leanly muscled build of an athlete, but shifters skewed tall and athletic, latent or not. It was just how the genes were.

Too bad I'd left my swords in the car.

"Do you have a beast?" she asked, her tone *just* skirting the line of disappointed.

"I don't have to answer that."

Shifters were backwards in a lot of ways, but the code on privacy regarding one's ability to shift or what type of beast they had was iron-clad and had been for decades.

Plenty of us revealed what we were, but it was never required.

She frowned, leaning back in her chair. "I can't condone you joining Guardian training, whether you have the enhanced strength of a beast or not. The only reason to do so is to become an actual Guardian, and that is a very dangerous job. Our females are too valuable to lose on the front lines."

Years of practice kept me from rolling my eyes. Our parents had fought alongside a few female shifters in the past, but none of them had been official Guardians, just as my dads hadn't been.

Guardians couldn't be everywhere, and in the past, they'd traveled around doing outreach to smaller, more isolated communities, teaching tactics and Moon-blessing blades so that those communities would have some hope of defending themselves in the event a stray wraith made an appearance. My parents had learned young, honed their skills, and passed them to us.

The small communities with fewer shifters living outside Guardian patrol zones needed all capable hands and couldn't afford to discriminate.

"I see," I replied with a tight smile. "I should focus on convincing one of your power quads to bond with me, right?"

If she pursed her lips any harder, they were going to get stuck that way. "I can hear the sarcasm there, Miss Baxter, but for our latent students, becoming the central bond to one of our Prime quads is just as important a job as that of a Guardian. As I'm certain you are aware, many male shifters experience a settling of their beast when they bond. And for many of our Primes, a bond can substantially increase their power. There's a reason the most successful quads in the Guardians are all bonded."

"Yeah, come on, Aves," Ian said with a shit-eating grin. "We won't have the next generation of Guardians without your help in popping out some Prime shifter babies."

I smacked him. "Quit it."

Mrs. Foley cleared her throat. "He isn't wrong, but of course that comes *later*. Many of our female students, both latent and our growing number of girls who do have the ability to shift, all go on to have successful careers in whatever magical or non-magical field they choose before settling down to start a family. The possibilities are endless, Miss Baxter."

I wasn't going to convince her to enroll me in training, but I didn't get into a fight with a Giant wraith, almost lose my leg, then agree to come all this way to give up that easily.

I'd figure something out.

She went back to her keyboard. "Do you have any secondary affinities?" she asked me.

I sighed. "I'm decent with runes and wards."

"Excellent," she said, perking right up. After a few more noisy keyboard strokes, she deflated. "Unfortunately, our entry-level runes class is full. But"—more typing—"I think we can get you a private tutor and have that approved for the full three credit hours."

"Sounds good to me."

"Great. I'll email Professor Blackwell. He'll be teaching your intro Lunar Magic course as well."

"Can't wait."

Ian snickered, and I swatted his arm again.

It only took about five more minutes for our official schedules to land in our new school email inboxes. Afterward, Mrs.

Foley ushered us out of her office and sent us down the hall to Housing, where the very flustered lady in charge profusely apologized that there were no available rooms in the underclassmen dorm for Ian, but there was an available suite in the upperclassmen dorm, and oh my gosh would he and I mind sharing even though the suites aren't usually co-ed but they'll make an exception this time because we're siblings?

We both stared at her for a solid five seconds before blurting, "Yes!"

No rolling the dice on the chance of a weird or creepy roommate? Not even a question.

Things were looking up.

THE DORMS LAY ACROSS THE LARGE GRASSY FIELD THAT separated the academic buildings from the residence halls and the athletic complex. Ian and I were directed to the correct parking lot for upperclassmen housing, and we found ourselves in front of a building that was a bit more modern than those on the academic side of campus. The ten-story dorm was made of similar redbrick, but it had the feel of an apartment complex that could've been on a swanky city block.

We weren't the only ones unloading our car. Students were returning from wherever they'd gone on holiday break, and we were getting some curious looks as we began to lug our stuff to the fourth floor.

Two hours later, I was unpacked, my bed was made, and my swords had been sharpened, sheathed, and hung over the back of my desk chair. Pleased with my progress, I decided that arranging my snacks and drinks in the little kitchenette would be next.

Ian's room connected to mine through a shared bathroom. I'd just crouched in front of my mini fridge when he burst in unannounced and flopped onto my bed.

He was wearing sweatpants and nothing else, so the silver fox tattoo that danced along his ribcage was on display. Ian was an inch taller than me and all svelte muscle, like a dancer. His fox didn't give him a huge boost in the raw strength department, but his speed was incredible.

"Look at us," he said, propping his chin on his hand, a swoop of his ash-blond hair falling over his forehead. "Real college kids."

"Sort of," I said as I shoved cans of cold brew coffee into the fridge. "This is shifter school. It's going to be cutthroat and weird."

He waggled his brows. "Good thing *I'm* cutthroat and weird."

I pointed at him. "Speaking of that, you better keep it down if you're going to be *entertaining* in your room. At least give me a heads-up so I can make sure I put my white noise machine right next to my head."

"Excuse you, let's not act like every single male we passed in the hallway wasn't checking you out. It's a smorgasbord of big, hot shifter men in this place, and you need to have a little fun on occasion too."

"Pass."

Sex with shifter men would never *not* be a way for their beast to sniff mine out for a potential bond, regardless of their power level. My beast bristled at the thought.

You and me both, sister.

He threw himself dramatically onto his back. "You're hopeless."

I *was* hopeless, but before I could invent reasons why I was not, a knock sounded at my door.

I opened it to find a slim redheaded girl with bright green eyes beaming a big, excited smile at me. "Avery?" she asked breathlessly.

I squinted at her. Fiery hair, smattering of freckles, infectious grin. Wait a minute… "Mallory?" I gasped.

She shrieked in delight. "It *is* you!" She launched herself at me, and I caught her in an awkward hug. "I thought that looked like you and Ian making trips to and from the parking lot! The whole dorm was abuzz, since we don't tend to get new students in the upperclassmen residence—"

Ian popped up behind me as Mallory released me from her clutches. "Is this *the* Mallory from Fulton Crescent Middle School basketball?"

"Yes!" she cried, and then it was Ian's turn to be smashed in a hug.

"Mal," I said, pulling her further into the room and shutting the door behind her, "how have you been? I haven't seen you since…"

"Since I disappeared from eighth grade without a word?" she asked, quirking a brow.

"Uh, yeah."

We hadn't been the best of friends or anything, but we'd played basketball together for two years. She'd been a fellow shifter girl and someone I genuinely enjoyed spending time around, which was rare in those rocky, awkward middle-school days.

I'd assumed she'd just moved away, which wasn't that odd, but it had been pretty abrupt—she was there one day, gone the next.

She helped herself to my desk chair. She frowned in confusion at my swords, still in their X-shaped harness and draped across the back of the chair, but then she shook it off. She'd probably seen weirder things around here.

Ian had sprawled out on my bed again, and I shoved him so I could have room to sit down.

"Well," Mallory began, taking a big breath, "a few months after I turned thirteen, I... shifted." Her smile faltered as her gaze bounced between Ian and me, like she was bracing for our reaction.

"That's amazing!" we both blurted with genuine excitement.

She blew out a breath, her shoulders sagging with relief. "Thank you. It is. My beast is a cat."

Excellent. A cat was an ordinary shifter on the lower end of the power scale, like Ian's fox. A useful and respectable beast entirely devoid of any desire or ability to play the dumb fucking dominance games the higher-powered shifters did.

"How did your parents take it?" Ian asked.

"Oh, they were thrilled," she gushed. "My mom thinks my great-grandmother had some kind of feline beast and just didn't tell anyone. Honestly, I've been lucky. There hasn't been *too* much crap about me being a shifting female —a lot of people seem to think it's high time there were more of us."

We'd just see about that, but it made sense that none of the big boys felt threatened by females with lesser-powered beasts, who were becoming more common in every generation.

"So, anyway," she went on, "when I got my beast, my parents sent me off to a private school exclusively for female shifters. A lot of latent girls went there to learn their secondary affinities, but it was also one of the few places I was able to be around other shifting girls in a place where that was celebrated."

"I'm really happy for you," I said, and I meant it. I'd

been lucky enough to get my beast during the summer between seventh and eighth grade, so the whole family had taken a two-month-long trip to the wilderness. I was able to get to know my new other half away from prying eyes.

"Thank you." She fidgeted absently with the hem of her Proteus College sweatshirt, and I noticed a tattooed band around her left ring finger.

I blinked wide eyes at her. "Mal, are you bonded?"

Those of us who could shift into a beast didn't wear rings or bracelets or anything that could be broken with the change in shape, so ring tattoos were in vogue. Piercings usually survived, because the holes remained in either form. I wore three titanium studs in each of my earlobes but nothing else.

She glanced down at her finger, and her grin grew impossibly wider. "Yes! I'm in a pair bond with my mate, Allen. He's a junior, like me, and he's a wolf."

Ian's blond brows bounced upward. "An Alpha?"

She waved a hand. "Oh, no, no. Respectably ordinary. You'll discover that, like, one in three of our shifting student body are ordinary wolves. They are everywhere and breed like... wolves."

We knew a few wolf shifters back home, and they all looked at my dad, Rand, like he'd hung the Moon herself. Wolves were common, but Prime Alphas were not.

"Also," Mallory said, leaning forward and affecting a conspiratorial whisper, "he's my Fated."

I stared at her with a slack jaw.

"Woah," Ian said. "Seriously?"

"Yes! It took me a while to get up the courage, but the first time I shifted in front of his wolf, we felt it. I don't know how to describe it, but our beasts just *knew*. We made the bond official last semester during the Full Moon bonding ceremony. The school has one every semester."

Fateds were rare, especially among heterosexual pairings, since they seemed to only occur when both or all parties had a beast. Shifting females were still uncommon, so most bonds were chosen by more normal means, like mutual attraction, social compatibility, or when the beast sniffed out something it liked.

Or whatever. I didn't date shifters, so what did I know?

One's Fated was supposedly the perfect match chosen by the Moon herself, two beast souls harmonizing in a divine song. Mallory and Allen were a rare and blessed couple, according to legend, and the thought almost made me gushy inside.

"That's amazing," I told her. "It's really good to see you, and it sounds like you've been doing awesome since we last hung out."

She sighed happily. "I have. I'm working on my healing affinity, training as a medic. It's been great. But enough about me—what brings you two here, like, in the middle of the year? Are you starting as upperclassmen? What's going on?"

Ian propped his chin in his hand and deployed an innocent, charming smile. "We both tried regular community college and just felt like we weren't... reaching our full potential. Right, Aves?"

Good one. "Right."

She beamed. "Well, it's amazing they let you transfer in so late! It's a little, you know, *different* here than human school, what with the dominance challenges and matings and hierarchy—" She laughed awkwardly. "—but it'll be *great*. You'll see. Probably!"

Well, that was reassuring.

She hopped to her feet and slinked to the door with feline grace. "Allen and I will come by tomorrow and grab you guys for breakfast in the dining hall. Sound good?"

"Yep," I said brightly. We could definitely use a guide, and I wasn't going to look a gift cat in the mouth. "See you then."

"Later!"

The door shut with a loud click behind her. Ian chuckled and rolled off my bed, landing on light feet. "Sounds like this place is a pressure cooker full of hotheaded hormonal shifters. It's gonna be fun."

"Ugh." I went to my desk and shrugged the harness holding my blades over my sweatshirt. It was getting dark outside, and while we were far enough into the lunar cycle that wraiths were unable to break out of their realm, it was better safe than sorry. "Let's go get sushi off campus before we're stuck here."

He laughed. "I'll get my sword."

4

AVERY

Mallory and her affable blond mate, Allen, arrived at my door at 8:00 a.m. sharp to hustle Ian and me out of our rooms. We trekked across the big field back to the main campus, and we picked up two of Allen's fellow wolf shifters along the way. He dragged them away from a gathering of a dozen other wolves, who were standing around in a haphazard circle, heckling and cheering as a couple of them fought each other in beast form.

Apparently this was a near-daily occurrence for the wolf students as they fought for their place in the hierarchy.

Now we were sitting at one of the tables in the college's only dining hall, which had probably been a church in its previous life. It was a cavernous space with cathedral ceilings, pointed arch windows, and stately wood paneling on every wall. Long banquet tables were arranged in neat rows around us. Ornate chandeliers hung from the rafters above us.

We piled our plates high with food from the breakfast

buffet, which smelled amazing, while our new friends gave us the lay of the land.

The tables where the various factions of wolves congregated.

The spots where the groups were more mixed and divided by class year or area of study.

The faculty tables tucked away in a smaller space off the main dining room, accessible through a wide, arched doorway.

"And over there are the avians," Mallory said, gesturing with her bagel at a table in the back corner. A large group of students sporting the big eyes and sharp, angular features of bird shifters chatted amiably amongst themselves. "They're pretty chill. Most of the ones who shift rank as minor and are drama averse, but there are a few raptors over there who are classed as ordinary and can be aggressive if you piss them off."

Yeah, it was never wise to fuck with a bird of prey, no matter how big and bad you thought you were.

"Ah, and the elite are beginning to arrive," Allen said with an exaggerated eye roll. "Try not to faint, everyone."

More students entered the hall and began to congregate at the open tables in the center of the room. The guys had the hulking, muscular builds of powerful Prime shifters, their worn jeans clinging to thick thighs and designer jackets struggling to contain wide shoulders. They moved with the swagger of shifter males who were a big deal and knew it.

Scattered among them were the elite shifter girls. Slim but curvy in the right places. Hair and makeup that would've taken me two hours to accomplish. Knee-high leather boots. Long wool coats and high-fashion scarves.

Feminine. Demure. Ideal latent females from wealthy Prime families.

Ian eyed the group lazily as he sipped Earl Grey from a mug sporting the Proteus College crest. "Quads?" he asked our friends. "And their bonds?"

"Some of them," Allen's friend, Chance, replied with a casual shrug. He wore his chestnut hair long, and his stacks of leather-corded necklaces gave him a distinct hippie vibe. "Most of the Primes have formed a trio or a quad by junior year or so. Some have already found their central and bonded, and the ones who haven't are definitely on the hunt."

I couldn't contain my snort. "Eager to use whichever lucky girl they choose as a power conductor?"

How the magic of bonding worked between shifters was mysterious, but it was well-known that the more powerful the beast, the greater the effect of the bond. Shifters like Mallory and Allen bonded for love, but Prime groups bonded for bloodlines and the ability to share power through their connection with their central.

But they probably didn't run around announcing that fact. The princesses wanted to be wooed by their princes, after all.

My comment elicited some raised eyebrows, but not from Allen's other friend, Ashley—or "Ash" as she'd instructed us to call her, on pain of death. Her black hair was shaved on the sides and styled in a sleek swoop on the top of her head. She'd pushed the sleeves of her black sweater to her elbows, exposing strong forearms covered in neat geometric tattoos. She wore several hoops pierced through her ears, one through her nose, and the dozen or so rings on her long fingers told me that, while she was from a wolf-shifter family, she was likely latent.

Ian and I had both questioned our sexualities for a hot second when Allen introduced her.

"That's a true statement," Ash replied with a husky chuckle, "but let's not pretend those girls aren't just as desperate to land a powerful quad with wealth and connections. The ones destined for the Guardians are also a hot commodity."

"I bet," I said. "An extra status bump, being bonded to future war heroes."

"I'm sure four huge dicks don't hurt either," Ian added.

I elbowed him.

Chance studied one of the tables full of large males. "I wonder if any of them have a shot at the top of the leaderboard this semester."

"Nah," Allen said with a dismissive wave. "My buddies in Support Squadron tell me that someone in Blackwell Quad would have to die before they gave up the lead, probably."

Ian and I exchanged confused glances. "The leaderboard?" Ian asked.

"And who are the Blackwell Quad?" I added.

Allen gestured at the back of a T-shirt worn by a male with long golden hair and huge shoulders. Printed on it was the logo of the Guardians—a beast claw bisected by a long sword. The words "Junior Champions 2024" were stamped beneath it.

"This is a Guardian training thing?" I asked.

Mallory nodded. "Yeah, it's how they decide who to cut and who makes it through the program to become a full-fledged Guardian. There's even a competition every spring that's open to spectators. Students like to go watch and make bets on the winners."

Uh. "Competition doing what, exactly?" Surely they

weren't letting wraiths loose on campus, if that was even a thing that was possible?

Allen laughed. "You'll see. It's fun to watch, that's for sure. Some of our wolf friends are still hanging in there in the Support Squadron group."

"Allen and I tried out when we were freshmen," Chance added. "It was just fitness drills and combat training the first year, and we were both shit with a blade."

Before Ian or I could articulate any more questions, heads began to swivel toward the entrance and whispers intensified, as if we were in the presence of celebrities.

Two male students strode into the room.

Mallory leaned in to whisper in my ear. "You asked who the Blackwell Quad is. There's two of them now."

I didn't need to be told that these two guys were top-of-the-food-chain Prime shifters. They were both well over six feet tall and built like they could toss a monster-truck tire like a frisbee while also being able to run a sub-six-minute mile. They oozed dominant energy as they breezed by our table, striding with the fluid grace of predators rather than the cocky swagger of their peers.

"The redhead is Wyatt Gale," Mallory went on. "His beast is a bear, believe it or not."

I blinked in shock, then immediately began to sneakily check him out from under my lashes.

Most Prime bear shifters were big burly guys built like offensive linemen on a professional football team. Wyatt was big—at least six-four by the look of him—but he had more of a linebacker's build, brutal but agile. His hair was a dark auburn shade, cut short on the sides but long and messy on the top. He wore distressed black jeans and boots with a white Henley molded to his broad chest. I could just make out small black plugs in his earlobes and the intricate tattoos that crawled out from under his collar and up the sides of his neck.

Unfortunately, he was probably the hottest guy I'd ever laid eyes on.

Except for the guy who'd come in with him.

Great.

"And the golden boy with Wyatt is Heath Blackwell," Allen said, his voice suddenly full of reverence. "He's the most dominant Alpha the school's had in a long time."

Chance nodded solemnly, and even Ash wore a look of profound respect as she watched Heath Blackwell nod a polite greeting to his fellow Primes.

Other wolf shifters acted that way around my dad on occasion. It was innate, the way they saw Alpha wolves as deities walking among mortals.

Heath was only an inch or so shorter than Wyatt but built just as solidly. He wore a gray long-sleeve shirt with the college crest and crisp blue jeans that hugged his very tight ass. His hair was darker at the roots before fading naturally into sandy-blond strands, wavy and artfully tousled. His exposed tan skin was tattoo free, and he sported just enough stubble to add a rough, masculine edge to what was a *very* pretty face. Greek-god-carved-from-marble pretty. Painted-on-the-roof-of-the-Sistine-Chapel pretty.

My beast half perked up, and I did the mental equivalent of swatting her on the nose.

No, ma'am.

Heath and Wyatt took their places at the end of one of the center tables. Wyatt wore a lazy smirk as he leaned back in his chair and took a swig from whatever was in his to-go cup. Heath studied his phone, unaffected by his surroundings and ignoring the cluster of students trying to get his attention.

"And the locusts descend," Mallory muttered as several of the girls at the table pranced over to talk to them. "There are still quite a few top quads who haven't bonded yet, but Blackwell is the holy grail."

I didn't doubt it. "Where are the rest of their quad?" I asked.

"Well, one of them is actually Heath's older brother," Allen said. "He graduated a few years ago, but he and Heath are so tight that Aiden put off joining a quad until his brother and the others started here."

"And no one ever knows when Elijah will be around," Ash added with a shrug. "He's one of the reasons their quad is so far and away ahead of all the others. He's a mythic."

I almost spit my iced coffee across the table. "Seriously? Are there any more at school?"

Mythic shifters were *extremely* rare and off the charts on the power scale. My dad, Joseph, claimed he met a Cerberus once, but the rest of us had never encountered one.

Mallory hummed. "Yeah, one of the senior quads has a griffin. But Elijah's a *basilisk*. Everyone is fucking terrified of him."

My beast half chuffed like she thought that was ridiculous and she'd enjoy meeting a giant raging snake monster.

Absolutely not.

Ian nudged me. "A *basilisk*, Aves. Sounds hot."

Mallory's blue eyes suddenly went comically wide. "By the *Moon*, Avery, isn't your dad an Alpha wolf?"

"One of my dads is, yes," I replied, now focused on shoveling bites of waffle into my mouth.

She barked out a loud laugh, attracting the attention of some of the tables around us. "No wonder they let you just drop into school in the middle of your junior year! If they think you're the latent daughter of a Prime...." She paused, frowning. "Wait, are you?"

I swallowed my waffle and sipped my coffee with a smile. "The administration thinks so."

The table was silent for the briefest moment before it was just shrugs all around.

"Sure," Mallory replied with a big grin, then waggled her eyebrows suggestively. "Shouldn't you be over there trying to cozy up to Wyatt and Heath like the other blue bloods, then?"

"Uh...." I waved a hand at my general state of being, "I don't think I'd fit in."

My loose sweater, comfy jeans, and low-maintenance ponytail were not really it.

Allen winked at me. "The *magic* doesn't really care about clothes, Avery. Go let those big powerful beasts take a sniff of you and see what happens."

Ian cackled. "See, Aves, our new friends have known you for all of an hour, and even they think you need to loosen up and get laid."

I punched his arm. "Shut up."

"Well, I for one am looking forward to getting to know all the big players on campus," he said in a lazy drawl. He leaned back in his chair and threw his hands behind his head. "I'm sure we'll see some of them in Guardian training. I'm signed up, and Avery is going to crash with me."

Chance choked on his French toast. Allen smothered a cough. Mallory and Ash stared at both of us like we'd sprouted tentacles.

"Way to play it cool," I said with a weary sigh. "You broke them."

Mallory recovered first. "Um, well, that's... ambitious.

The Support Squadron is mostly ordinary shifters, so I guess that would apply to you, Ian?"

"My beast is a fox," he announced with a cheeky grin.

"Right." She cleared her throat. I admired her valiant attempt to keep an encouraging smile on her face. "I'm sure you've realized Guardian training is extremely competitive, and starting in the middle of your sophomore year will put you behind, but... good luck?"

"Thank you."

The rest of the group hadn't taken their wide-eyed stares off me. "You're going to crash Guardian training?" Chance asked, looking very bewildered. "They, uh.... There aren't any females in the Guardians. Not even in the Support Squadron."

Which was bullshit, obviously. I shrugged. "Seems silly. The Guardian forces need all the skilled bodies they can muster."

"Avery," Mallory hissed, her green eyes wide with panic. "Can you shift? You won't stand a chance otherwise. You could get seriously hurt!"

I patted her hand. She meant well, and her worry for me was actually kind of nice. "I'll manage, Mal. It's what I came here to do."

She frowned. "It is?"

Ian nudged me, and we both got to our feet. I slung my backpack over my shoulder and pasted a light-hearted smile on my face. "Well, we're off to remedial magic class. Thanks for giving us the lay of the land. See you guys at lunch?"

They all just nodded silently back at me.

As I followed Ian out of the dining hall, I turned to give one more friendly wave to Mal. She probably thought I was nuts, but hopefully she'd still want to be my friend. It'd be nice to have one at school who wasn't my brother.

My gaze collided with a pair of hazel eyes over Mallory's shoulder. Eyes that focused on me with such intensity that they had me pinned momentarily to the floor.

Heath Blackwell was staring at me, and not in a casual manner.

My beast rumbled a challenge.

Settle down.

Tearing my attention from Heath, I couldn't help but glance at Wyatt next to him. Wyatt's bright green eyes did a little dip down my body and back up again, like he was checking me out and didn't care if I knew it. His air of lazy amusement was a stark contrast to his serious quadmate.

I turned away and stomped off after Ian, groaning inwardly. I didn't want the attention of the Blackwell Quad or *any* Primes, but I wasn't naive.

I was going to attract attention sooner rather than later.

It was time to ready myself for the consequences.

5

———

AVERY

Lunar Magic 101 was held in a large auditorium-style classroom in the nearby Magical Education building. Ian and I managed to find a couple of open seats near the front, as most of the two hundred freshmen also taking this class had beat us here.

We were getting some looks. Proteus College was small enough that most of the students would recognize one another by sight, so two random new students in a spring-semester freshman class would've been noticeable, and that was before they found out neither of us was actually a freshman.

Right at the stroke of 9:00 a.m., our professor strode into the classroom.

A girl let out an audible sigh somewhere behind me.

Ian chuckled. "Maybe remedial magic won't be so bad after all."

Our professor was, first and foremost, *young*. He couldn't have been more than two or three years older than I was. He was at least six-foot-two, with broad shoulders and a solid torso that tapered down to trim hips and strong thighs. His chocolate-brown hair was wavy, curling over his forehead and at his temples. He wore stylish dark-framed glasses, tailored gray slacks, and a black dress shirt with the sleeves rolled to his elbows, which put his corded forearms on display.

He also moved with a languid grace that hid the coiled power of a Prime shifter.

"Feline," I whispered to Ian.

"Definitely."

Our professor was also the third utterly gorgeous Prime male to wander into my path on the first damn day of school, when I'd arrived here adamant that I wanted nothing to do with them. Was the Moon playing a trick on me?

"Good morning," he said briskly as he pulled a laptop from his leather bag and set it on the lectern. "I'm Professor Aiden Blackwell. Welcome to Lunar Magic 101."

I snorted under my breath, and Ian elbowed me.

Aiden *Blackwell*. The third member of the school's power quad. Heath Blackwell's older brother.

Of course he was as hot as the other two.

My beast gave a little rustle of interest.

Nope, stop that.

Aiden pressed a few keys on his laptop, and the day's slide deck appeared on the large screen that hung over the top of the blackboard at the front of the room.

"Now," he began, observing the class with only fleeting interest, "I understand that much of what we'll cover in this class, especially in the beginning, may feel extremely rudimentary to some of you. But there are many of you for whom the Proteus curriculum is your first magical education, and the school requires that everyone have a solid grasp on the basics before you can move onto more exciting things."

Some girls giggled behind me. "My parents had me in magical training by the age of five, but I'd take this class every semester if I could," one of them whispered.

Her friend snickered some more. "Yes, Bernice, Professor Blackwell is going to just pluck a freshman girl out of his class to present to his quad for bonding."

"We can all *dream*, Madeline."

On Aiden's first slide was a simple lunar calendar—this month's, by the look of it—with the phases of the Moon illustrated and set off by the week. "We'll begin with what I hope is not a revelation to any of you—the source of all magic that we as shifters are able to harness and use, to varying degrees. The Moon."

While neither Ian nor I had ever attended anything other than human school, our dads were not slouches in either the magic department or the teaching department. None of this would be news to us. Still, I found myself at least mildly interested in what a formal magical education looked like.

And Aiden seemed only mildly interested in teaching it. His tenure as a professor here might've had more to do with his need to stick around with his quad until they graduated than his desire to be in the profession. He was likely bound for the Guardians when Heath and the others graduated.

"All shifters are born with the Moon's magic in our blood," Aiden continued, "whether you develop the ability to shift or not. We believe it is both genetics and luck that determine whether the magic within you can meld with a beast soul."

"Do you think he'll give us a demonstration and shift?" Bernice asked breathlessly behind me.

"You just want to see him naked," Madeline replied.

Couldn't say I blamed her there.

"Obviously," Bernice said, "but I've heard his jaguar is one of the largest and fastest felines the school's ever seen. We're all curious."

Another flick of the ears from my beast.

Cut it out.

Madeline sighed. "Hopefully we'll get to see it at the Guardian competition in the spring."

"The strength of the Moon's magic—and our sensitivity to it," Aiden went on, "is determined by the lunar cycle. Our magic is the strongest at the Full Moon and the days surrounding it, while our ability to wield magic weakens as we approach the New Moon."

On his slide, a bright border lit up, surrounding the January New Moon and the two days on either side of it.

My family had been in the streets on those nights last week, culling the few swarmers that'd managed to find their way into the city.

Down the row from us, a girl raised her hand.

Aiden nodded at her. "Yes?"

"Why isn't the strength of your beast affected by the phases of the Moon? My dad's wolf doesn't seem to experience any dips in power around the New Moon."

"Good question," he replied. "We don't *truly* know, but it's theorized that once the beast soul has melded with our own, usually around age twelve or thirteen, it is magically stable within us. It's really only our secondary affinities that wax and wane with the Moon."

Another hand went up. "Is that why shifting doesn't feel any different day or night?"

"Yes. The gift of the beast soul is permanent. Our secondary affinities require skill and practice to channel the

Moon's power into that activity, whether it be healing, rune work, apothecary work, constructs and illusions, or the techno-magic specialties that have developed over the past few decades. But the most talented of us are able to store magic like a battery to work secondary magic all throughout the cycle."

"Professor!" Bernice said, no doubt raising an eager hand behind me. "Do you subscribe to the theory that latent shifters can often become *extra* proficient in secondary affinities because we're able to devote all of our focus and magical abilities to those abilities?"

The preening in her voice was not subtle. Many of the girls in the class perked up, eager for his answer.

Aiden ran his long fingers through his thick brown hair, and anyone closely studying his face—which of course I was *not*—might've caught him smothering an eye roll.

"That is often the case, Miss...?"

"Tanner," she replied breathlessly. "Bernice Tanner."

"You are correct, Miss Tanner, that we've observed generations of latent shifters, both male and female, who often rise to the top of their field in whichever secondary affinity they've developed. Some of the nation's top surgeons are latent shifters with powerful healing affinities, for example. Plenty of us who can shift are proficient with secondary affinities, but it is true that often our animals can muddle the different types of magic and also... divide our power and focus a bit."

Bernice was a dog with a bone now. "But bonding helps steady the beast and increases your powers and abilities, right?"

I did not smother *my* eye roll.

Aiden's hazel gaze landed on me, and he paused for a

moment longer than was necessary, his eyes narrowing, before his attention moved over my head, back to Bernice.

"That is often the case, yes," he replied evenly. "Particularly for those of us with Prime-level beasts."

I could just *feel* Ian grinning like a loon next to me.

As Aiden took a few more questions from the class about the mechanics of lunar magic as applied to secondary affinities, I zoned out, doodling a little jaguar on my syllabus.

Then some guy in the back blurted question that ripped my attention away from my drawing.

"So how exactly did the wraiths happen, then? The higher powers sure fucked us with that shit."

Aiden grimaced. "We will have a whole unit on wraiths later this semester."

"Come on, Professor," another guy said. "Give us a preview. You train with the Guardians, so you have all the gory details."

Ian huffed a disgusted snort, and I was right there with him. It was hitting us how many of our fellow students may have never seen a wraith in their entire lives. Must be nice to hide behind the wards of whatever fancy shifter community these kids came from where the Guardians actually patrolled.

Aiden relented, vacating his spot behind the lectern and taking a seat on the table next to it, his long legs stretched out in front of him. He leaned back on his hands, which caused the veins in his forearms to pop in a way that was far too sexual for this classroom. "Fine. I'm aware this is the topic everyone seems to find the most interesting. Does anyone know the general magical theory behind the origin of the wraiths?"

A few hands shot up, and he called on a girl seated a few

chairs away from me in the front row. "The wraiths are thought to be perversions of beast souls not destined to become part of one of us."

Aiden nodded. "Or not compatible with our bodies or our magic. Instead, they fester in their realm, which is a cesspool of darkness and rot. Unfortunately for us, the veil between our world and theirs is thin, and when the Moon is at its weakest, they are able to tear through and attack us."

"Why do they attack us?" someone asked from the back of the room.

I had to stop myself from turning around to shoot an incredulous look in that direction. Was this really something people didn't know?

"They feed on our souls," Aiden replied, his tone the appropriate level of foreboding. "It's thought that wraiths need to consume shifter souls to sustain their forms, and with enough bites at that apple, they become stronger. They can power up and become even more dangerous."

Bernice jumped in. "Is that why only those of us with shifter blood can see them? And why they don't affect humans at all?"

What?

Aiden hummed in agreement. "They are attracted to a high concentration of shifter souls, and when the Moon's power wanes enough to allow them to escape, they tear straight through at the points where we're the most numerous—in particular where there are large numbers of Primes. It's why their attacks are almost always around where our largest communities are based, like here in Northern Georgia, the Pacific Northwest, or the big settlements in Virginia."

My hand was up in the air before I could stop it.

Aiden almost looked surprised. "Yes, Miss...?"

"Avery Baxter."

His eyes widened behind his glasses for the briefest of seconds. *Yes, I am the new student you will have the pleasure of tutoring in introductory runes.*

"Miss Baxter. Something to add?"

"It isn't true that wraiths don't attack humans, or that they can't harm them. They do and they can."

The class began tittering, and he arched a dark brow. "Is that so?"

That was a haughty fucking stare, and I didn't appreciate it.

"While it's true that humans can neither see nor feel wraiths," I said, "they are still susceptible to an attack, especially when there are no shifters in the area to draw the wraiths' attention elsewhere."

He was unmoved. "We have no human deaths on record from a wraith attack."

"That's because the Shifter Councils don't give a shit," I snapped.

Ian cleared his throat, but I forged on. This nonsense pissed me off. "Wraiths *can* feed on human souls. No, they can't kill a human in one fell swoop like they can a shifter, but human souls can still be damaged beyond repair. Some get sick for a few days and recover. Some slowly descend into madness. Some just physically waste away over a period of years. They're often diagnosed with a human disease that has similar symptoms, but the decline always starts after wraiths have been spotted in the area. If the Guardians deigned to occasionally patrol the human cities, it would be common knowledge."

The scandalized chatter of the class intensified.

Aiden's jaw tensed, and his eyes flared, a hint of bright

turquoise lighting up around his irises—his beast peeking through.

Bring it, cat.

He smothered that shit fast. "I suggest you save your editorial comments for essay assignments during our wraith unit, Miss Baxter."

If he ever showed his face at Guardian training, I would punch it.

I settled for a shitty smile. "Understood, Professor."

He rose from the table, returned to his laptop, and then launched into his lecture on the next slide's topic—historical evidence of shifting and magic use in early human societies.

I went back to my doodling. I had plans to draw an even bigger cat putting the jaguar's head in its mouth.

Ian chuckled. "If that man doesn't anger-bang you before the end of the semester, I will eat my shoe."

"You're delusional," I snapped out of the side of my mouth.

Aiden was able to lecture for ten solid minutes before he was interrupted once more. The classroom door creaked open, just a sliver, and the girls seated closest to the door shrieked and began to scramble out of their chairs.

A *python* slithered into the classroom, winding its leisurely way across the floor toward Aiden. It had shiny purple scales, embellished with even shinier golden scales that wove a geometric pattern down its back, and was at least six or seven feet long.

Aiden blew out a breath, removing his glasses to pinch his brow. "George, we've talked about interrupting my classes."

The snake ignored him, continuing his casual slither

across the floor, mere feet from those of us seated in the front row.

One guy stuck his foot out like he was going to try to kick the snake. George reared up and hissed at the kid.

His friend, who was seated next to him, punched the guy in the arm. "Dude, don't fuck with that snake. Just because he isn't venomous doesn't mean he won't fuck you up. Tyler thought it would be hilarious to try to shove him into a cabinet last semester, and the snake wrapped itself around his neck and nearly choked him to death."

"He's correct," Aiden said to the class. "Do not touch George. Don't approach him, don't talk to him. I apologize that he's decided to invade our classroom. Elijah's off campus currently, and I'm the only other person George seems to like. He's bored."

Fascinating. The basilisk shifter had a pretty purple snake as a pet!

George paused his journey right in front of where Ian and I were sitting. He looked at Aiden like he was finally ready to meander over to his second-favorite person, but then he turned to take a little last-second sniff of my shoe.

I didn't move a muscle. He was a gorgeous snake, but I wasn't dumb enough to ignore Aiden's warning.

George perked up, changing tactics and slithering under my chair.

"George," Aiden barked. "Get over here. Now."

George ignored him once again, inching closer and lifting his shiny head to nose at my thigh.

"Hi, buddy," I murmured. "You're so pretty, but I think you're going to be in trouble with your second daddy if you don't do what he says."

George, apparently an intelligent snake, gave Aiden the stink eye, and then he continued his climb under the desktop and into my lap. Madeline and Bernice squealed behind me and vacated their seats as he wound his way up my body and settled his upper half around my shoulders.

"Shit," Aiden swore. "I apologize, Miss Baxter."

"It's fine" I replied. I rubbed a fingertip along George's scales. He sniffed my hair and then settled in to doze on my shoulders. "He's very friendly."

"He isn't, actually," Aiden said, crossing his arms over his chest with another slutty flexing of his forearms. "I don't know what's gotten into him. I can remove him and lock him in my office."

George hissed at him.

"I don't think he likes that idea," I replied, grinning at our unflappable professor, who was a little flapped right now. "He can sit with me until class is over."

Ian held a cautious hand out to the snake. George lifted his head and took a tentative sniff. He eyed Ian for a few seconds, then settled back onto my shoulders.

"Did I pass?" Ian asked, laughing. "You don't get a choice, G-man. Avery's my sister, so if you wanna hang out with her, I'm part of the package."

Aiden's narrow-eyed stare at me rivaled the intensity of his brother's—the already too familiar hazel gaze that I'd tangled with earlier in the dining hall. "Right," he said after a long moment. He hit a few keys on his laptop, and a new slide appeared. "Everyone settle down. Class isn't over yet."

I stroked George some more as I tuned back out. A ridiculous start to the day, but at least it hadn't been boring.

6

AVERY

George decided it was time to obediently slither over to Aiden about two minutes before class ended, so Ian and I were able to make a quick escape the moment we were dismissed.

Ian departed, headed for his Organic Chemistry class in the Math and Science building, while I only had to shuffle a few doors down to another lecture hall for Shifter History and Culture. I pouted about Ian's absence for a second, but then I slapped my game face back on because I was a big girl.

This time I was earlier to class, so I was able to have my pick of seats. I settled on a spot in the middle, intending to disappear into the sea of faces as other students began to file in. As long as I didn't get into a standoff with the professor or have George come looking for me, I had a real shot at this plan.

After a few minutes of peace, my beast twitched, snapping my attention from emails on my phone. A second later, Wyatt Gale and Heath Blackwell entered the room. Every eye turned their way as they prowled up the shallow stairs and made their way into the row behind mine. They stopped—because of course they did—at the chairs directly behind me and sat down.

"If Elijah doesn't check in by the end of training today, one of us should go after him," Heath said in a low voice. It was a deep, resonant sound that carried the power of the most dominant and deadly of our kind. "We shouldn't have let him go alone in the first place."

"He'll be fine," Wyatt replied. His voice had a similar gravity but with a lighter, more lyrical tone—another surprise from this supposedly legendary bear shifter. Bears were always big burly dudes with beards and the deepest baritone imaginable. He chuckled, and it irked me to no end that I'd never heard a sexier sound in my life. "If only he gave training and school the focus he's giving this side project."

"I think him being this focused on anything is a positive," Heath said. He cleared his throat, and then he muttered, "Incoming."

"Hey, Wyatt," a female voice purred. "Is this seat taken?"

Wyatt's voice took on a classic fuckboy lilt. "Taken by *you*, Callista."

She let out a flirtatious giggle.

Heath snorted, and his whisper just reached my ears. "No one to blame but yourself for this one."

"Laugh it up, asshole. Looks like you've got company too."

"Heath, *hi*," another saccharine voice cooed. "Okay if I sit here?"

"Hey, Phoebe," Heath replied diplomatically. "Sure, go ahead."

"Perfect," Phoebe said lightly. "Hi, Wyatt." She paused, and her voice lost all the bubbly sweetness. "Callista."

"Phoebe," Callista replied, her tone just as caustic.

I couldn't help my chuckle. *Testy, aren't we?*

"Something funny, new girl?" Callista drawled at the back of my head.

Damn it. Where was George when I needed him to be a menace?

Not one to cower, I craned my neck around to look at her over my shoulder. Callista was one of the girls from the blue-bloods table in the dining hall this morning. She'd styled her dark hair in perfect waves, and her contouring was on point.

I could just make out Wyatt's hot, stupid smirk from the corner of my eye.

"I apologize," I said to Callista with my best contrite face. "As you pointed out, I'm new here, so it's my first time being exposed to the hostile atmosphere of the competition for a Prime quad's bond. I'm sure I'll adjust soon."

Wyatt snorted a laugh before he smothered it with a cough.

Callista's dark-brown eyes narrowed to slits. "Watch yourself, b—"

"Wait." Heath's command had just the edge of a bark to it, the dominance saturating the air. It shut Callista up instantly. He leaned forward, his breath ghosting against the back of my neck. "What's this?"

His fingers just brushed my shoulder. My beast's ears flattened against her head, and I tensed at his touch.

"These look like George's scales."

Oh. I blew out a breath, glancing down at my other shoulder. A few tiny, sparkly purple scales were embedded in the thick fabric of my sweater. I met Heath's burning hazel gaze over my shoulder. He had more golden brown in his irises than his brother did, and I hated that I knew that.

"They are George's scales. He came to visit my last class and decided he wanted to snuggle with me for a while."

Heath blinked, and then his eyes narrowed, hitting me with the full weight of that Alpha stare. "You're lying."

I scowled. *Fuck you, wolf.* "Ask your brother."

Phoebe gave his arm a sympathetic squeeze. "Ignore her, Heath. Just a new girl making a desperate bid for your attention."

Ooh, burn. "Nice friends you have there, *Alpha*," I said drolly to Heath.

He continued to glare at me, the golden starbursts around his pupils flaring with the pulse of dominance from his beast. My own beast rumbled a warning within me, and I whirled around in my chair to face the front of the class before my eyes lit up like fireworks.

Just in time, too, because our professor had arrived.

"Good morning, everyone," she said brightly. "Welcome to the first day of Shifter History and Culture."

Professor Oglethorpe was middle-aged, with the tall, solid build of a female with shifter blood while also appearing soft around her generous curves. She wore a stack of diamond-encrusted bands on her ring finger—the modern hallmark of a latent female who was the central bond of several partners. I was sitting too far away to be able to count the bands.

She sauntered over to the desk at the front of the room and dropped her heavy beaded bag on top of it. Unlike the illustrious Professor Blackwell, she eschewed the lectern and slide deck for a more informal vibe, hopping up on top of the desk and taking a seat, cross-legged like she was a kindergarten teacher about to read us a story.

"I've been teaching this class for a decade," she said, beaming her pleasant smile around the room. "And I've discovered that my students are most interested in beginning with the seminal legend of our people."

I ground my teeth together. *Fucking perfect.*

"And that is the legend of the First Guardians," she continued. "Who can tell me a little bit about them?"

A few hands went up, and she called on an eager girl sitting in the front.

"They were the first Prime shifters," she chirped. "An Alpha wolf, a polar bear, a Barbary lion, and the White Tiger. The tiger was the only female and the central bond of the group, but most people today still call them a quad, since they were four Prime beasts."

Right. The formal erasure of the bonded mate came later.

The "bonded quads" running around this place were actually a *quintet* with the addition of their central bond. A bonded trio would be three shifters and their central. It was considered the ideal formation among Primes, and some of the more powerful ordinary shifters worked the same way. The further down the power and dominance scale you slid, the less necessary it was for the beasts to form a quad or trio and bond around a central. Some animals, like wolves, preferred the mini-pack structure of a group of four or five, but most of us ended up in monogamous pair bonds like Mallory and Allen. In the modern age, a pair bond could get legally married, which made navigating the normal human world as a couple easier.

My parents had been a *true* quad, a mix of Prime and ordinary shifters, before my mother was murdered.

Professor Oglethorpe nodded at the girl. "Very good, yes. While we suspect the existence of Prime shifters dates back much further than this, shifter culture only began keeping records a few thousand years ago, at the time our First

Guardians lived in a small settlement on the European continent. We believe this was the first appearance of the wraiths, as the legend suggests, which spurred our ancestors into more meticulous record keeping."

Another hand went up. "Was that when the wraiths first came into existence? Or was it just the first time they broke out of their realm?"

She shrugged. "I'm sure you'll cover this in Lunar Magic class, but we don't really know. We can theorize that as long as the Moon has been blessing our kind with beast souls, there have been the souls unfit to meld with us that go on to become so violently corrupted. The magical universe requires balance, and the wraiths are the darkness to our light. Now...." She cast her gaze around the room, an encouraging smile on her face. "Who can tell me the story of the First Guardians and how it endures this day?"

By being fodder for zealots.

She shot a sly smile over my head. "How about you, Mr. Blackwell? I suspect our top Guardian candidates are well-versed in their history."

Heath blew out a quiet breath that was only *just* tinged with annoyance. "Sure. The legend says that the first wraiths attacked the shifter settlement during a New Moon. They took many lives. The First Guardians, as the strongest shifters, fought valiantly through the night. They'd tear the wraiths apart, but then they'd regenerate and continue to attack. It was the leader of the quad, the Alpha wolf, who discovered that it took a Moon-blessed blade to truly kill a wraith. They vanquished the remaining wraiths and held the line until the sun rose that morning."

"Excellent," the professor said with an indulgent smile at Heath. "But the story doesn't end there, does it?" She glanced to Heath's left, where Phoebe was sitting. "Yes, Miss Atkins? What happened next?"

"The Great Betrayal," she said in a hushed whisper, like she was divulging a dark secret. "The village only had a few weeks to recover because there was a lunar eclipse at the next Full Moon. The First Guardians and others in the settlement fought them off at the gates, protecting the village with the knowledge they'd gained from the first attack. But the White Tiger was approached at her post by the wraith leader, said to be an all-powerful Apex wraith the likes of which hasn't been seen since. He seduced the tiger with promises of extra power and the gift of fertility, since it's believed she was barren."

Such bullshit. Wraiths were mindless soul-sucking killing machines. Seduction wasn't in their skill set.

"She let the wraith through the warded gates," Phoebe continued, "and of course it didn't reward her—it killed her. The wraith leader then unleashed his horde and massacred half the village before the other Guardians were able to kill them. Then they disappeared, ashamed of the tiger's betrayal and mourning the pain of the loss of their bond."

Professor Oglethorpe nodded sagely. "That is indeed the legend our ancestors have passed down through the generations. Modern shifter historians have debated the veracity of the story for many years, but we can all agree that whatever happened, it had a seismic effect on our people."

"The Curse," a girl whispered reverently from the front row.

"Indeed. Our ancestors believed that in retribution for the White Tiger's betrayal of her people, the Moon cursed shifting females. Texts from this age posit that it was the Moon's divine will that females weren't fit to meld with a beast soul, especially powerful ones." She paused, a placid look on her face. "After these events, fewer females were born with the ability to shift. And for those that were, many experienced struggles with infertility, as the tiger was believed to. This has become known as the Curse."

"Do you believe the Curse is real?" the same girl asked. "And that the disappearance of shifting females was the Moon's will?"

The professor gave another diplomatic shrug of her shoulders. "I don't know. What matters is that our ancestors did, and their beliefs may have caused them to selectively breed the female shifting gene out of existence. Whether this was also divine providence is anyone's guess. It has only been in the past two hundred years or so that female beasts have begun to revive within our ranks, and the vast majority are minor or ordinary in power."

Phoebe cleared her throat. "Yes, because the White Tiger was supposedly a very powerful Prime. She was tasked with guarding the gates, just like her mates, and but as a female, she was more vulnerable to the wraith's lies. The Moon deity, in its great and infinite wisdom, has decided that Prime beast souls are best gifted to our males, while our latent shifters, both male and female, are called to glorify our kind by excelling at our secondary affinities and carrying on the shifter lines."

Was that the lie the regressive types were touting nowadays? What a bunch of horseshit.

The Professor nodded sagely. "Perhaps, Miss Atkins. There have been records of females with a Prime beast popping up over the past five hundred years or so, but they are very few and far between. There are some matriarchal wolf packs in the northwest lead by female Alphas, but I don't believe we have record of any female Primes in our region currently."

A guy in the front row scoffed. "Female Primes are an affront to the natural order, which is why they barely exist."

Spoken like a shifter of lesser power with a small dick.

Murmurs of agreement sounded, including two feminine ones behind me. To their credit, Wyatt and Heath remained silent as the dead.

"At any rate," the Professor went on, raising her voice, "in magical academia, we do not teach that the disappearance of shifting females is or is not the Moon's divine will, nor do we take a position on the existence of a curse. We study our ancestors' *belief* in those things and how they affect us today."

A hand went up on the front row. "Like with quad bonding?"

Another serene smile. "Indeed. It is still a widely accepted theory today, adopted by our ancestors after the death of the White Tiger, that the latent shifter is a more ideal choice for a bond than a shifter with a beast soul. Who can tell me why that is?" Her gaze jumped over my other shoulder, to where Callista sat on Wyatt's other side. "Yes, Miss Jackson?"

"Well, we can pretend all we want that the Curse isn't real," she began, sounding smug, "but females who can shift are more likely to be infertile. I don't know the statistics, but—"

"It's mostly anecdotal at this point," the professor interjected mildly, "but we think its somewhere around one in three shifting females experience some form of infertility."

"Right, and also, the presence of a beast soul in a central bond can disrupt the magical connection with the quad, or trio, or whatever. Our most powerful males need a *settled* soul and a large magical well that doesn't compete with a beast for their quad to properly share power with one other.

Especially our Guardians, who need to be as strong as possible to protect us all. Right, Wyatt?"

Wyatt gave a half-hearted grunt in response.

"Yes, very good, Miss Jackson," the professor replied indulgently. She must be pleased as punch to be doing her part to power up her own bonded mates. "Again, we have a lot of *theory* and very little hard data, as there have not been many centrally bonded *females* with the reported ability to shift, but it is believed a bond with a beast soul is less stable and can disrupt the ability of the group to share power. But of course, we can only make educated guesses when it comes to interpreting the Moon's will."

I'd roll my eyes, but this pervasive bias in our culture was the reason I'd been let into the school in the first place, so I would award it a single kudo.

Professor Oglethorpe clapped her hands, her smile brightening even further. "That said, however, I do believe it is wonderful that more and more shifting females are born with every generation. Love is love, and bonding is a personal choice for all involved. Not everyone needs to prioritize power or stability in a potential match. There's plenty of room for everyone, and discrimination has no place in my classroom."

How diplomatic.

Hands started shooting up, but students stopped waiting to be called on before they started offering their opinions.

"Yeah, someday we'll have equality!"

"Fuck that. We'll go extinct if more chicks start shifting."

"Oh, whatever, the Curse isn't fucking real."

"The wraiths will kill us all, and the Moon will curse us all *again* for this woke bullshit."

The professor waved her arms in the air. "All right, all right! We're not here to debate theology or politics. For purposes of this class, we only need to agree that our ancestors believed that the story of the First Guardians happened a certain way, which influenced their actions, and that has affected our kind for many generations. It is a foundational aspect of our culture. Your personal beliefs are between you and the Moon."

Wyatt's throaty chuckle sent tingles along the back of my neck. "Good thing your dad isn't teaching this class, man."

Heath let out a humorless laugh. "We get so many lectures at home, we could get an entire degree in this shit."

I'd heard enough chatter in the short time since I'd left my dorm this morning to surmise that another reason Heath and Aiden were so revered around here was because they had two fathers on the Southeastern Council, which was one of the four governing bodies for our kind in the U.S.

Color me the opposite of surprised that one of the Blackwell dads had staunch beliefs surrounding female shifters, and I'd bet my swords they weren't the progressive type.

Thankfully, the professor steered the discussion into much more boring territory, regaling us with tales of the diaspora of those early shifters across Europe, Africa, and Asia, each culture bringing with it the knowledge of how to effectively counter wraith attacks, which would only follow them across the world.

When we were finally dismissed, I hopped to my feet, eager to go investigate the lunch spread in the dining hall before Ian and I would need to get warmed up for what was probably going to be an eventful afternoon.

"Hold up there, new girl."

I glanced behind me to find Wyatt still lazing in his seat, his broad shoulders hardly fitting in it. He was checking me out the same way he had at breakfast. Callista noticed, and she did not look pleased.

"What's your name?" he asked.

"Avery Baxter."

He mulled that over. Heath looked on silently, feigning disinterest while Phoebe lingered in the aisle to stare longingly at him.

"Where'd you come from, Avery Baxter?" Wyatt asked.

I arched a brow. "Why do you care, Wyatt Gale?"

He chuckled. "I see my reputation precedes me. I'm just curious, is all. I don't think we've ever had an upperclassman show up in the middle of the school year. This place rarely takes transfers, and usually only those starting sophomore year. What's special about you?"

"A few things, actually. Is this interrogation over?"

He grinned. "Sure. See you around."

I hustled out of there, leaving Wyatt to enjoy Callista's whining and Heath to continue pretending Phoebe wasn't trying to eat him alive with her eyes.

7
___

AVERY

A few more of Allen's wolf friends joined us at lunch. While I enjoyed a delicious pita, piled high with chicken kebab and all the fixings, Ian and I made polite but enjoyable conversation with those seated next to us. There were two gregarious male wolves, who were definitely dating given where they had their hands most of the meal, and a soft-spoken brunette, who gave me her extra tzatziki and spent the entirety of lunch staring longingly at Ash.

After returning to my dorm to decompress, organize my assignments, and get changed, I tagged along with Ian as we hiked the short distance to where his schedule indicated Guardian training was held.

Neither of us knew what to expect from today, but it was safe to assume we wouldn't be fighting any actual wraiths in the daytime, behind powerful wards, and weeks away from the New Moon. So I ditched my trusty dark cargo pants and thermal shirt for workout leggings and a racerback tank top, which I wore under my oversized zip-up hoodie. Instead of my beat-up combat boots, I'd slipped on my running shoes.

My blades sat in their comforting position pressed between my shoulder blades.

Ian was dressed similarly in track pants and a T-shirt from our high school swim team, his katana slung across his back.

We passed the state-of-the-art gym, which was set back a little further than the dorms. It housed a large weight room, dozens of rows of cardio equipment, and an indoor track.

Just beyond the gym lay what I'd have thought was a basketball arena if I'd been on a normal college campus. The building was round, like a little Colosseum, and completely enclosed by a domed roof. It had a sleek, modern look to it that didn't match the historical feel of the rest of the buildings on campus.

That was our destination this afternoon.

Other students made their way in that direction, the Prime quads easily identifiable as they marched along, radiating smug confidence and barely constrained aggression. Ordinary shifters were headed that way, too, some alone and deep in focus, while others laughed and joked with their friends. I recognized a few of the wolf contingent.

Everyone was male, and they all wore some form of gym clothes in the black-and-gold colors of the Guardians—a stark contrast to the forest-green-and-silver colors of the college.

I shot Ian a confused look as we observed the others. "Almost no one has a weapon?"

He shrugged, his blue eyes sparkling. "More fun for us, then."

We entered the building, following in the wake of the other trainees. After a short trek through a dim hallway containing offices and locker rooms, we emerged into a vast arena. The floor was maybe three times larger than a basketball court, and like the building itself, it was perfectly round. Bleachers ringed the space, and a jumbotron hung from the domed ceiling.

While the bleachers were dark, fluorescent bulbs overhead lit the arena floor in harsh white light. A few rows of benches and some equipment storage lockers surrounded the edge of the arena floor. The floor itself was slightly springy, like the thin rubber mats you'd find in an average weight room.

Ian nudged me. "What in the world is that?" He pointed at a nearby raised platform that overlooked the arena floor. It resembled the control booth you'd see at a concert, except in places of the knobs and switches, there were rows and rows of softly glowing silver runes.

It was the most complicated array I'd ever seen.

"I have no idea," I replied.

As we continued gawking at the space, it was slow to dawn on me that most of the class was gawking at *us*. It wasn't until my beast flicked her ears in mildly aggressive interest, alerting me to the arrival of Heath and Wyatt, that I dropped back into the here and now.

Wyatt's eyebrows hit his hairline as he realized that it was indeed the new girl from Shifter History class standing in the Guardian training class with two blades strapped to her back. Heath was also staring at me, his brow furrowed like I was a concerning situation he didn't know what to do with.

The whispers of the dozens of trainees surrounding us intensified.

"You know, I get that this is a bit of a sexist operation," I said to Ian, "but they could just let me train with them for an hour or two before they decide how aghast to be at my presence. Do they think my swords are just decoration?"

He laughed. "You're adorable. Of course they think that."

"All right, all right, everyone shut the fuck up," a deep voice barked.

Several men strode into the room. The leader, the one who'd spoken, wore dark combat fatigues. The black T-shirt plastered to his enormous chest bore the golden Guardians logo over the left chest. He looked a few years older than us, maybe midtwenties, and his dark blond hair was shorn close to his head in a military-style cut.

Flanking him were three other males dressed similarly, all of them radiating both irritation and menace. Probably the rest of his quad.

"Why is everyone standing around whispering like a bunch of fucking schoolgirls?" the leader demanded, marching onto the arena floor and turning to face us where we all lingered around the edges.

"Sir," a guy piped up from somewhere to my right, "there's two random new students here, and one of them's a chick."

"What?" he barked, his pale eyes narrowing as he scanned the group of us.

I sighed heavily. *This better be worth it, Dads.*

With my chin up, I stepped out of the crowd and under the harsh lights of the arena floor. Ian followed, sticking tight to my side.

The hostile stares of the entire room pricked my skin, but Heath's and Wyatt's were the only ones that burned the side of my face like a brand.

I gave the guy who I assumed was our trainer a friendly wave. "Yeah, hi. I'm Avery Baxter, junior. This is my brother, Ian. He's a sophomore. We're new trainees."

He glared at me, his lip curled. "Is this a joke? We don't allow females in the Guardian program."

Murmurs of agreement sounded around me.

"We do have an Ian Baxter on our roster, Cash," one of the other trainers announced, examining the tablet he held. "Fox shifter, Support Squadron candidate."

"That's not fucking fair," someone griped from nearby. "The rest of us had to survive the freshman year cull to make it to the sophomore program."

The lead trainer, Cash, flapped a dismissive hand at his quadmate's announcement. "I don't give a fuck. No one is allowed in this program without the points and experience required for their class and section. And you two"—he swung his glare back to us—"have exactly *zero* points or experience. Get the fuck out of my class."

Ian snorted. Glad *he* thought this was all hilarious.

"That's not true," I protested. "I've killed hundreds of wraiths. So has Ian."

Cash scoffed. He nodded to the trainer with the tablet, who tapped away at it.

The jumbotron lit up. On the screens was a list of student names.

It was titled "Guardian - Quads," showing Blackwell Quad leading by several hundred thousand points. The next list was "Guardian - Individual." Heath Blackwell was at the top by a nose, followed closely by Wyatt Gale, then Elijah Harrow. Aiden Blackwell was a bit further down the list, but I suspected this had more to do with his lack of attendance at training than his skill. The list flashed again, and "Support Squadron - Individual" appeared. I recognized none of the names but noted that the point totals were a fair bit lower than the Guardian lists. It was tough for a non-Prime shifter to kill a higher-powered wraith alone, so I supposed this made sense.

"I do not see any *Baxters* on this list," Cash said with a sneer. "No points, no entrance into this program."

Ian and I exchanged what was probably our seventh confused look of the day. "Are points for wraith kills?" I asked. "How do you track that out in the chaos? Is it an honor system or—"

A throat cleared politely next to us. A cute guy wearing the student training gear had sidled up next to Ian. His big brown eyes were kind, and he had tawny brown skin and some seriously luscious dark curls. "We accumulate points by facing the Simulated Wraith Invasion Magic, known as the SWIM," he said, waving a hand at the rune-decorated control booth with an apologetic smile. "It's a marvel of complex and sophisticated magical constructs and illusions and the pride of the Guardian training program. In sophomore and junior year training, we fight the SWIM's conjured wraiths. At the end of each school year, the bottom half of the leaderboard is cut. Only those who make it to senior year start training out in the field against real wraiths."

I blinked, trying to process that.

Ian had no comment except to very unsubtly check out this very helpful and also very attractive student. Said student noticed, and a flirtatious smirk appeared on his face.

"Wait." I squinted at Cash the Dickhead. "You mean all of the kills you guys are talking about are against magical illusions?" I waved up at the jumbotron. "All of those points are for killing *pretend* wraiths?"

"Watch your tone," Cash snapped at me. "The SWIM is a near-perfect replica of the experience of a wraith attack and has been the foundation for the most successful Guardian classes in the history of the force since its inception. Our Guardian candidates come out of this program *trained* instead of *dead*."

I gaped at him. Disbelief and anger coiled in my gut. My beast growled, pressing against the bars of her cage.

Ian's beast was always sensitive to mine, and he squeezed my hand. "Calm, Aves."

I shut my eyes, tamping down the fireworks. When I opened them, I speared Cash with a distasteful glare. "Ian and I have walked the streets of Fulton City with my family every lunar cycle since I was fourteen years old, trying to limit casualties in our small urban community, where the Guardians don't patrol." Harried whispers started up around me again, but I was on a roll. "We lost *two* shifters just last month to a particularly bad attack. We've lost more over the years. And you're telling me that all these capable power quads and other trainees have been here, less than ninety minutes away, slaying magical constructs when they could be lending a hand to vulnerable areas during the New Moon?"

Heath and Wyatt had inched into my peripheral vision as I finished my tirade. They wore identical frowns, like they were suspended somewhere between disbelief and anger.

"That's the biggest crock of shit I've ever heard," Cash snapped. "Fulton City? A female killing wraiths? Get the fuck out of my class. I won't tell you again—"

"Cash," a deep voice boomed from somewhere in the darkness of the bleachers. "She stays. They both do."

I searched for the source of that surprising and kind of bone-chilling order. With the slightly enhanced vision my beast afforded me, I could just make out an enormous man reclining in the first row of the bleachers near the back of the arena. He wore the same fatigues Cash and crew did, but he was much older. He had a bushy beard and a bald head, and his tree-trunk-sized arms were crossed over his burly chest. He was watching the proceedings like it was a mildly interesting football game.

Ian's new friend whispered, "That's Ward Gale. Actual head of the Guardian training division. He's rarely here, but he's the big boss in charge."

Gale. Wyatt's dad? Probably. Unlike his son, Ward Gale was exactly what you'd expect a Prime bear shifter to look like.

"Ward, come on," Cash griped. "You don't believe that shit, do you?"

"I think a few rounds against the SWIM will determine the veracity of Miss Baxter's claims, don't you?"

Cash engaged in a short stare-off with his much larger and scarier superior before he huffed, relenting. "Have it your way." He motioned to the booth, and one of the other trainers climbed inside.

This guy was as tall as Cash and only slightly leaner, and he had white-blond hair that contrasted sharply with his dark eyebrows. He began chanting under his breath, his fingers tracing the runes, their silver hue brightening as he channeled what could only have been the lightest touch of magic into them, since it was the middle of the day. The system itself would have to store a shit ton of magic, re-upped during a Full Moon, like an enchanted solar panel.

The overhead lights dimmed, and the ethereal light-blue glow of Moon magic consumed the arena floor. "Because we have *new* trainees today, and because some of your brains are so fucking porous that I assume most of what you learned last semester has leaked out your ears over the holiday break, we're going to review and demo like it's your first fucking day," Cash announced.

A few groans sounded.

"Look at us, making friends already," Ian said, chuckling.

"You did make an actual friend, you butthead," I griped, jerking my chin at Mr. Adorable Curls.

The boy grinned. "Brody," he said, holding a hand out to me. "Ordinary lynx, junior, and number two on the Support Squadron leaderboard."

"Hot," Ian whispered.

I shook Brody's hand. "Avery, undisclosed, soon-to-be top of the Guardian leaderboard."

His big brown eyes widened, and then he barked a loud laugh. "This is fantastic! Those meatheads won't know what hit them."

"Blackwell! Gale!" Cash barked. "On the floor. I presume our current leaders are willing to demo even though you're missing half your quad?"

My irritation receded and my interest was piqued. Even if I got nothing useful out of today, I'd at least get to watch half of the fabled Blackwell Quad put on a show.

Show me what you've got, boys.

8

AVERY

Heath and Wyatt did not appear surprised to have been volunteered to demo. They dropped their gym bags to the floor, and Wyatt ambled over to one of the storage lockers. He pulled a battle-ax from the locker, and then he followed Heath as he trudged out into the middle of the glowing arena floor. It was only then that I realized Heath was one of the few students who had arrived wearing a blade. He pulled a long, slightly curved sword from the sheath on his back—a saber, and a fine one by the look of it.

As they swung their weapons a few times to limber up, Cash directed everyone to clear the floor. We climbed into the bleachers and spread out around the perimeter. No one sat down. Instead, we all leaned over the railing, ready to watch half of the Blackwell Quad do whatever they were about to do out in the middle of all that brewing magic.

"As a reminder," Cash said, his voice echoing around the arena as he held a microphone in front of his face, "we don't train against Lɪ wraiths, colloquially known as 'wisps.'"

The glow brightened, and several wraiths appeared in

the middle of the arena. I had to hand it to them—the illusion magic was extremely realistic. Wisps took the vague shape of an animal and were barely corporeal, and they tended to leak and spread like an oil spill from the source of a rift in danger of tearing.

"And why is that, Anderson?" Cash asked, pointing a finger in the direction of a beefy guy leaning over the railing near the control booth.

"Li wisps are harmless and don't have a corporeal form that can be slain," the guy recited.

"And why do we learn to identify them anyway?"

"Because they are often seen in the location of a rift that will tear and release higher-powered wraiths within the next few lunar cycles."

"Correct."

Well, at least they weren't teaching total bullshit here.

The wisps winked out, and a dozen swarmers materialized onto the floor. Again, the magical construct was dead-on. A wraith's form was always a mixed bag, but we could count on a swarmer to range anywhere from a poodle to a small pony in size. A swarmer usually couldn't kill a shifter on its own, but they became lethal when they would pool together and, as their name suggested, swarm.

And the illusion wraiths were definitely gearing up for a swarm. Half of them took the form of a bat-like body the size of a Doberman, but the bat had eight gnarly spider legs and a mouthful of tiny, spiked teeth. The others had more of a chimpanzee shape, if a chimp were a dried-up husk with fangs and no eyes bent into a quadrupedal form with legs twice as long as its body.

All of them had chunks of skin and hair missing, exposing decaying ribs and pieces of skull.

Like all wraiths, they were a colorless dark gray, but the magic gave them a soft ice-blue glow around the edges.

Some of the bat-spiders screeched, and all the swarmers converged on Wyatt and Heath.

It was immediately obvious that those two had been training as a team a lot longer than just the two years they'd been here at the college. They worked through the horde methodically, dodging teeth and claws and slicing off limbs. Heath slashed his saber through the necks of two of the chimps, lopping off their heads. The wraiths flashed and faded away, the "kill" releasing the magic holding the construct together.

The trainer with the tablet tapped the screen, and the jumbotron chimed above us, awarding Heath a hundred points for each kill and Blackwell Quad the same amount.

The SWIM rules appeared to mirror those in the real world—you had to decapitate a wraith to kill it. We'd learned you could also gouge its heart from its body, but that was trickier and messier. Anything else, and the wraith could regenerate.

Wyatt kicked a spider away that'd launched itself at his chest. He spun wildly, swinging his ax and severing the head of another spider that'd attacked him from behind. The wraith winked out, and Wyatt's points went up on the board.

"It really looks like they're slicing limbs," I mused. "And taking real hits when they collide with the magical simulations."

"They are," Brody agreed. "That's seriously advanced—and seriously expensive—magic. The Guardians hired the world's best construct and illusion specialists to design this program about twenty years ago. If you ever sneak up into the control booth, you'll see thousands of runes etched into the equipment. There are a bunch in the arena floor too.

The specialists visit each region's programs quarterly to recharge the magic when the Moon is at full power."

"Wow," I said. "That's impressive, but you know what's even easier than paying through the nose for specialized magic like that?"

Ian snorted. "Going outside at the New Moon?"

"Bingo."

"You two are so fun," Brody gushed. "But fair warning. The injuries we sustain against SWIM aren't real, but the magic makes it so your body *thinks* it's real. If you get slashed with mutant razor claws, it will feel like your arm is falling off. If a six-foot-long tentacle smacks you in the head, it can knock you out. You can even 'die'. If you take a lethal hit, you'll pass out right there on the floor and need to be revived. The magic also knows when you've been down long enough for the SWIM to devour your soul and kill you that way. And if you die or flee, you *lose* the points you'd have won from the kill. It's happened to almost all of us."

"Hear that, Aves? Next time a Giant almost takes your leg off, you won't have to spend the night in the hospital."

Brody sputtered a cough, his eyes going comically wide. Some of the other nearby trainees were giving us some dubious looks. Being surrounded solely by shifters with sensitive hearing was going to take some getting used to.

Heath and Wyatt made quick work of the rest of the wraiths. The last of them winked out, leaving the two of them standing in the middle of an empty floor, their breathing labored but barely a sweat broken. The soft glow of the active magic seeped into the carved lines of Wyatt's bicep as he slung his ax casually over his shoulder. Heath sheathed his saber behind his back in a smooth practiced movement.

They waited, looking almost bored, as Cash got back on

the microphone. "That was a textbook elimination of an L2 swarm, gentlemen. As blades are needed for the kill, there should be no reason to shift in a fight with an L2. It is all about quick and efficient weapons work. Support Squadron trainees take note, as culling these swarms will be your main job in the field while the Guardian teams take on the larger, deadlier wraiths. Now"—he nodded to his buddy in the control booth—"we're going to run a randomized sequence of higher-level specimens at Gale and Blackwell. Normally a sequence like this is reserved for quads only, but Gale and Blackwell like to show off, right, boys?"

Neither of them acknowledged him.

"And if one of them is KIA on this one, then consider it my gift to you chumps who are trailing so far behind them on the board."

Without warning, two Rippers materialized on the floor and charged straight for the guys.

Rippers were the equivalent of fighting a Prime shifter. Apex predators, always larger than the version of the animal found in the wild, but the wraith version came in the form of a fucked-up mutant with appendages, claws, and teeth in places you couldn't predict.

Heath and Wyatt were being treated to a pair of hellhounds the size of an Alpha wolf—putting them somewhere around five feet tall at the shoulder. These came with dinosaur spikes down their backs, extra-long tails that looked like they had scorpion stingers on the ends, and gaping jaws that oozed orange flames around drooping gray skin and exposed jawbones.

I'd seen a few of those around. The tail forms varied, and sometimes they spewed noxious purple gas instead of flames, but either way, they were a bitch to deal with. Iterations of wraiths tended to repeat, and they usually spawned in multiples. Whatever was happening in their realm was seriously fucked-up.

The hounds snarled, leaping straight for Heath. He pulled his sword and ducked under one beast, then sprang up just in time to lop its tail off before stabbing the other in the throat. It lurched, and Wyatt was quick to behead it with his ax. He pivoted, wound up, and launched a baseball swing at the other, who'd just recovered from losing its tail and was back on the attack. The flat of the ax hit it in the face, and it staggered away.

Two more Rippers appeared. Seven-foot-tall gorilla things with ram horns and four-inch claws. I'd seen similar versions of these in the wild, as well.

Those thick necks were challenging to cut through, and the wraiths were so much faster than they looked.

Wyatt tossed his ax to the floor, and the blade embedded there as if it were soft ground, the handle sticking up in the air. He shifted instantly, his training gear coming apart at the seams and falling into a heap on the floor. A large but *sleek* bear tore from his body, his dusty-red fur appearing almost purple in the icy-blue light. He charged the gorillas as Heath managed to behead the remaining hound, earning the kill.

The bear barreled into a gorilla, knocking it to the floor. Wyatt was the fastest bear I'd ever seen—nimble but still enormous and solid enough to plow through a wraith that size. He roared in its face and slashed his bear claws across its throat. Then he sprang away, allowing Heath to jump in with the head-severing blow.

As Heath hacked away at that thick neck, Wyatt was already charging the remaining gorilla. It took a few additional maneuvers to get the thing down, but he managed to rip its arm off with his strong bear jaws. It shrieked, throwing Wyatt off, and then it used its remaining arm to swipe at Heath as he approached. He dodged, but the entire crowd hissed in unison when the gorilla raked its claws across Heath's back. His shirt tore, and he winced in real pain, but I could see no blood or open wounds.

Wyatt's bear circled the gorilla and leapt for it when he spied an opening. They grappled until they crashed to the floor. Wyatt roared in pain as the gorilla landed on top of him, but he managed to flip them and roll quickly away before Heath was back for the final beheading.

Or so I thought. After a moment of quiet, the bodies of the dead wraiths flickering out of sight, one final wraith materialized at the back of the arena, motionless as if on pause.

"That was four L3 Ripper kills," Cash announced. "Four thousand points to both Gale and Blackwell individually and to their quad. Note the efficiency of working with one shifted beast and one blade-wielder. This is vital when dealing with most L3s, and certainly any L4s. Let's see if the boys have one more in them. If not, there goes ten thousand points from both columns."

He was throwing a Giant at them. Kind of a dick move after the four Rippers, but since it wasn't real, I didn't feel sorry for them.

Giants were exactly what the name passed down from the days of the First Guardians implied—gargantuan, horrifying monsters. Bigger and stronger than any Prime shifter, with the possible exception of some of the mythics. If you were lucky, they might be a little slower than their Ripper brethren, but that was where your luck usually ran out.

This guy was a humanoid werewolf thing, maybe twelve feet tall and standing on two massive legs with clawed paws the size of car tires. Its head was entirely too big for its body, its wolf jaw unhinging at an unnatural angle and displaying two rows of grotesque teeth, like a mouthful of porcupine quills. Its hands were only slightly smaller than its feet, the claws curved like little daggers. Dark gray fur stood on end like tiny spikes over the parts of its body where flesh hadn't melted away. Its eyes glowed with the blue light of the magic.

Wyatt, still a bear, exchanged a look with Heath that managed to convey exasperation even on his bear face. Heath just nodded and walked a few feet away to impale his saber in the ground next to Wyatt's ax.

The trainer working the runes in the booth released the wraith, and it let out a howl that sounded more like glass shards being dragged across cement than an actual lupine noise.

A huge golden wolf tore from Heath's body. I snapped my mouth closed, irritated that the form of Heath's wolf had surprised me. He was as big as my dad, who was the largest wolf I'd ever laid eyes on until today. Heath's wolf was nearly as big as Wyatt's bear, but he was—somehow—the thicker of the two, his solid muscles bunching under his lush golden coat as he ran.

Wyatt's bear ran after him, both beasts charging straight for the wraith. It lumbered forward, moving quickly for a Giant that size and swinging its lethal claws in challenge.

Heath skirted the wraith and attacked the back of its legs, sinking his jaws savagely into the gnarled muscle. The wraith roared and whirled, taking a hard swipe at Heath's head.

He released the wraith and dodged, but the monster still managed to clip his hind legs, sending him spinning like a top across the floor.

Wyatt roared, goading the wraith into following him.

Heath recovered, and they both sprinted toward the side of the arena where their blades impaled the ground.

As the wraith rushed them, they turned in unison and attacked. Two large, savage beasts snarling and tearing at an even larger savage beast for minutes that felt like hours until they finally managed to fell the thing. It hit the ground with a screeching roar, and Heath buried his teeth in its neck. Wyatt danced away, shifting back to a nude man with liquid grace.

He plucked his ax from the floor and hefted it high. "Now!" he bellowed.

Heath released the wraith and darted away. Wyatt's ax came down across the wraith's neck, severing it entirely in one stroke.

The wraith blinked out of existence, and the jumbotron's chime echoed through the arena. Ten thousand more points to each of them and also to their quad.

Polite applause sounded.

I took one tantalizing moment to soak in the sight of the naked bodies of Heath Blackwell and Wyatt Gale. Wyatt's pale skin was covered in tattoos that dripped down from his neck, expanded across his broad chest, then flowed down his arms. Heath, the golden boy, had an intricate wolf inked in the middle of his tanned chest. Both were male shifter perfection, chiseled abs and thick thighs and round asses you could bounce a tire iron off of.

I tore my gaze away as they began to dress. "What a show," I said to Ian. "They should sell tickets."

"I'd buy one," he replied, grinning salaciously as he checked out Wyatt's ass.

"Do you think it's over?" I asked. "Surely they aren't going to release an Apex wraith on someone."

Brody made a pained noise. "No, definitely not. They

don't train us on L5s, since they're only ever seen during a lunar eclipse, and you can't really kill them, anyway. Though we can volunteer to try to *outlast* one in the SWIM, no one does because it's basically a guarantee you'll die and lose 100,000 points. Elijah's the only one in recent memory to try it. That's how he's so high on the board even though he misses half our classes."

The thought gave me a shiver. I hoped I never had the pleasure of meeting an Apex wraith. Or Elijah's basilisk, if he somehow took one on and didn't die.

Then I scowled, remembering that it was a *fake* Apex wraith he'd challenged.

"Bravo," Cash said into his microphone. "An impressive fight, as always, from the Blackwell Quad. The rest of you need to step your shit up if you ever hope to come in even a respectable second place on the junior class leaderboard." He paused, scanning the bleachers until his beady gaze landed on me. "And now that we've all been refreshed on wraith classification, battle tactics, and how the SWIM works, I think it's time we let our gatecrashing female impress us with her street smarts."

Half the class snickered.

The others looked mildly concerned.

Cash gave me a mocking grin. "Let's go, Baxter. On the floor."

9
____

HEATH

Wyatt and I climbed into the stands behind the control booth. I was exhausted, though the power of my beast would recharge me quickly. My back still ached with the phantom pain of claws tearing out my skin, and I was lucky I didn't have a broken leg where the Giant had smashed my wolf's hindquarters like it was returning a tennis serve.

Still, my beast was thrumming with the sated bloodlust he experienced from even the simulated kills of high-powered wraiths. I loved the arena, the competition, and even more, I loved showing the other quads who thought they were nipping at our heels why they'd never be as good as we were in their wildest fucking dreams.

"New girl sure is full of surprises," Wyatt mused as we watched Avery Baxter stride confidently onto the arena floor. "We thought we had her figured out, didn't we?"

"Yeah." I swallowed, then tried to figure out where the hell that flash of anxiety had come from. "There's no way the school fast-tracked her admission for *this*."

We didn't take an interest in every transfer student, but the school so rarely took upperclassmen transfers, especially those with no previous magical education. Avery's arrival in the second semester of her junior year was notable.

Also notable—the fact that she was smoking hot.

Hot girls were abundant at a shifter college, but my wolf half had decided to take particular notice of this one. She'd challenged me in class earlier, and my beast was very interested in getting her underneath us.

Wyatt was experiencing similar urges, so after class this morning, I sent a demand-disguised-as-a-request to one of the ordinary wolves who was a computer science major. Within an hour, I had her university file on my phone.

Junior. Fulton City resident. Community college credits. Shifter blood—obviously, since no one was allowed admission to Proteus without it—but undisclosed status. The file did contain a conspicuous note that Avery's father was an Alpha wolf named Rand Baxter.

Case closed, or so I'd told Wyatt. A female, likely latent despite her apparent unwillingness to disclose it, from a Prime bloodline.

The administration was tossing her to the unbonded quads like a piece of meat.

Because the situation at the Blackwell home had escalated over the holiday break, my quad had resolved to get focused on finding the right girl for our central, and soon. If Avery was on the menu, all the better.

Then she showed up to Guardian training, wearing two wakizashi blades strapped to her back, and our little bubble of cautious interest had burst into fucking vapor.

Prime-blooded latent or not, it appeared she was here to stir up trouble and get herself killed.

Wyatt chuckled at my disapproval. "You heard Trent—they enrolled her brother in training, but not her. The admission staff has no idea what kind of female they let in here."

Avery reached behind her head with both hands and unsheathed her short swords. She spun the grips expertly before slashing the blades in a pattern as she warmed up. She moved like a dancer, her lean muscles flexing deliciously. Her long blonde hair appeared almost silver in the soft glow of the magic that was still thick on the floor. She still wore it in the no-nonsense ponytail from earlier today, when I'd spent half of class trying not to salivate over the elegant curve of her neck and her enticing scent, which reminded me of springtime. Her skin-tight leggings left no part of her toned legs and ass to the imagination, and every guy in this room had fucking noticed.

I shook off my wolf's irritation. *Cut that shit out.*

"Damn," Wyatt muttered, his gaze glued to her every move. "Check out the runes etched into her blades. Those are Moon-blessed, man. Maybe she really has killed a wraith?"

"It would be a weird thing to lie about," I agreed. "But wraith attacks in the city? Where it's mostly humans? That makes no sense."

Wraiths were attracted to shifters because they needed to feed on them to survive, and they were especially attracted to *powerful* shifters. The higher the concentration of Primes in an area, the higher frequency of attacks and the more dangerous breed of wraiths involved. While there were certainly a few shifters scattered around the urban areas, they were few and far between. I wouldn't be surprised if Avery's Alpha father was the only Prime living within the Fulton City limits.

"All right, Baxter," Cash said into the mic, sneering at her. He was a dick, but his quad were three-year veterans of the Guardians and had the most kills in their division, an especially impressive feat given they weren't bonded yet. I tolerated him because he and his team knew their shit. "No training wheels. You clearly think you're hot shit, so you're getting the real deal, same as everyone else in your class year."

"Except that none of this is actually *real*," she shot back, glaring at him.

Wyatt laughed. "She really is disgusted with all of us. Is that hot? Why do I think that's hot?"

"That's your bear talking. She provokes the urge to dominate."

His grin widened, slow and lascivious. "Mmm, yeah. That does sound like fun."

Cash rolled his shoulders, and we heard him mutter, "Cocky fucking bitch," before he nodded at Trent, who was still behind the SWIM controls.

Eight swarmers materialized on the floor.

Wyatt swore. "What the fuck is he doing?"

"Trying to humiliate her," I replied, grimacing.

A SWIM sequence of eight L2 swarmers was a quad challenge in our sophomore year, or one for a full Support Squadron unit of six ordinary shifters in the junior year.

It was not something we threw at single fighters, and certainly not at a non-shifting *female* on the first day of training.

Avery's brother, Ian, was leaning over the bleacher railing across the way, watching his sister with something like lazy amusement on his face—not an ounce of concern to be found. He was snuggled up next to Brody Dara, a lynx shifter and one of the more talented Support Squadron trainees in the junior class. It would've been unlike Brody not to warn Ian how bad this was about to get for his sister.

Both Baxter siblings were too fucking cocky.

The wraiths coalesced into their swarm and charged at Avery. This group were all identical mutant crocodile things, if crocodiles had agile feline legs and four vacant eyes brimming with the SWIM's magical glow. They were the size of pit bulls and would be ten times as aggressive.

She twirled her swords, unbothered, and then ran straight into the fray.

My dread morphed into confusion and then into... something else, as I watched Avery Baxter skillfully and systematically destroy every single wraith on the floor.

Every croc that lunged for her with a gaping maw received a violent stab straight into the mouth and through the brain. She whirled, chopping off legs, leaping onto backs and hacking at those thick necks, the kills ringing up as she went. It'd been an even bigger dick move by Cash to choose this form of swarmer from the magical array because the thick croc-like neck made decapitation difficult work, unless you were swinging a battle-ax like Wyatt's.

When the last wraith flickered out, a few whistles sounded from the crowd.

"Fuck" was all I had to say.

"Fuck," Wyatt agreed.

"She's better with a blade than just about everyone in this room."

"Yeah, and there's not a chance she's latent," Wyatt muttered. "Not with how she moves. She has to have a beast soul."

"Disappointed?" I asked wryly.

"Not sure." He peeled his eyes off Avery, who stood defiantly in the middle of the floor, catching her breath as she gave Cash a cold stare. Wyatt waggled his dark red brows at me. "Doesn't mean I—*we*—can't fuck her."

"That's the worst idea you've ever had."

He grinned. "Liar."

Cash was back on the mic. "What the fuck was that?" he demanded. "You can clearly shift, Baxter. What's your beast?"

"I don't have to disclose my status to you or anyone else," she shot back.

My wolf half rumbled irritably, and I agreed. *What are you hiding, Avery Baxter?*

Cash snapped his fingers angrily at Trent, and without warning, two L3 Rippers appeared on the floor. They were vaguely bear shaped and just as huge as Wyatt or any of his fathers, except they had curved demon horns, snouts the size of a wolf's, and sickles for claws that could run a girl of Avery's size straight through.

"Cash, what the fuck?" I snapped over the railing.

"Problem, Blackwell?" he drawled.

"We only let *Prime* shifters go one-on-*one* with a Ripper, you asshole."

"This bitch needs to be put in her place. Or do you want her in this training class? How about at camp this summer? Or running around the front lines during the lunar eclipse this fall?"

I scowled. He was implying that she was a weak link and would fuck everything up once we were allowed out in the field, but that shit bothered me for a different reason I wasn't able to examine because the wraith bears roared and converged on Avery.

She remained where she was, shifting lightly on her feet.

Her shocking blue eyes pinned to the wraith that reached her first.

It leapt at her. She ducked underneath it and thrust both of her blades straight up into its gut as it soared over her head.

"Holy shit," Wyatt said.

Bellowing in outrage, the wraith crashed to the floor.

The second wraith swiped its claws at her head. She dodged, rolling to the floor and severing the wraith's hind leg as she went. It screeched, losing its balance and toppling over. She sprang from the floor and ran for its head. In two vicious swings of the blade in her right hand, she'd hacked its head from its body.

"Trent!" Cash barked, his face turning a deep shade of maroon.

A collective gasp sounded as a *fucking Giant* materialized on the floor. We never trained single individuals against an L4 Giant unless that person volunteered, usually in a desperate bid for points on the leaderboard, which almost always backfired and ended with the person's "death" and the loss of those points. Even my quad had only ever gone up against a Giant in at least a pair, and certainly not without a shifted Prime beast.

Cash was a sadistic asshole.

The remaining Ripper had recovered from Avery's impaling it through the gut and was lumbering her way. Now she also had a ten-foot-tall serpent-shaped thing with six legs and a crocodile mouth full of six-inch needle teeth to contend with.

Avery slashed at the mutant bear, keeping it at bay while the serpent crawled along the edge of the arena, stalking her.

"Ian!" Avery shouted.

Without hesitation, Avery's brother vaulted the railing and landed in a crouch at the arena's edge. He unsheathed his katana from his back and sprinted straight for Avery and the bear.

Wyatt whistled. "Shit, he's fast."

Ian ran at the bear head-on, ducking a swipe of its claws before slashing his blade across its chest. It roared, too distracted by trying to maul Ian again to notice Avery until she'd jumped straight onto its back, the magical construct holding her weight as if it was a real, corporeal thing. She raised both of her blades and stabbed the bear right through the back, severing its spine.

She dove from its back as it collapsed. Ian took its head off with one swing of his katana, and then they turned to face the Giant together.

"This has backfired spectacularly on Cash," Wyatt mused, chuckling.

I blew out a breath. "It's going to make her a target."

He sighed. "Maybe."

Across the way, Wyatt's father watched all of this without a hint of emotion. He'd stayed silent as Cash tossed a criminally overpowered SWIM sequence at a brand-new, unknown female with no experience in feeling the blows or the "deaths" that the magic could deliver. I suspected Ward's presence was the only reason Cash hadn't pulled the plug and accused Avery of cheating the second her brother dropped in to help her.

Because we all knew it didn't fucking matter. It would have hardly been a fair fight against an L4 if *I'd* jumped in there with her, much less her brother, the fox shifter.

The serpent screeched a terrible noise and attacked.

Ian began to run circles around the arena, using his

impressive speed to try to draw the wraith's attention. It struck at him, its mouthful of teeth nearly sinking into Ian's leg. Avery shouted in alarm. As Ian rolled away, Avery hurdled him and landed in front of the wraith in time to catch its next strike.

It lunged for her, mouth gaping, the rows of needles in its jaws aimed straight at Avery's face. It would be an excruciating hit and probably an instant "death." I tensed, my knuckles turning white where I gripped the railing.

Avery rammed one of her blades right up into the wraith's mouth, impaling it through its skull.

The wraith shrieked and flailed, wrenching its head away from Avery and taking her sword with it. She swore, cradling her arm with her free hand. The teeth must've still gotten her.

Ian bolted for the wraith. He tossed his sword to Avery as he ran by her, shifting mid-stride into a hardy silver fox.

"The fuck?" Wyatt said. "That fox can't do shit against an L4."

As the serpent thrashed, Avery's blade still stuck in its mouth, Ian's fox scurried up its back until he was on top of the flailing head. The fox snarled and sank its claws into the wraith's void eyes, blinding it while he held on tight.

Avery shook out her arm and charged, holding Ian's katana in her dominant hand and using her remaining wakizashi blade as a companion sword. The magic would allow the wraith to sense her location despite it not having the use of its eyes, just like real Giants were supposedly able to do. It spun, shaking its head violently as it lunged, and its serpentine neck caught Avery in the torso, knocking her across the floor.

Ian's fox clawed and bit at its head.

Avery climbed to her feet, wincing, and then she squared up again.

"Ian! Now!"

The fox shifted instantly into a nude Ian. As the extra weight tipped the serpent's head back, he reached into the monster's mouth and ripped out Avery's blade. He launched himself down onto its back, using the momentum of his fall to stab the wraith through its spine just as Avery approached to deliver the final killing blows.

She buried her shorter blade in its chest before grasping Ian's katana with both hands and swinging the blade straight through the wraith's thick neck like she was knocking a baseball out of the park.

"Holy *fuck*," Wyatt exclaimed.

The wraith flickered and disappeared.

The arena was dead silent.

Jared, assistant trainer and the quietest of Cash's quad of douches, logged the points on his tablet, and the jumbotron populated new scores. Ten thousand each to both Avery and Ian Baxter. Avery had been here for a single day, and she was now at the top of the Support Squadron leaderboard. Ian's points for just the one Ripper kill and the Giant had him solidly in the upper middle of the pack.

Cash didn't have shit to say.

Frankly, neither did I.

Finally, Ward Gale stood up from his lone perch in the bleachers. "Well, I'd say we can make room for both these new trainees in our program. I think perhaps our trainers should take a moment to reflect on our teaching methods, as I'm certain not a single pair of students in this room could do what those two just did without the aid of a Prime beast. Welcome to the Support Squadron, both of you."

Ian had pulled his pants back on, and he gave Ward a jaunty little salute and then a shallow bow.

Avery cleared her throat. "Thank you, sir, but I'm actually here to be a Guardian."

I blinked.

The room burst into grumbles, gasps, and annoyed protests.

Cash finally found his voice. "Absolutely the fuck not."

Ward just shrugged. "Earn it, then, Miss Baxter."

"Ward! You can't be serious."

Wyatt's chuckle was humorless for once. "My dad, always the shit-stirrer."

Avery smiled at Ward. She had a gorgeous fucking smile, and that old bastard was a goner. Wyatt had four little sisters, and the man adored every one of them. "Thank you, sir, I will," she said brightly.

Cash threw his hands into the air and then growled into the mic. "Class dismissed. Everyone better have their shit together at Wednesday's training or there will be hell to pay."

Wyatt and I didn't move as the class filed out around us, opting to linger and watch Avery and her brother as they gathered up their swords and Ian's clothes, amicably chatting as if they'd just finished a fucking pilates class together and instead of singlehandedly destroying the order of the entire Guardian training program. Brody Dara joined them, staring at Ian like he wanted to eat him for dinner.

Fortunately, it was dark up here in the stands, so Avery couldn't see Wyatt looking at her the same way.

"Cut that out," I told him. "This is going to be a shitstorm."

"I think our quad leader doth protest too much. Who knew skill with a blade could get me so hot?"

I didn't want to think about how much blood had rushed to my dick through that whole display, so I growled at Wyatt. "It doesn't matter how skilled she is. Or how many real wraiths she's supposedly killed. Here, within these walls, she is only going to cause trouble."

And trouble was something my quad had in abundance. We didn't need any more.

10

WYATT

Heath and I hit the showers in the arena locker room—solo, since no one else had done shit during today's session except stand around and gape like assholes as a female and a fox shifter made them all look like fucking chumps. We didn't speak as we toweled off and redressed. Heath was deep in thought, the default mode for our quad leader, so I left him alone to process the half dozen conflicting thoughts I knew were banging around in his head.

"Let's swing by Aiden's office before dinner," he suggested as we marched back across the lawn toward the main campus, huddled under our sweatshirts as we braced ourselves against the bitter wind. Shifters ran hot, but it was cold as fuck out. "We should probably update him on this mess."

"Maybe he has thoughts on our new little wildcat," I added, smirking. "Since she apparently had his class this morning."

Heath quirked a blond brow. "You think she's a feline?"

I shrugged. "No idea. You're better at reading a beast than I am. If she has one."

His jaw tensed. "I don't have a read on her at all. She was such a machine against the SWIM. Her strength and speed indicate a body enhanced by a beast soul, but she and her brother have also clearly had superior training. It could just be that she really has been fighting actual wraiths for years, and it shows."

"While the rest of us were taking combat class in prep school and poking each other's beasts with training weapons."

"Yeah," he grumbled irritably.

And we'd thought we'd been ahead of the curve. Only shifter kids from wealthy families or those with Prime beasts—often one and the same—were able to attend the exclusive private schools that catered to the supernatural, and those of us who knew we wanted to serve in the Guardians from a young age would begin training well ahead of our arrival at Proteus College.

We'd learned to wield our blades of choice and were given advanced combat training by expensive private tutors. Aiden, Heath, Elijah, and I had even had the extra good fortune to meet and resonate with one another when I was in middle school, so by the time we entered Proteus, we were a fully formed quad. We met up with Aiden here in his senior year when we started as freshmen, and the rest was history.

Blackwell Quad had been at the top the leaderboard since day one for a reason. We'd taken every advantage afforded to us and worked our asses off to achieve our goals.

For me, the Guardians were always endgame; my dads were vets, and I'd follow in their footsteps. I had talent, and

I'd been raised with a sense of duty that I should use it to protect the community.

For Heath and Aiden, becoming Guardians would earn them a level of freedom and independence from their fathers and the Council that nothing else could.

And for Elijah.... Well, he needed to be seen as disciplined and useful rather than uncontrollable and deadly.

So yeah, we were going to graduate Guardian training in the top spot, making us the most valuable asset in our class as we entered the forces.

Except it appeared the thing we'd needed to do to *really* excel was run around outside the borders of Guardian patrol as high school students, pick fights with real wraiths, and hope we didn't die.

Heath was undoubtedly frustrated by this news.

I thought it was kind of hilarious.

"Stop looking so fucking... giddy," he griped at me. "I know you think this whole thing is entertaining, but it's also going to become a major distraction."

I clapped him on the shoulder. "Relax, dude. It's been a day. We'll handle our own shit, like we always do, and I bet Avery the sexy wildcat bails on this whole thing before the semester's over. She'll decide occasional off-the-books wraith vigilantism in Fulton City is preferable to dealing with Cash and a lot of other bad attitudes."

Though it'd be nice to have a taste of her before she stomped out of here in a huff, middle fingers thrown high. My beast hadn't taken special notice of a female in a long while, but something about Avery had perked him right up. Heath was suffering from the same affliction.

When we arrived at Aiden's office on the third floor of the Magical Education building, we were just in time to catch Professor Eleanor Tally as she exited, tossing a flirty smile and a little wave over her shoulder as she went.

"Thanks so much, Aiden. See you bright and early tomorrow!" She startled when she spotted Heath and me, and her smile turned even more coy. "Oh, hello, boys. Dropping by to visit Aiden? I'm sorry to be missing you, but I have a student conference in five minutes." She stuck out her lower lip in a little pout she only used around Aiden and occasionally the rest of our quad. At all other times, she was firmly in her hard-ass professor mode.

Heath managed not to roll his eyes. "We have quad business anyway, Professor Tally. Not really here for a social call."

"How many times do I need to ask you boys to call me Eleanor?" she said with a little swat to his shoulder, and then she winked. "Aiden's quad has special privileges."

Yeah. Those privileges included fucking her, if any of us so chose. Tally was the same age as Aiden and had been a senior when we were freshmen. She wanted Aiden in the worst way and the rest of us in a slightly less-than-worst way. A pedigreed latent, she was angling to become our central bond, and for her, Aiden was the way in.

He was probably going to be in a mood after this.

"Thanks, *Eleanor*," I purred at her, shoving Heath into the office. I slipped inside behind him and slammed the door before she could bat her eyelashes at us again.

Aiden sat behind his large oak desk, reclining in his chair with his arms crossed over his chest, his face pinched. George was curled up on a couch cushion that Aiden had thrown in front of the small fireplace. Ignoring our entrance, he sunned himself in quiet bliss.

I nudged George with my shoe. "There you are, you little slut. I heard you were groping the new girl."

He lifted his head an inch, yellow eyes narrowed as he hissed at me, then went right back to his nap.

"Is that true?" Heath asked his brother as we both took our seats in the chairs facing Aiden's desk. "George decided to crawl all over Avery Baxter this morning?"

Aiden's brows bounced upward. "It is true. He slithered into my class, then lost his mind and climbed right onto her lap. How did you hear about that?"

"We sat behind her in Shifter History. He left some scales behind in her sweater."

Aiden raked a hand through his wavy brown hair. "It was the strangest thing. She didn't care in the slightest either."

"Not surprising," Heath muttered.

Aiden's hazel eyes narrowed behind his stuffy professor glasses. "Is that why you two are here? To ask about Avery? Not that I mind the intrusion—Eleanor is growing more insistent."

I chuckled. "That blouse was unbuttoned a little lower than usual."

He rolled his eyes. "If it's not her, it's a student. This is the price I pay for refusing to join a quad my own fucking age." He pinned Heath with a scrutinizing stare. "Why are you in my office, asking about the new girl?"

Heath leaned forward in his chair. "What did you think of her?"

"She's a mouthy brat," he replied instantly, his nostrils flaring.

I snorted a laugh. "Coming from you, that's as good as saying you'll be bending her over your desk before the semester's over."

He glared at me. "She lectured *me*, in my own fucking class, about how wraiths supposedly harm humans."

Heath grimaced, and I could only casually scratch the back of my head.

"I'm inclined to believe her, man," Heath said quietly. "She showed up uninvited to Guardian training this afternoon."

Aiden stared at him. "She what?"

We took turns describing what went down at training. Aiden's eyes had widened to saucers by the time we finished.

"What the hell is your dad thinking, Wyatt?" he asked me, incredulous. "She'll get torn apart for this. If not by an actual wraith in the near future, then by the ignorant meat-headed beasts in this school."

"He was thinking that she dominated the fuck out of that arena, man. You weren't there. She took down a fucking L4 with only her brother's help, and he is a *fox*."

He sighed. "Great. Well, I've failed to mention that I'm also tutoring her in runes twice a week. The intro class is full, and apparently that's her strongest secondary affinity."

"Lucky you," I said, waggling my brows.

Heath punched me in the shoulder. "I wish you would take this seriously."

"Why? None of this is our problem. We all got a little excited when we found out that not only is she gorgeous, but her father is an Alpha wolf—"

"He is?" Aiden asked, brows creeping upward once again.

"—and now we've had to file that little flash of cautious optimism away as *something else* because it's pretty damn clear she has a beast but is being real fucking shady about it—"

"This girl wants to be a *Guardian* but won't shift or even admit she has a beast?" Aiden pressed.

"—and yeah, it sucks because our backs are kind of up

against the wall, and having a new, hot, Prime-blooded latent female, who caught all *three* of our interests, not to mention fucking *George's* interest, had been a positive development on the bonding front—"

"Jumping the gun a little bit to claim I was *interested* in her," Aiden grumbled.

"—but I guess it's not to be," I finished. "So, yes, bummer, but if she wants to make waves in the Guardians or the school, it isn't our problem."

Heath sighed. "As the strongest quad on campus, waves in the Guardians or the school inevitably become our problem, Wyatt. Or a distraction, at the very least, and we don't need that shit." He glanced at his brother, as glum a look on his face as I'd ever seen. "I don't suppose you've heard anything from home?"

"I called Richard," he replied, sounding resigned.

Heath slumped in his chair. "And?"

"Useless," Aiden spat. "He and Charles just do not give a fuck anymore."

Richard Blackwell was an attorney and ran one of the most influential law firms in the Georgia shifter community. He was also a Prime panther and Aiden's biological dad. He and Charles—another of their fathers, who was an investment banker—spent the majority of their time away from home. Business trips, long stints at their respective apartments nearer to Fulton City for "work," vacations with college buddies, bullshit like that. They'd make appearances at the Blackwell family home with just enough frequency to tend to their bond with Heath and Aiden's mother, providing what I assumed was just enough physical intimacy so that it didn't wither and die. Then they'd bounce again.

It wasn't how a bonded quad was meant to operate, but

if I had to spend a significant amount of time around the two other Blackwell dads, I'd probably be looking for a way to make myself scarce too.

"It's not like either of them has the ability to do anything short of kidnapping Clara and hiding her," Heath said, "even if they did care, which they don't. Holden is too fucking powerful and runs our entire family with an iron paw."

"But you're closing in on him," Aiden said softly. "Not to mention, you're light-years better trained, since none of our parents ever deigned to serve in the Guardians. You have to believe in yourself, Heath."

"I do," he growled. "And I'd do anything to save Clara from their twisted machinations. But I can't save her if I die challenging Dad."

My bear's rage had been clawing under my skin since the conversation took this turn, and a guttural growl finally broke through.

"Easy, Wyatt," Aiden said gently.

I relaxed my jaw and blinked away what I was sure were ruby-red headlights. Discussion of Heath and Aiden's little sister's situation never failed to set off the bear inside. I had four little sisters between the ages of twelve and seventeen, and if one of my dads had tried to pull something like this on any of them, he'd already be dead. "Sorry. Remind me again why we can't just unleash Elijah at your parents' next garden party and call Holden's death a tragic accident?"

Aiden removed his glasses and pinched his brow. "Because even if Elijah did manage to kill him without losing control and killing everyone else in a one-mile radius, which would then put a target on his back, it would leave the question of Clara's custody up in the air. It would take months if not years in the legal system to resolve it, and by then it would be too late."

Clara was sixteen years old, the light of Heath's and Aiden's lives and best friend to my oldest sister, Willow. She was also the only latent daughter of the most powerful shifter in the Southeast Region. This made her a highly desirable potential bond for the sons and soon-to-be-formed quads of our community's most influential families.

Holden, along with Stephen, their fourth father, who was an Alpha wolf, decided to take full advantage of this and planned to sell her to the highest bidder.

We'd found this out over the holiday break.

While simply offering their daughter up for cash would've been scandalous and in poor taste for a family of the Blackwell's status, the two of them had begun entertaining proposals involving business connections, investments in the Blackwell companies, and Council favors from a bunch of other rich pricks attempting to secure a powerful legacy for their sons.

We'd formed a plan to deal with it, but Heath needed to be stronger to have a shot at taking his father in a challenge.

"And that brings us back to why we're all so salty," I said, going for light but just sounding tired. "We've decided to quit fucking around and attempt to find a suitable girl to bond, but not one of us is excited about the prospect, nor do we have any candidates that have vibed with all of us *and* our beasts. The new girl was an interesting little beacon of hope, but she is perhaps not what we thought she was, so we remain at square one."

"Even if she doesn't have a beast," Heath said, "she will likely get herself killed if she continues this farce about becoming a Guardian. We need to bond for reasons beyond dealing with my parents—we're headed for a dangerous job and need the ability to share power that a latent central bond is supposed to provide. Not to mention Elijah needs a solid bond for the rest of his fucking life."

We sat in silence for a few minutes. Heath stared broodily into the fire. Aiden glared at his computer screen. George snoozed, the reflection of the flames dancing on his glossy purple scales. I fucked around with my phone, first requesting to follow Avery on Instagram, then sending off another text to Elijah in our quad group chat.

> When the fuck are you coming back?

After a few minutes, he finally replied.

ELIJAH

> I'm on the way.

Heath jerked his phone from his pocket. His eyes narrowed as he read.

HEATH

> Did you get anything useful?

ELIJAH

> The guy won the knife off a member of the Low Country Kings in a poker game over the summer.

"Oh, perfect," Aiden said, tipping his head back with a groan. "A shifter motorcycle gang."

I stood up and stretched my aching muscles, then shrugged my backpack onto my shoulders. "I'll tell him to meet us at Aiden's house so we can chat in private. If I order pizza now, he can grab it at the guard station on his way into campus."

"Good idea," Heath said, also rising from his chair. "I don't feel like being in the middle of whatever will be stewing in the dining hall tonight anyway."

Aiden stood up from his desk and began to pack his shit. "Make sure Elijah's pizza has the dairy-free cheese."

"Like I haven't been dealing with Elijah's bullshit dietary restrictions for years," I replied with a roll of my eyes. I poked George again with the toe of my shoe. "Let's go, asshole. Your daddy is on his way."

He didn't acknowledge me, but he did slowly unwind his body and begin a leisurely slither toward the door.

11

AVERY

Breakfast this morning was a tenser affair than it'd been yesterday. Mal kept the conversation upbeat, but the weird stares and whispers surrounding us in the dining hall weren't exactly subtle.

"So, uh," Allen said around a mouthful of bacon, "did everything go okay at Guardian training yesterday, Avery?"

Chance stared at me with wide eyes. "They didn't toss you out, did they?"

"They did try," I told him, narrowing my eyes at some freshmen who were sneering and pointing in my direction from a few tables over.

"Yeah, the lead trainer would've had Avery bodily removed from the arena if Intense Bear Daddy hadn't stepped in," Ian added, grinning. "I think he likes her."

I pinched my brow. "Can we please stop calling him that?"

Allen gaped at me. "Ward Gale was there? You crashed Guardian training when the big bear was around?"

I shrugged. "He seems nice."

Mallory pointed her spoon at me. "First the snake, now

this. I think you've been living away from shifters for too long, friend, and it's warped your judgment. Try to remember that we're all violent, untrustworthy beasts and proceed with more caution. No petting."

"I am not going to pet any bears," I retorted.

Wyatt chose that moment to stride into the dining hall, dressed to incinerate panties in fitted dark jeans, combat boots, and a tight long-sleeved T-shirt that hugged his broad chest. A black beanie covered his red hair, and his cheeks were flushed from the cold outside. He grabbed two coffees from the beverage bar, gave a friendly bro nod to one of the tables full of quads I recognized from training, and then sauntered back toward the door.

I watched him over the rim of my mug. As if he could feel my gaze on him, he glanced my way, and our eyes met. A sheen rolled over his emerald irises—his beast peeking out to say hello. My own beast rose in response, gliding like silk under my skin.

Wyatt grinned, a look of smug satisfaction on his handsome face. He winked at me, and then he disappeared through the hall's arched entrance and out of sight.

Mal cleared her throat. "Well, I wouldn't blame you if you wanted to pet *that* bear," she muttered under her breath.

"Me neither," Ash added, studying the now-empty doorway. "I'm gay as hell, but that's an ass."

As I'd seen that ass naked yesterday, I could confirm.

I pushed my chair back from the table and got to my feet, slinging my backpack over my shoulder. "On that note, I'm off to class," I told everyone. "Regular, boring, non-magical literature class. No bears."

Famous last words.

Early to class, I was able to grab a seat in a quiet row near the back of the room. The space, smaller than my classrooms yesterday, since it was an upper-level class, was arranged in a semicircle with auditorium-style seating. We were in an older part of the Humanities building, so the room came with wood paneling, a chalkboard instead of a whiteboard, and chairs that creaked loudly when sat in.

Students filed in around me. Most didn't look my way, but there were a few who stared, whispered something to their friends, or made a face.

I couldn't let it bother me, or else I'd go nuts. It was only my second day.

Now that I was here, did I think it would've been nice to have a normal college experience, as much as a shifter-only school could be considered normal? Going to class, making friends, parties, boys, and all without signing up for the staring and whispers and near-death experiences?

Yeah, sure I did.

It was probably still within my reach if I wanted to put my swords away, bow out of Guardian training, and pretend to be a normal shifter girl for the next year and a half. The risk of someone coming after me because of the rumor of what I was would probably dissipate over time. I could work on convincing my dads of that fact, and they wouldn't pull me out of school if I wanted to stay here without becoming a Guardian.

But fuck that.

After yesterday, I wasn't just joining the Guardians because my family thought I needed it to be safe or because I had the skills to succeed there.

It wasn't even about the real need for those with my skill

set to protect our community from the horrors of the wraiths. I could do that at home.

No. Now I was joining the Guardian training program because I *wanted* to be there.

It was the somewhat ridiculous discovery that trainees didn't go anywhere near a real wraith until senior year that did it. I wanted to be a constant reminder that this was cowardly and negligent when nearby unpatrolled areas were experiencing casualties at higher rates every year. I'd be a thorn in the sides of Cash the Dick and his bro-squad when I performed as good as or better than their best, all because I'd had real-world experience instead of being sheltered inside their magical "near-perfect replica" that supposedly churned out the best Guardians in a generation.

But it was also that arena. I'd never felt so moondamned *alive* as I had out there, slaying wraiths that looked and moved like real ones, all without the low thrum of fear I was used to when facing the actual threat of grievous bodily harm or death. Ian and I had worked that Giant monstrosity together like we did that kind of thing every day, and we really didn't. I'd seen a Giant all of twice in my life, and the second time was the night that brought me here.

The only injuries I'd walked away with were some bruised ribs and the phantom pain from the magic making my body think I'd almost had my arm bitten off by a needle-toothed serpent creature.

When Cash had thrown that thing onto the floor, I'd worried that I'd be fighting the urge to shift the whole time. But with Ian's help and the knowledge that I was facing a magical construct and not actually fighting for my life, my beast had been content to ride the adrenaline wave and let me work.

I couldn't wait to do it again.

The chatter around me quieted. I glanced up from my laptop, expecting to see the professor entering the room, but instead it was a student. He seemed impervious to the stares, his gait stealthy and graceful as he made his way to the shallow staircase that bisected the rows of desks. He was tall—maybe six-two or three—with a lean build that still showed off corded muscle all over.

He radiated raw power, barely contained within that sinewy body. It felt cold and brutal.

My beast was immediately on edge.

As he climbed the stairs, he finally looked up from his phone, shoving it lazily in the pocket of his ripped jeans. Our gazes slammed together like magnets, and I strangled a gasp.

He was beautiful, this guy. His eyes were an eerie yellow gold—a unique color, even for a shifter. His inky black hair hung in tousled waves over his forehead and around his ears. A thin gold hoop hugged each of his earlobes, and he had another looped through his nostril. He wore no jacket or sweatshirt, only a loose linen shirt that was unbuttoned halfway down his sternum, showcasing olive skin and a sculpted chest. A tattoo peeked from his collar—a snake, wrapped around the back of his neck and draped over his shoulders, the head and tail each dipping just below his collarbone.

This had to be Elijah.

The basilisk shifter.

Fourth and final member of the Blackwell Quad.

George's daddy.

He stared at me for a second, and then he broke into a big, beaming smile as if I was the most exciting thing he'd ever seen.

He resumed his climb, headed straight for me.

The small hairs rose on my neck. My beast surged under my skin, her fur standing on end, coiled and ready.

Elijah licked his lips, and a sly smile appeared on his face. He kept those yellow eyes pinned to me as he slinked into my row. He dropped his weathered backpack to the floor and sat down beside me, sprawling lazily in the creaky chair, his long legs stretching into the row below. He smelled minty and a little tropical, like fresh citrus or a fruity drink.

"If it isn't the new girl," he said, his voice a silky rasp. "I've heard *so* much about you, Avery Baxter."

Students were fully turned around in their chairs, gawking at us. He either didn't notice or didn't care.

"I've heard quite a bit about you, too, Elijah Harrow," I replied.

He grinned. His teeth were blinding white, his canines sharper than anyone's human form had a right to be. "I can't believe my luck, getting to share my Tuesday and Thursday mornings with the girl who has my quad in a bit of a tizzy. Not to mention my snake."

I decided to ignore the insinuation that his quad had been talking about me, even though it made me feel weirdly tingly. I made a show of looking at the floor around us. "Where is George? I haven't seen him since yesterday morning."

He only grinned wider. "I see how it is. You prefer his company to mine?"

"I just met you."

"True." He reached under the desk, rummaged in his bag, and pulled out a scuffed laptop. "I fed him this morning, so he's sleeping it off. Hopefully by the time he's out and about again, I'll be your favorite snake on campus."

Something not entirely unpleasant burned in my belly.

My beast went from one fang-flash away from ready to kill to making a preening little rumble in my chest.

Why are you like this?

"Are you this welcoming to all the new girls?" I asked him under my breath, since the professor had finally strode into the room.

"Certainly not. Just the ones who make Cash Rogers look like an imbecile in front of the entire sophomore and junior training classes. Aiden has faculty access to the security camera footage in the arena, babe. I got to watch you in all your glory last night."

I shoved down the urge to squirm. The fact that Heath and Wyatt had watched my wraith battle in real time hadn't registered at the time—too much other fun and exciting shit going on—but imagining the entire Blackwell Quad sitting around a laptop to study me after the fact?

My beast lounged within me, tail flicking as she casually cleaned a claw, preening again. We were constantly bouncing between the urge to *challenge, dominate, kill* the Blackwell Quad and rolling over and showing our belly to each of them.

Seriously, what is wrong with you?

Time to redirect. "Cash is a prick. I think you should eat him."

Elijah waggled his dark brows. "Maybe someday."

The professor began her lecture, and I tried to relax as I sat nearly shoulder to shoulder with the most dangerous predator I'd ever encountered.

It was easier than it should've been. Maybe Mal was right about my shifter instincts being rusty.

An hour passed. Elijah didn't move even an inch out of the cozy little space between us, but he appeared to be dutifully taking notes through the entire lecture. For the last thirty minutes of class, we were assigned a short story to read followed by some discussion questions that we were to go over with our neighbor.

"You feel so... bright," Elijah mused. His golden stare was heavy on my face as I finished the reading. Probing. *Just* this side of predatory. "I'd love to know what you are," he went on, "but I hear we aren't being particularly forthcoming about that?"

I fought the blush that was threatening to rise under his curious gaze. He was as mesmerizing as he was dangerous. "I bet you wish you could walk these halls occasionally without people knowing what you are."

He sobered a bit. "That's true enough. It was never in the cards for me, though. Not as a mythic. And my beast would struggle with... discretion, anyway."

I gave him a sympathetic smile. The more powerful the beast half of one's soul, the more difficult the fight for control could become. I couldn't imagine what that was like for a mythic, and especially one like him.

His cheeky grin returned, and he leaned even closer to me, whispering, "Don't think I didn't notice you dodging my question, but fine. Keep your secrets."

I would, thank you, at least until I had the might and the respect of the Guardians at my back.

When class was dismissed, he escorted me down the stairs and out into the hall. I got the sense that this was unusual behavior for him, given the stares and hushed conversations had started up again.

"I really was normal before I came here," I told Elijah with a sigh. "No one special. Nothing to be whispered about in the halls."

He stopped, turning to face me. With gentle fingers pressed under my chin, he tilted my face so that I was looking him right in those yellow eyes. "I sincerely doubt you've been normal a day in your life, Dove. No more hiding for you."

I could only stand there, transfixed, as his eyes began to glow. His pupils turned to slits, and I sucked in a quiet gasp.

His coy smile fell. He shut his eyes and dropped his fingers from my chin, curling them into a fist.

I stepped back to give him some space. "See you later, Elijah," I whispered before I hurried away.

"Until tomorrow, Dove."

12

AVERY

The hike back across campus to my dorm room was welcome despite the frigid bite of the air. I needed to breathe in something other than Elijah's heady mint and citrus. That was probably how a terrifying snake monster lured his prey—by smelling so good. I had about an hour before I was meeting Ian and our friends for lunch, so I was going to spend it decompressing in my room and finishing our reading assignment from this morning.

I dug my hands into the pocket of my hoodie and braced myself against the wind as I walked. Maybe Ian would be willing to spar with me later this afternoon before I had to meet Aiden Blackwell for tutoring? Might be a good idea to expend all the pent-up energy I was accumulating before being in close quarters with that jaguar.

I hadn't made it halfway across the lawn before my way was blocked.

"If it isn't the bitch who thinks she's better than us."

Four large males stood in the grass, spread out in front of me, arms crossed over beefy chests, menacing smiles on their faces. A quad, likely all Prime shifters, looking like they were here to pick a fight with little old me.

The one who'd spoken stood about six inches in front of the others, designating him the leader of this merry band of predators. He had shaggy brown hair and a day's worth of stubble, and he'd managed to squeeze his enormous shoulders into a denim jacket with a fur-lined collar. His smirk was lazy as he sized me up like he was both checking me out and probing for weaknesses.

"I'm sorry," I said, keeping my tone light even as my beast had woken all the way up, wound tight and ready to strike, "but I have no idea who the hell you are. I couldn't have an opinion as to whether I am or am not better than you, whatever that's supposed to mean."

"Don't play dumb," the lead asshole barked. "We're the Ashton Quad, and our families practically *own* Starburg."

Starburg was one of the picturesque little cities in the Hills. Definitely high on powerful shifters and low on human residents.

"Congratulations," I said. "If I acknowledge how special your quad is, will you go away? I want to get a head start on my homework."

The guy looming off Lead Asshole's right shoulder rumbled a sound of disgust. He was enormous—barrel-chested, bearded, and probably six-foot-five, at least. "She's a mouthy bitch, Rip," he said to the leader.

"Females don't talk to us like that," the male standing to Rip's left added, sneering at me. He had brown skin and black hair buzzed close to his scalp. He was as big as Rip but leaner, and he gave off distinctly feline energy as a golden sheen flashed across his dark eyes. "Females get on their knees and say please for us."

"She wishes," the last guy said with a derisive snort. He

looked just like Rip, minus an inch of height and about twenty pounds of muscle. Little brother, probably. "I wouldn't let an *abomination* within ten feet of my cock."

"And yet here I stand, within five feet of the lot of you because you've decided to harass me on my walk back to my room," I said blandly. "You're a special quad. I'm an abomination. We're all on the same page. Are we finished?" I moved to step around them.

"No," Rip snarled, thrusting an arm out in front of me. "You think you can just show up here, shake your ass at the trainers, and waltz right into the Guardians? My quad put in two years of training and work only to get fucking *cut* at the end of last year. It's bullshit, and I won't allow it."

Ah, now their hostility made more sense. Word had gotten out, and my name on that leaderboard was hurting their fragile egos. An affliction of many shifter males.

"Feel free to express your displeasure to Ward Gale," I told him. "Now, if you'll excuse me—"

"I challenge the new girl," the Rip look-alike announced, his voice booming across the field.

Nearby students stopped in their tracks.

Great.

I took a step back and squared my shoulders. "To what end? There's no pack hierarchy between us to fight over, and membership in the Guardian training program isn't decided by challenge."

Rip rolled his eyes. "You really are a dumb bitch. Since you're new here, I'll explain. You seem to think you belong among the school's top males, so we'll treat you like one. We challenge each other to establish dominance and pecking order on this campus. Get your ass kicked enough, and it will be clear to the entire student body that you're weak and shouldn't be anywhere near the Guardians. And once we all see that you really are an abomination, we'll also know you aren't fit to lick the cum from any Prime male's dick."

My beast rumbled dangerously within me. *Yes, they're gross and terrible, but now is not the time. Keep it together.*

Little Rip stepped forward. "We go until one of us can't go anymore—knockout or submission. Unfortunately, the college forbids challenges to the death, but severe maiming is always on the table. We usually fight as beasts, but since whatever weak-ass fucking animal you're harboring probably won't help you much, human form is allowed a weapon. If you can find one." He winked at me.

Looked like I wouldn't be traversing campus without my blades from now on, even in the daylight.

"Get on with it, Ranger," Rip griped.

Ranger rolled his eyes. "How about I go easy on you, new girl? I'll stay in human form, and who knows? I might be feeling charitable. You're hot enough, so maybe I *will* grant you the honor of sucking my cock in exchange for not breaking your arm in three places."

"I really pity any poor girl you four may have your eyes on for bonding," I replied. I set my backpack down and windmilled my arms. While I had no doubt I could turn around and sprint away faster than they could catch me, it would make me look even weaker than if I let Ranger the perv beat the shit out of me until I bled all over the grass. "Egos so fragile, you have to pick a fight with an unarmed female. Coercing sexual favors from an *abomination* with threats of violence. Real winners, all of you. The town of Starburg must be so proud of its exalted sons."

My words had the intended effect. Ranger's nostrils flared like a bull's, and he charged straight at me. The small crowd that had gathered around us gasped like they hadn't thought he would actually go full force at a female.

I ducked his first attempt to knock me out cold with a wild swing of his fist at my head.

"No wonder you got cut from the Guardians," I said as I danced away. "Your aim is shit."

"Shut the fuck up." He lunged again, throwing his whole body into a tackle.

I dropped to a crouch and caught his bulk, using his momentum to flip him hard over my shoulder. He landed hard on his back, shouting obscenities.

I whirled and pounced on him before he could get his feet back under him. One hard stomp to the groin and one solid punch to the temple, and he was out.

The silence around me was deafening. I stood up, shaking my hand out. That fucker's head was rock-hard, and I'd split the skin on my knuckles. The whole thing had taken less than sixty seconds, which I could only hope was a decisive enough victory that I could be on my way.

"Yes, I'm stronger than I look," I told Rip, who'd lost that asshole smirk and just looked stunned and quite pissed. "So, with that settled, are we finished?"

"Barrett!" he barked. "Get her."

The huge bearded guy shoved to the front. His muscles swelled, and then a giant brown bear burst from his body, leaving his clothes in shreds on the lawn.

"Fuck," I swore through clenched teeth as gasps and screams erupted around me. My beast clawed at her cage, but I couldn't let her out. Not unless I was desperate and near death.

But with a giant brown bear charging at me, she might just get her wish.

The bear reared up on his hind legs when he reached me, and he swiped sharp claws at my head. I dove away, but he still managed to rake them across my shoulder before I hit the ground. Unlike the magically simulated injuries I experienced yesterday, this one opened my skin. I could feel the blood seeping from my stinging flesh and into my sweatshirt as I rolled to my feet.

The bear roared, rearing up again to smash me. I darted away, just missing what would've been more deep scores in my back. Barrett was enormous, bigger than Wyatt's bear, but in what was probably my only sliver of good luck, he was a hell of a lot slower.

"Avery!"

Ian's terrified voice cut through the noise of the crowd. He elbowed his way to the front, Brody the lynx at his side. Ian lunged like he was going to jump into the fight with me, but Brody grabbed his jacket and held him back.

"It's a challenge, you can't intervene!" he shouted in Ian's ear. "But this will help." He unsheathed a sword from his back and tossed it to me.

I caught it by the hilt and immediately slashed at the bear's face. He roared and lumbered backward a few feet.

"Brody, what the fuck is this?" I yelled, swinging the sword a few times. It was a thin double-edged blade, light and easy to wield, with a guard made of several intricate twisted braids of steel. Pretty, but you'd have a hell of a time slicing the head off any wraith more powerful than a swarmer with this thing, so I had no idea why he had it.

"It's a rapier!" he shouted back. "Beggars can't be choosers when there's a giant bear trying to rip your head off, Baxter!"

"Damn it," I groaned.

The bear roared again, rattling my bones. He stood up on two legs once more and attacked, this time with his big fucking teeth. Bears liked to clamp down on your neck and shake you like a rag doll, and there would be no keeping my beast inside if I let this bear get his teeth around my throat.

I thrust the rapier upward with all my strength, ripping a huge gash in the bear's stomach as he came down on top of me. He roared in agony. Unfortunately, while I was strong enough to toss Ranger the large human over my shoulder, I could not say the same for a 900-pound bear.

His bulk smashed me, and I fell under him, my sword still buried in his gut. The impact knocked the wind from my chest, and I felt a rib crack. Still, I jammed that sword into the bear with everything I had.

"Avery!"

That was Ian again. I hated how scared he sounded.

Barrett didn't enjoy being impaled on my blade, so he quickly rolled off me, staggering and bleeding on the grass. I sucked in a shaky breath. Adrenaline surged, my beast pumping an overload of aggression and rage through my body. I rolled to my feet and launched myself onto the bear's back.

With a mighty heave, I drove my blade through his spine. He roared a cracked, terrible sound and collapsed.

"Get a healer!" Rip shouted into the crowd.

I limped away from the bear. I was breathing hard, and it kind of hurt. I pointed my rapier at Rip. "Fuck you. He'll regenerate in an hour if he just lies still." A thing I wished I could do to heal all my fun new aches and pains. "Had enough?"

The dark-haired guy stepped forward. He held a dagger in each hand, which meant he was going to fight me in human form—at least to start.

"I challenge you, new girl," he said, twirling the knives in his hands. "I might even slip up and cut your fucking jugular. They'd probably expel me for that, but I bet my parents can take care of it."

Good to know that killing in a challenge on campus meant expulsion. My parents definitely did not have the kind of fuck-you money it would take to buy me back in.

"My name is Avery," I said. "Not 'new girl.' What's yours?"

"Victor," he replied, his lip curling like it was beneath him to have answered me.

"You've got this, Avery!"

That was Mallory. Her bright orange hair was easily spotted where she huddled next to Ian, looking concerned, to put it mildly. Allen watched somberly behind her, and Ash was there, too, her tattooed arms crossed over her chest as she glared at Victor.

"You hear that?" I said to Victor. "The crowd thinks I can take you even though I've been smashed by a giant bear, while you're standing there looking fresh as a daisy."

"You talk too much," he snapped, and then he struck.

He slashed the knife in his right hand right at my throat in a fast backhand. I leaned out of the way, so he swiped through empty air, and then I thrust my rapier at his stomach. I managed to stab him, but he shoved me off before I could bury the blade deep. He came quickly at me then, one hand then the other, and I parried just as fast, moving my sword to block each strike and wishing I had my two wakizashis instead of Brody's toothpick. I blocked and stabbed and sliced as we danced across the lawn.

My ribs hurt. The deep gouges where Barrett had slashed my shoulder stung even as I could feel them beginning to close. My arm was sore from taking the bear's weight onto my sword.

But I was also *very* pissed off. The nerve of these

assholes, all because *they* couldn't hack it in the Guardians. Not only were they trying to humiliate me, they were also trying to force me to shift. The Ashton Quad were old-school bigots, the type that believed the Moon had deemed females were unworthy of a beast soul and cursed those of us who had one because of the White Tiger's "betrayal." They wanted to goad me into showing my animal both because it would paint me as an "undesirable" female and because they assumed she was something unimpressive. They wanted to prove to the school that not only was I an abomination but a weak shifter who had no business playing with Primes.

I sliced into Victor's bicep for the fourth time, finally causing him to lose the ability to use his arm properly. He bellowed in pain and frustration, tossing his knives to the ground.

A pulse of aggression pierced the air. His tall frame stretched, and his skin rippled.

Oh shit.

His body morphed into a giant black panther. A Prime panther was substantially larger than one found in the wild, almost a foot taller at the shoulder and a hundred pounds heavier.

My beast slammed against the bars of her cage. She wanted *out*. My skin tightened, but I pushed back with everything I had.

The panther leapt, snarling, claws extended. I slashed his chest with my sword, then dove out of the way.

I hit the ground, rolling onto my back. The panther pounced again, blood dripping from the deep gash in his chest. He swiped at me with his claws. I blocked him with my sword, but his teeth were next, and he buried them in my side with a guttural snarl.

I screamed. It fucking hurt. Someone else was screaming —sounded like Mal. Ian was shouting, and Brody and Allen were shouting back at him.

I managed to twist, yanking my body away from his teeth, then twisting again to bring my elbow down on his head. He yelped, staggering, and I scrambled to my feet.

My vision tunneled. I'd been this injured before, and I'd been fighting fucked-up shifter spirits who could eat my soul if they managed to incapacitate me. This asshole couldn't kill me even if he wanted to—I wasn't going to let it get that far, but I sure didn't want to blow my cover on the second fucking day of school.

I dug deep and took a running leap at the panther, slashing Brody's rapier in a downward strike. The panther snarled, bracing like he was going to pounce, but my sword sliced through his neck.

Students screamed.

I stopped, yanking the blade out before it could hit the spinal cord. I'd have to really hack away with this thing before I could actually take the beast's head off, but it was still a devastating hit. He'd be out for hours healing that in his beast form.

The big cat fell to the ground. I staggered away and knelt in the grass, catching my breath.

A few yards away, the bear still lay in his healing sleep.

Ranger had shifted to heal the head injury I'd given him with my fist. He was a nasty-looking canine thing—a jackal, maybe?—and he sat silently at Rip's flank.

Ian shook off Brody and Allen and sprinted to me. He slid to his knees next to me in the grass. "*Aves.* Fuck, are you okay?"

"Yeah, I've had worse."

He glared. "That does not make me feel better."

"But I'm kicking ass, Ian," I said, gesturing to the carnage on the field.

He fought a smile. "You totally are. Prime quads aren't shit, are they?"

"You, fox," Rip barked. "Get the fuck out of here. We're not finished."

A harsh wave of shifter dominance slammed into us. Ian winced, and a shock of rage blasted through me. I climbed to my feet and pointed at Rip. "Don't you dare *bark* at my brother, asshole."

"You're dead, you little bitch," he snarled. "This challenge isn't over until I say it is. You should've just gotten on your knees and fucking taken it like females are supposed to."

"Ian, go," I pleaded. "He'll bring his brother and Moon knows who else into this if I break the rules of the challenge."

"I don't give a shit, Avery," he snapped. "You're torn up, and this *challenge* is bullshit."

Rip tore his shirt off. Fur rippled across his skin, and then a large gray wolf tore from his body. An Alpha, but only just.

He howled, preparing to attack.

I raised my sword.

"Enough," a deep voice boomed.

Heath Blackwell stepped in front of me.

13

AVERY

"Take one more step, and it'll be your last, Ashton." Rip the wolf growled, showing Heath a mouthful of sharp teeth.

"Sure, try me," Heath said, folding his arms across his chest, appearing casual, almost bored. "I'd love to smear your ass all over this field. It would be fun for me. I haven't worked out today, and it would save me the trouble."

Thank the Moon. I sat down in the grass, finally taking a load off. Ian flopped down next to me, rested his elbow on his knee, and propped his chin in his hand. We both had an excellent view of Heath's ass in snug denim.

Rip snarled, and with a contraction of his body and a fast cracking of bones, he shifted back into human form. Naked Rip stood barefoot in the grass, glaring at Heath, his thick slabs of muscle glistening from the exertion of such a quick shift to and from beast form. "What the fuck, Blackwell? You're interfering in a challenge."

"Is that what this is?" Heath asked lazily.

"You know it is," Rip bit out. "You don't win a challenge against a quad until there's no member left standing."

"That would be true in a challenge against *another fucking quad*, Ashton," Heath said, his voice icing over. "No, instead you four have decided to gang up on a lone female. That's embarrassing enough by itself, but then that female has apparently incapacitated"—he made a show of looking around at the animal bodies strewn around us—"three of your quad, and without the aid of a beast. I'm doing you a favor by ending this now."

"Fuck you, Blackwell," Rip said, sneering. "That bitch is done. I'm finishing this. You can't possibly want this bullshit with her joining the Guardians to continue."

"It doesn't matter what I want," Heath replied, back to sounding bored. "Ward Gale makes the rules, not me, and not you. If you'd have spent a fraction of the energy you just used to attack a female on fixing the shitty teamwork your quad displayed in the arena last year, maybe you wouldn't have been cut."

It was mildly comforting to hear that the Guardian training program, even with dickheads like Cash at the helm, still had the wherewithal to toss to the curb assholes who didn't know how to work as a team.

"For the last time, Blackwell," Rip snarled. "Get the fuck out of my way."

They glared at each other. I couldn't see Heath's face, but I imagined his eyes had lit up like golden sparklers. Rip's eyes pulsed with a deep amber glow, like he was pressing his beast's will against Heath and then getting slapped back. The flavor of dominance unique to Alpha wolves was thick and soupy in the air around us. Students standing in the splash zone fidgeted. Swimming in a dominance battle between Primes was off-putting for most shifters, and Heath in particular was a very heavy hitter.

I reached for Ian's hand and found it trembling ever so

slightly. I squeezed it, sending calming energy from my beast to his.

After a long, tense minute that felt like an hour, Rip swore violently and dropped his gaze. Heath had submitted him, and it appeared even Rip wasn't dumb enough to challenge Heath wolf to wolf.

Rip pulled a pair of sweatpants from his backpack—those who could shift tended to carry extra clothes around because unexpected shifting happened and destroyed clothes when it did—and he yanked them on before ordering his brother to shift back to human form and do the same. Once dressed, they stalked off, arguing with each other, leaving the rest of their quad to finish healing in a heap on the lawn.

Heath turned around and held out a hand as he looked down at me. "Can you stand?"

I stared at his hand, blinking dumbly, until Ian nudged me. "Yes, I can stand," I grumbled.

I took his hand, which I found pleasantly warm and calloused. His grip was firm as he pulled me to my feet.

My beast chuffed at his touch, flicking her tail.

Stop that.

Once steady on my feet, I let go of Heath's hand, but he had other ideas. He slid that strong grip right up to my bicep, wrapping it snugly around my arm and ushering me forward.

"Woah, what the hell, Blackwell?"

"I'm taking you to the infirmary."

"No, thanks. I'm fine."

"Bullshit. You're bleeding in two different places, and Brody informed me when I arrived at the scene of this nonsense that Barrett's bear crushed you. You're seeing a healer."

Damn it, Brody.

I craned my neck around to give Ian a pleading look. "You're going to let this wolf manhandle me?"

He grinned, reclining in the grass like he didn't have a care in the world. "I, too, would like you to see a healer. Blackwell's saving me at least an hour of arguing with you."

"Ian!"

He just waved.

Heath dragged me past where my friends stood, observing my newest predicament with slack jaws. Mallory gave me an enthusiastic thumbs-up, while Ash's eyes were wide with more of a "what the fuck is happening" sort of look.

"Here," I said to Brody, holding out the rapier. "This pointy toothpick was handy after all. I owe you."

He took it from me with a satisfied smile. "You wielded it like a pro. I can give you lessons if you're ready to ditch your little Japanese sticks."

"Never."

He tutted. "Snob."

"I won't apologize for having good taste in blades, Brody."

"Come on," Heath huffed, pulling on my arm. "I don't have all day."

"I didn't ask you to throw your big Alpha dick around and treat me like an unruly child."

"*Avery*," Allen hissed. "You do remember that's *Heath Blackwell*?"

I rolled my eyes. These wolves and their worship of the Alpha. "Yes, Allen. He's very impressive, but as he's neither my Alpha nor my *father*, this is out of line."

Mal brushed a hand lightly over my side. "That's a broken rib, Avery. If you don't go with Heath to get healed,

I'll have Brody, Ash, and Allen hold you down while I try my hand at it, and I'm only a medic-healer in training." She shrugged, her lips quirking. "I might mess it all up."

"Totally," Allen added, nodding vigorously. "I'm not afraid of you, Baxter!"

"Some friends you all are," I hissed over my shoulder as Heath dragged me away, though I was kind of touched they cared after knowing me for all of two days.

"Thank the Moon," Allen muttered behind me, "because I'm actually very afraid of her."

HEATH SAT IN A PLASTIC CHAIR IN THE CORNER OF THE SMALL med room I'd been assigned upon arrival at the college infirmary. He'd folded his arms over his big chest, and his face was firmly fixed in a fuck-around-and-find-out sort of glower. He'd shucked his jacket and wore only a tight gray T-shirt, so the nurse and I were being treated to the view of his carved biceps flexing under golden skin.

The nurse hadn't questioned Heath's presence even once, and she'd just ordered me to take my shirt off so she could clean my wounds.

"How about a little privacy, Blackwell?" I said testily. "I'm here. I'm getting treated. Why don't you go see if the two assholes whose spinal cords I nearly severed are recovering?"

He was unmoved. "We're shifters, *Baxter*. Nudity isn't a thing."

That was mostly true, except it was more of a thing for females because most of us couldn't shift. Except he knew that I was here to play with the big boys, so he was daring me to act like one.

Holding his glare, I pulled my sweatshirt over my head. My Fulton City FC T-shirt followed, leaving me in my strappy sports bra and jeans.

His hazel eyes flashed, the golden starburst that surrounded his pupils glowing from within as he dragged his hard gaze down my body. He paid particular attention to the deep gouges in my shoulder left by the bear and the bite marks just above my hip from the panther, making a show of examining my wounds rather than checking out my nearly nude torso.

Heath Blackwell had no doubt seen his share of naked girls since he was old enough to get a hard-on and know what to do with it. Shifters were hot-blooded and horny, and it would take more than my modest C-cups shoved into a sports bra to interest the leader of the most in-demand quad on campus.

Not that I cared.

The nurse cleaned my wounds and stitched a few of the deeper gashes closed. Often modern medicine was quicker and more reliable than magical healing for simple things like closing wounds, but she told me to sit tight and wait for the doctor to come see to my ribs.

Heath and I sat in silence for one long minute after she left, and then he spoke. "Why didn't you shift?"

I raised an eyebrow. "You're so sure I have a beast?"

"There's no other explanation for how you move. Your speed, your strength, and your bullheadedness in facing down *four* Prime shifter males in a challenge. Your animal may not be an asset in a fight against a Prime beast, but you could've at least shifted to accelerate your healing."

"I know you were late to the party, Blackwell, but I won three challenges one right after the other, all without the aid of an animal. You should've let me finish them off."

He clenched his jaw. "Rip was going to kill you. You'd embarrassed the absolute fuck out of his entire quad, and he was about to completely lose control. My wolf felt it."

"I'm touched you care."

"Believe it or not, a Prime quad challenging and killing a single female, beast or not, isn't something anyone with sense condones." He dragged a hand through his thick blond hair. "We can't have that kind of anarchy. We're a brutal and violent species at our core, but this is the twenty-first century, and we're here to go to fucking *college*. We don't kill females in an unfair challenge just because they can swing a sword better than the average male."

I stared at him. What a reasonable, level-headed argument that also disclaimed any feeling whatsoever about me personally.

Fine.

"I think you know my skill with a blade is a lot more than *better than average*," I said with a taunting smile.

He leaned forward, resting his elbows on his knees, a shark smelling blood in the water. Now I got a view of his corded forearms flexing along with those biceps as he studied me intently. "Where did you and your brother learn how to fight wraiths—and apparently other shifters—like that?"

"You're aware we've been in the streets, fighting actual wraiths for years, Blackwell."

"So you've said. Who taught you wraith combat? Your parents were never in the Guardians. I checked."

I shifted on my cot, moving to sit cross-legged on the mattress. It was less than a month ago that I sat almost the same way on a hospital bed, though less naked, while another overbearing Alpha wolf loomed in the corner. I needed to not make this a habit.

This part of my family history was mostly a safe subject. "My parents were trained by the traveling Guardians back when they were making a big push for their outreach programs. They lived in a small mountain town in Colorado and were the primary force that kept the occasional wraith attacks there at bay. My Alpha father also grew up in a hostile and old-school wolf pack, so he learned to fight early. My cougar dad, Kaito, was trained in kenjutsu from a young age by both his father and grandfather. My fox dad had a father and an uncle who served in the Support Squadron. And—" I paused, bracing against the brief wave of sadness that smacked me every time I thought of her. "—my mother died when I was three, so our dads have been pretty zealous in making sure we can protect ourselves."

Heath's expression softened. "How did your mom die? Was it wraiths?"

The million-dollar question. "No. She was murdered."

His brows hit his hairline. "What happened?"

And that was where story time ended. "We still don't really know," I replied, shrugging. "It's like you said—we're a brutal and violent species. I should probably stop being a surly bitch and thank you for ensuring that I was not also murdered on the campus lawn today, because it would've broken my family."

His scowl returned. "Then why the *hell* are you trying to become a Guardian? The casualty rate is ten percent in the first year."

"Worry about yourself, Blackwell."

A growl erupted from him with the subtlety of a buzz saw. "You are the most infuriating female I've ever met."

Finally, some praise. "Thank you."

"Knock, knock."

We ceased our stare-off as an attractive man wearing a

white lab coat over form-fitting scrubs strolled into the room. He had straight, shiny black hair, dark eyes that radiated kindness, and cheekbones carved by the Moon herself. His features hinted at an East Asian heritage, and he looked to be about thirty.

"Hello, Miss Baxter," he said warmly. "I'm Dr. Lee. I hear we have some broken ribs?"

"Um, yes," I replied, hyper-aware of how hot my face suddenly felt. "A bear might've, um, crushed me a little bit."

He frowned. "That's unfortunate." He stepped to my side and began to feel around my ribs with gentle pressure. "Hmm, yes, there they are. Let's see what we can do about that, shall we?"

Warmth seeped into his fingers. My right side flared with a sharp pain, and I hissed, but then the pain gradually receded, replaced with a warm tingling feeling.

Heath was watching Dr. Lee's hands on my skin like he was moments from shifting and biting them off.

I shot him a squinty-eyed glare. "If you're going to be pissy, you can leave, Blackwell."

"Hmm, yes," Dr. Lee said absently as he worked. "I'm not sure why you're in here, Mr. Blackwell. Miss Baxter is in good hands."

I sighed happily. The pain was a distant echo now.

"Clearly," Heath bit out. "I'm just here to ensure our promising new trainee doesn't dip out of treatment before she's fully healed."

Dr. Lee lifted a sculpted brow at me. "Trainee, huh?"

"I like killing wraiths," I said with a demure little shrug, "and I'm good at it."

"Are you? Color me impressed, though it sounds like we may be seeing more of you in the infirmary, then," he added, winking at me.

Heath cleared his throat, loudly.

Dr. Lee chuckled. "All right, that should do it. It wouldn't be a terrible thing if you iced these ribs later. And keep your sutures clean and dry for twenty-four hours, please."

"Will do, Doc."

"Fantastic." He grabbed my chart from the little table by the door and shot Heath a pointed look. "I'm sure I'll be seeing both of you again soon."

After he'd gone, I stretched my arms over my head. I did feel a hell of a lot better. I wasn't a stranger to visiting the clinic in our neighborhood after a particularly bad night, but I usually preferred to heal at home with the help of one of my dad Joseph's elixirs or by spending time lazing around as my beast within the privacy of my bedroom.

Heath stood up and prowled over to me. I became acutely aware of the heat of his body as it came within two feet of mine, and then I remembered I was still shirtless.

He brushed a hand over the healing bruises on my side. "They aren't going to stop coming for you, Avery. And I won't always be around to save you."

My beast, who had been practically purring at his nearness, flattened her ears and hissed her displeasure in my head. "I didn't ask you to save me, Blackwell. Not this time, and I won't any other time. That's the whole point of all of this—I'm just as dangerous as you are, and the Guardians are exactly where I need to be."

He leaned down, his hand still pressed gently to my ribs, and he rasped next to my ear, "My name is Heath. Use it."

I could only sit there, staring like an idiot, as he snagged his jacket from the chair and then strode confidently from the room.

14

AIDEN

We were less than two days into this semester, and it felt like it'd been two years.

After decades of pain and confusion, followed by a semester of stalking and torturing people for information, Elijah finally had a solid lead in his hunt for his mother's killer. It had also given him a single-minded focus that we could only hope would keep his beast occupied for the time being.

And, after years of holding out hope that Richard and Charles, who were the least tyrannical and backwards of my fathers, would find it within themselves to step up to protect my sister, I'd finally cut off contact with both of them with one final heated phone call last night.

And, after being challenged on the first day of class by one of my female students, I later watched, with my jaw on the floor, the footage of said female student destroying some of the toughest SWIM sequences in the Guardian training program with only the aid of her blades and her fox brother.

And finally, after a morning spent in relative peace with my coffee, research, and one uneventful class, I happened upon several injured students in their beast forms out on the campus lawn as I walked from the Magical Ed building to the dining hall. I was then informed by a gaggle of chatty freshmen that *the new girl* had defeated three Prime challengers with only her fists and a sword and that *my brother* had hauled her off the infirmary afterward.

All of that in two fucking days.

Things were perilously close to spinning out of control already, and we still had a long road ahead of us.

It was now midafternoon, and I'd dismissed my last class of the day. Normally, I'd wind down in my office, answering emails, meeting with the occasional student, or reviewing lesson plans. But not today.

Today I found myself stomping up the stairs to the top floor of the upperclassmen dorm, where the rest of my quad had a three-room suite.

They spent their downtime here during the week, and on the weekends, they often escaped to my house in the faculty complex on the far west side of campus. I'd bitch about them invading my space, but the truth was that it felt more like home when they were there.

My brother and I had been inseparable since he learned to walk and could chase me around the house. When Heath was twelve years old, he met Wyatt and Elijah at the private shifter boarding school we'd all attended. I was fifteen at the time, but they spent more time in my room than theirs. We ate, trained, and spent most of our time together until I graduated, which was how I ended up with two extra younger brothers and an overpowered quad with a laundry list of problems.

I let myself into their suite and found Wyatt on the couch, shirtless, his sweatpants slung so low, we were lucky his dick wasn't out, a Playstation controller in his hands.

Elijah was sprawled out in the nearby recliner, reading a paperback that he'd propped on his knee. My brother sat at the small kitchen table, aggressively typing on his laptop.

George slept in the huge terrarium that Housing had not wanted installed in the suite's living room but was too terrified of Elijah to forbid him from doing it.

Only Heath looked up at my entrance.

"You interfered in a formal challenge, submitted Rip Ashton, and then physically dragged Avery Baxter to the infirmary in front of half the school?" I asked him dubiously.

"Rip's a little bitch," Wyatt hollered from the couch. "But I agree with Aiden. Should've let the wildcat stab him through the skull."

Elijah hummed in agreement. "My dove is so vicious. I'm devastated I missed her slicing the Ashton Quad to ribbons."

I arched a brow at him. "Your *dove*? How are you in pet-name territory with Avery when you've been back on this campus for less than twenty-four hours?"

"It is my excellent fortune to have Folklore class with our stunning new student," he replied, shooting me a smug, fangy grin. "And to sit next to her. I was only able to taste the barest hint of fear from her, but it was delicious."

Great. Another fixation for our most unstable quad member.

"Rip was going to kill her," Heath said darkly. "I sensed his loss of control, and Avery was pretty beat up by that point. And she refused to shift, even to heal. I should hope that any one of you would've stepped in if you happened across a quad issuing back-to-back challenges to a single student, especially one without a Prime beast."

I shifted my messenger bag around to my front and

sagged against the door. "I've never seen that happen in all my time here as a student or a teacher. I guess I don't blame you, if you really thought she was in that much danger."

Wyatt scoffed. "Heath tells us he got there just in time to watch her nearly hack that panther's head off with a fucking rapier. She was doing fine."

I scrubbed a hand down my face and groaned. "Fuck."

"She ended up with a bunch of stitches and some broken ribs," Heath told me. He shifted his attention back to his laptop screen, muttering, "and Dr. Lee had to put his hands all over her to fix them."

I rolled my eyes. "Dr. Lee has had his hands all over every single one of us, many times. What's your deal? Is it your wolf?"

"Maybe," he growled. "I don't fucking know. She was reckless, she got hurt, and it pissed me off."

"Our fearless leader has never met a female he couldn't boss around," Wyatt quipped. "Why don't you give Phoebe a call, Heath? After your two dates with her last semester that were, in your words, 'perfectly fine,' I'm sure she's waiting by her phone and at your beck and call."

Heath scowled at him. We all knew there was a reason he'd failed to contact Phoebe Atkins, latent daughter of a quad of Alpha wolves who were also the biggest real estate moguls in Northern Georgia, even once over the holiday break.

No spark. No flash of interest from the beast. No pull toward a lifetime commitment. We'd all been through the same once we started getting serious about dating.

My brother's practical reading of the situation was that while a girl like Phoebe was mostly his type (pretty, well-mannered, wolf blood) and kind of *my* type (pretty, smart, agreeable), she wasn't Wyatt's (hot, mouthy, wild), and she sure as hell wasn't Elijah's (we'd yet to unlock this mystery).

Or had we?

Damn it.

"Shut up, dickhead," Heath growled at Wyatt. "I wonder how many times Callista will knock on our door this week after you let her blow you at the Bergs' holiday party."

"Mmm, yes, she did give that her all, didn't she?" Elijah said, chuckling. "So generous of Wyatt to let me watch."

"Heath's just salty because his dick's about to atrophy from lack of use," Wyatt drawled.

I sighed and banged the back of my head against the door. "*Anyway.* I'm meeting Avery in a few hours for runes tutoring. No—" I held up a hand as Elijah sat up in his chair, his face brightening. "—none of you are invited. Get your heads on straight about her. She's a beautiful novelty, but that's it."

Wyatt rolled his eyes. Heath glowered—at who or what, I wasn't sure.

Elijah's smile was a dare, his pupils slitting. A flash of his insane beast. "Have fun, Aiden," he purred.

AVERY ARRIVED AT MY OFFICE EXACTLY ON TIME. I'D SET OUR tutoring session to begin at 5:00 p.m., when the winter sun would begin setting. Those of us who chose to hone a secondary affinity could become skilled enough to work the magic even in the daylight, but it was easier to do under the Moon, and the strongest spells were always performed under the Full Moon.

We were at the first quarter Moon tonight, so it would be a good time to see what my new pupil was made of.

"Welcome, Miss Baxter," I said as she entered.

She closed the door behind her with a click. My beast stirred, watching her with a level of interest he showed in very little else.

"Professor," she said, rolling the word in her mouth like she was only using it to humor me. "Thanks for taking the time. My guidance counselor seemed insistent I hone a secondary affinity so I can be a proper latent shifter, and I apologize you got roped into it."

She slinked toward the chair in front of my desk, her gait fluid, her steps light. She wore a sweater cropped just high enough above her jeans that I could glimpse a sliver of her toned stomach. Her jeans molded to a round ass and strong, lean thighs. She smelled good, too, like jasmine and lavender.

Her presence set my beast on edge with a wary anticipation that was more exciting than off-putting. She appeared relaxed, seeming almost soft under that lithe, strong figure, but I sensed that she was also tightly coiled and ready to strike at any time.

She was a trained killer, yes, but I wondered now if she was also a feline.

Is that what your fucking problem is? I thought at my beast half.

I leaned back in my chair and crossed my arms over my chest, watching her closely as she approached. She dropped her backpack to the floor, slung the harness containing her two swords onto the back of the chair, and sat down. Her striking blue gaze dipped to my forearms, where I'd rolled my dress shirt sleeves to my elbows. I smothered a primal, satisfied smirk.

"If I'm going to spend my evenings helping you work your magic," I said drolly, "I'd appreciate it if you'd dispense with the bullshit. We both know you're not latent, which means we'll need to work on the balance of the beast and the magic in our lessons."

She just shrugged, a coy smile pulling at pink lips. "If you say so."

And in a blink, I went from maintaining a semblance of professional calm to riding the urge to dominate and submit this female, preferably by marking her ass with my palm while she was draped over my lap.

"Oh, I see the jaguar wants to come out and play," she teased.

Shit. The ring around my irises would light up a neon blue-green when my beast was really pushing, which he rarely did except in the heat of battle. Before I could blink it away, her blue eyes flashed lighter, *hotter*, like the center of a blazing flame.

"You think he could take me?" she asked, her silvery-blond ponytail caressing her slender neck as she leaned forward in her chair.

My beast half wanted nothing more than to try, apparently. I was as bad as the rest of my fucking quad.

"Put it away," I growled, and she fucking *smiled*. "In this office and in my classroom, I'm the professor, and you're my student. If you want to play power games with Primes, save it for training."

She relaxed back in her chair. The headlights were off, but she was still eyeing me with something that may have been amusement.

What a fucking *brat*.

"I'll take you up on that," she replied. "If you ever decide to show up to training. Did you already go through it when you were a student?"

"I did. I competed as an individual in the Guardian class,

and I practiced quad tactics with other Primes who needed an extra to make a full four. I drop into training every so often to practice as a quad with Heath and the others, and I'll rejoin the program full-time this summer for camp."

"Camp?"

"It's what we call the off-campus field training that all of us who make the final-year cut must complete before the start of senior year. We'll start going out on patrols. I used my senior year to start working with my own quad, so I didn't go to camp."

She nodded, her teasing smile returning. "I see. Are you excited to see a real wraith? Will it be your first time?"

I flashed her a warning look. I didn't want to think about it, for some reason—the fact that she'd been out fighting wraiths with just her family, only one of whom was a Prime, for years. It was emasculating, yes, but it also sent something like dread creeping through my body.

She could have—and by all accounts, should have—been killed. Those vibrant blue eyes closed forever, never quite making it here, to school, to challenge me in my own space.

My beast rumbled an angry noise in my chest.

"I have seen a wraith," I told her. "Two Giants once made it through the wards that surround the small suburb where my family has a lake house. I was ten. The local Guardian patrol was able to kill them, but I watched through the bedroom window as the wraiths killed four innocent shifters and ripped apart two Guardians before they were put down."

Most shifter communities had wards to keep wraiths on the outskirts, though the quality varied depending on how deep the pockets were of the city and the locals. But even the best wards, like those that surrounded this campus, could be breached by a high-level wraith, especially if it were able to consume a soul beforehand.

"I'm sorry," she said, and she sounded like she meant it. "I never had to witness something that horrible at such a young age. I didn't see a wraith kill someone until I was sixteen."

Her tone was so matter-of-fact, it took me a moment to process that statement.

"Who was it?" I asked quietly.

"Montana Mark." She smiled, and it was sad. "He'd moved down to Fulton City from Montana a year before it happened. His beast was a mountain lion. Ordinary size and power, but feisty and a little crazy. He ran a construction crew in the neighborhood, and some cycles he'd go out on patrol to help. We had a particularly bad one that month, and two Rippers ambushed him. Shredded his beast to pieces, then consumed his soul. My family and I got there right as they'd finished, and it took all five of us to kill them."

"Shit."

"Yeah. And I know you don't believe me, but before they killed Mark, those two wraiths had managed to take some serious bites out of two drunk college students while they waited for a rideshare, completely oblivious to what was happening to them. We found out later that one of them was in a coma for a year, and the other suffers from what human doctors think is young-onset dementia, but it isn't. It's because a wraith turned his soul into Swiss cheese."

I sighed. "I do believe you, Avery. I just don't understand why human injuries aren't reported or tracked among wraith scholars, the Council, or Guardian leadership."

"Oh I don't know, Aiden, maybe because shifters don't really give a fuck about humans?"

I didn't correct her use of my first name because I liked the way it sounded coming out of her mouth, even if we were back to a borderline hostile tone. "I suppose we don't. We're an insular species, and we have enough problems keeping our supernatural existence secret and maintaining a civilized society."

She studied me. "True. It's rough out here. Who do you think kills more of us, wraiths or other shifters?"

It was time to get focused on what we were supposed to be doing, which was Runes 101. I had my own opinions on our archaic and often savage culture, but the way she asked the question was probing and serious, like she thought no one was truly safe.

That wasn't a discussion I was up for tonight. Not with a student I met only yesterday.

I adjusted my glasses and put my professor face back on. "How about we begin your lesson, Miss Baxter? I'd prefer not to be here all night."

15

———

AVERY

I didn't know what it was about the Blackwell brothers that made me enjoy riling them up. They both had a stick up their respective tight asses, but it affected them in different ways.

Heath's brand of domineering boss-hole was familiar to me. He was an Alpha wolf and the most dominant shifter in his quad, like my dad, Rand. He expected to be obeyed when he gave orders and was used to being worshiped by lesser shifters (which was pretty much all of them) and females alike. He probably cared about only three things—his quad, his family, and order. Maybe the prestige of becoming a top Guardian recruit was in there too. I was an unpredictable thing fucking up his world, and it was scrambling his brain.

Aiden's dominance was sneakier than his brother's, but that was the feline way. Alpha wolves were in your face, daring you to fuck with them, staring you down and ripping your throat out when you did. A powerful feline pounced when you least expected it and would gut you without remorse. Aiden wanted obedience, too, but because he was

Professor Aiden Blackwell. He wanted it because he was older, smarter, and one of the most respected names on campus, not because he stared you down, showed his teeth, and demanded it. He probably didn't know what to do with me, the student whose first words to him had been to tell him that he was wrong.

All this sexual tension didn't help, either, but maybe that was just on my end.

Aiden's hazel eyes had returned to factory settings behind those slutty glasses. No more enthralling turquoise glow around his irises, which meant he'd packed the beast away for the night.

I was enjoying cataloging the differences between the brothers. For example, both Heath and Aiden had hazel eyes, but Aiden's were a chocolate brown around the pupils that faded into that vibrant green at the edges of the irises, while Heath had burnished gold starbursts around his pupils that bled into a lighter brown shot through with thin striations of forest green.

My beast chuffed and licked a paw at the thought.

"By all means," I told him with a tight smile. "Let's get started. I've had a long day."

He arched a perfect chocolate brow. "So I heard."

I just bet he had. "Just so you know, I'm not new to rune work. I haven't had any formal magical training, but my dads know their stuff, and they love to teach."

"I see." He leaned back in his chair again, studying me. His dress shirt was dark gray today, unbuttoned just enough to tease a peek at the tip-top of a defined chest, right below the collarbone. His shoulders were wide—not quite the breadth of Heath's or Wyatt's, but close. Biceps and pectorals both strained under the fabric of his shirt, but in a way that said his clothes had been perfectly tailored to his strong body, not the way many huge muscly shifter men stuffed themselves into clothes like sausages into a casing. His scent lingered in the air, woodsy and masculine and a little bit like the rain. "Tell me why we use runes, then," he said, waving a hand.

"For spellwork," I replied easily. "Each rune has a unique meaning, and putting them together creates the recipe for whatever spell you're trying to accomplish."

He nodded, a smile pulling at the corner of his lush lips. "Correct. A shifter with this affinity is adept at creating, assembling, and casting a spell, using the act of carving or drawing the runes to channel the lunar magic and energy needed to create it."

"And the more permanent the writing or carving, the longer the magic will last," I added. I reached behind my chair and unsheathed one of my blades, and then I held it out to him, parallel to my chest. The soft yellow light of his desk lamp illuminated the runes carved into the steel. "Hand engraved with a rotary tool because using modern methods like lasers or electro-chemical means to engrave doesn't channel the magic properly. The engraving is done with the initial Moon blessing, and then we recharge under each Full Moon by tracing the runes with a simpler tool. I just use a drypoint needle."

He eyed the runes on my blade with covetous interest. "So it's true. You have a real Moon-blessed weapon."

"Of course I do." I slid the sword back in its sheath, and he suddenly looked like a kid whose toy had been taken away. "Can't kill a wraith without one."

"Who does the Moon blessing?" he asked. "That's advanced rune work that's usually left to experts. I've tried it, but I'd much rather trust my saber to the Guardians' specialists when the time comes."

So he and Heath were both saber users. They were probably the primary blade wielders in the quad, while Wyatt and Elijah would do most of their fighting in beast form.

It's what I would do with that mix, anyway.

"I do it," I replied. His jaw slackened, and I enjoyed it immensely. "My dad Kaito's rune affinity is pretty strong. He taught me, and I started blessing my own blades every Full Moon a couple of years ago." I shrugged. "So far it's worked fine? I guess I haven't had a chance to slice the head off a Giant wraith since I started doing my own blessings, but the Rippers I've decapitated have stayed dead."

I couldn't claim success for Ian's blade, which he'd used to kill the Giant that shredded my leg and was the reason I was sitting here today. That had been Kai's work.

Aiden stared at me for a beat, and then he huffed a laugh. "Next Full Moon, you can show me what you've got. We'll bless my saber. The guys will be so jealous."

I shrugged again, casually, like the idea of impressing Aiden and by extension the rest of his quad by doing something they couldn't was not extremely appealing to me. "Sure. Then we can go beyond the school's wards at the New Moon together and see if it worked," I added, winking.

His face lost all mirth. "Absolutely not. I know you're skilled, and I know you've managed to stay alive after all these years of wraith vigilantism despite the odds, but you're here now. You're a Guardian trainee and a Proteus student, which means you stay behind the school wards after curfew the day before the New Moon through the day after. The invasions up here, where the concentration of powerful shifters is highest, are not a joke. It would be nothing like it is down in the city."

I rolled my eyes. "You and the powers that be didn't even know there were wraiths in the city at all until I told you."

"I mean it, Avery."

"Okay, Aiden."

He clenched his teeth in frustration, his eyes threatening to blaze again. I soaked up the little hit of adrenaline it gave me, like a junkie.

After blowing a harsh breath through his nose, he shoved back from his desk and stood up, spearing me with a *look*. "Get your shit. We're going outside."

"You want me to ward this flowerbed?" I asked Aiden dubiously.

"Why the tone?" he replied, his grin sharklike. I almost squirmed. "This isn't even intro work. We're jumping straight to wards, which, as I'm sure you know, is a specific subset of rune work that is the purview of security specialists. Wards involve learning specialized runes, channeling a lot of power, and crafting the spell to fit the specific security need."

"Uh-huh."

"Let's go, Moon-blesser," he said, still wearing that cocky grin. Weird. Maybe it was the fresh air? "A simple ward to repel animals from the flowerbed, and it only has to last as long as I need to check your work."

We were in a courtyard off the Magical Education building. I examined the small flowerbed in front of me, which contained a variety of night-blooming plants. I spied evening primrose, gardenia, and angel's trumpet, but Ian would've been able to identify a lot more. Night-blooming plants absorbed the Moon's magic better than any other kind of plant, and shifters like Ian, who had a secondary affinity for apothecary magic, could use them to create potions and elixirs, activated and strengthened by his ability to channel his own inherent lunar magic.

Night had fallen, and the first quarter Moon joined the lamps that lined the campus sidewalks softly illuminating our little corner of the courtyard. Aiden was sitting on a nearby bench, his long legs spread, elbows propped on his knees as he watched me closely.

"All right," I said, crouching down next to the bed. I dug into my backpack and pulled out an old pen. "Here goes."

I'd learned the gist of the wraith repellent wards Kai used around our house, and this would need to be something similar without packing near the punch. Using my pen, I scratched the first rune into the dirt at the edge of the bed. Almost all wards began with the rune for *Protection*, and then I decided to go with *Disruption* and *Travel*, ensuring *Travel* pointed away from the bed, urging any animal that approached to turn around and head the other direction. I threw *Stability* in there, even though this ward wouldn't last past the next wind gust strong enough to toss the dirt around.

Now to power them. I felt for the magic reservoir my shifter blood gifted me. For those of us with a beast, it was often hard to distinguish the difference between that magical soul we shared a body with and the more fluid power we could learn to harness in other ways, but I could usually grab onto it within a minute or so. On a night like tonight, it was like dipping my hand in the gentle current of a river. Under a Full Moon, that river would be a torrent.

Clinging to the feeling, bolstered by the soft rays of the Moon, I let the power flow through my fingertips as I traced my runes, channeling magic into each to create the full ward spell.

"Good," Aiden murmured. "This magic has a different

sensation than the more potent part of us that houses the beast. Do you feel it?"

"I'm sure I don't know what you mean," I replied. Adding one last etching in the dirt, I finished the spell and released my hold on the flow of the river.

"Avery," he growled.

"Would you like to come check my work?" I asked, blinking big doe eyes at him.

He prowled over and knelt next to me, the heat of him searing through layers of my jacket and sweater even though we weren't touching. He held a hand over the dirt, his long fingers splayed as he felt for the magical vibrations of the ward. "Excellent work," he told me, almost reluctantly. "I might've gone with *Resistance*, but *Disruption* appears to have done the trick just as well."

"Thanks," I said brightly. I capped my pen and slid it back into the front pouch of my bag. "So, since this is supposed to be Runes 101 tutoring, if you want to just give me an A and cancel for the rest of the semester, you can have two evenings a week back."

Instead of an immediate reply, Aiden rolled gracefully to standing, and then he held out a hand. After shaking off the momentary surprise, I grasped his hand and let him pull me to my feet. Like his brother's, his grip was firm, warm, and bossy.

He didn't release me right away. He stood there, gripping me tightly, while he studied my face for yet another time tonight. "Nice try, Miss Baxter. You still have to put in the hours if you want the credit. Maybe after a few weeks, you'll trust me with the knowledge of the nature of your beast."

Unlikely, but if his jaguar wanted to goad my beast some more, he might get more than he bargained for.

"Does your knowledge of whether I have the ability to

shift or what animal I may or may not be able to shift into have any bearing on your ability to grade my work?"

His eyes narrowed. I was daring him to admit he'd stomped right into questionable legal territory, and he knew it. "No."

"Then stop asking," I said, smiling with all my teeth.

His nostrils flared, and he leaned in closer to me, his hand still wrapped firmly around mine. "What are you hiding?" he rumbled, a low hoarse purr.

Nope. I extricated myself from his grip with a basic self-defense move. "Goodnight, Professor," I purred right back at him.

Neon ignited once more around his irises, and he looked for all the world like he wanted to grab me again. I turned and stalked away before I decided to let him.

16

AVERY

After not so pleasant dreams of running through the dark streets of the city, being chased by jackals and trying but failing to reach a pair of glowing hazel eyes, I dragged myself to the dining hall with the usual crew.

Brody had joined us for dinner last night and was back for breakfast, but he hadn't stayed the night in Ian's room. I knew this because I was a nosy bitch and had burst in unannounced sometime after 11:00 p.m., but Ian had been sound asleep all by his lonesome. If Ian was taking it slow, it meant he liked Brody *a lot*, and so far, I approved.

Said lynx had brought a few pals with him this morning, so Mal and I were crammed between some friendly Support Squadron trainees and Allen's wolf friends.

"I don't know, Avery," Mal said, biting her lip. "You would think that after how you fared yesterday against the Ashtons, everyone would've gotten the message to leave you alone, but I worry."

Ash spun one of her many rings around on her finger, her dark gaze sweeping the room like she was assessing it for threats. "It's typical. Half the student body will think it was high time those assholes got put in their place, but the other half are the type who are still engrained in 'tradition' and freaked out by females who can shift. They'll have to get the hell over it."

"Well, I've never claimed to be able to shift," I replied with a shrug, but then her words registered. I narrowed my eyes at Mal. "Have people been targeting you?"

She waved a hand. "No. Well, not that much. Especially now that I'm always with Allen. He only associates with the wolves who think shifting females are cool and normal, and they make for good backup."

Unease leached into my stomach. In some ways, I'd lived a sheltered life down in the city, away from the heart of the region's shifter community. I'd known a few women with beast souls, and I'd never seen any of them directly targeted by hate. Those of us who lived where we did tended to be the types to eschew shifter norms, so strong beliefs regarding Moon curses or any of that bullshit weren't really a thing.

I still took great pains to avoid shifting in front of others, but that was a *me* problem.

And yet here I was, bulldozing my way through the college and inflaming the zealots. My actions could make things worse for girls like Mallory, and I did not like that.

I pointed at her with my fork. "If something happens, don't be a hero. Shift and scurry your little cat butt away."

"Says the lady who was literally underneath a bear less than twenty-four hours ago," she retorted, and then her gaze snagged on something over my shoulder, a sly grin forming on her face. "And not in the fun way."

Wyatt had just breezed into the room, dressed to kill in a dark green Henley and his usual distressed denim. Heath and Aiden entered behind him, deep in conversation with each other. Heath wore a long-sleeved black T-shirt sporting the Guardian logo and snug blue jeans. Aiden's dress shirt was navy blue today and tucked into fitted gray pants.

Behind them walked Elijah, wearing only a loose cream-colored tank top with his jeans, the inked snake wrapped around his neck on full display, the thin gold hoops in his ears and nose glinting under the light of the chandeliers.

I had to tamp down the little thrill his presence elicited. I'd yet to see him in the dining hall, and by the blatant staring of 80 percent of the room, it must not have been a regular occurrence.

"Ooh, if Elijah's here, does that mean—"

Shrieks from the tables near the entrance answered my question.

"Oh, fuck no," Allen said, grabbing Mallory and lifting her on top of the table like she was a doll. He scrambled up after her, while Chance and one of Brody's friends stood on their chairs.

A seven-foot train of sparkly purple scales wound its way into the room. Elijah and the rest of his quad went about piling their plates with food in the buffet lines, blatantly ignoring the fact that people were crawling on tables and fleeing the room behind them.

George slithered under our table. Ian laughed, and Brody, to his immense credit, had gone only slightly pale. Ash pulled her feet up underneath her body on her chair but otherwise seemed unaffected.

"Yes, hello to you too," I cooed at George as he climbed into my lap. "Who's the prettiest snake in the world? You are, that's who. Did you have a nice long nap after your daddy fed you?"

"Avery, *why*?" Mallory moaned.

"Did you know snakes only eat a few times a month, and they have to nap for several days afterwards while they digest, depending on the size of the prey?" I asked her. "Fascinating."

"Avery, we are *eating*," Allen whispered urgently. "Put the snake down."

George slanted Allen a snakey glare, and then he continued his climb to his favorite spot, wrapping himself around my shoulders, where he could sniff my hair.

"Pythons aren't venomous, Allen," I said. "You guys all need to calm down."

"No way, I've seen him choke a guy out," Chance said, still standing on his chair. "That thing is vicious, and I don't know if you realize this, Avery, but he is wound around your *neck*."

"George won't harm her," Elijah announced, popping up behind me and jump-scaring half the table. He stroked George's head with one long finger, and the snake made a pleased sort of hissing noise. "He's partial to our dove."

"Hi," I said to him, lamely. His yellow-gold eyes were full of mirth as he observed me wearing his snake like a scarf. "Do you want George back? Or can I take him to Aiden's class with me?"

He grinned. "You think I can tell him what to do? He'll go where he wants to, and right now, I suspect that's with you."

"Aiden will be thrilled," I said.

With that thought, I darted a glance at the faculty dining area, set apart from us by a wide arched doorway. Aiden was sitting next to a young female professor, who looked like the polished version of a teenage boy's hot-for-teacher fantasy. She gazed at him adoringly, but his eyes were on me—or my situation, at least. He appeared as exasperated by George and me as he had been on the first day of class. I fluttered my fingers at him in a wave, and he shut his eyes like he was praying to the Moon for peace.

"Don't let Aiden fool you," Elijah said in a conspiratorial whisper. "He and George are practically best friends."

"Who wouldn't want to be your best friend?" I crooned at the snake. "You're so pretty and smart and cuddly."

"Avery, honestly, I think you may have hit your head when that bear crushed you," Mallory said. "Did Dr. Lee check you for a concussion?"

Heath and Wyatt strolled up, plates in hand. "Dude, we only have, like, fifteen minutes to eat," Wyatt said to Elijah. "I'm sure the wildcat will take good care of George while you scarf down a sweet potato bowl or whatever vegan bullshit you're eating today."

A jolt of adrenaline sizzled through my veins. "Wildcat?"

Wyatt's grin was wicked. "What, Elijah can have a pet name for you, and I can't?"

"Uh—"

"How are you today, Avery?" Heath asked diplomatically. "Any lingering problems?"

"I'm well, thank you for asking, *Heath*," I replied, matching his tone but adding one dash of sarcasm.

His hazel eyes blazed, but he snuffed it out instantly. "Good. We have training this afternoon, and you'll want to be in full health for that."

I resisted rolling my eyes and turned back to Elijah. "Heath thinks he's my dad," I told him.

He barked out a laugh. "I can promise you, Dove, that he does not."

Heath shoved Elijah. "Table. Food. Now."

As they shuffled off to join the elite student tables, Wyatt cast one heated, lingering look at me over his shoulder, sinking perfect white teeth into his lower lip before he turned around.

I ate the rest of my breakfast pretending that there wasn't a python wrapped around my shoulders, that the entire room wasn't staring at me, and that my dear brother wasn't laughing at me with his eyeballs.

GEORGE STAYED WITH ME THROUGH AIDEN'S CLASS AND THEN took off for parts unknown. Then it was Shifter History and Culture, which I found to be much less tense and much more boring than it'd been the first day, thanks to the lecture topic on shifters in medieval times.

The fact that Heath and Wyatt had to find open seats much further away from me also helped. My beast was aware of them, though, ears perked and tail flicking, but I did my best to ignore the heat of their stares on the back of my neck.

When class ended, I packed my stuff away unhurriedly, so my butt was still in my seat when Phoebe swanned by and gave me a hateful look, her perfect little nose turned up.

I got it. I really did. Girls like Phoebe had been raised to believe that their ultimate purpose in this life was to become the central bond of a power quad like the Black-wells. She seemed to have some kind of connection with Heath—or a serious crush, at the very least—which meant he represented the thing she wanted most. Heath was also powerful, dominant, and stunning. A Prime-blooded girl's wet dream.

But then I showed up out of absolutely nowhere, swinging my swords and being otherwise annoying to half the campus, and I had Heath marching me to the infirmary and stopping by my table in the dining hall like he gave a shit. I wouldn't be my favorite person, either, if I were her.

Since it was all our backwards-ass culture's fault, I'd let the mean-girl behavior slide. I was proud of my maturity.

The patting myself on the back lasted all of three minutes, until I'd finally packed my bag and exited the classroom.

"Hey, new bitch."

I whirled. There was Callista, the Veronica to Phoebe's Betty, her arms crossed over her black cashmere turtleneck and her lips—colored dark red and perfectly lined—pursed.

Great.

I blew out a resigned breath. "Can I help you?"

"You sure can. You can keep your *claws* off Wyatt and the rest of his quad."

I pasted on a confused face. "Shouldn't you be addressing your concerns to Phoebe and maybe that hot professor lady I saw pawing at Aiden earlier? They're the ones who seem to have their eyes on your prize. I'm just here to become certified to kill wraiths."

She scoffed. "Whatever. You're here pretending to be latent, which is clearly bullshit. You're the shiny new thing right now, but that won't last. Wyatt will quickly see you for what you really are—a desperate bitch trying to climb the social ladder on the back of a high-status quad."

Deep breaths. Zen. "Sure."

Her cheeks tinged pink, and she pointed a long maroon nail at me. "All you are is the *maybe*-daughter of an Alpha who stooped to form a trio with *ordinary* shifters and then stooped *again* to living in the human city. Then they had *you*, a freak of nature, and your brother, a weak fox shifter, for kids, and they probably have shit for power because their central bond is dead—"

My blade was out of the special pocket I'd fashioned for it on the side of my backpack and at her throat before she could blink. She shrieked as I slammed her against the wall and pressed the sharp edge right up under her chin.

"Do not talk about my family," I growled in her face. "If you insult them again—in front of me or behind my back, I don't fucking care—I will break your pretty face and then poke you so full of holes that you'll be laid up in the infirmary for months."

"You deranged bitch—*ahhh!*"

I pressed harder. Tiny beads of blood sprouted under my blade. "And you will keep all references to my dead mother out of your fucking mouth, or I'll slit your throat—"

"Uh-oh, that's enough of that."

A large hand deftly removed my sword from my grip and Callista's neck, and then I was unceremoniously thrown over a large shoulder.

"*Wyatt,*" I growled. "Put me the *fuck* down."

"Wyatt!" Callista screamed. "Where are you going? She hurt me!"

He ignored her and marched us down the hall. I thrashed, but he'd wrapped his arm around the back of my thighs like a steel band. He also had my blade in his other hand, spinning it leisurely like it was a pencil and he was bored in class. Students darted out of our way, not one of them appearing concerned for my predicament.

He kicked the doors of the building open and hauled me outside into the bright, chilly day. A few quick, purposeful strides around the corner, and we were in a small courtyard similar to the one Aiden had taken me to work runes in last night.

"Are you going to behave if I put you down?" he asked lightly, coming to a stop next to a crape myrtle tree.

"Try it and find out," I hissed. He was lucky my beast wasn't rattling the bars of her enclosure. Anyone else would've had teeth in their neck by now, but *nooo*, Wyatt got to manhandle me while she flicked her tail, merely curious and alert.

He chuckled, a pleasing rumble I could feel where my boobs were smashed against his back. "Game on, then, Wildcat."

In a swift and graceful move, he set me on my feet, then stepped clear of my reach. He still had my sword, so he knew I wasn't going to bolt, and he probably suspected I wasn't dumb enough to attack him—a Prime bear shifter armed with a blade.

I wasn't dumb, but I was really pissed off, so there was still a chance.

"This is nice," he said, making a few slashes with my sword as he examined it. "But way too lightweight for my taste. Perfect for you, though. I don't think we have anyone in the program who can dual-wield as well as you."

"Thank you. Give it back, please."

He raised a dark-red brow, and his green eyes sparkled with predatory amusement, like I was a feisty little mouse he was excited to have caught. "Are you going to threaten any more students whose fathers are on the college's Board of Trustees? I've decided I might be disappointed to see you expelled so soon."

I glared at him. "Your girlfriend isn't allowed to talk shit about my family or my dead mother. She can insult me all day and call me a social-climbing whore and warn me off you, but she can't—"

"Callista warned you off me?"

I rolled my eyes. "Come on, Wyatt, don't play dumb."

"She isn't my girlfriend, but you knew that." He grinned lasciviously. "Are you jealous, Wildcat?"

"No."

"Not even a little bit?" He crept closer to me, stashing my poor sword away by slipping it through his belt as he moved.

I went on high alert, slowly shuffling backward until my legs hit a stone bench, which knocked me off balance. I sat down, and Wyatt kept coming. My jaw went slack as he knelt between my legs, crowding me, a huge sculpted arm coming down on either side of me.

Our eyes met, and he spoke again in a low, flirty purr. "Callista is beautiful, sure. She's a little louder and bolder than your average blue-blooded shifter girl, which I like, but I *don't* like hearing that she let petty jealousy turn her into someone who would be callous about your mother." He paused, moving closer, his lips brushing my ear as he whispered, "She isn't my girlfriend, though I suppose she thinks she's the current lead contender because I let her suck my cock at a party last month."

Uncomfortable, conflicting emotions burned in my stomach. My beast flattened her ears and growled.

"I don't need to hear about where your cock has been, asshole," I said through clenched teeth.

He chuckled, and it sounded like sex because now I was *thinking* about sex, moondamn him. He leaned back again, a deceptively earnest look in his eyes. "All I'm trying to say is, there's no need to be jealous, baby. One blow job does not a claim on me make, though I definitely wouldn't be opposed to you giving it your best shot."

I surged forward and wrapped a hand around his throat. His eyes widened. My grip was probably much stronger than he was expecting, though my hand was little and his neck was thick. He lifted his chin and *leaned* into my grip, his green eyes blazing as his beast surged to the surface, a wild smile on his lips.

"Are you finished?" I snarled in his face. There was no way my own eyes weren't lit up like the northern-fucking-lights, but that ship had well and truly sailed. "Give me back my sword, and keep your groupies in line if you don't want to clean their blood off the walls of the Magical Ed building. And if you proposition me again, I will cut off that cock you're so fond of using to make all those poor girls think they have a chance. Understood?"

"*Fuck*, you're hot," he said, his voice a guttural growl. "Tell me what you are. Tell me why my bear is so fucking fixated on you. Then you can do whatever the fuck you want to my cock."

I shoved him away, and then I jammed the flat of my shoe into his wide, hard chest for good measure. He let me move him, and I scrambled to my feet, swiping my sword from his belt as I went.

He stood up and turned to face me, smiling like it was the best day of his life.

I raised my sword and pointed it at him. "Don't ever touch this again."

"Your sword? Or your sexy fucking body?"

I groaned and stomped off.

He didn't follow me.

17

ELIJAH

"What did you do to agitate my dove earlier?" I asked Wyatt lightly, as if I wasn't half-contemplating shifting and letting my beast put his head in its mouth. We stood shoulder to shoulder, dressed in our Guardians training gear, and were surveying the arena as some of the sophomores dragged the practice weapon stash from the storage room.

He arched an amused brow. Wyatt was the member of our quad who took the challenges of packing up with a mythic the most in stride, and I did appreciate the levity he brought to our little brotherhood.

Usually.

But if he hurt my dove, he could spend the afternoon healing in the infirmary.

"Stalking her, are you?" he asked, chuckling. "Why am I not surprised? Though I'm not sure how you're going to fit stalking the wildcat into your packed schedule."

"I'll manage. Answer my question."

Because he'd done *something* to her. I knew this because I'd wandered over to the Magical Education building after my morning class had let out, hoping I might catch a glimpse of Avery on her way out of the class she shared with Wyatt and Heath.

I'd lingered for a few minutes, tucked nonthreateningly into the shadows of a copse of trees. Minutes passed, and I figured I'd missed her, until she came storming around the corner from one of the building's courtyards, her lovely face flushed and her hand in a death grip around her little blade.

Seconds later, Wyatt had trotted out after her, looking pleased with himself. I'd watched him amble off in the opposite direction, and the only thing that stopped me from chasing him down and interrogating him had been the sudden and alarming pressure of my beast slithering up under my skin as I bounced between suspicious anger that he'd done something to upset my dove and seething jealousy that he'd gotten to be near her at all.

Now we were under control, so it was time for answers.

He sighed and shook his head, his wild auburn hair flopping onto his forehead with the movement. "Callista said something shitty to Avery, and it set her off. She had her blade to Callista's throat when I ran into them in the hallway. So I... diffused the situation."

I cocked my head at him.

"Fine. I stole her sword and carried her out of there over my shoulder. She wasn't pleased with our encounter." His eyes went hazy, a far-off look crossing his face, and he grinned. "But I sure was."

"Mmm," I said, pondering that. When faced with the same situation, I probably would've seized the same opportunity to... seize *her*. "I suppose I'm relieved you intervened. I'd hate for her to be expelled so soon." I kicked at the floor and huffed in irritation. "Especially because I keep missing her mouthwatering little displays of viciousness."

It was why I'd shown up to training this afternoon. I wouldn't be missing any more.

"With the way you're behaving about her, that's been a good thing," Heath said, striding up with all his quad leader energy. He gave me a chastising look. "If you'd have been there yesterday when Rip and those idiots challenged her, I suspect they'd all be dead, and we'd have a really fucking big mess to clean up."

"There's still time," I replied, waggling my brows.

He pointed a finger at my face. "Do not kill anyone on this campus. And no stalking Avery either. We're supposed to be focused on... other shit."

Still smiling, I snapped my teeth at his finger. "Sure thing, boss."

He rolled his eyes, but then his attention snagged on something across the arena. Wyatt and I followed his gaze, and there she was.

Avery, walking out onto the floor, wearing an easy smile and chatting with her brother.

My gorgeous new fascination.

Our campus was home to many lovely ladies, but none of them were vigilante wraith slayers, nor were any of them harboring quite the delicious secret that was my dove's inner beast.

I wanted to know everything about her.

How many freckles decorated her pale cheeks.

How many wraiths she'd ended with her little swords.

Why my ornery pet snake was obsessed with her.

Why she was hiding her inner magic from us all when her aura was so bright.

What her body looked like under those tight leggings and her loose Guardian trainee T-shirt.

How her tongue would taste if I stroked it with mine.

How her pert tits would feel in my hands.

And, most urgently, why my control of my beast was most threatened when she was near.

As she meandered in our general direction, all three of us stood up a little straighter.

I elbowed Heath. "It's delightful how full of shit you are."

"Shut up," he growled.

Cash chose that moment to stomp into the arena, the rest of his quad and fellow trainers in tow. Because of my relationship with Wyatt, I'd had the opportunity over the years to meet many of those in Guardian leadership, and I'd judged most of them to be decent shifters. It took at least some degree of self-sacrifice and genuine desire to protect others to want to become a Guardian, even with the prestige and benefits that came with it.

Cash and his quad weren't decent or altruistic or valorous. They were power-hungry sadists who hid behind their stellar kill record and family members on the Northeastern Council.

Heath and Aiden tolerated them because they knew how to kill wraiths, and that was what we were all here to learn. Wyatt thought they were mostly full of shit but dismissed them as a threat because they weren't—to us. Cash was a Prime lion shifter, but he was practically a cub compared to Holden Blackwell. The rest of the quad was comprised of two Alpha wolves and a snow leopard, none of whom could take Heath, Aiden, or Wyatt in a challenge.

And they certainly couldn't handle *me* in a fight, but my beast never got to have that kind of fun.

I wasn't convinced Cash was harmless, though. I'd tasted his fear once, during one of the very few times I'd let my beast out in the arena, and there was something *off* there. Sour. Dark, even.

And right now, if he didn't take his slimy fucking glare off my dove, I'd be tasting more than just his fear.

"Everyone shut up and line up!" he shouted across the floor. "We're doing conditioning first today. Maybe if you were all in better shape, you wouldn't be such fucking embarrassments."

I groaned. "This is what I get for deciding to actually show up today."

"Look alive, man," Wyatt said, nudging me. "If we hustle, we can position ourselves so that we're right behind Avery. Staring at that perfect ass while we run bleachers will make it all worth it."

I snapped my fingers and grinned at him. "Excellent thinking."

"Damn it," Heath said, a growl scratching inside his chest. At this point, I feared he might be stuck that way permanently. "Can you two behave?"

"Is that a serious question?" I asked.

Unfortunately, we did not make it into line behind Avery, who was surrounded by Brody Dara's little squad of feline friends. Fortunately, Brody only had eyes for Avery's brother, and the rest of the group appeared to be wary enough of her that they kept a respectable distance. I'd hate to have to maim any of our Support Squadron.

After we were all required to strap our weapon of choice to our backs, we began our conditioning. Heath wore his saber like a second skin and was one of the few of us—along with the Baxter siblings—who used his own blade rather than those provided by the program. Wyatt bitched, but he was the strongest of our quad pound-for-pound in human form, so running around with a massive ax strapped to his body would hardly register. I didn't use a weapon when facing the SWIM, but I did carry a dagger for certain emergencies.

For half an hour, we ran laps up and down the bleachers. Heath, Wyatt, and I paced each other perfectly, as always, and by the end, I was feeling invigorated. Physical activity in my human form had a way of lulling my beast into a relaxed state, and I'd been remiss with that sort of thing lately.

As we lined up on the arena floor again, I drifted Avery's way. She sparkled under the arena's fluorescent overhead lighting, a light sheen of sweat coating her pale skin. I was delighted to find that she'd shed her ill-fitting Guardians T-shirt and was gracing us with a view of her lithe torso and perfect tits in a sports bra.

Heath and Wyatt drifted with me, both eyeing the same prize. Wyatt was grinning like it was his birthday, while Heath looked to be on the verge of apoplexy.

"Dove," I purred as I sidled up to her. I couldn't smell her as well as my quad brothers would be able to, but a pass of my tongue over my lips told me she was wary but not fearful of me. Perfect. "You look delectable."

Her brother, who was standing next to her, unsheathed his katana in a flash and pointed it at my chin. "Thinking of taking a bite of my sister, snake?" he asked, which would've had a bit more teeth if he wasn't wearing an amused grin.

"Ian!" Avery gasped.

Heath rumbled a displeased noise, and Wyatt snorted.

"Always," I replied, returning his grin.

"Hey!" Trent, Cash's second, barked in our direction. "Break it the fuck up over there. Baxter, you set off that snake, and I will toss your ass out of here—if he doesn't kill you first."

Oddly, my beast had little interest in killing Ian Baxter.

I'd been told that George tolerated him as well—the privileges that came with being so closely related to our dove.

Ian sheathed his blade, but not before he darted an ill-advised, threatening look at Wyatt, and then another at Heath. "You assholes need to tread *very* lightly around my sister. Hurt her, and I will kill you."

I laughed. Wyatt's smile had turned evil, and Heath had gone stone cold.

"Excuse him," Avery said, exasperated, stepping in front of Ian and blocking him from our view. "He enjoys being provocative, and he is aware that I do not need his help to kill any one of you."

"There she is," Wyatt said, green eyes blazing. "Our savage girl. Wrap that hand around my throat again anytime, Wildcat."

Heath and I both slanted a look at him. Avery had choked Wyatt? Not fair.

"Control your brother," Heath growled at her. "That shit can get him killed. He's lucky Wyatt and I have superior control over our beasts and that Elijah just ran his into a lull."

Her eyes flashed electric blue, and she stepped toward Heath. Fuck *yes*. "Are you threatening my brother, *Alpha*?"

A gold sheen rolled over Heath's irises, his beast's energy surging in the space around us. Wyatt's bear prickled, and mine opened a curious eye.

"Pair up!" Cash bellowed, snapping the tension. "Weapons drills for the next half hour!"

Ian snatched his sister's hand, pulling her back from her confrontation with Heath. "C'mon, Aves. We haven't sparred in a million years."

Trent took that moment to butt into our huddle. "Nice

try, fox. Go pair up with someone in Support Squadron. Cash wants *Miss* Baxter paired with Harrow."

"Absolutely the fuck not," Heath snapped. "Does he think we're stupid?"

Trent sneered. "If the bitch doesn't want to spar with a Prime mythic, she can see herself out. Or does she still claim to have what it takes to become a Guardian?"

"Why don't you ask *Cash* if he'd like to spar with Elijah?" Wyatt said, his voice taunting. "He's top of the Guardians, and yet, I don't think *he's* ever had the pleasure of sparring with a mythic."

"Watch your fucking tone, Gale," Trent growled. "You don't get special treatment just because of who your daddy is, and he isn't here to save your ass today."

"How about you and I spar, Trent, and I'll show you special treatment."

Avery's gorgeous gaze had bounced around the group, a confused frown on her face. "What is everyone's problem? I don't mind working with Elijah."

I sighed, reaching for her hand. I rubbed my thumb across her palm, and she softened, peering up at me curiously. "My beast is unpredictable in combat situations, Dove," I said in a low voice. "Cash is purposefully putting you in danger. As much as I'd like to think we would never harm you, I can't exactly guarantee it."

In fact, her hand in mine had awoken my beast, the tension inside intensifying rather rapidly. Color leached from my vision, and my teeth throbbed. I sucked in a deep breath and released her hand.

She studied me. Her heartbeat had jumped, but I tasted no fear. "We can't let Cash win, Elijah. Heath and Wyatt can work out right next to us. I have faith in you."

Was this love? If her existence didn't make my beast so fucking feral, I would've thought so.

"Not happening," Heath said, then he turned his scowl on Trent. "Tell Cash I'm working with Avery, and Wyatt will take Elijah."

"Only if Baxter wants to get tossed out on her tight little ass, Blackwell."

Avery's lip curled, and I gritted my teeth as the pressure doubled. Luckily, Wyatt stepped right into Trent's stupid, smirking face, his bear's sudden rage heavy in the air, which mollified the monster within me. "Talk about her like that again, you sniveling dickhead, and I will rip your snowy white hide apart."

"What the hell is this? Are you fucking her, Gale? Are you, Blackwell? Not that I blame you. She looks like she has a tight—"

"That's enough." Avery shouldered in front of Wyatt, separating him from Trent. "We're wasting training time. Trent, please tell Cash I will be working with Elijah under the condition that Wyatt and Heath will be nearby." She didn't wait for him to respond, whirling on her heel. "Come on, Elijah," she said over her shoulder as she marched out onto the arena floor, ripping her swords from their sheaths on her back as she went.

A pleasant feeling bloomed in my chest, the buoyancy releasing me from the clutches of my beast, at least for now. I strolled after her, a pep in my step.

Heath and Wyatt fell in next to me. "You sure?" Heath asked quietly.

"Yes," I replied easily. "About *something*, anyway."

18

AVERY

Once Ian was sure I had the situation under control, he slipped away to spar with Brody. Now I was alone with Elijah, except that Heath and Wyatt were standing fifteen feet away, pretending they were paying attention to each other and not us.

Color me shocked that Trent, like Cash, was an enormous asshole, but the Prime dick energy that Heath's quad had brought to that situation had been a little much.

They were *all* a little much and had been every single day since school began. There was no escaping them in training, though, and I might've actually been pleased to work with Elijah if everyone hadn't acted like it was a death sentence.

"Well, Dove," Elijah began, his golden eyes drinking me in, "the bad news here is that I don't use a sword. I do carry a dagger, but as you've undoubtedly guessed, I fight wraiths only in beast form, and only when I am truly needed."

"Wanna try one of my blades?" I asked him. "The wakizashi isn't as short as a dagger, but I bet you'll manage." I tossed him the sword in my left hand.

He caught it easily and spun it in his grip. "Sure," he said, his sharp grin returning. "Why not?"

"What the fuck?" Wyatt griped, leaning on the long handle of his ax. "You threatened to chop my dick off for touching your sword, Wildcat. How come Elijah gets a pass?"

"You *stole* my sword," I retorted. "I am *allowing* Elijah to borrow it."

Elijah slashed my blade through the air a few times. He was full of shit—he looked pretty proficient to me. "It's a well-made, nimble little blade," he told Wyatt with a shit-eating grin. "Just like my dove."

I rolled my eyes. "I can't believe you're even here," I told him. "Don't you just come kill a few Giants or spar with an Apex wraith when you need points and then fuck off again?"

His laugh was almost musical. "Usually, but then I wouldn't get to spend as much time with you."

My beast preened.

Quit that.

I narrowed my eyes at him. "Why me, Elijah?"

"Why not you, Dove?"

"You know why."

His smile dipped, but Cash started shouting orders into his microphone before Elijah could respond. We were to spar with our partner, no holds barred, until someone tapped out. These were not blunted practice weapons either. They were the real deal, so if any of us were seriously injured, our trainers were probably counting on our ability to shift or the soft magical hands of Dr. Lee to heal us.

"Ready?" I asked, raising my blade.

"For you? Always."

We lunged at each other. Our blades clashed, the force

reverberating down my arm, the familiar thrill beginning its song in my body. Elijah's grin never wavered as we went back and forth. He'd strike, I'd parry. I'd strike, he'd parry. Faster and faster, we moved in a rhythmic dance I'd have sworn we'd rehearsed.

"You are exquisite, Dove," he said brightly as I blocked a particularly sneaky attack.

"Thank you. You're unfairly good at this for someone who claims not to ever train," I said, trying not to sound sulky.

He was truly a worthy opponent—almost as technically skilled as Ian but with a whole hell of a lot more force behind his strikes. I couldn't remember the last time I'd had this much fun training with my blade.

The sounds of steel-on-steel had filled the arena, and then the roars and growls of beasts followed, as some students shifted to work blades against beasts.

Nearby, Wyatt had shifted and was doing his level best to maul Heath to death, while Heath was doing *his* level best to poke as many holes in that bear as possible with his saber.

Throughout, Cash and the other trainers wandered the floor, critiquing forms and barking instructions. They were wise enough to leave our little corner alone even as heads turned our way constantly. It seemed much of the class was on the edge of its seat, waiting for Elijah to lose it and bite me in half.

After fifteen minutes of an intense and dead-even heat, Elijah and I paused to drink water from the Guardian-branded sports bottles we'd all been issued. We watched as Wyatt roared and swiped sharp claws at Heath, who dove out of the way before rolling to his feet and slicing at Wyatt's hindquarters. I suppressed a wince, and something like dread roiled inside me at the thought of either of them seriously injuring the other one.

I needed to get over that shit fast, as serious injury was one hundred percent guaranteed for all of us if we continued down our chosen paths. Also, why did I care if Heath or Wyatt was injured?

Wyatt especially needed his ass kicked today.

I'd never been more grateful to already be overheated and red-faced as when Elijah shucked his T-shirt and used it to wipe the sweat from his face before tossing it aside. That smooth olive skin, the grooves of his abs, the carved muscles of his arms, the snake tattoo draped around his neck... all of it there for me to peruse without guilt because I was supposed to be finding ways to stab that work of art with my sword.

"Careful, Dove," he said, the low rasp of his voice making my small hairs stand on end. "The way you look at me—it makes me want to do things to you."

At least my face couldn't get any redder. "Sorry. I know we need to be mindful of your control."

"The things I want to do to you have nothing to do with me losing control of my *beast*," he replied, his sharp grin turning even more wicked.

Warmth pooled low in my belly, and my beast flicked her tail in interest.

"But, to your point, sparring with you hasn't tested my control at all. You're not trying very hard to actually injure me, and this whole exercise has been nothing but enjoyable so far. I'm dying to see how that body can move in... other ways."

"Mmm" was all I managed, taking a rough swallow of my water. I needed to steer him in a different direction before this unbearable sexual tension made me do something stupid. "So, with all of your supposed, um, issues, why become a Guardian?" I asked him. "I'm sure the rest of your quad would still be top recruits even without you."

Elijah twirled my sword lazily as he pondered my question. "A few reasons. My beast is a violent bastard who needs to kill, and setting him loose on wraiths is the best way to sate that bloodlust."

I nodded. At least the constant threat of extermination of our kind was good for something. "Does it work the same with the simulations?"

"We'll find out when we finally go out into the field, won't we?" he replied, grinning. "The SWIM works well enough for now."

"What's another of the reasons?"

He tapped his chin, his yellow eyes assessing me like my interest in him was a curious thing. "Do you know, Dove, that killing a mythic is seen in some circles as a badge of honor?"

I frowned. "I'd never met one until you. Who would dare challenge a mythic? That's near certain death."

He shrugged. "Lesser Primes who want bragging rights. And you're correct, it often is a death sentence, unless said challenge was unfair. Cheating and all that. Someone managed to kill one of the Chinese dragons just last year, and the details are shady as hell. But you can bet the *challenger* is the king of the castle now."

It dawned on me then. Elijah was here, at least partially, for the same reason I was. "A mythic in the Guardians would be better protected from illegal challenges or any other sort of shady murder attempt because it would bring the wrath of the most deadly group of Primes down on that person. A much bigger risk."

A slow smile spread across his face. "That's exactly

right." He gave me a knowing look, like we were sharing a secret.

I swallowed another glug of water. *Abort.*

"And there are also certain types not without power in our society who think mythics are too dangerous to be allowed to live," he said matter-of-factly. "Best to make myself useful, wouldn't you say?"

I nodded, looking away so he wouldn't know how close to home that also hit. "Then there is the added bonus of, you know, saving our people from having their souls eaten, right?" I asked.

"Indeed." He was quiet for a moment, seeming lost in thought. "I do feel a sense of duty to protect others from wraith attacks. That was how my fathers died. Did you know that?"

Profound sadness swept over me. "I didn't know. How old were you?"

"Two, so I don't remember it. They lived on a ranch, a ways outside our warded communities, but they rarely saw wraiths and rested on the assumption they were skilled enough to protect themselves as a quad of powerful Primes. But you know how total lunar eclipses go."

I did. They happened every few years, but some were worse than others, depending on how long the totality lasted. Sometimes it was less than ten minutes, but it was the ones that lasted nearly two hours that were the most deadly. Wraiths could escape their realm in overwhelming numbers, and it was during these times that the rare Apex could make an appearance.

That was something the legend of the First Guardians got right, anyway.

We hadn't had an eclipse like that in this area of the country since I began patrolling, but there was one coming up this fall. The totality was predicted to last an hour and fifty-three minutes.

"I'm sorry, Elijah," I said softly. "Did any of your parents survive?"

He gave me a sad smile. "My mom managed to escape with me as her bondmates were overwhelmed by several Giants and an Apex wraith. She saved my life, and then she was murdered six months later."

Horror punched me. "What?" I croaked.

"An allegedly random stabbing by a mugger when she was walking down the street. Isn't that terrible?"

"Elijah, I...." I hardly had words. "And a healer couldn't save her?"

A latent female wouldn't have been able to shift to accelerate the healing process, but that was why we had magical doctors.

"Her body didn't take the magic," Elijah said. "And it was too late for non-magical means."

Her body didn't take the magic. A wave of nausea rolled over me.

"Dove?"

My heart pounded in my throat, and my beast curled in on herself. I shut my eyes and sucked in a deep breath.

A warm, rough hand wrapped around mine. "What's wrong?" Elijah rasped.

"I just need a second."

"I can taste your fear," he whispered. His voice trembled. "*We* can taste it."

"Avery?" That was Heath. "What the—oh shit. Elijah, step away from her."

"No," Elijah hissed. Actually *hissed,* then he dropped my hand like I'd burned him.

I opened my eyes. Heath had wedged himself between

Elijah and me, his big hands pressed against Elijah's bare chest. Elijah's pupils had slitted, the basilisk rising to the surface, his golden eyes laser-focused on me.

My heart now pounded for a different reason. I scooped my second blade from the floor where Elijah had dropped it, and I took a few wary steps backward, swords raised. My beast growled, her fur standing on end and her claws out.

"Avery, go," Heath demanded between clenched teeth. "If he loses it, we'll have to clear the entire arena as a precaution."

I looked at the pair of them, feeling utterly helpless. "I don't know what happened. Elijah, everything is fine. *I'm* fine. Come back and we'll spar some more?"

Elijah closed his eyes, nostrils flaring as he shook his head. Dark green-gray scales ghosted across his chest and down his arms before winking out.

"Get the fuck away from us right now, Avery," Heath barked.

An enormous rust-red bear butted into me. A furry head the size of a tire shoved me toward the arena's exit.

I swatted Wyatt's nose, and he growled at me. "Stop that," I told him. "I'm going."

Trent stomped toward us. "What the fuck, Baxter? We still have ten minutes of weapons drills. Get your ass back over to your *partner* or you're out."

Wyatt bared his teeth in a savage growl.

"Trent," Heath snapped from behind me. "This is what happens when you play games with a mythic. Tell Cash to clear the arena and conjure up an L4. Elijah needs to let his beast out to run off some steam, and it is *your* fucking fault."

"What?" Trent barked.

Elijah hissed.

"Oh, fuck."

With a flash and the crunch of muscle and bone rearranging itself, Wyatt returned to human form. He stood gloriously naked next to me, his green gaze livid and pinned on our asshole trainer. He wrapped a large, firm hand around the back of my neck, keeping me pointed in the correct direction while he had it out with Trent. "You happy now, you absolute fucking jackass? You and Cash not only endangered Avery but also the entire moondamned program. Clear. It. Out."

"Fuck, fine. Cash!" he bellowed as he strode away.

"Let's go," Wyatt said, his voice completely devoid of its usual mirth. He steered me toward the other side of the arena, headed for Ian and Brody.

My brother and his maybe-boyfriend stood there, sweating and panting from exertion while they watched Wyatt frog-march me across the floor. Ian frowned, and Brody's dark eyebrows bounced straight to his hairline.

"Wyatt, I don't know what happened," I said softly. "Everything was fine, and he said something that upset me for just, like, a minute, and—"

"Elijah's beast is volatile, Wildcat. Don't beat yourself up."

"All right, we're wrapping up early today!" Cash announced on the microphone. "Everyone get the fuck out of here unless you want to be basilisk food."

Our fellow trainees dropped their weapons where they stood, grabbed their bags, and began a semi-organized retreat toward the door.

Wyatt deposited me with Ian. "Take her out of here right the fuck now."

"Ok-aay," Ian said slowly, sheathing his katana. He glanced over my shoulder, and his blue eyes narrowed. "What's all the fuss? Elijah seems fine."

I whirled and caught a glimpse of Elijah standing quietly in the center of the arena, still shirtless. In profile, he seemed pensive, pointedly not looking my way. Heath hovered at the edge of the arena, arms crossed over his broad chest, radiating impatience.

Wyatt slid in front of me, his chiseled nude body blocking my view. "Don't make me throw you over my shoulder again, baby. I will carry you out of here if I have to."

"Only if you want to get stabbed," I replied tersely. "I said I was going. Come on, Ian."

Wyatt didn't move a muscle, watching as I left with Ian and Brody. As we approached the door, the overhead lights cut out and the arena floor lit up with the magical fog of the SWIM.

The last thing I heard as the doors slammed behind us was the guttural bellow of a monster.

19

AVERY

I didn't see Elijah for the next two weeks. Not in our shared class, not in the hallways of our dorm, and not in the dining hall or anywhere else on campus. I finally asked Aiden about it during one of our tutoring sessions, and he assured me—tersely and without embellishment—that Elijah hadn't gone far and was fine.

My meetings with Aiden had been less tense and sexually charged than our first session together, mostly due to his deciding to teach me the driest fucking rune theory imaginable and his deliberately keeping the desk between our bodies at all times. I pretended I was listening instead of sneaking glances at his forearms and hands, while he pretended my apathy wasn't making his eye twitch behind his glasses.

Heath and Wyatt had been almost as elusive as Elijah. They made it to class most days and were often in the dining hall, but we rarely had reason to directly interact. A few times I'd considered approaching one of them to see if they would give me more information on Elijah than Aiden had, but my better judgment stopped me each time.

The Blackwell Quad was consuming too much space in my brain, and I didn't like or understand it.

The tempo of classes had picked up, which kept me busy. Most of my free time was spent staying on top of my assignments or working out with Ian.

The structure of Guardian training over the past few weeks had shifted, too, which accounted for my lack of quality time with most of the Prime Guardian candidates, not just Heath, Wyatt, and Elijah. We were starting our first individual challenges against the SWIM, and it was going to take some time to get through all the trainees. Cash had emailed out a schedule, and small groups went in shifts every afternoon until each of us had gone several rounds alone against simulated wraiths of escalating difficulty.

I'd had a thoroughly enjoyable time completing my challenges, and after managing to take down two Rippers all by my lonesome and not "die," I was sitting comfortably inside the top quarter on the individual Guardian leaderboard. Ian had rocketed to the top slot on the Support Squadron rankings, and not even Cash the Dickhead could come up with a reason why he shouldn't have been allowed in the program.

Tales of my meteoric rise in the program continued to fan the flames of loathing for the segment of the student body that saw female shifters in male-centered spaces as barbarism or whatever, but no one had attacked or challenged me again. I'd been allowed to go about my business unmolested, and I'd begun to think that just *maybe* I could have a regular college experience after all.

"It's been quiet, hasn't it?" I asked George, who was curled in a ball and half buried in the pile of pillows next to me on my bed. "Maybe the school is getting over the Guardian thing and the does-she-or-doesn't-she-have-a-beast thing, and everything will be totally *normal* from here on out."

His forked tongue darted out of his mouth, and he made a soft hissing noise.

"If *normal* is what you're going for, you may want to ditch the sparkly purple python that's been following you around like a puppy," Mallory drawled from where she sat at my desk, pouring over a biology textbook.

Ian snorted. He and Brody were sprawled out on my rug, Brody on his back and scrolling his tablet while Ian used Brody's stomach as a pillow, a pharmacology textbook in his hands. "Come on, Mal—leave my boy alone. He's giving us major street cred among the beasts that roam these halls."

"Is that why it's been quiet?" I cooed at George, tickling his chin. "No one's bothered me since the first week of school because you've been such a faithful companion?"

George had joined Wyatt, Heath, and Aiden in the dining hall most mornings but would inevitably end up in my lap or curled up at my feet. He usually spent my morning classes with me before heading off, probably to take a glorious midday nap. I'd also found him sleeping in Aiden's office when I arrived one evening for tutoring, so I got to stroke his pretty scales while Aiden tried his damnedest to make our lesson as unsexy as possible.

If George was keeping the haters away, I had no complaints.

Though I might've liked to see Elijah, too, just to make sure he was okay.

And to tell him I was sorry that the story of his mother's murder had thrown me for a second.

Because the fact that her body rejected magic after an attempt to kill her? It was eerily similar to my own mother's story.

"This curfew bullshit blows," Ian griped. "There should be an exemption when the beginning of the lunar cycle is on a weekend."

Brody ran an affectionate hand through Ian's blond hair. "I'll take you out next weekend. I don't trust you or Avery not to go looking for wraiths if we sneak off campus now."

This cycle's nightly curfew had started sundown last night and would end at sunrise Monday morning. It was currently Saturday night and the New Moon, and Brody wasn't wrong. I was feeling extra itchy for my swords.

"It just feels wrong to be lying in my bed, reading about Slavic folklore, while our neighbors back home may be under attack," I said.

"Dad told us on our last Sunday-night video call to take a few cycles off, Aves," Ian replied. "They can handle it."

I knew that, but it didn't make me want to climb the walls any less.

"We can always go down to the study room and see how Allen and Chance's D&D campaign is progressing," Mallory said, tossing me a teasing grin over her shoulder. "It's always the highlight of the nights we have curfew."

Over the past few weeks, I'd learned that Allen was adorably nerdy and extremely obsessed with Mal. I loved it.

Maybe I should go down to the D&D room to see if I can catch myself a nice nerdy boyfriend. Plenty of males around here weren't Primes or part of a quad on the hunt for a central bond, after all.

If I had other male distractions, maybe I'd stop thinking about how much Heath seemed to care when I was injured, or the feel of his rough, possessive hand against my bare skin, like he was trying to erase Dr. Lee's touch.

Or about how Wyatt's green eyes had blazed with desire

and his powerful body trembled when I'd grabbed him by the throat.

Or about how Aiden pointedly avoided looking at me when I had his class but rarely took his probing hazel gaze from my face during our tutoring time together.

Or about how Elijah's jovial-but-dangerous edge thrilled me and sparring with him had felt like we'd been doing it for years.

Who was I kidding? D&D wasn't going to do it.

I slid off my bed and toed on my fuzzy boots. "Mal, I'll walk you down to see Allen if you want. I think I'm going to go outside and just... get some air."

She slammed her textbook closed. "Sure. If you're leaving, I should go anyway, so Brody and Ian can get it on or whatever it is they do in their private time."

Brody coughed, and Ian aimed a beatific smile at Mal. "So thoughtful." His smile faded as he turned narrowed eyes on me. "Aves, I see you drifting toward your swords like you think I don't know what you're up to."

"Can I please just... go walk the perimeter so I'm able to *pretend* I'm doing something?" I asked. "I'll take George. He needs some exercise anyway. He's been loafing around in here all day."

Ian stared at me. I stared back.

Are you going to be difficult? his eyes asked.

You bet, mine replied with a twitch of my brow.

He let out a defeated sigh. "If you so much as put a *toe* outside the wards without me, sister dearest, I will steal three pairs of your most revealing underwear and deliver them to Wyatt."

I gasped. "You wouldn't."

"I would."

"He would," Brody added, nodding sagely. "I wouldn't help him, though, Avery! I like my balls where they are."

Ian tilted his head to give Brody his most suggestive grin. "Care to show me where, exactly?"

"Well, that's our cue, Mal," I announced, slinging my swords over my sweatshirt before glancing at my bed. "Come on, George. Let's go see if these wards are really worth the silver they're etched on." As George began to unwind and slither off the bed, I pointed a stern finger at Ian and Brody. "Do *not* fuck on my rug."

"You know, you're very quiet for such a large snake," I said to George as he slithered silently through the grass next to me. He was able to blend into the thick brush that grew outside the manicured lawns of the main buildings, the cloudy moonless night allowing even his shiny purple scales to appear dark and dull. "Is this how you hunt? Or do you just lounge around and wait for your daddy to feed you dead things?"

If a snake could roll its eyes, he would've. He hissed softly and picked up the pace, his long, thick body winding like a corkscrew through the dry grass.

"That wasn't me being judgmental, George!" I called out, hurrying after him. "I don't go out and kill my own food, either, you know? I show up to the dining hall and someone hands it to me. No need to exert ourselves for a meal when we don't have to."

The echo of a beastly screech sounded in the distance. If I concentrated, my sensitive ears could just pick up the muffled shouting of men in response. I'd been walking the perimeter of the campus for about half an hour, and this was the second time I'd caught the sounds of wraith battle in the distance. There were several Guardian posts in the surrounding area, and they were out doing their jobs.

Frustration welled. On the one hand, I still resented the Guardians for leaving the city-dwelling shifters high and dry, but on the other, I *itched* to be out there with them, slaying wraiths, my blades singing, riding the adrenaline of the kills, which was a high like none other.

I ran my hand along the campus's warded brick wall next to me. The school must employ a small army of security experts to recharge the wards under the Full Moon, because I could feel the soft buzz of the magic under my fingertips even from the interior side of the thick wall. This level of magic would blaze like a bonfire under the Full Moon, but that was the unfortunate nature of our wraith problem—they could only appear when our magic was the weakest.

The crunch of tires on gravel caught my attention. George and I were nearing the front gates, which were closed and locked with a silver chain and padlock during curfew nights. No one in or out, and good luck picking that lock without melting your fingertips off. The sound of a car approaching the campus entrance was unexpected, to say the least.

George must've thought the same because he darted in front of me and increased his speed, both of us hurrying over to peek through the wrought iron bars.

A large black Cadillac SUV had skidded to a stop a few yards away from the gate, next to the little hut where the guard normally sat. The hut was abandoned tonight since we were on lockdown.

The door opened, and a teenage girl tumbled out. "Shit!"

she shouted, banging her small fist on the glass of the hut. "Moon*damn* it." She cast a harried look around, raking a manicured hand through perfect brown curls and stumbling a bit in her heeled leather boots. She was also wearing a skirt under her wool peacoat, so I doubted breaking and entering into the Proteus College campus had been on her to-do list when she'd picked out her outfit for the evening.

"Hey!" I whisper-shouted through the bars of the gate. "What are you doing? It's dangerous to be out right now."

Her frantic gaze jerked to me, and her shoulders slumped in what might have been relief. She scurried up to the gate to meet me. "I know it's a New Moon. It's so reckless, but I just... I didn't know what to do," she told me, her lip quivering. She hardly looked old enough to drive the car she'd abandoned, and words began to spill out of her at breakneck speed. "I was, um, on a date over in Frederickstown, and it was going badly. I needed to get away, but I can't go home. My brothers go here, and it was the only place I could think to come. Do you know them? Heath and Aiden Blackwell. I'm Clara Blackwell—wait, is that Elijah's snake?"

I blinked at her for two seconds before my brain switched into action mode. "Yes, I know your brothers, and yes, that's George," I told her. "And I'm Avery. Did you call your brothers?"

Clara shook her head frantically. "I turned my phone off. I don't want my parents to be able to track me."

"Why?" I asked slowly. The idea of my dads not being the first place I'd run to for safety was foreign to me. "What's going on?"

"They're making me go on, um, dates," she whispered. "My dads are very powerful Primes, and I'm their only daughter, so they've, um.... They've decided to arrange an *advantageous* bonding for me." She gripped the iron bars and leaned closer to me. "I don't want it, but they don't care. And the guys tonight were terrible. One of them kept grabbing my thigh under my skirt, and they kept talking about how they, um, couldn't wait to see if 'latent Prime pussy was as good as everyone says.'"

I bit my cheek so the rage that blasted through me wouldn't force my body to sprout fur. This girl couldn't be older than sixteen. "So you ran away from your dates?"

She nodded again. "I swiped the car keys off the table when they weren't looking, went to the bathroom, and climbed out the window. Then I stole their car and drove here. Outside the town's wards during curfew—I know, so *stupid*, but I was panicking. They're probably tracking me, though. One of them is an Alpha wolf, so he'd be able to find the scent. *Shit*." She jerked on the bars.

Shit, okay—think, Avery. "Good for you, Clara. That was still good thinking, getting away like you did. How many guys are we talking about?"

"Two. Brothers. A wolf and a lion. My dad really wants me to bond with a lion."

Fuck lions, and two was better than a whole quad. "Okay, let's figure out how to get you inside the gates, and then we'll go find your brothers and let them deal with your dates. Unless.... They aren't involved in this shit, right?" I couldn't imagine Heath or Aiden being complicit in shopping their baby teenage sister for an *advantageous* bonding against her will, but if they were, I'd stab them myself.

She shook her head vehemently. "No, they call my dads to yell at them about it all the time. They just can't... do anything, really. Not now."

The immense relief I felt at hearing that Heath and Aiden didn't actually suck was unnecessary, but no time to dwell. "Okay, I'm going to try to climb over the gate, and then I'll give you a boost—"

A roar sounded from deep in the forest. A wolfy snarl followed.

Those were not wraiths.

Clara tensed, and then she turned wide hazel eyes to me. "That's them! They found me!"

"Shit, okay. It wouldn't make sense for them to try to hurt you, but let's not chance it. George, slither out there and stand guard."

George oozed his scaly body between the iron bars of the gate and curled up in the ten-foot space between Clara and the car. I had no idea what he could do against a baby Prime shifter, but we'd find out.

Tears leaked from Clara's terrified eyes. "I don't want them to catch me. They're probably really angry."

I wrapped my hands around hers on the bars. "Listen, Clara. I am going to get over this wall, and I will make sure they don't touch you. I have my swords, and I'll tell you a secret: I also have a beast, so I'm very strong."

She hiccupped. "You... you do?"

There were more roars and snarls, louder ones, and they were getting closer. "Yep. Okay, here goes nothing."

I backpedaled about fifteen feet, and then I sprinted straight for the gate. With everything I had, I took a running leap and landed halfway up the gate, my feet pressed against the bars while I gripped the same bars above my head for dear life. I shoved off the bars with my legs and propelled myself upward until I was able to grasp the top of the gate. I swung my body over, readying myself to jump down.

A large brown wolf came charging out of the trees and onto the road right behind the SUV.

Clara screamed.

Then came a dark gray lion, tearing out of the forest behind his brother.

I was out of time.

With a fortifying breath, I launched myself off the gate and dropped into the fray.

20

AVERY

"Avery!" Clara shrieked as the wolf hurdled the SUV and launched himself at her.

He wasn't as big as Heath or my dad or even that shithead Rip, but he would be close when he fully matured.

I landed next to Clara, and the force of it rocked me hard, even with my enhanced strength. I ripped my swords from their sheaths, ready to impale an out-of-control teenage Prime. I could only hope Clara wasn't injured in the process.

I needn't have worried.

George sprang from the ground, launching his upper half like a dart at the wolf. He struck, sinking his rows of curved teeth into the wolf's thick neck and knocking him right out of the air. The wolf yelped, and then he snarled and shook his head violently, but to no avail. George was already wrapping his long body around that furry neck.

"By the Moon," Clara gasped.

"He's constricting," I told her. "George! Do not kill him."

I had to trust he would listen to me because there was no

time for me to interfere. The lion was on us, roaring as he leapt right at me.

My beast pounded ruthlessly against my skin. It would be so much easier to let her out to handle this asshole. Like all Primes, he was larger than the average lion found in the wild, but he wasn't as big as a mature Prime feline. My beast would tear this little shit apart, but I had no idea if the school had cameras out here.

So swords it would be, like it always fucking was.

I shoved Clara out of the way and then dove in the opposite direction. The lion flew past me, skidding to a stop against the gate before he turned and jumped at me again, mouth open and teeth aimed at my neck.

I ducked and jammed both swords in an upward strike, impaling one in his furry chest, the other only managing a glancing slice to his shoulder. He roared in pain, and I was able to yank my sword out and hit the deck, but not before the lion's hindquarters smashed right into my skull.

"Avery!" Clara shouted again. "Paul! Leave her alone!"

Paul the lion snarled viciously at Clara, blood dripping from his chest and matting his dark fur. I crawled to my feet, my ears ringing. Something warm dripped down my temple. I must've busted my head open when I hit the pavement.

"Now I'm pissed, Paul," I told the lion. "Shift back and walk away, or George is going to suffocate your brother to death."

He roared, baring deadly teeth.

"Wrong answer," I said, my voice dropping to a guttural growl as my beast snarled and raked at my skin.

Paul charged me, staying lower to the ground this time. He swiped at me with sharp claws, and I parried with my blade, slicing his front leg deep. He recovered quickly and pounced, his big body slamming into me. His hotheaded teenaged shifter brain was in overdrive, my swords be damned.

I shouted in frustration as I went down under him, burying both blades in his stomach. Clara was screaming again, but there wasn't much I could do at this point, outside of shifting into my beast. Paul roared and wheezed, the weight of him crushing, but my swords weren't going anywhere. He was bleeding profusely now—I just needed to wait for him to weaken.

But I'd forgotten my ace in the hole.

George had released his prey, who lay motionless on the ground right in front of the SUV, a few feet away. He zipped over to me and struck at Paul, then wound himself around the lion's neck just as he had the wolf. The force of George's strike shifted Paul's lion body off me enough that I was able to roll out from under him.

I flopped onto my back and lay motionless for a minute, staring up at the cloudy, dark sky. Clara appeared above me and held out a hand.

"They're both, um, passed out," she said quietly as she helped me to my feet. "I thought George might've killed them, but I can see their bellies moving. They're breathing."

George slithered quietly over to us, a gleam in his snaky eyes. "You did so good," I crooned at him. "What an efficient little fighter. The best ever—yes, you are."

"He's terrifying," Clara whispered. "Elijah's not allowed to bring him into our house. My mom thinks he'll eat Bonbon and Parfait."

"Who?"

"Her corgis."

I snorted a laugh, then sheathed my swords and rolled out my neck and shoulders. My head still hurt, and I was covered in lion blood.

This was a giant fucking mess, but I wouldn't be cleaning it up. I'd done my part.

I directed Clara to the gate, and I used what strength I had left to boost her over. I followed, using the same run, leap, and climb method I had the first time, and after George had slipped through the bars, we trudged off in search of the Blackwell brothers.

"I KNOW AIDEN'S HOUSE IS OVER HERE SOMEWHERE," CLARA mused. "This is faculty housing, right?"

I took in the narrow street illuminated by the soft light of the streetlamps and lined with quaint redbrick homes. "I've only been going here for, like, a month," I replied with a shrug. "I'm a transfer."

Clara tapped her lips, still perfectly lined and colored even after all the nonsense earlier. I'd have to ask her what brand of lipstick she used. "It's here somewhere. Heath always stays with Aiden on the weekends, and they wouldn't be off campus during curfew, right?"

"We'll find out." I was just glad Clara had insisted on tracking Aiden down at his house instead of marching us through the dorm, looking for Heath's room. I was a little too blood-spattered for polite company, and faculty housing was much more isolated over on the west side of campus.

"Oh! Do you think George knows the way?" she asked.

I must've taken a harder hit to the head than I'd thought, because *duh*. At the moment, George was gliding lazily through the manicured lawn next to the sidewalk. "Hey, buddy, can you show us the way to Aiden's house?"

He dipped his head in a nod.

Perfect.

We followed him down the street to the first intersection, where he made a right turn, and then he slithered up the stone walkway and onto the porch of the house on the corner. It was a two-story home with a sloping roof and windows framed by dark blue shutters. Thin white columns stretched from the edge of the roof down to the porch floor. Under one of the large front windows, there were a couple of weathered rocking chairs with a small table between them. A black coffee mug sat abandoned on the table, forgotten from sometime earlier.

I jammed my finger into the doorbell, then rapped a fist on the door for good measure. I was out of patience. This night needed to be over already.

The door swung open. It appeared the Moon had decided I deserved a reward for my suffering tonight, because there stood Aiden, wearing only a pair of navy sweatpants. Unlike his brother, he did not have his beast tattooed across his broad chest. No, he was all smooth, tan skin over taut muscles. The dim light from the bulb above us seeped into the grooves of his abs, and I allowed myself a single second to trace those lines with my tired gaze until the V-cut at his hips disappeared into the waistband of his pants.

"Clara? Avery? What the hell—"

Clara sobbed and threw herself into his arms. He caught her, wrapping her in a hug, his defined biceps flexing as he squeezed her tight. His gaze was pinned on me, though, confusion and alarm written there as he took in the state of me.

"Woah, Clara? What's going on?"

Heath appeared over Aiden's shoulder, disappointingly fully clothed in a simple white T-shirt and soft gray pants. He took one look at Clara crying into Aiden's bare shoulder, and then he saw me. His jaw slackened, and then his eyes narrowed dangerously.

"Good, you're both here." I sounded as exhausted as I felt. "We have a problem, and you're going to need to clean it up."

Heath lunged past Aiden and Clara and grabbed me by the arm. He pulled me into the house, slammed the door behind us, and maneuvered me right onto the couch in the cozy little living room.

"What happened?" he growled as he hovered over me, grasping my chin in his hand and using the other to gently probe the cut on my head. "You reek of feline hair and blood. Are you hurt anywhere else? Take your sweatshirt off."

He reached for the hem of my shirt, and I swatted his hands away. "Stop that. This blood isn't mine. That would be Paul's, the piece of shit your parents sent your sister on a date with."

Aiden set Clara on the couch next to me, and now we had two bossy Blackwells staring down at us, concern warring with rage across both of their stony faces. Clara sniffed and grabbed my hand. She was trembling again, so I gave her fingers an encouraging squeeze.

"Clara," Heath said, forcing some softness into his voice that he hadn't bothered with when speaking to me. "Did Dad send you on a date with Paul Blankenship? How did you end up all the way up here?"

She nodded. "It was Paul and Harrison. They were... they were *awful*, Heath. I had to get away, and I didn't know where else to go."

She recounted the details of her date, her escape, her frantic drive to the school's front gates, and the events that unfolded when Harrison and Paul tracked her here. Gold rolled over Heath's irises as she spoke, and Aiden's had lit up in my favorite neon turquoise, both riled and fighting the urge to murder.

Good.

"I don't know what would've happened if Avery and George hadn't been there," she said, sniffling. "I mean, they would've been in a lot of trouble if they'd have hurt me, but teenage shifters…"

"Aren't always in control of their beasts," Aiden finished for her. He ran a hand through his wavy hair, and then he speared me with a *look*. "Avery, for fuck's sake. You took on two Prime beasts with only your swords?"

"Really, it was just the lion," I replied. I flapped a hand at George, who had curled up in front of the fireplace and was snoozing away like he hadn't choked out two large animals tonight. "George took the wolf down all on his own, and then he finished the lion off for me. If he hadn't, I might still be underneath that little bastard, waiting for him to bleed out."

Heath scrubbed a hand down his face and groaned. "Shit. *Fuck.* I don't know whose throat I want to rip out first —Dad's or those shitty little assholes'. Clara, I am *so* sorry this happened."

"It's not your fault, Heath."

He stared at her, his hazel eyes despondent. "We're going to figure it out, okay? Just keep… being disruptive when they force you to meet these dickhead Primes. Buy us some time."

Clara gasped. "Oh! Can Avery teach me how to use a sword? That way when someone touches me in a way I don't like, I can stab them."

"No," they both replied.

"Yes," I said, glaring at them. "I would be happy to,

though it's not like your brothers aren't good with a blade. You should ask Elijah to teach you to use a dagger."

"Ooh, you're right, I should," she said and hummed thoughtfully. "He doesn't say no to me either. Not like these two."

The front door blew open, and Wyatt stomped into the living room. He wore workout clothes and smelled like sweat and delicious male pheromones. "Hey, why the fuck isn't anyone answering their phone? Willow just called, and she said Clara's fucking *missing*—oh."

Clara waved at him. "Hi, Wyatt. Did my mom call your mom, looking for me?"

"Yep." His gaze slid from Clara to me, two dark emeralds boring straight into my chest. A red sheen rolled over those emeralds, a fucking siren call to my beast. "What in the actual fuck is going on here?"

"Good, you're back," Heath said. "I need you to stay with Clara. She can sleep in my room tonight—I'll bunk with Aiden."

Wyatt was still looking at me. "Someone needs to start fucking talking. Why is the wildcat covered in blood and stinking of feline?"

"Clara will explain," Aiden replied. "Heath and I have to go take care of something, and we need you to watch over her while we're gone. Do not answer the door for anyone except us, and if your parents call again, don't tell them she's here."

He blew out a breath, his big shoulders dropping. "Okay, I got it. Go."

Heath held out a hand to me. "Let's go, Killer. You're coming with us."

"Me?" I stared dumbly at his hand. "No, I did my part. I'm going to *bed*."

"Yes, you did a whole hell of a lot tonight, but I'm not letting you out of my sight. We're going to go deal with the two little shitheads who thought they could put their hands on my sister, and then you're going to the infirmary, even if I have to hogtie you and drag you there myself."

I lifted my chin. "I don't take orders from you, Heath Blackwell."

Clara snickered.

Aiden shouldered Heath aside. He leaned in, hovering over me, and placed one hand on the couch's armrest to my right, his long fingers curling over the leather in a way that shouldn't have been hot, but *ugh*, it was. He bent down further, our noses nearly touching as he growled softly, "You'll take orders from your professor, *Miss Baxter*. You'll get that perfect ass off my couch, and you'll stick with Heath and me until I release you to go back to your dorm. Understood?"

His eyes blazed turquoise behind his glasses, challenging me. Instead of the appropriate response of wanting to bite the head off this presumptuous jaguar, my beast flicked her tail lazily, ears perked in interest.

YOU. ARE. NOT. HELPING.

I glared at Aiden as he stood up again and waited for my response with his bare arms folded over his chest, a perfect brow arched. Heath watched me intently, and Wyatt smirked at my plight. Clara, the ungrateful traitor, just giggled more.

"Fine," I said. "But no infirmary. Mallory can stitch the cut in my head closed and magic away my headache. There's nothing else wrong with me."

Heath and Aiden shared a look.

"Deal," Heath said. "Let's go. I want to get to those

fuckers before they become wraith food. They'd deserve it, but it would be a hell of a lot harder to clean up."

HEATH AND AIDEN WERE SILENT ON OUR WALK BACK OUT TO the front gates. They marched stoically on either side of me, and I could sense both tamping down the beastly rage that had to be roiling inside them. Few things were harder on our control than threats to a loved one.

I could attest. One of the few times I nearly lost it and let my beast out in the middle of the hallway of my human high school was during my sophomore year, when I'd happened upon a couple of meat-headed jocks spewing homophobic slurs at Ian, who'd been a new freshman at the time.

Ian had to drag me into the girls' locker room and shove me under a cold shower before I'd been allowed to go back to class.

So, while I was supremely irritated that I was not on the way to my room because the Blackwell brothers had decided to boss me around *again*, I also understood the need for a cooler head on this little outing, and that could only be mine.

When we approached the gate, we found Harrison the wolf, back in nude human boy form, frantically dragging Paul the lion's beastly body toward the SUV, leaving a trail of dark blood in his wake. Even with his enhanced strength as a burgeoning Prime shifter, it would be a feat for him to get that unconscious lion's bulk into the backseat of the car.

Unearthly screeches and bellows echoed in the woods behind him. The Guardians must've been chasing wraiths this way, so he was understandably panicking, and he hadn't even spotted Clara's incensed brothers yet.

Heath blew out an angry breath. He stood next to me, his shoulder pressed against mine, as we observed Harrison's plight. Aiden, now tragically dressed in a T-shirt and a fleece jacket, was on my other side, as close as he could possibly be without touching me. He was silent and still as the grave—if you ignored the rapidly coiling aggression leaking from his every pore.

"I see Paul's still down," Heath said through clenched teeth. "How many holes did you put in him, Killer?"

I thought back to the fight, counting on my fingers. "Really only, like, three. George is the one who ultimately took both of them down, so make sure he gets an extra juicy ferret or whatever he likes best next time Elijah feeds him."

"Even so, Paul's lucky his spine is still intact." Heath glanced over my head at Aiden. "Think you can force a shift?"

Aiden scoffed. "He's, what, seventeen?"

Harrison took a break from his efforts, dropping the lion and wiping the sweat from his brow. At that moment, he finally looked up and saw the three of us watching him from behind the gate's iron bars. His eyes went comically wide, and he took off running into the woods without a backwards glance at his fallen brother.

Heath barked a laugh and jumped four feet off the ground, grabbing the bars of the gate and propelling himself over the top in a much more efficient fashion than I had. He took off after Harrison, who had, like an idiot, just engaged Heath's predator instinct by fleeing like prey.

"Stay here, please, Avery," Aiden murmured. "Like you said, you've done enough tonight."

"Okay." I didn't desire a climb over that gate a third or

fourth time tonight, nor was I in the mood to slay any wraiths that wandered this direction, which was a testament to how tired I was. "Keep it together, though, both of you, or I'll have to come out there and take you down before you kill one of those idiots."

Aiden turned to me, his neon eyes lighting up the narrow space between us. "My brother and I are extremely skilled at *restraint*," he rumbled, his voice a low purr rolling gently over me like a lullaby. "When we lose control, it's because we *let* it happen. Stay. Here."

He vaulted over the gate somehow even faster than Heath had, and then he stalked with feline grace toward the prone lion.

I sat down on the ground, crossed my legs, and settled in for a show, a little thrill zipping through my body at the thought of watching Heath and Aiden work those shitty boys over.

21

HEATH

"Whatever she told you, she's fucking lying!" Harrison Blankenship sputtered as I slammed him up against the side of his SUV. "She stole our fucking car!"

I jammed my knee into his exposed groin, and he keened like a wounded lamb and not the fucking Alpha he was supposed to be. "You're calling my baby sister a liar?" I growled in his face. "My sister, who was so put off by the things you said to her—by your touching her without her permission—that she ran away from you and drove your car thirty minutes under a New fucking Moon just to get to me?"

"I don't know why crazy-ass females do the things they d—"

I slammed my fist into his face. Bone crunched under my knuckles, and blood seeped from his nose.

Behind me, Aiden had his foot on Paul's furry throat. "Shift back," he commanded, the force of his dominance making even Harrison wince.

The lion's body trembled, and with lightning-fast rearranging of bone and muscle, the beast retreated, leaving only a blond shaggy-haired teenage boy in its place.

Aiden hauled him off the ground and threw him against the side of the car. He bounced off and landed in a pathetic heap by my feet. I released Harrison long enough to kick Paul in the ribs, the satisfying crack of bone and groan of pain fanning the bloodlust I was keeping carefully contained.

"Get up," Aiden barked at Paul.

"He was still healing!" Harrison whined. "Just let us go. We get it. We won't see your sister again. We don't want to bond with her anyway! Our dads made us take her out."

I buried my fist in his stomach, and he doubled over. "You're only walking away from this alive because I don't feel like exerting the effort to clean up your deaths," I told him. "Because you didn't just misbehave on your date, did you? You chased my sister to this school, and then you attacked an innocent female."

"I didn't—"

Aiden picked Paul up from the ground like he was a rag doll and shoved him against the car next to his brother. "Yes, your brother got his ass kicked by a *snake*, but you, Paul, attacked an innocent female at the front gates of this college. Do you have anything to say about that?"

"She's not an innocent fucking female!" Paul rasped. "She's clearly got a beast. She should be put down."

It was Paul's turn to get a fist in the face. Aiden probably shattered his cheekbone with that shot.

It was woefully typical that the Blankenships' views on females with a beast were as backwards as my fucking dads' were. They'd selected them as potential mates for Clara, after all.

"Listen up, both of you," I said quietly, the violence of

my beast threaded through every word. "You will get into your fucking car and drive home. You will explain to your parents and mine that you said some things that were too forward and aggressive for a first date, and that Clara got nervous and ran away. You tracked her here, where Aiden and I were waiting for you. We tuned you up, taught you a lesson in dating etiquette, and sent you on your way. You did not get your ass kicked by a female and a snake. Got it?"

Harrison couldn't meet my eyes, but he nodded at his feet.

"Fine," Paul choked out, coughing up some blood as he did. "We're going."

A monstrous roar sounded in the woods. An alarmed shout followed.

"You better hurry," Aiden said. "The Guardians like to herd wraiths up against our wards sometimes."

True, though it was supposedly a last resort. The college had some of the strongest anti-wraith wards in existence.

I released Harrison, and he ran around to the driver's side door. Paul limped his bloody body over to the passenger door, flung it open, and crawled inside like the rodent he was.

My beast shuddered within me, almost in pain from the cage I was keeping him in. I could sense Aiden's jaguar experiencing the same struggle.

As Harrison jerked the SUV around and gunned the engine, racing away like the coward he was, Aiden and I turned our attention back to the girl who'd saved our sister from the Moon only knew what at the hands of two out-of-control teenage shifters.

Avery's gaze was glued to my brother and me as we stalked slowly back toward the gate. She was sitting on the ground, her swords sheathed in their harness lying next to her. She looked tired, but she also wore a satisfied smirk that pleased me more than it should have.

I hadn't been lying when I'd told her that I was making her stay with us so that I could make sure she got treatment for her injuries. She'd been fucking reckless yet again, taking on two Prime shifters with only her swords and no equivalent beast at her disposal. If it hadn't been for George taking an inexplicable liking to her and following her all over campus while Elijah was away, she'd be a lot more fucking hurt right now, and who knew what that would've meant for Clara.

But I'd also dragged her here because she'd done something I couldn't—she'd been there to save my sister, and the wolf within me had needed to show this female that we could take care of our own business.

And now the wolf within me wanted something else, and I'd lost the will to maintain control of that beastly urge.

Aiden boosted me over the gate, and he followed right behind me, scrambling up and over with ease. He'd always been a better climber than me.

Avery stood up and dusted herself off. Even in a blood-stained sweatshirt, more blood caked in her blonde hair and dried on her face, and exhaustion weighing down her ethereal blue eyes, she'd never looked more beautiful to me.

"Well, now that *that's* done, I'll just be going—"

With a snarl, I pushed her into Aiden's waiting arms. She gasped as her back hit his chest. He held her tight and pulled her away from the gate, bracing against the brick wall that separated the college from the rest of the world.

Avery didn't breathe as I pressed into her, crowding her front while Aiden held her in place, one arm banded across her stomach and the other over the top of her chest. No question that Aiden and I were on the same wavelength. My brother had cut the cord and wanted this as badly as I did.

"I am so fucking *frustrated*, Avery," I growled softly, wrapping my hands around her hips. They fit perfectly in my grip, and it pissed me off even more. "I'm furious at you for traipsing around this campus *alone* during a New Moon. Our wards are excellent, but nothing is infallible."

She writhed in my grasp, but she sure wasn't trying very hard to escape. "Fuck you, Blackwell. I had my swords and George, and for the last moondamned time, I don't take orders from *you*."

She gasped again as Aiden chuckled, his mouth up against her neck. "Such a brat."

"But you know why I'm so frustrated, Killer?" I went on, running my nose up the side of her pale neck that Aiden wasn't occupying. She smelled of sweat and blood and fucking flowers. "Because I'm also *thankful* you were wandering around tonight because you found Clara and put yourself in harm's way for her, a girl you'd never even met before."

"We don't know what to do with you," Aiden said. "You saved Clara, just like you try to save everyone in your neighborhood each lunar cycle, but you're also on a path that's going to get you killed."

"Mmm," I grunted in agreement, caving to the urge to taste her skin. I licked a stripe from her collarbone to her ear, and the tiny moan it elicited destroyed every brake I had left. "Can't have that. We could threaten you, but you don't appear to fear anything."

"Would love to fuck some sense into you," Aiden mused, and she shuddered in my hands, "but I don't think that would work, either."

"We really are at a loss," I whispered in her ear. "So, for now, I'm just going to... thank you."

Her hooded eyes fluttered. "What—"

I dropped to my knees and ripped her leggings down to her ankles. She gasped and clawed at Aiden's arm, but he only chuckled and nipped her ear. I yanked one of her boots off and pulled her foot free from her pants. I tossed that smooth, shapely fucking leg over my shoulder, and then I buried my face in her hot, wet cunt.

"Oh *shit*," she moaned as I took a luxurious lick of the tastiest pussy I'd ever encountered. I was going to be so fucked after this, but my rational brain had left the building. "Don't stop, Heath."

A Giant could've barreled through the wall, and I wouldn't have stopped. I was in this until she came all over my face. Her little moans and mewls spurred me on at a breakneck pace, and I *devoured* her.

Aiden did his part, crooning dirty shit in her ear. "You're shaking, sweetheart. Does that feel good, having Heath's tongue between your gorgeous thighs? I'm so damn jealous of my brother right now. I'd love to be the one making you moan."

"Aiden," she said, sounding breathless. "Are you even supposed to be touching me like this?"

We both laughed at that. "That's the thing about being a Prime in an unbonded quad," he whispered, like he was telling her a secret. "I could rut you like an animal up against the Magical Ed building, and the dean would give me a hearty slap on the back for trying to find our bond. Well, he would, if you weren't lying about being latent."

She groaned. "If I'm not a special blue-blooded latent, then why does Heath have my clit in his mouth?"

It was my turn to groan, her dirty words turning me on

even more, which I hadn't thought was possible. I sucked hard on her clit in retaliation, threading a finger into her hot center as I lashed her with my tongue. She was tight and wet and fucking perfect.

"Heath doesn't go down on those girls, sweetheart," Aiden murmured. "He takes them on boring dates, where they talk about school and family and what kind of boat their parents just bought for the lake house."

I rumbled a noise of agreement, then added a second finger. I hammered them into her because she was the strongest female I'd ever met and could take everything I wanted to give her.

She screamed, her muscles contracting around my fingers as she climaxed, gushing hard just for me.

"Fuck *yes*," I groaned against her slick skin.

"Good girl," Aiden said. "I could listen to that beautiful sound all night."

She moaned, sagging in his arms, still spasming around my fingers. My dick had never been harder in my life, and my beast lounged with a level of primal satisfaction he'd never cared to feel when I hooked up with a girl.

I gave her a few more languid licks, and then I helped her back into her pants. Aiden pulled them up her legs while I slid her boot back onto her foot. Satisfied she was dressed and comfortable, I stood up and wrapped my arms around her. She buried her face in my T-shirt while Aiden ran a gentle hand up and down her back.

My brother and I exchanged a look over her shoulder. We'd just done something neither of us could take back, but he didn't look like he regretted his part in it even a little bit, and neither did I. Sex wasn't a declaration of intent to date or bond, and Avery wasn't the type to make this something it wasn't.

But she deserved to feel something tonight other than the pain inflicted on her by more powerful shifters, and I'd wanted to give it to her. Soon, I would have to scrub this *fascination* with her from my soul—as would the rest of my quad—but tonight, I'd let myself have what I wanted, and it'd been fucking glorious.

"Let's get you to your room," I said into her hair. "Call your medic friend and have her meet you there."

"Okay," she replied easily.

Aiden chuckled. "Maybe fucking the sass out of you actually does work."

"Maybe," she replied, releasing me and stepping out of my arms. It took everything I had not to grab her again. "Or you might get your dick sliced off the next time you try. Still want to chance it?"

"Yep," I said.

"Sure do," Aiden added.

She rolled her eyes, a smile tugging at the corner of her lips. She swiped her swords from the ground and shrugged them on, then pulled her phone from her pocket. "Hey, Mal, you still up? Oh.... No, I didn't need to know that.... Uh-huh.... Well, can you put some clothes on and meet me at my room with your first aid kit?... No, just some minor scrapes and bruises.... Yep, okay, thanks."

We walked her back to the upperclassmen dorm in comfortable silence. It was nearing one in the morning, and since it was a curfew night, no one was out and about. That relative privacy was all I needed to chance holding Avery's hand on the walk. I was shocked she allowed it—or the hand Aiden kept on the small of her back as we went.

Aiden made her hand over her blood-soaked sweatshirt and sent her inside wearing his fleece jacket instead. We watched her disappear through the doors of the dorm, and once we were satisfied she wasn't going to sneak back out, we began the hike to Aiden's house.

After a few minutes of walking in silence, Aiden said softly, "I don't know what to do about her."

I knew what he meant. "Me neither," I replied with a sigh. "But right now, unfortunately, it's time to deal with Dad."

His face hardened. Getting lost in Avery had been a nice little interlude before what we really needed to accomplish, but I hadn't forgotten, and neither had he. "Yeah," he said. "We have to end this soon."

He was right—on several counts.

22

AIDEN

Wyatt had showered and waited up for us, and he was extra surly when we finally trudged into my living room.

"About fucking time," he griped. He was sitting on the couch, his arms crossed over his bare chest, his eyes slits. "I can't believe you left me here while you got to go tear apart those handsy little fucks."

"You know exactly why we left you," Heath retorted. "Besides the fact that one of us who is not a python needed to watch over Clara, how long did you have to stand in a cold shower to get your bear's rage under control?"

"An hour," he muttered. "And I texted all of my sisters to tell them they aren't allowed to go on dates with males, or someone might die."

Willow, who was seventeen, was too wily to let Wyatt catch her on a date with anyone. Winona was fifteen and learning from her sister, and no doubt that knowledge would later be passed down to Wendy and Winnifred, who were twelve and thirteen. Wyatt was going to have a lot on his hands.

"Is Clara sleeping?" I asked.

He nodded. "Like a baby. With her big scary brothers and her new best friend Avery on the case, she calmed right down."

My lip twitched at the mention of Avery's name, and Heath was no better. Wyatt's suspicious gaze pinged between the two of us, and then he was on his feet, prowling toward my brother.

He sniffed the air in front of Heath, and then a mean smile spread across his face. "Why does our fearless leader *reek* of sex?"

I stifled a groan. If we weren't about to have to deal with my asshole father, I'd be in the shower finishing myself off to the memory of Avery's sweet moans and delicious screams. Tutoring her was going to be a special form of torture after tonight.

One I deserved.

Heath stared Wyatt down, unrepentant. "Avery jumped in front of two Prime beasts for my sister, so I got on my knees and thanked her for it."

Wyatt shut his eyes and groaned like he was in horrible pain. "Fuck you, Heath. I cannot believe after all the bullshit you've been spouting about keeping our distance from her, *you* are the one who caved." He opened his eyes and pointed at me. "*Both* of you. I know you didn't just sit on the sidelines, Aiden."

I met his accusing stare. "I held her. Got to feel her shake in my arms while she came all over Heath's face. Happy?"

"No," he growled. "I won't be happy until I'm *bathing* in that girl's cum."

"Right. Great." I threw up my hands. "We're all fucked for her, but our situation has not changed, as the events of tonight have so clearly demonstrated."

The fight went out of Wyatt, and his shoulders slumped. "Fuck your fucking parents. I assume they know where Clara is by now?"

Heath pulled his phone from his pocket and stared at the screen. "I have five missed calls from Holden, two from Stephen, and one from Mom," he said. My phone had been buzzing incessantly in my pocket, too, but I didn't care to check it. "So, yes. It's time."

Wyatt nodded. The three of us padded quietly through the kitchen and into the small sunroom I used as my home office. Clara was asleep upstairs, and hopefully she would stay that way through this call.

I sat behind the small wooden desk I'd shoved up against the windows and opened my laptop. Heath took up a power stance behind me, his arms folded and his jaw tense. Wyatt flopped into one of the armchairs by the wall. He'd listen but wouldn't be on camera.

The ceiling fan whirled quietly above us. I took one fortifying breath before I hit the video call button, and my dick stirred in my pants as I caught the faint scent of Avery wafting off my brother. I tossed him an annoyed look over my shoulder. He licked his lips and winked at me, the asshole. Wyatt grumbled at us both.

It all blinked right out of my brain as my dad Holden appeared on the screen.

Holden Blackwell looked a decade younger than his fifty years, as age took longer to wear on the most powerful of our kind. He was broad, grizzled, and wore his dark brown hair long—a point of pride for lion shifters. He had a permanent five o'clock shadow, and his hair had only just started to dapple gray at the temples, all of it adding to his air of distinguished and dangerous power. There wasn't an ounce of exhaustion or worry on his face even though his only daughter had been missing for several hours tonight.

The depthless voids that were his gray eyes focused on me like lasers through the computer screen. "Aiden. Heath. It appears you've finally deigned to return my calls."

"We had a problem to deal with," I replied evenly, sounding bored even though I was anything but. "You're welcome, by the way, for cleaning up a mess that *you* created by forcing Clara to go out with two teenage perverts with embarrassingly little control over their animals."

He waved a hand. "I'm certain you have all overreacted. Clara fleeing like a scared child. The two of you attacking the boys like they were common criminals. Ridiculous, all of it."

I clenched my jaw, and Heath blew out a frustrated breath behind me.

"This is a sign that Clara isn't ready for this, Dad," Heath said with impressive patience. "So call off the auction for her bond."

"As I have told you numerous times, son, this is not an *auction*," Dad bit out. "How uncouth. We are procuring a bonding for our precious daughter that will be most advantageous for her and for this family."

"Against her will," I snapped. "She's a *child*, Dad."

He scoffed. "The legal bonding age is seventeen, which you know, and that's mere months away for Clara. The fact that you two continue to coddle her doesn't make her a child. She is a latent female and *my* daughter. She has a single purpose in this privileged life of hers, and she will fulfill it. End of discussion."

Heath leaned over my shoulder to glare into the camera. "Keep it up, Dad. Next time one of her dates puts a hand on her, I will tear out his throat, and I'll leave you to deal with the consequences."

Holden sighed and pinched his brow. "I am both disappointed in your attitude and yet so damn proud of the Prime you've become, Heath. You and your brother have created an outstanding quad that will ensure the Blackwell legacy remains as powerful and revered as it always has been." He leaned back in his chair and gave us both a pointed look. "That is, once you decide to actually choose a bond from that school's veritable *buffet* of females from quality bloodlines, whom I'm certain are throwing themselves at you night and day."

"We'll bond on our own time, Dad," I said wearily, as I always did. He didn't need to know the urgency we felt around the search for our bond because it had nothing to do with his fucking *legacy*.

"Yes, yes, you are all focused on your noble quest to become Guardians," he replied with a flippant wave of his hand. "I wish I could call it a waste of time for males of your pedigree, but I can't argue against the prestige that can be gained as highly decorated soldiers in the Guardian force. With that and the Blackwell name, there truly are no doors that won't be opened for you in shifter society across the entire country."

Because the Guardians' role in the safety of our community wasn't a thing he valued. Our parents hid behind the expensive wards surrounding their estate in the Hills, and I doubted any one of them had laid eyes on a wraith in over a decade.

"We appreciate your full-throated support of our life choices," Heath said, his tone flat. "And I will insist, yet again, that Clara deserves to make her own life ch—"

"Also, what's this I'm hearing about a *female* being

allowed into the Guardian training program?" Dad asked, spitting the word like a curse. Wyatt's attention snapped to the computer screen, and it was only our many years of practice that kept all traces of emotion from my face and my brother's. "Arthur Mahoney called me the other day to complain about it. According to his son, it's an embarrassing farce."

"Sounds like sour grapes to me, Dad," Heath said with a careless shrug. "Kace Mahoney's trio still hasn't found a fourth, and they're sagging on the leaderboard because they're a fucking mess against the SWIM. None of that is the fault of a random female."

"Still, it's unseemly, Heath," he went on. "I called Ward Gale to insist he stop this madness, but that stubborn bear seems to think this *female* can actually kill wraiths."

No one in this room was going to give Holden Blackwell an ounce of information about Avery, even to come to her defense. "Dad, if the girl can hack it in the program, she'll advance, and if she can't, she'll be cut," I said. "It doesn't have anything to do with us."

"We remain at the top of the leaderboard," Heath added.

"I'm pleased to hear that, but I still don't like this," Dad growled. "If this nonsense goes much further, the Council will issue a censure letter to the Guardians. With Stephen and I, we only need three more votes for a majority, which I know we'll have."

Wyatt rolled his eyes. The Guardian leadership would take one look at that letter and then have a good laugh as they fed it through the shredder. The Guardians existed as a completely autonomous entity outside the control of any of the regional councils, and Dad hated it.

We, on the other hand, counted on it.

"Good luck with that," Heath said simply. "Back to Clara—"

Dad slammed his fist on his desk. "Son, we can't have females—females with a *beast*, especially—running around in the Guardians and doing the Moon knows what else. It is against the divine will—"

"Dad, it's late," I said. It was time to end this insufferable call before he really got going. "We'll bring Clara back to the house when it's safe to do so. Tell Mom we said hello."

He leaned into the screen, his stark gray eyes flashing molten silver for the briefest of seconds. "Fine. Your mother will be sad to have missed an opportunity to see you, but the events of the evening were upsetting to her, so she's taken one of her elixirs. She needs her sleep."

Our mother, Octavia, had a shockingly strong affinity for apothecary magic for a woman who cared more about the brand name on her clothes and jewelry than she did training the affinity. It was her little hobby, and she put some effort into it when she needed a potent draft of something, which was at just about every inconvenience.

"Right," Heath said. "Good night, Dad."

He reached over my shoulder and slammed my laptop closed.

All three of us glared silently at the computer for a moment, and then Wyatt got to his feet. "I'm going to bed," he declared, stretching his arms over his head and yawning. "Well, I'm going to jack off first, since I've had to smell the wildcat's delicious pussy on Heath's face for the last hour."

Heath's cocky smirk flashed, but he wiped it away quickly. He pointed at Wyatt. "Don't get any ideas."

Wyatt strode from the room, throwing a middle finger over his shoulder as he went. "Fuck off."

I watched him go, then slumped in my chair. "That went well," I muttered. "Maybe all our problems will disappear when we wake up in the morning."

"Keep dreaming, man," Heath replied, staring at his phone. "At least Elijah's checked in. He'll be at home with his aunt and uncle until curfew is over, then he says he's going to make one more trip to South Fulton before he heads back to campus."

I removed my glasses and scrubbed a hand down my face. "Are we being reckless, letting him go on this crusade alone?"

"Probably, but we can't all be gone from campus for weeks at a time. Until we see clips of a twelve-foot basilisk raging through the streets of Fulton City trending on Clock-Tok, we have to just let him do this."

He deserved answers, after all, and none of us would get in his way.

Except that his control had started slipping again, and it seemed to be happening mostly around Avery. None of us knew what to make of that, especially not him. I had no doubt he was as entranced by her as the rest of us, but he'd figured out long ago how to keep the beast at bay when he was aroused. He'd never had even a near miss when he'd hooked up with girls in the past, and he swore up and down that he hadn't touched Avery beyond briefly holding her hand.

Just another entry on the list of reasons why we needed to find our central—the stability offered by bonding with a magically strong but latent shifter was said to settle even the most volatile beasts.

My head hurt.

"I'm going the fuck to bed," I told Heath with a defeated

sigh. I did not mention that I, like Wyatt, would be getting myself off to the thought of Avery before I finally let sleep take me.

23

AVERY

When I finally stumbled my bedraggled ass into the bathroom sometime well after the sun had risen, I was met by Brody, who was wearing only tight boxer briefs as he casually brushed his teeth at Ian's sink. I should've grabbed some sunglasses—that was a lot of bronze skin and toned muscle on display for this early in the morning.

His big brown eyes widened at the sight of me in only an oversized T-shirt and panties—not that he cared about that part—and he hurriedly spat toothpaste into the sink. "What happened to you?"

I took in my reflection in the mirror over my sink. Mal had stitched up the gash in my head last night while Ian hovered over the entire process, as pissed as I'd ever seen him. The stitches were hidden well enough in my hair, but I had a spectacular purple bruise blooming across my cheekbone where the lion had decked me.

And wait until Brody got a load of the road rash on my back. Mal had to clean that, too, while Ian had screeched something along the lines of, "What does not a *toe* outside the wards mean to you, Avery?" at me.

"Oh, hey, Brody," I said lightly. "Ian didn't, uh, wake you up last night, I guess?"

"I sleep like the dead. But it makes sense he didn't really sleep until you made it back." He looked me over, scanning for more injuries. "Did you get into it with a *wraith*?"

I flapped a hand. "Oh, nothing like that—"

The door to Ian's room burst open, and my brother stalked into the bathroom. He wore nothing but an open silk robe and his tiniest briefs.

"My eyes!" I whined, throwing an arm over my face.

"Save it," he snapped. "Now that you are no longer actively bleeding or covered in the stench and fluids of the teenaged lion you skewered last night—"

"*What?*" Brody barked. "What lion—"

"—we are going to discuss the fact that last night you also smelled a little bit like *sex* and a lot like a certain Alpha wolf *and* a certain feline professor of ours."

I grimaced. "You caught that, huh?"

He threw his hands in the air, his robe swishing to reveal a glimpse of the fox tattoo on his ribs. "Of course I caught that. You're lucky Mallory and I decided one insane story was enough to pull out of you while you were injured."

Brody leaned against the counter, shaking his head like he was dizzy. "What the hell did I sleep through last night?"

So fucking much, Brody.

"It's not a big deal," I shot back at Ian. "Should I start stomping around like a pissed-off elephant every time *you* stink like sex? I'd never get anything accomplished."

"Spill it, Avery," Ian growled.

"Fine." I grabbed my toothbrush, squeezed toothpaste

on the bristles, and shoved it in my mouth. "*Heathmight'veg-onedownonme*," I mumbled as I brushed.

"*What?*" they both exclaimed.

I spat the toothpaste into the sink, rinsed, and wiped my mouth on my purple hand towel. "Look, everyone was really keyed up after all the violence." I gave Ian a pointed look. "The *beasts* were keyed up. Things happened, I enjoyed it, and they both treated me nicely afterward. It didn't mean anything."

I'd chanted that last part over and over in my head—at my beast—as I fell asleep in my bed, and I was doing it again now. Heath and Aiden had shocked the absolute hell out of me last night, and it was the hottest experience of my life. I would treasure it as such.

What I would not be doing was throwing myself into their arms the next time I saw them.

Even though my beast seemed to want exactly that. She'd always been an inexplicable slut for all members of the Blackwell Quad, and last night had made the problem ten times worse.

Ian and Brody both blinked at me like I was an alien before Brody finally asked in a low voice, "Was it good?"

Ian elbowed him. "Don't encourage her."

"You're the one who's been acting like my vagina will shrivel into dust if I don't get laid soon," I retorted.

He clicked his tongue. "If you want to get laid, Brody and I can marshal up a line of eager suitors from the ranks of the numerous attractive males in this school who are *not* members of a fancy Prime quad."

Brody nodded solemnly. "Ask and you shall receive, Avery."

"Especially *that* quad. I just worry they're going to hurt

you, Aves. Maybe not today, maybe not even this year, but eventually it will happen. I won't have it."

I sighed. "Ian, it was just a post-fight hookup. I'll be okay."

Because I had to be. I was here to become a Guardian and earn myself a cocoon of safety and relative freedom, full stop. I was not here to fall for the hottest, most powerful, and most coveted males on campus.

Ian and I had a thirty-second stare-off, and then Brody broke the tension. "Is anyone going to explain the whole lion-skewering part of the evening?"

"Yeah." I waved my hands, shooing them away. "Get the fuck out so I can do my business, and then we'll catch Brody up on the way to breakfast."

They grumbled but complied. As they moved toward the door, Ian tossed me a look over his shoulder that was only concerned, devoid of all the ire from earlier.

"*Love you,*" I mouthed.

He rolled his eyes. "*Love you too,*" he mouthed back, before he shut the door behind him.

BY THE TIME WE ARRIVED AT THE DINING HALL FOR WHAT WAS more brunch than breakfast, Brody was caught up. Since this month's curfew nights had fallen over the weekend, most students had remained on campus, and the dining hall was hopping.

As we sat down at our table, I ignored the fact that Heath, Wyatt, and Aiden were also here. They were sitting at one of their usual central tables, surrounded by their fan club. Clara was also with them, wearing what looked like one of Heath's sweatshirts over her skirt from last night. She seemed cheerful, so I relaxed and tucked into the tall stack of pancakes I'd meticulously assembled at the buffet.

"Avery!"

Somehow, I already knew that voice well. Clara was waving exuberantly at me from her table, the girls seated nearby looking at her like she'd stripped naked and thrown her panties at me.

And now I also had the attention of her brothers and Wyatt. They each wore their default facial expressions: Heath, serious and commanding; Aiden, aloof and slightly bored; Wyatt, cocky and smirking. The difference was in their eyes. Three intense, probing, *knowing* gazes were aimed at me while my beast groomed a paw and preened under them.

Brody cleared his throat. "Is it hot in here, or—"

"Avery!" Clara called out again, now pushing to her feet, then trotting over to my table. She wore her tall, heeled boots from last night, and they thunked loudly on the wood floors, drawing even more attention. "Hi!" she chirped happily as she slid into the chair next to me. "How are you feeling? Did you get all patched up?"

"I did. My friend is a healer and medic-in-training, and she took care of me."

Clara blew out a satisfied breath. "Good."

I couldn't help but go a little gooey at her sincere hazel eyes. They were more reminiscent of Heath's than Aiden's, and I was yet again irritated that I knew that. She patted my hand, then she noticed Ian and Brody.

"Hello, I'm Clara Blackwell." She reached a delicate, manicured hand across the table.

Ian snagged it first. "Aren't you adorable? I'm Ian, Avery's brother and a wily fox shifter."

She gasped in delight as she shook Ian's hand. "Avery, you have a brother? He's *so* cute."

"He knows," I replied drolly.

Brody snatched Clara's hand from Ian and gave her his winning smile. "I'm Brody. Lynx shifter and Ian's boyfriend."

"Aw," she cooed. "So nice to meet you both."

"I hear we had a bit of a ruckus at the gates last night, Miss Clara," Ian said gently. "I'm so glad you're okay."

She sobered a bit. "Thanks to Avery. She was amazing."

"It was mostly George," I muttered. That harsh reality had set in over the course of the morning. Without George, that fight would've gone a lot differently, and I probably would've ended up letting my beast out of her cage and creating another huge mess. I could do a lot with my swords, but I'd always be hobbled without the ability to freely shift. "And," I went on, nudging Clara, "your brothers are the ones who really put the fear of the Moon's wrath into those little shitheads."

"Yeah," she replied, wringing her hands. "Is it too much to hope that Paul and Harrison will tell all the other boys in our social group that I'm not worth the trouble?"

The anxiety simmering in my stomach from rehashing last night's fight twisted into a ball of rage. "You know what, Clara?" I slapped my hand on the table and stood up. "We were headed to the gym after this to train for a few hours. Wanna come? We'll go through some basics with a blade. Ian's actually a better teacher than I am."

"Yes!" she shrieked, jumping to her feet and clapping her hands. "Let's go. Wait—can I borrow a sports bra and some shorts?"

"Yep." We were close to the same size. I had a few inches of height on her, and she definitely had a cup size on me, but we'd make it work.

Brody and Ian were immediately on board. As we all gathered our things, Heath appeared at our table. He wore a snug-fitting white Henley and gray sweatpants that should be illegal, and he smelled like a forest after a rainstorm.

I became very focused on pouring my coffee into a to-go cup.

"Clara," he growled. "Where are you going?"

She lifted her chin. "Avery, Ian, and Brody are taking me to learn swords."

He sighed. "Clara—"

"Heath," she said quietly. "Let me do this."

He was no match for those big doe eyes. "Fine. One hour, and then we're taking you home."

"Yay, thank you!" She threw her arms around his neck.

He hugged her gently, but he was now focused only on me.

He didn't say anything—just let his gaze roam over my face, pausing on my bruised cheekbone. His jaw tensed and his nostrils flared. I was in trouble all over again for last night, and warmth pooled low in my belly at the thought.

"We'll be at the arena," I told him briskly, and then I turned and high-tailed it out of there before my face flushed redder than Wyatt's hair.

CLARA'S OVERBEARING BROTHERS LET US HAVE HER FOR FIFTY-two minutes undisturbed.

Brody assigned her a short practice sword that he'd swiped from the storage lockers, and each of us had gone a few rounds with her, walking through some basics.

She was with Ian now, swords down, while they worked on self-defense moves. Brody and I were using the time to go full-on at each other, him with his rapier and me with Ian's katana. I was a sweaty mess, and I'd need to take another one of Ian's concoctions that was like ibuprofen on steroids, but it felt good to work the soreness and kinks out of my body after last night's activities.

At minute fifty-three, Wyatt sauntered through the doors. A few other Guardian trainees were utilizing their free Sunday afternoon to run combat drills nearby, and all heads turned to Wyatt as he stepped onto the arena floor, his auburn hair glowing like garnets under the fluorescent lighting above us. He had on athletic pants that molded to his thick thighs and a soft-looking V-neck T-shirt under an unzipped fleece, the tattoos that covered his chest visible through the sheer white fabric of his shirt.

"Wildcat," he purred as he approached our corner of the arena. Brody and I paused our assault on each other, and both of us pretended we hadn't been momentarily distracted by Wyatt's pecs. "I'm here to retrieve our Blackwell princess. Thanks for helping her sharpen her claws."

"I'm not finished yet, Wyatt!" Clara hollered. Ian lunged for her, and she managed to flip him over her shoulder. It was a bit clunky but a huge improvement from earlier.

I wiped the sweat from my forehead and arched a brow at Wyatt. "Did the bosses send you to charm her into leaving?"

He chuckled. "Something like that."

"Let her go a few more minutes," I said quietly. "It's helping her feel safer, even if it's mostly an illusion."

Because when it came down to it, a latent shifter couldn't do much against a Prime, especially in beast form.

Wyatt turned serious for a moment, his focus shifting to Clara and Ian as they grappled. Frustration radiated from him, his huge shoulders tense and his emerald eyes hard.

He shook it off quickly and returned his attention to me, a sly smile creeping onto his face.

"Fine. How about a little wager while we wait, Wildcat?"

That sounded dangerous. "What did you have in mind?"

"My bear, your sword. If you can best me, I'll leave and convince Heath and Aiden to let Clara hang with you guys for another couple of hours."

"And if I can't?"

His grin grew, and he stepped into my personal space, leaning in to whisper in my ear, "Then I get a kiss."

I shoved him away. "Game on, Gale."

24

WYATT

Hell yeah. I loved fighting with this girl, and my bear wanted to be on top of her *now*.

I backed away from her slowly. She watched me, expertly twirling her brother's katana in her dominant hand. Her pale skin glistened under the arena lights, her tight body on display in her sports bra, flimsy tank top, and spandex shorts. Strands of her blonde hair had escaped her ponytail in a wild mess, and her blue eyes shone, bright and defiant, in a direct challenge to me and my bear.

She was so fucking hot, I wanted to punch something.

Later, I'd need to have a discussion with Franks, Guilford, and Holmes, sophomore Guardian trainees who were working out nearby. I'd caught all three of them staring at Avery's ass multiple times in the five minutes I'd been here. The urge to gouge their eyes out was strong, and I had little desire to prevent my beast from getting what he wanted.

On second thought, I'd just report them to Heath. That sneaky, obsessed motherfucker would deal with it. It was obvious he was still high on the wildcat's taste this morning, and it was driving me fucking *nuts*.

I shucked my fleece jacket and toed off my sneakers. Next came my shirt, which I pulled over my head with deliberate slowness so Avery could look her fill. She was made of tough stuff, though, her focus never straying from my face.

Brody whistled. "Ian, I think this resistance is futile," he said over his shoulder. Behind Avery, her brother was sprawled on the floor, Clara digging her knee into his back. "The chemistry over here is about to melt my face off."

"Just be ready to use your sword if any genitals start touching," Ian ordered, his voice strained.

I chuckled, sliding my pants to the floor and stepping out of them. I was commando today, as usual, so I was now naked and ready to shift. My bear rumbled a pleased noise in my head, the shock of rage he usually felt when we were on the verge of shifting for a fight noticeably absent.

"Ready, baby girl?"

She scowled. "Call me that again, and I'll make sure they're wiping your blood from this mat for days."

Fuck me. It was time to go furry before my dick turned into a moondamned steel rod.

I called my bear forward and threw open the mental gate I kept him locked behind. The hot sting of the shift was over in an instant, and I hit the ground on all fours, shaking out my coat with a menacing growl.

"Yes, very scary," Avery said, still twirling her sword. "You're such a big, sleek boy, aren't you? If you yield now, I'll give you some pets and ear scratches."

As much as I was still ultimately in control, the bear's instincts and desires were at the forefront now. He shocked the hell out of me by rumbling his approval, as if he was ready to forfeit the fight for some head rubs.

Cut that shit out. We have a bet to win.

I darted forward. My speed never failed to surprise those who expected a bear of my size to be lumbering and slow, but Avery was ready for me. She spun out of the way with her usual easy finesse, a deadly little dancer.

I whirled and attacked again, swatting at her with my giant paw. She ducked and slashed at my planted front leg, opening a shallow cut on my shoulder. We were both holding back—she could've cut me a hell of a lot deeper, and I'd avoided using my claws when I struck at her.

We went around and around like this for several minutes —I'd swat, she'd cut, we'd break apart and go again. Her face was flushed from the exertion and sweaty as fuck, but she still smelled like lavender.

I wanted a taste.

She was tiring, though, because she'd been at this for over an hour, while I had endless energy to burn.

After my particularly vicious strike at her abdomen, she stumbled a bit, and I had her. I reared up onto my hind legs, roaring, and I threw my weight right on top of her. The force knocked her off her feet, and I followed her down.

Right before her back hit the floor and my enormous bear body would've crushed her, I shifted back into a man.

"Wyatt!" she shrieked. Her fist hit the ground beside us, knocking her sword from her grip. It clattered to the floor.

"Hey, baby," I said, my voice like silk. I straddled her thighs, clamping them together with mine, then I gathered her hands in my grip and pinned them above her head. "Time to yield."

And she better do it quickly because pinning her underneath me like this had my dick half hard. There was no surer way of losing my most important body part than pressing a full erection against this girl without her consent.

"By the Moon," Brody murmured from somewhere nearby. "That is a *monster*. Clara, avert your eyes."

"I am *not* looking. Gross."

"Well, he is a bear," Ian mused. "Aves, just letting you know—if you take another temporary leave from your senses and slip and fall on that cock, you may end up in the infirmary."

My grin was very smug. "Don't listen to them, Wildcat. I'd make it good for you."

My sweaty, beautiful girl bucked underneath me, but to no avail. I was a lot fucking bigger than her, and I had her solidly in my clutches. "Get off me," she ordered through clenched teeth.

"Do you yield?"

"*Wyatt*," she snarled.

"Yes, very scary," I said with a little shiver, throwing her teasing from earlier right back at her. I dipped even lower, my nose now almost touching hers as I whispered, "Yield, baby. I want to collect my prize."

A frustrated and *beastly* rumble sounded in her chest. Her eyes flashed the same electric blue that'd mesmerized the shit out of me back when she'd wrapped her hand around my throat, and her body warmed beneath me. "Fuck you," she said, her voice a deep, inhuman growl.

"*Yes*," I hissed. "There she is. Let that beast out, Wildcat. I want to meet her."

My bear had shoved back to the surface, the eager motherfucker. I couldn't remember the last time he'd tested my control like this when feeling something other than raw, terrifying rage.

The urge to slam my lips onto hers and shove my tongue into her mouth consumed me, but I wanted her to yield. I wanted her to *want it*.

"What the fuck is going on in here? Gale, get the hell off Baxter and put your cock away, for the love of the fucking Moon."

I blew out the world's most frustrated breath, and Avery sagged in my hold, Cash's obnoxious fucking voice snapping the tension between us like a twig.

His presence was also an instant cure for my erection.

With an annoyed sigh, I climbed to my feet, and then I offered Avery a hand up. Brody threw my pants at my head, and in about five seconds, I was half dressed and ready to deal with whatever fresh bullshit Cash had in store.

"What is this, Baxter?" Cash demanded, his lip curling as he glared at Avery. He'd freshly buzzed his dark-blond hair—so fucking weird for a lion—and he wore cargo pants, boots, and a black Guardian T-shirt, which meant he was dressed for work tonight. "You opening your legs for Gale and the rest of that quad now? Ballsy, given you managed to set off the fucking snake."

"Hey—" I started to say, but he barreled on.

"You know, Baxter, my quad was out on patrol last night. We chased a horde of swarmers and a few Rippers near the campus walls on the southwest side, so as a matter of proto-col, I went over last night's security camera footage this morning. I saw your pathetic little perimeter walk."

To Avery's immense credit, she just stared at him like he was boring the shit out of her.

Heath had made sure one of his little techy wolf minions had erased the footage of the shit that went down at the front gate last night and looped a non-incriminating few hours so no one would suspect anything. It appeared his foresight had paid off.

"What did you think you were gonna do, huh?" Cash continued, sneering. "The Board of Trustees and the

Council spend a huge chunk of the college's endowment on those wards, and they pay the best security specialists to reinforce them monthly. But even if they failed, you have no fucking chance against an entire horde of *actual* wraiths. They'd tear you apart, devour your soul, then go on to kill every weak-ass shifter in this place."

"I'm not sure why you're so concerned," Avery said in the world's most blasé tone. "If a wraith eats my soul, I won't sully the Guardian training program with my presence any longer."

He gave her a slimy smile. "How true that is. Are you fucking Ward Gale too? I can't think of any other reason for him to be so insistent on this farce—"

I stepped right into that motherfucker's face. His shitty attitude was on my last nerve, and I wished for the eightieth time that Cash's quad wasn't so skilled at wraith combat. Not only would it have spared us from being subjected to them as our trainers, but they'd probably have been tossed from the Guardians by now. My dad had taught me that the Guardians valued integrity and independence above almost everything, but Cash was so far up the asses of not only the members of the Northeastern Council, where several of his fathers served, but also our local Council members, including the asshole Blackwells, that his loyalty was real fucking questionable.

His quad was in the small minority of the force that were in it only for the prestige and the money, and it made them terrible team players.

"That's enough," I said to him, a lazy smile on my face, while my tone was one of barely restrained violence. "We get it, man. You're embarrassed about how small your dick is, so you take it out on the only female who's forced to be in your presence on a regular basis. I have to tell you, man, none of us are buying the act, and if you piss Avery off more, she's going to relieve you of that small dick, and my dad isn't going to have shit to say about it."

Cash's amber eyes went molten gold, his lion popping up to say hello. Dominance pulsed from him and battered against me, like cresting waves against a seawall. He was trying to force me and my beast into submission by sheer will alone.

In a horrifying turn of events, I stumbled a few steps backward before I was able to dig in and hold against him. My bear, loath to give a shit about Cash normally, jolted to life within me.

Avery put a gentle hand on my bare back to steady me, probably unconsciously, but she quickly dropped it. Her gorgeous eyes narrowed, studying Cash, a mere hint of her beast glinting there.

Few things in my life had ever infuriated me as much as Cash's smug fucking smirk did in this moment. "Oh, did I forget to mention?" He lifted a hand and flashed us a view of the new bonding tattoo encircling his ring finger. "My quad bonded under this past Full Moon. She's lovely—a latent from a *long* line of Prime lions. She just graduated from the shifter finishing school in Virginia, and our fathers introduced us over the holidays. No sense in waiting when you find *the one*, am I right, Gale?"

Just fucking perfect. Cash's quad now had their central, which meant their beasts were all connected, able to share power with each other through their bond with her. I'd trained under Cash since the start of this school year, and what he'd just blasted me with was a noticeable and substantial difference in the force and dominance of his beast. As their quad's leader, he would reap the most benefit.

I would still crush him, but this had caught me off guard, damn it.

"Mazel tov," I said flippantly. "Is there anything else you needed? We're not in training, so you have no reason to be harassing Avery or any of the rest of us."

"Watch yourself, Gale. Eventually, you and your girl-friend won't be cradled in the soft embrace of the SWIM and the training program and your father. You'll be out in the field with the rest of us, and well...." He smiled at Avery. "Things can happen."

I gritted my teeth and bore the next onslaught—this one from within. My bear was about to rip out Cash's throat.

"Can't wait," Avery said, smiling serenely back at him. "When I become a Guardian, we'll settle this shit like real shifters, Cash."

"*Avery*," Ian hissed from somewhere behind us.

Cash barked a loud laugh. "Sure we will."

He turned and strolled out of the arena without a back-ward glance.

I shook out my limbs and took a few cleansing breaths. The bear had settled, and my boner was well and truly gone.

I turned to Clara, my good humor also vanished. "Let's go, princess. Your brothers need time to take you home and then get back onto campus before curfew."

She didn't argue. "Okay. I'm coming." With a sad smile, she handed Avery one of her little swords, which she must've borrowed at some point. She hugged Ian, then Brody, and then Avery last. "I'll wash the clothes I borrowed and send them back with Heath when I can," Clara told her.

"Don't worry about it," Avery replied, giving her one last squeeze before pulling back and giving her a pointed look. "You have my number, so call if you need anything, okay?"

Clara nodded, releasing her reluctantly, like leaving her new friends was the saddest thing she'd ever experienced.

I jerked my head toward the doors and ensured my attention was anywhere but on Avery. "Come on."

Clara followed me obediently as I strode from the arena, away from those electric blue eyes and the harsh fucking dose of reality I'd just been handed.

25

———

ELIJAH

For an organization full of supposedly hardened criminals, the members of the Low Country Kings Motorcycle Club with whom I'd had the pleasure of spending time had been exceptionally easy to break. Unfortunately, the two I'd pulled aside for a chat prior to this had very little useful to tell me.

I was hoping my conversation with the gentleman chained to the chair in front of me would be more fruitful. I'd been away from campus for a few weeks already, and while the administration would've loved for me to stay away for an extended period, my beast and I needed to reconvene with our quad sooner rather than later. We were a unit, always better together, and I missed those lovable assholes.

And I was ready to see my dove again. We had things to discuss.

"Hey," I said, lightly slapping the biker on his stubbled cheek. His road name was Buzz, according to the ridiculous leather cut he wore over a faded flannel shirt. "Wakey, wakey."

Milky blue eyes fluttered open. Buzz hadn't been asleep,

exactly, but rather in a bit of a daze. According to lore propagated mostly by humans, a man who looked into the eyes of a basilisk would die a horrible death. The reality was less macabre and, in my opinion, much more useful. If I called the beast forward enough to let him look through my eyes, I was able to temporarily stun all but the most powerful shifters.

Buzz, who I deduced was a shifter of minor power because his defenses were weak and his pheromones tasted of rodent, hadn't stood a chance.

"Where... where am I?" he asked, his voice a sleepy rasp. "And who the fuck are you?"

I sat down in the second metal chair, which I'd positioned a few feet in front of him. Deciding on a relaxed posture to begin, I crossed my legs and took a lazy sip of my cashew milk latte. It was lavender flavored, in honor of my dove's sweet scent and George's scales.

I did wish my python was by my side, but I was supremely glad he'd stayed behind at school to follow Avery around, given the situation they'd both had to handle for Clara.

"You, my friend, are in an abandoned warehouse in South Fulton, not far from the dilapidated bachelor pad your club calls its headquarters," I said. "My name is Elijah. We met briefly in the parking lot of the liquor store you frequent on Thursday nights."

It'd taken thirty seconds of conversation for Buzz to slip under, and I'd helped him into the back seat of my Bronco. A seven-minute drive later, and here we were.

He jerked on the silver-laced chains that bound his hands and feet to the chair. They'd be blistering his skin by now, and in weaker shifters like Buzz, the silver would cut off his access to his animal. "Do you have a death wish, man? My club will chop you into tiny pieces and bury you behind our compound."

I rolled my eyes. "Please be serious, Buzz. Your club is a bunch of bored males with minor beasts pretending to be biker criminals. Your leaders are ordinary wolves who want to play at being alphas of a pack. Do I need to remind you what I am?"

I let the beast creep forward again, just enough to shift my eyes.

He reared back and sucked in a startled breath. "Shit. Fucking fuck."

"Wonderful," I said with a quick lick of my lips. His fear was certainly hearty, if a little sour. "We're now on the same page."

He glowered at me. "What do you want?"

"I want to tell you a story from about twenty years ago, and I'm hoping parts of it might jog your memories." My backpack was on the floor by my feet, and I reached inside. I pulled out the item that had started me on this crusade a few short months ago.

Buzz's eyes widened, a flash of recognition on his face before he wiped it all away to look surly again.

My pulse began to race. *Finally.*

"No, no, Buzz," I purred, holding up the beautiful dagger so he could get a nice long look at it. "You don't need to pretend. It's gorgeous, right? Hard to forget a piece like this."

The dagger was a double-edge steel blade, a bit dull after a few decades of moldering in the cesspit of the MC. It's hilt, though—that had remained stunning. A light brown wood with intricate carvings of a flowering plant with wide, flat leaves and purple blossoms. The blossoms were inlaid with amethyst gems in a rich purple, while other blooms contained small black pearls that gave the appearance of dark, deadly berries.

"I don't know what you're talking about," Buzz said, swallowing roughly.

"I think you do. You see, Buzz, it was by sheer dumb luck that I happened into a bar last semester with my quadmate, Wyatt. It was in a nearby college town where we shifter students like to go to... blow off steam with humans, if you catch my drift." I waggled my eyebrows at him, but he wasn't amused. *Fine.* "And one of the human students in the bar that night had a few too many shots of whiskey. He had this lovely dagger out, right on the bar top, and was bragging about how he stole it from his brother."

Yes, it was a unique and memorable dagger. So much so that the bystanders who witnessed the five seconds it took my mother's assailant to kill her were able to describe the murder weapon in great detail.

"So?" Buzz grunted.

"So." I gave him an indulgent smile. "Do you think it could be a coincidence that this dagger matched the exact description of the one used to slit my mother's throat in the middle of a crowded farmers market almost twenty years ago?"

Buzz swallowed again, and he was starting to sweat now, despite the chilly draft in the warehouse.

"Right, me either," I said, pointing at him. "So, Wyatt and I had a private chat with this human. He was resistant at first, but we convinced him to disclose the whereabouts of his brother with some gentle encouragement."

Wyatt had beaten the shit out of him, actually, while I played the good cop. It was certainly better him than me because I'd been a bit blindsided by the sudden appearance of the dagger. Any attempt at controlled violence on my part would've undoubtedly resulted in poor drunk Dave becoming a meal.

"And then," I went on, "a few weeks ago, I was finally able to finagle some alone time with said brother. And guess what he told me?"

Buzz stared at the floor, his jaw tense.

"Yes, you've no doubt guessed correctly. He won this one-of-a-kind, likely priceless dagger off a member of the Low Country Kings in a poker game last summer. So, that's why I've come calling. I spoke with a few of your... brothers? Partners in crime? Anyway, they fingered you as the most prolific gambler, and you look to be in your late thirties, which makes you *just* old enough to perhaps have been around when someone used this dagger to murder my mother." I leaned forward and let the beast peer through my eyes again. "Let me repeat that one more time, in case you're not grasping the gravity of the situation. This dagger was used, likely by someone in your club, to *murder my mother*."

He trembled, the terror radiating from him an utter *feast*. "Okay, okay! Yes, I lost the dagger in the poker game. But I don't know anything about your mother! I swear."

"Think harder, Buzz," I growled. "Where did you get the dagger?"

"I stole it from the chapter safe a few months back. I've been, uh... a bit low on funds for my weekly poker games."

"And you just happened to stumble upon this dagger when you were raiding the safe?"

He hesitated. "Yes."

I lunged from my chair and wrapped a hand around his throat. The basilisk rose, my vision narrowing and my fangs elongating. Scales rippled up my arm before fading away.

Easy. We can't find out what he knows if he's dead.

"Try again," I hissed.

"Okay! Shit, okay!" He shook in my hold, and he began to babble. "I recognized it. I'd forgotten about it, but yeah, like you said, it's pretty unique, and way back when I was a prospect, I remembered seeing the Prez with it one afternoon. Most of the club was out on a road trip, so it was just me and Johnny Weasel hanging around the clubhouse, being the cleaning bitches. The Prez and the VP at the time stayed behind too. They'd been taking some jobs from these rich fucking Primes because we needed the money, but they didn't tell anyone what they were doing. It was real secretive shit. They'd come back to the club wearing street clothes, which usually meant they were on one of *those* jobs. They were stressed out, arguing with each other about something, but then I never saw them with the dagger again. So I guess it's been in the safe all these years. They quit taking the jobs after that."

I released him and sat back down in my chair. I blew out a breath and crossed my ankle over my knee again, taking a slow sip of my latte as the beast retreated. "And where are that President and VP now? They can't be the current holders of those titles, as those gentlemen aren't much older than you are."

"Dead," he croaked. "They both died in a crash about six months later."

That was the least surprising thing he'd said in the past five minutes. "And do you happen to know who the rich Primes were that they were working for? Ever see them? Get a name or a face?"

He shook his head. "No. Like I said, they were real secretive about it all. It was weird at first because this club doesn't fuck with Primes, but then everyone got over it because for about a year there, the chapter had some real cash."

"And do you happen to recall the date you last saw the

Prez and VP with the dagger? Was it sometime around September 30th, 2004?"

"Uh... yeah, maybe? I patched in back in the spring of '05, right after the Prez and VP died. So I guess it could've been around then."

I took a moment to mull over everything Buzz had told me. He'd all but confirmed my theory that my mother was not killed by a mugger. It was too close to the deaths of my fathers. The weapon was too showy. Her killer had stolen her purse, but that was an easy ruse. And even though she was latent and her wound would've been fatal to a human, there was no reason for her body to be resistant to the magical healing that should've saved her life. The shifter medical examiner theorized it had to do with the fact that she'd lost her bonded mates so recently. She may have given up. Let go, body and soul, to return to them.

As I grew older, I knew that couldn't be true either. My mother had risked her life to save me, her two-year-old son, while her mates were torn apart under a lunar eclipse by a half-dozen high-powered wraiths, including an Apex. My dads managed to kill most of them, but they'd died doing it. They'd died to save my mother and me, and Mom wouldn't have let that sacrifice be in vain.

She wouldn't have just *given up*.

Someone rich and powerful within the Prime shifter community had wanted my mother dead, and they'd hired the Low Country Kings—a group with whom no one among our richest and most powerful would be caught dead associating with—to kill her.

I just had no fucking idea why.

I rose from my chair and patted Buzz lightly on the cheek. "Thank you, my friend. You've been most helpful. I can see your wrists are pretty blistered, and I apologize for that. They should heal right up after I unlock the chains."

He scowled in silence.

"Right. Your cell phone's in your pocket if you want to call for a ride after I've gone. And of course, I'd appreciate your discretion about our little talk. The other two members of your club I've interviewed were kind enough not to mention it. I'd hate to have to come back for a much more uncomfortable chat, yeah?"

He winced. "I won't say anything."

I believed him. Not only was he terrified of my beast, but like the others, he'd never want to admit to his club of criminals that he'd been nabbed by a college student, chained to a chair, and then sang like a canary.

After stashing the dagger carefully back in my backpack, I slipped my work gloves on and unlocked Buzz's silver chains. He sat still as a statue, and I licked the cloying taste of his apprehension from my lips as I worked. I stashed the chains away as well, then slipped off my gloves.

"Karma's a persistent bitch, Buzz. I'd suggest the Low Country Kings be on their best behavior for the foreseeable future." I gave him one last salute as I headed for the exit.

I slammed the metal door behind me, and then I was on my way home.

MY AUNT, KATERINA, AND UNCLE, HORATIO, WERE SAINTS OF the highest order.

Horatio was my father Cassius's younger brother. My fathers had all been Prime felines from long lines of Prime felines, but Horatio had drawn the genetic short straw and never manifested a beast. He and his wife had only just returned from their honeymoon when they'd taken my mother and me into their home in the wake of our terrible tragedy.

They were both accountants, and they lived in a suburban neighborhood in Lion Valley, a quiet middle-class town tucked snugly in the center of the North Georgia shifter community. It was on a bustling street in the Lion Valley town center, where my mother had been perusing the local farmer's market, intent on buying something nice to contribute to our new home, that she was murdered.

I'd been home with Aunt Kat, taking a nap.

After that, my aunt and uncle had a toddler to raise, which they did with enthusiasm and love. When that toddler became a preteen and manifested not as a Prime feline but a rare mythical basilisk, they rolled with it. My parents' estate had provided me with a small nest egg, and it was enough to send me to the best shifter boarding school in the South for budding Prime males. There I met Heath, Wyatt, and Aiden, and the rest was history.

It was to my uncle and aunt's same quiet suburban home that I returned after my meeting with Buzz. The late-afternoon sun had just begun to sink low on the horizon, the chill in the air hardening into a more oppressive cold as I let myself in the back door.

A few minutes later, Horatio eyed me over the frames of his reading glasses, his laptop in front of him on the kitchen table. "You think members of this motorcycle club were hired by mysterious rich Primes to kill your mother." A statement, not a question.

"Yes."

Aunt Kat set a glass of sweet tea in front of me and ruffled my hair fondly before she pulled up a chair next to her husband. She'd braided her long black hair over her shoulder, which she did every evening when she returned home from work. "We've always suspected, Hor. What happened to Amara could not have been just some random mugging."

"But *why*?" Horatio crossed his arms over his broad chest, his biceps bulging under his dress shirt. My uncle had the body of a Prime, just not the beast to match. "Who could've wanted her dead so badly that they resorted to this? Back-alley deals with bikers, fancy knives, unknown magic that interferes with healing? She was a grieving young widow, and no one back then had any reason to suspect that her son's beast would manifest as one of the most dangerous classes of mythic alive. She wasn't a threat to *anyone*."

I sipped my tea. Peach, my favorite. "I'm going to find out, Uncle. And when I do, what my mother went through will seem like a day at the spa compared to what will happen to those responsible."

Aunt Kat gave me a fond smile. "That's right, baby. No mercy. You just let us know if you need anything."

Horatio tapped his chin. "Do you know if either the deceased President or Vice President left behind a wife?"

"I think they call them *old ladies*," Kat said, nudging Horatio with a grin.

I shook my head. "I can find out, though."

Horatio waved a hand. "No, let me take this one. The firm has some forensic accountants and investigators on staff. I can get one of them to discreetly look into it."

Perfect. "Thank you, Uncle."

"Are you caught up on your schoolwork?" he asked, and just like that, we were back to the mundane things. "Not that your aunt and I don't enjoy having you around, Elijah, but you are paying tuition to that very fine institution."

"I'm on top of everything, do not worry." My professors

were only too happy to email my assignments, and I did take my degree seriously. "I'll head back in a few days. I'm feeling pretty settled now."

My uncle studied me. "Good. You're too hard on yourself, son. It takes most mythics several decades to gain true control over their beasts, bonded or not. And with your chosen career path, you're turning the bloodlust and the unpredictability into something productive. You'll be saving lives. I'm proud of you."

Kat beamed at me. "We both are."

See? Saints.

I hadn't mentioned the particular struggle my beast and I were having over luscious Avery. Kat and Horatio put on brave faces, but they did worry about me, and I didn't want to add to the pile.

Plus, I had a plan.

I'll be seeing you soon, Dove.

26

AVERY

You could've knocked me over with a feather when Elijah strolled into Folklore class, his shoulders relaxed and his gait easy, like he hadn't been missing for almost a month.

George slithered happily along next to him, clearing the front row as he went. Elijah chuckled and rolled his eyes playfully in my direction, as if the students scrambling out of their seats and clawing their way into the rows behind them were just so silly.

"Mr. Harrow," the professor said, sounding exasperated but also a little wary. "While I am, um, pleased to have you back in class, is the snake necessary?"

Elijah paused on the stairs that bisected the room's tiered seating. George continued on without him, headed my way. "George goes where he wants to, Professor," Elijah said over his shoulder. "He's his own snake. I promise he'll behave." Elijah took in the rest of the class, amusement glinting in his golden eyes. "Unless someone provokes him, of course."

The professor sighed heavily. "Fine. Take your seat, please. All of you. We're starting class."

George curled up under my feet as Elijah dropped into the seat next to me, which no one else had dared occupy in his absence. The sweet, tempting scent of citrus, mint, and *male* floated around me.

"Hello, Dove. I've missed you terribly."

I'd saved up a lot of thoughts and questions for him. The last time I saw him, he'd looked so forlorn, like the fact that he needed to let his beast out to rampage against a Giant wraith had been a tragic failure on his part.

And I wanted to know more about his mother.

But all I managed was to angrily hiss, "Where the fuck have you *been*?"

His smile was blinding white, those deadly sharp canines taunting me. "Oh, here and there."

"What does that mean?"

"It's okay to admit you missed me, too, Dove."

I looked away and stuck my nose in the air. "I had George to keep me company."

"Yes, I hear you two had some exciting times together."

Of course he knew about that.

He leaned in, his warm breath ghosting along the side of my neck. "I hear you had some exciting times with Heath and Aiden as well."

My face heated and warmth bloomed low in my belly. Of course he knew about *that* too.

"You boys gossip like church ladies," I muttered.

His chuckle was sinful and dirty. "A quad becomes very comfortable with that kind of thing, Dove. After all, a painfully heterosexual group like ours is meant to settle down and fuck the same girl together for the rest of our lives."

It took every ounce of my willpower to control the full-body shiver that threatened to consume me at that thought. My beast rolled over, ready to show her belly to the dangerous predator. *He doesn't mean* me, *you ridiculous animal.*

"And what a lucky girl she'll be," I said, going for flippant but just sounding hoarse.

"I'd like to think so. But you're right, Dove. Class is starting, and if we're going to discuss... *arousing* things, I'd rather we be alone."

"We aren't going to be discussing—"

"Okay, settle down everyone!" the professor said, projecting her voice over the low hum of student chatter. "Today we begin our unit on the Heroic Journey."

Elijah scooted ever so slightly out of my personal space and began typing notes on his laptop. He appeared genuinely interested in the lecture, as usual. It was ridiculously endearing.

When class ended, Elijah and George followed close on my heels as I made my way out of the classroom and into the stuffy wood-paneled hallway. George slithered out ahead of me, and students swore and scattered out of our way. I rolled my eyes. Not everyone who walked the halls of this school had a powerful predator living inside them, but come on. This was a seven-foot-long python with shiny purple scales, not a wraith stalking down the hall.

"Dove, may I have a word?"

"Um—"

Long fingers threaded through mine, and Elijah pulled me gently into a small alcove between classrooms. An oil painting featuring one of the 19th-century founders of the college hung there, the grizzled old shifter watching us with judgy black eyes.

My back hit the wall next to the painting. Elijah stepped into my personal space, leaning an elbow against the wall by my head. It was intimate, and he was too close, but I had no desire to demand he move.

This was not a private area, but George had curled himself into a pile out in the hallway in front of us, a glittering purple traffic cone that had the few students wandering this way turning around and hurrying back the way they came.

Yellow-gold eyes drank me in, sinful, dangerous, but also playful.

That was Elijah in a nutshell, wasn't it?

"I'm sorry for what happened when we sparred, Dove," he said in a low voice. He swiped his thumb softly across my cheekbone. "I've worked very hard to maintain my hold over my beast. I've gotten good at controlling the urge to shift, but once he's out, I'm not in the driver's seat as much as you would expect from a strong predator Prime. The basilisk is a bit more volatile around you, for some reason, and I'm sorry if I frightened you."

"It's okay," I whispered. "I wasn't scared, Elijah. Just worried about you, I guess."

A pleased grin spread across his face. "Were you, now?"

I swatted his chest. He wore his usual breezy linen shirt, unbuttoned low enough to show off the snake draped around his neck and the top of his defined pecs. "Don't read into it. Are you sure you should be this close to me? If I set the basilisk off in this hallway, I'll never hear the end of it from Heath."

And yet, even knowing his loss of control was a distinct possibility, I felt no fear. My beast wasn't even tentatively on edge, which she normally would be at the slightest whiff of danger.

I know you think you can handle the beasts in this quad, but this basilisk can and will kill us.

She licked a paw and flicked her tail. Great.

Elijah just chuckled. He slid his hand lower to wrap it possessively around the back of my neck. "Mmm, true. And what happened the last time you got in trouble with Heath?"

A hot blush flared from my face all the way to my chest. He knew exactly what happened, so I wouldn't dignify that question with an answer. I just scowled at him.

He grinned even wider. "Heath's a lucky bastard. I'm insanely jealous. Not sure if I mentioned that."

"You did not," I replied, clearing my throat.

"But, to your point, Dove, I've decided to work on this little issue of mine." He leaned in, his nose a hair's breadth from mine, and whispered, "Exposure therapy. Plus, if our ruthlessly by-the-book quad leader is going to misbehave, it's only fair I get to."

"What—"

He kissed me.

Soft, insistent lips pressed to mine. His hand tightened around my neck while the other landed on my hip, and he pulled me closer.

My body went slack, and I kissed him back. Elijah rumbled a soft male noise of satisfaction. He licked the seam of my lips, and I opened for him. A skilled tongue caressed mine, coaxing little moans from me as he explored my mouth.

I buried my hands in his shirt. Wet heat burned between my legs. "*Elijah,*" I gasped against his mouth.

He ripped his lips from mine and took a big step backward. Slitted pupils inside glowing golden irises stared at me, hungry and predatory.

My beast awoke from her lusty little haze and began to pace.

Elijah slammed his eyes shut and shook his head like he was trying to clear it, his nostrils flaring like a bull's and his fists clenched at his sides.

"Hey, it's okay—"

His eyes snapped open. Round pupils greeted me, and his irises had returned to their usual non-glowing gold.

After a cleansing breath, he smiled at me once more. "Thank you, Dove. Baby steps, I think, but all progress is good progress, wouldn't you agree?"

He didn't wait for me to answer. He turned around, whistled at George like he was a dog, and strode off down the hall. George glanced my way, his little snake face sorrowful, before he slithered off after Elijah.

I just stood there, shellshocked and confused, as they both disappeared from view.

AFTER THAT, ELIJAH JOINED HEATH AND WYATT IN KEEPING A respectable distance from me. None of them engaged with me—not in the dining hall, in our shared classes, or during Guardian training. Wyatt didn't openly flirt with me. Heath didn't boss me around. Elijah didn't try to kiss me again or even touch me beyond the inadvertent brushing of our arms on occasion when he sat next to me in class.

I knew better. Despite appearances, they weren't ignoring me. They were watching me, all three of them, like hungry dogs watched the family's pet rabbit that they'd been forbidden to eat.

Aiden was the worst of them all, or maybe it just felt that way because we were forced into spending so much one-on-

one time together. He continued to pay me no mind in class, but our tutoring sessions were rife with sexual tension, his beast constantly peeking through his eyes, studying me from across his desk. Both of us struggled to pretend that I hadn't shattered in his arms while I'd come the hardest I ever had in my life.

Unfortunately, he did not decide to rut me like an animal against the side of the Magical Ed building, despite his claim that he had a free pass to do so.

George still came around. Elijah and I were splitting custody of him at this point, and he even spent a little time with Ian, who'd bought George's affection by shifting into his fox and taking George out hunting for rodents one night.

Cash continued to hate me, but there was little he could do about my holding steady in the top quarter on the Guardian leaderboard. Wyatt's dad dropped in to observe training once every couple of weeks, and that big bear had little tolerance for anyone's bullshit—especially from Cash and the other trainers, who were extra fucking obnoxious now that they were bonded and juiced up.

We'd spent the past few weeks working on formation and battle tactics, which involved a lot of slow-motion breakdowns against the SWIM, with various wraith combinations. There'd been little opportunity for leaderboard movement as a result, so the quads were getting antsy.

When the first Friday in March rolled around, tensions and excitement in training were high. The quad groups were going to be released to go all out against the simulations. Support Squadron had gone in their six person groups against lower-level swarms the day before, with Ian and Brody's group coming out on top by a mile.

"Cash is trying to tank you by sticking you with the Mahoney Trio," Ian muttered. We were perched in the bleachers, watching as the Valente Quad limped through a challenge that'd thrown four Ripper-level leonine creatures with pincers and scorpion tails at them. One of them had been stabbed in the stomach with that tail and was being subjected to the feeling of bleeding out on the floor while the rest of his team got their asses kicked. Ian winced as their leader, an enormous jackal, took a pincer right to the face. "The Mahoneys are a fucking mess," he went on. "It's no wonder they can't find a fourth to become a quad."

"Plenty of shifters bond as a trio," I pointed out.

Our dads did—sort of. And there wasn't a *requirement* among Primes to form a quad. It was just seen as the ideal, especially among the wealthy and influential families, because it projected maximum strength and was an even number, or whatever.

I didn't tend to care what the *elites* of our kind got up to, but I couldn't avoid it now that I was surrounded by them.

"But you're right," I went on. "The Mahoneys will be every man for himself out there."

But I had to go along with it because I needed to complete challenges in quad formation if I wanted to keep my position on the leaderboard. There wouldn't be another full quad competition until next month.

Ward Gale was also here today. He needed to see me prove myself fighting within a traditional team of four if I wanted a role among the Guardians and not the Support Squadron, because Cash sure as shit wasn't going to recommend me for it.

I caught Kace Mahoney glaring up in my direction. He had white-blond hair, soulless gray eyes, and a white wolf for a beast. He was an Alpha in size and physical strength only, because he sure didn't lead like one.

I sent him a shitty salute. He could stow the attitude

because he needed me as much as I needed him right now. His trio was low on the leaderboard and in real danger of getting cut at the end of the semester, and my addition to their team would mean more kills in today's run.

Trent cut the simulation magic from the control booth, and Cash brought the house lights up. As the Valente Quad limped off the arena floor, Cash announced the next team to go.

"Yes, yes, hold your applause," he said irritably into the microphone. "The *full* Blackwell Quad has decided to grace us with their presence today. Looks like none of you have a shot at the top of the leaderboard yet again."

I sat up straighter in my seat. Ian snorted a laugh at me, and I deserved it for nearly pulling a muscle in my neck trying to catch a glimpse of Aiden in his Guardian-issued tight black T-shirt and sweatpants. He stood next to Heath at the edge of the arena floor, warming up his sword arm with controlled practice strikes of his saber.

There were the carved biceps and the corded forearms I already knew well. His ass filled out those sweatpants spectacularly, and he'd stashed his glasses away somewhere in preparation to shift. He must've just shown up because he hadn't been here for warm-ups.

Heath stood there with his arms folded over his broad chest, scowling at the empty arena. Wyatt twirled his huge battle-ax like a baton, and Elijah was engaged in some sort of stretching.

"Is that warrior two?" I asked Ian, gesturing at Elijah.

"Might be. Yoga's good for peaceful connection to the beast."

At least Elijah had a few tools in his arsenal. Maybe if we tried yoga together....

"All right, Blackwell Quad!" Cash barked into the mic. "Get your asses out there. I don't have all fucking day."

The crowd quieted as the lights went down and the soft blue glow of the magic fired up and spread across the arena. I was as enthralled as everyone else as Heath, Wyatt, Elijah, and Aiden stepped onto the floor.

27

AVERY

The guys dealt with the swarmers without even breaking a sweat. They set Wyatt up to be a human guillotine and herded the monsters at him. The next phase sent four Rippers at them, and as expected, Wyatt went furry to batter the wraiths while Heath and Aiden took turns slicing heads off with their sabers.

Elijah remained a mostly casual observer at the edge of the floor, occasionally slashing a dagger at the wraiths if they strayed too close to him.

When the magic conjured a Giant, accompanied by more Ripper mutants, I finally got what I wanted.

Aiden tossed his saber to Elijah, ripped off his shirt, then let his jaguar burst free.

Ian whistled. "Damn."

Damn was right. Aiden was exceptionally large for a jaguar, Prime or not. His fur was a rich brown, dotted with darker rosettes all over his lithe, muscular feline body. Blue-green eyes glowed as the jaguar snarled at the Giant. He and Wyatt's bear were preparing to attack it together.

My beast's ears perked up, and she stretched languidly within me.

Yes, yes, he is a very majestic feline.

Aiden's jaguar was as impressive a fighter as Heath's wolf or Wyatt's bear, but he had the agile feline quickness that the others lacked. It was of particular use against this Giant —a twelve-foot-tall humanoid monstrosity with a bird head and three spiked tails.

Like how Wyatt and Heath had worked together in animal form to take down the Giant on my first day of training, Aiden and Wyatt were able to topple the wraith after a long and brutal fight. Heath was there with Wyatt's ax to chop off its head, while Elijah had been forced off the sidelines to decapitate a faltering Ripper that Heath had taken down earlier that looked like it was about to regenerate.

When all was said and done, they were awarded thousands of additional points, both to their quad and to them as individuals. No one would be touching them in the top spot, and they deserved it. They were far and away the most talented group in this program.

Talent that was wasted in a magical simulation. At least they'd be let out of this cage in a few short months and allowed to put their skills to use protecting people outside the warded walls of the school.

Aiden and Wyatt padded off the arena floor to shift and dress, the shadows obscuring my ability to check out Aiden's naked body.

I'd already seen Wyatt's multiple times, but I wouldn't have said no to another viewing.

"All right, Mahoney is up next!" Cash barked. "Three minutes."

Ian patted my shoulder. "Stay sharp and don't trust any of them to have your back."

"Right."

I stood up, shrugged on my swords, and made my way down to the arena floor. Kace Mahoney waited near the control booth with the other two members of his trio— Blaine, a big burly bear, and Drew, a lanky panther.

No one spoke to me as I took my place next to them.

"Nice of you to join us, Baxter," Cash said. "I'd tell you all to play nice, but that's not how shit works in the real world, is it? Get your asses out there."

I trudged to the center of the floor behind my temporary teammates. As the lights dimmed and the magic flooded the arena, I reached behind my head to unsheathe my blades.

"Just stay out of our way, bitch," Kace said, still not looking at me.

Off to a great start.

I didn't reply, keeping my focus on the periphery of the floor, where the first wraiths would appear. Heath was there, lurking and grinding his jaw, his attention squarely on me. Aiden stood behind him, glasses back on, eyes narrowed at Kace. Wyatt was nearby, too, arms crossed over his shirtless chest and his amused smile nowhere to be found. Elijah slouched against the wall of the bleachers behind Wyatt, his posture relaxed, but his mouth was set in a tight line instead of his trademark breezy smile.

A dozen catlike wraiths with bat wings flickered to life on the northern edge of the arena. Each was the size of a Rottweiler and flashed us double rows of needle teeth. They screeched in unison, formed a swarm, and attacked us head-on.

We had no battle plan here, of course, except to just hack away at whichever monsters ended up in each person's general vicinity. Fine by me. The little cat bastards were spry and fast, but their necks were spindly, so lopping off their grotesque heads took less effort than it could've.

By the end of the wave, I'd killed eight wraiths, while the rest of my team had managed the other four. Blaine was limping with some kind of simulated injury. Maybe he'd ended up with those nasty teeth in his leg—the guy was lumbering and slow in human form and only slightly less so as a bear, so he wouldn't have been hard for a swarmer to catch.

"I'm not impressed, Mahoney," Cash spat through the speaker system. "A *female* is getting more kills than your entire trio. Act like fucking Primes."

I received three hateful glares for that comment. *Thank you, Cash.*

"We all share the points," I told my teammates, gesturing above us with my sword as Jared, the quiet tablet-wielding trainer with a bad case of resting asshole face, loaded our scores onto the jumbotron. "So, you're welcome."

"Shut the fuck up," Kace snapped. "You're an embarrassment to this program, this school, and to shifter females in general."

I sighed. "If you have a small dick, just say that, Mahoney."

A few snickers sounded from the gallery.

His eyes flashed silver, and a growl ripped from his chest. "You fucking dare—"

Two Rippers materialized in front of us, tearing Kace's attention from me. He charged the wraith on the left, sword drawn for the kill. Blaine shifted into his bear and loped off after him. Drew ran into the fray, shifting into his panther mid-stride.

That left me to deal with the second wraith alone. *Thanks, guys.*

This one was as big as my dad was in his wolf form, but it had a horselike body, its dark-gray flesh twisted in knots like tree bark. A triangular head sat atop its abnormally long, thick neck, and a mass of antlers sprang in gnarled branches from the top of the head. They looked extremely sharp. Its void eyes glowed with the soft blue magic holding it together.

The wraith snorted, pawed the ground, and then charged me. I braced myself, keeping my body loose and my blades at the ready. It tucked its head, ready to spear me with that tangle of antlers, so I ducked low and slid to my knees, arching my back. I sacrificed one sword, burying it in the creature's chest as it trampled over me.

It roared and stumbled away, my sword still embedded in its rotting gray flesh. I climbed to my feet and sucked in a harsh breath. One of the wraith's thick legs had slammed into my side, and I was being subjected to a magical simulation of at least a couple cracked ribs.

The wraith circled, ready to run at me again. In the periphery, Blaine's bear reared on his hind legs and then tackled their wraith to the ground. Drew's panther slashed at its face, while Kace, still a human, began hacking away at its neck with his blade.

My wraith lunged at me again, this time with its teeth. I slashed with my remaining sword, keeping it at bay. My ribs screamed at me.

It's not real, I screamed back internally.

The wraith snapped at me again, and again I slashed. It was moving slower, though it wasn't exactly sluggish. It had to be feeling the sword impaled in its chest, gray sludge oozing from the wound.

The right move here was to hold—continue this dance with the wraith, letting it attack and bleed and slowly lose energy, until my partners finished with their kill and could jump in for an assist. It's what I would've done if it'd been my dads or Ian on the floor with me now.

But it wasn't. I had to assume I was on my own.

On its next attack, the wraith lowered its head, switching back to trying to spear me with those antlers. The move protected its face from my sword, but it also meant it took its eyes off me for at least a few seconds.

As it charged me, I dropped to my knees again, ducking the thrust of the antlers and sliding to its side. As I went, I swung my sword upwards into the wraith's neck in a two-handed slash meant to inflict maximum damage.

My blade cut deep into the thick, gnarly muscle. The wraith gurgled a horrifying screech and staggered.

It was enough.

I sprang from the floor and rammed my sword straight into its ribs, shoving its body with everything I had.

The wraith stumbled again, squawking like a flock of dying barn owls, and it tripped and fell onto its side.

I ripped my sword from its ribs, grasped it with both hands, and sliced through the wraith's neck in a vicious downward strike.

Cleaved from its body, the head hit the floor with a disgusting thud.

Kill managed.

The wraith flickered and disappeared as the magic released. My chest rose and fell in a harsh rhythm as I fought to catch my breath. I bent to pick my other sword off the padded floor.

As I stood up, I caught sight of Aiden pacing on the side-lines, his frustrated stalking still executed with feline grace. Elijah was with him, his hands shoved casually into the pockets of his athletic pants, eyes glowing yellow and focused only on me.

Kace's team must've finished their kill about when I did. Their wraith blinked out of existence, surrounded by the beasts in the group, who heaved big panting breaths, and Kace, who cradled his non-sword arm.

Cash didn't waste time. The magic pulsed, and two Giants appeared on the floor.

"Fuck," Kace barked.

I agreed. Two Giants were a bitch, but so was one Giant with a handful of Rippers. They liked to change it up at this stage.

These wraiths were ten-foot-tall humanoid werewolves, bipedal with clawed feet, even larger clawed hands, and thick muscles rippling under dark-gray fur. Ribs were visible where chunks of skin and fur were missing. A stripe of porcupine quills ran the length of their spines, their wolf eyes lit up with the white-blue of the magic.

Since Drew and Blaine were still in beast form, they elected to charge one of the werewolves as it took its first steps. Kace tossed his sword to the floor and ran straight for the second wraith as it let loose an eardrum-shattering shriek.

He rounded the backside of the wraith, then turned and sprinted toward me, his eyes sparking and white fur rippling down his arms. He was inviting the Giant to chase him in my direction.

Looked like our team leader had finally wised up. We needed to take these insane wraiths in teams of two if we had any shot at killing them both.

He streaked toward me, the wraith hot on his heels. I braced, readying my blades. Ten yards from me, Kace completed the shift to his big white wolf, landing on four paws and continuing his sprint. Ideally, he would complete another circle behind me, and then we could attack this thing head-on together.

Except he didn't do any of that.

Kace leapt straight at me. I'd been so focused on the monster behind him that I wasn't ready. I hadn't expected to have to defend myself against the large Alpha wolf, who was supposed to be my teammate.

I moved too slowly, raised my swords too late.

He tackled me to the ground, and my back slammed into the floor, knocking the air from my lungs. I fought, but my swords were pinned under his big wolf body. Kace snarled and bit down on my shoulder, tearing at my flesh, his teeth hitting bone.

The pain was excruciating. White light shot through my vision.

This wasn't part of the simulation. This was fucking *real*.

I screamed.

In a flash, the wolf was gone, darting out of the way of the wraith as it pounced on top of me.

Huge clawed hands held me down.

My beast roared and slammed against the bars of her cage.

And then I lost her.

Icy pain spiked in my chest and radiated through my limbs. I couldn't move. Everything was heavy. I blinked and blinked, but the room began to darken.

The magic is forcing my body to feel the wraith consuming my soul.

My head rolled to the side. Ian was at the edge of the floor, thrashing in Wyatt's hold and screaming words I couldn't hear.

Then everything went black.

28

AVERY

I came to under the bright lights of the college's infirmary. I recognized the same small med room Heath had dragged me to after Rip and his gang of idiots had challenged me on the campus lawn the first week of school.

"Awake now, Killer?"

Think of the devil, and he shall appear.

Heath sat in his usual chair in the corner of the room, arms crossed, reproachful quad-leader face out in full force.

Yes, he had a "usual chair" now that we'd done this twice together. I had no idea if we were in the same room or if all the patient rooms looked the same in our infirmary, but wasn't it nice for Heath to always have his chair?

I groaned and attempted to sit up on the bed. My shoulder ached, but it was a dull, persistent ache rather than the horrendous screaming pain from earlier. I no longer wore my Guardian T-shirt—probably destroyed by that traitorous fucking wolf—and was in my sports bra, leggings, and a lovely bandage that was wrapped snugly around my injured shoulder.

"Don't start with me, Blackwell," I said wearily. "Why are you in here?"

He cocked his head, studying me intently. "I think we're on a first-name basis now, since I've had my tongue in your pussy, don't you?"

I looked for something to throw at him, but all I had were the clothes left on my body and the treatment table underneath me, and its pillow was firmly attached. "You want to bring that up *now*?"

He was unmoved. "To answer your question, I'm in here because I'm the one who brought you to the infirmary. Again."

"I didn't ask you to do that. Where's Ian?"

He jerked his chin at the door. "In the waiting room. Under guard."

"He's *what*?" I snapped.

Heath raised his brows like he was inviting me to change my tone.

I glared daggers at his stupid, perfect face.

"Wyatt's watching him, or did you want your brother to run off and try to kill Kace Mahoney? Because he's tried twice."

My beast, thankfully back online, roared in my chest.

"He can get in line," I growled.

"You're not going to kill him either." He pointed at my eyes. "Put her away. I have enough to deal with between you, your brother, and Elijah, who Aiden had to drag outside to run laps around the school so that Kace didn't end up basilisk food."

"No one asked you to *deal* with me or Ian, and you should've let Elijah eat that backstabbing asshole—"

A polite knock sounded at the door. Dr. Lee slipped into the room, all sharp cheekbones and kind eyes. His shiny black hair was a little disheveled, like he'd been rushing around saving lives all afternoon. Swoon factor: doubled.

"Oh, good, you're awake," he said cheerfully. He rolled his little doctor stool next to my bed and sat down, and then he gently prodded my bandaged shoulder. "Usually the magically simulated soul death will knock you out for about half an hour, but we thought the, ah, non-simulated injury and blood loss might keep you down longer. I'm pleased to see that it did not."

I arched a brow. "Is that what we're calling it? A *non-simulated injury*? I was attacked and sabotaged by my own teammate."

His dark eyes were full of sympathy. "You were. Treating injuries inflicted by students upon one another is very common in my job as lead physician at a shifter college. This isn't even the first time I've treated *you*, Miss Baxter, for injuries caused by other students. But your outrage is valid. I've never seen an unprovoked attack like this from within a team training with the Guardians." He glanced over his shoulder to give Heath a pointed look. "Have you, Mr. Blackwell?"

"No," Heath grunted. He was eyeballing Dr. Lee's hands on my skin like they were a personal affront.

Dr. Lee unwound my bandage and checked my injury. "We did a combination of regular sutures and magical healing to treat your shoulder. Your bone and muscle should be back to normal within a few days, and the stitches will dissolve in a couple of weeks."

After he rewrapped me, I did a little arm circle. Stiff, and there was a small pinch of pain. "Thanks, Doc. When am I cleared for full combat?"

His amused smile could've launched a thousand Tumblrs. "Can you give me two weeks?"

I shrugged, very casual and coy. "I can try."

Heath muttered something unintelligible.

"You do that, Miss Baxter." Dr. Lee pushed his rolling stool back from my table and stood up. "I'll process your discharge, and then you can be on your way, okay?"

As he exited the room, he had to squeeze past the imposing figure that had just appeared in the doorway.

Ward Gale. The big bear, in the flesh.

Paying me a personal visit.

"Miss Baxter, may I have a moment?" The deep rumble of his voice might've rattled the door hinges.

"Um, sure." I waved him in.

Heath didn't appear particularly surprised by Ward's visit. He blew out a breath and slumped a little in his chair. Maybe he was relieved it was Wyatt's dad here instead of Cash to address the *incident*.

That would make two of us, even though of the two, Ward Gale was the one who intimidated the shit out of me.

Ward shut the door and leaned against it, folding enormous arms over his barrel chest. He wore top-to-bottom Guardian fatigues today, and his bald head shone under the harsh light of the room. This close, I could see his bushy beard was a rust-red color, more like Wyatt-the-bear's fur than Wyatt-the-man's dark auburn hair, and his eyes were a deep coffee brown, unlike Wyatt's vibrant green.

It was possible he was Wyatt's bio-dad, but I'd gathered from chatter among the trainees that all four of Wyatt's dads were Prime bears, and they'd all done at least some stint in the Guardians. Like me, Wyatt probably didn't know which father had sired him and liked it that way.

"I've come to inform you of the state of things after what happened today," Ward said. He looked me over briefly and seemed satisfied I was in one piece. "Despite the blatant sabotage from your teammate, there is no way to undo the loss of points for the L4 death you experienced against the SWIM—"

I sucked in a harsh breath. "*What?*"

"—as well as the loss of points for the second L4, which your teammates also failed to kill."

I cut Heath an incredulous look. "What the hell?"

He sighed and ran a hand through his lush blond hair. Hair I didn't get to dig my fingers into while he had his head between my thighs because Aiden had trapped my arms in his unyielding hold. "Kace ran out of bounds rather than be killed," Heath said, "which, as you know, causes the same points deduction as a death. Drew got knocked out by the other wraith, and Blaine didn't manage to inflict enough damage to matter before they cut the program off."

"As a result, the Mahoneys have fallen so low on the leaderboard, they have no shot at making the cut for the summer field training," Ward went on. "Normally, we don't make cuts until the end of the semester, but in this case, I've informed them that they've been dismissed and are not welcome to return to training."

"Oh." I chewed on that, then gave Ward a curt nod. "That's good, then."

"I don't think I have to tell you, Miss Baxter, that losing this many points this late in the year leaves you with a bit of an uphill battle to make the cut as a Guardian. You'll be sidelined for a few weeks until Dr. Lee clears you for full-contact combat, and there's only one more quad competition on the schedule for the semester."

He was right. I'd need to earn points as both an individual fighter and with a group of four, specifically to kill Giants, if I had any hope of making it to the next stage of training.

I lifted my chin. "I'll be ready by then. As long as I'm assigned to a group that doesn't try to kill me."

Ward's face softened the tiniest bit, giving me a glimpse of the man rumored to be the doting father of four daughters. "I believe you, Avery. But I also wanted to let you know that if you don't make the cut, we'd welcome you back next year in the Support Squadron, even if that isn't the usual course for a Guardian candidate who fails to advance. You and your brother are both extremely talented. I admire your tenacity, but the odds were always going to be against you to become a true Guardian without a Prime beast."

Props to him for not also including my lack of penis in that statement.

"I appreciate that, sir, but I'm here to become a Guardian. Any assumptions about the existence or nature of my beast are, at the moment, just that. *Assumptions.*"

Heath dropped his head into his hands and fisted his hair with a very put-upon groan.

"What's wrong with him?" I asked. I jerked a thumb at Heath and blinked big innocent eyes at Ward.

Ward grinned, and *there* was a hint of Wyatt. "Go easy on him. It will take these boys a while before they're a bit less flummoxed by the mysteries of the female."

Heath snapped to attention. "Come on, Ward."

Ward ignored him. "Rest up, Miss Baxter. I hope to see you back in the top half of the leaderboard soon."

"Thank you, sir."

After Ward left, I didn't have to look at Heath to know his full focus had slid back to me. The hot blaze of his stare did things to my body, and in this state, I didn't have the energy to fight against it.

"I wish you'd reconsider," he said after a minute.

I frowned. "Reconsider what?"

"All of this." He leaned forward, resting his elbows on his knees, and a golden sheen rolled over his hazel eyes. "It isn't safe, Killer. We've just seen what can happen against a fucking magical *simulation*, which, as you have shouted repeatedly at all of us, isn't even real wraith combat. You refuse to shift when you're injured, and I can't promise that you, as a female, won't always be a target for the backwards, small-dicked assholes among us, whose beast brains can't handle a female in battle. At some point, it isn't worth it."

Sexy tingles—gone. Rage hackles—up.

"After everything I've done since the day I showed up to this ridiculous school—" I said, seething. "My performance in training. Putting down student challenges. Helping your sister." I looked down at my feet where they dangled over the edge of the table, wishing I didn't care so much. "You *still* don't believe in me."

"What I *believe* is that I'm tired of watching you get hurt!"

He stood up suddenly and began to pace the small space between us.

I sighed. "It isn't your concern—"

"It is *agonizing*, Avery." He stopped pacing, his stoic face slipping into something that looked almost despondent. "I just want it to stop."

We stared at each other. I didn't know what to say to that, and I wasn't going to give him the answer he appeared to want, which was something along the lines of, "Okay, Daddy, I'll put down my swords, quit the Guardians, and go back to pretending to be a well-behaved latent female just here for some bonds and a degree in Literature."

But I didn't like that my tendency to get banged up was hurting Heath. I didn't ask for him to care about me like that, but I couldn't pretend the thought didn't make me gooey in my girly center.

And if I sat with my own feelings for two seconds instead of trying to pretend they didn't exist, I'd probably find the idea of Heath being seriously injured in any way was pretty agonizing to me too.

What the hell was I supposed to do with that?

We were saved from having to continue this conversation when a nurse bustled in and announced that I'd been discharged. I slid from the table and made my way to the door. Heath followed silently behind me.

In the waiting room, I found a very surly Ian glaring at Wyatt from his seat in an uncomfortable-looking plastic chair. Wyatt leaned against the wall across from him, arms crossed over his black T-shirt, cocky smirk affixed to his handsome face.

Brody sat on one side of Ian, and my swords and gym bag occupied the chair on his other side.

"You can't watch me 24/7, Gale," Ian was saying, his tone taunting. "You gonna become Mahoney's bodyguard full time? I won't even need to lift a finger. I'll just ask my buddy George to slither through Mahoney's window and suffocate him in his sleep. You know he'd do it for my sister."

Wyatt rolled his eyes. "George doesn't take orders from anyone, Baxter. You need to chill the fuck out. Your boyfriend and I both agree that your sister will burn down the school if we let you run off and get yourself killed by Kace Mahoney."

"He's right," I said as I strode into the room. "It's been dealt with for now, Ian."

He launched himself out of his chair and threw his arms around me. "*Fuck* this, Aves. That was the second-worst thing you've made me watch in the past three months. I can't do any more."

Wyatt shot me an incredulous look. "What the fuck happened to you that was worse than this—"

Nope, not talking about the reason I was in this entire mess to begin with. I ignored him and squeezed my brother. "I'm sorry," I told Ian, really meaning it. "But Dr. Lee fixed me up. Make me one of your painkiller elixirs after this, and I'll be right as rain."

Ian released me, took a moment to scan my body for any stray damage, and then he waggled his blond eyebrows. "Dr. Lee came to give me a status report earlier. I think I might let Mahoney maul me if that man will be the one to put me back together."

Brody sighed wistfully. "He healed my broken leg once. I've been waiting for the opportunity to break the other one."

Heath grumbled some kind of annoyed nonsense.

Wyatt snatched my hand and pulled me away from Ian, who huffed irritably. He looked me over, his gaze caressing my entire torso, and I became acutely aware that I still did not have a shirt on. "Better now, Wildcat?"

"Yep, I'll live."

His jaw tensed, and his eyes flashed a red hue as he ran a gentle hand over the bandage on my shoulder. "I would hope so."

I stepped away from him before I caved to the urge to melt into those strong arms. I was very tired, and it would be very easy to let Wyatt carry me out of here and all the way to my bed.

After a quick dig through my gym bag, I located a long-sleeved T-shirt. I pulled it on, and then I carefully affixed my swords to my back, the press of their weight between my shoulder blades soothing the itchy feeling within me.

"Let's go," I said to my brother. "I want ice cream, a bath, and ten hours of sleep tonight."

He grinned. "Coming right up."

I left the infirmary with Ian and Brody flanking my sides like two adorably unnecessary sentinels. I didn't have to look back to know that Heath and Wyatt watched me until I disappeared through the front doors.

29

AVERY

I spent most of the next day convalescing in bed and watching the gayest anime I could rustle up from the buffet of streaming apps on my phone. Mal showed up to check my wound every few hours while she delivered the latest gossip.

The report was that the whole school knew what'd happened to me in the arena yesterday, and opinion was divided on whether I was the victim of an underhanded attack by a more powerful shifter or I'd been asking for it.

After a light run with Ian and Brody around campus, a giant burger for dinner, and a long, hot shower, I gathered my supplies and wandered outside, headed to one of the Magical Ed building's smaller courtyards. It was nearing midnight, and I wanted to take advantage of the Full Moon at its zenith and the relative quiet of the school on a Saturday night.

Many students left campus on Saturday nights for the local bars and clubs in the nearby shifter towns. For example, Ian, Brody, Mal, and Allen were out tonight, listening to some band that was playing at a gin distillery half an hour away. I'd learned that others liked to head west to a neighboring college town to parade their hot shifter bodies in front of unsuspecting human students in an attempt to get laid.

I liked to get out as much as the next person, but I had work to do tonight.

When I entered my favorite courtyard, I found it blessedly deserted. I loved the mood of this space. The bright rays of the Moon illuminated beds of night-blooming jasmine and other pretty plants. A few stone benches were tucked against the landscaping. Classroom windows, which were completely dark on a Saturday night, abutted this side of the building. The professors' offices overlooked the larger courtyard on the other side, and there was always at least one night owl up there with the light on, ruining the perfect moonlit space below.

I laid my swords on the bench that had the fewest trees surrounding it. The moonlight bathed my steel blades, and the rune etchings on the steel sparked with a soft glow, beginning their charge. Next, I dipped into the pocket of my hoodie and retrieved my drypoint etching needle. I placed it next to my swords and then sat down on the ground in front of the bench. I'd need to meditate for a few minutes, establishing my connection to the Moon's magic flowing through me alongside my beast.

I'd been in this quiet mental space for ten whole seconds when the sound of light footsteps on the sidewalk behind me told me I was no longer alone.

"Avery?"

My beast unfurled her body and flicked her tail.

"Aiden," I said, releasing a resigned sigh. I glanced over my shoulder, and sure enough, there he was. Professor Blackwell, dressed in nice jeans and a long-sleeved shirt sporting the college's coat of arms, the strap of his leather messenger bag draped across his body. Draped in the other direction was the strap of the leather harness that held his sword, the handle of his saber just peeking over his shoulder.

"What are you doing out here?" he asked, creeping closer.

"What are *you* doing out here?" I retorted.

He arched an imperious brow. "I was in my office, catching up on the work I did not get done yesterday because I had to show up to Guardian training. And because I had to watch Elijah after... what happened."

"After I was attacked by my own teammate, you mean?"

His eyes sparked turquoise for a second, and then he blinked it away. "Yes. You don't need to remind me. I was there."

I turned back to my swords and picked up my needle. The thin wooden handle was smooth and comforting in my grip. "Is Elijah okay?" I asked casually.

"He's fine." More footsteps sounded, inching closer. "We had a dicey couple of minutes after Mahoney first attacked you, but after that, it was more about keeping human Elijah occupied. Elijah's beast isn't the only part of him capable of murder."

That gave me a little shiver, and it wasn't from fear. "I see."

"Are you blessing your blades?" he asked, suddenly eager. He shrugged off his bag and sat down on the ground next to me. We weren't touching, but his knee hovered about an inch from mine. Reaching behind his head, he unsheathed his saber. "Let's do mine too."

"You'll need a drill—"

He pulled a handheld rotary drill from his bag. "I come

prepared," he announced with a smug grin. "Most runes teachers have something for permanent etching."

"How convenient," I drawled. "What do you need a Moon-blessed blade for, *Professor*? Planning on dipping outside the state's best wards during curfew to try your hand at killing something that can actually kill *you*?"

He gave me a droll look. "Are you going to impress me with your magical prowess or are you going to be a brat?"

I bristled, but my beast rumbled a little purr and flicked her tail. *Quit that.*

"Fine. Do you have the sequence you want to use?"

He peered at the etchings on my swords. "I like yours just fine."

Runes used for any given spell would differ by practitioner, and the Moon blessing was no different. I presumed everyone stuck within a standard theme, but the real trick was in the casting of the spell and channeling the Moon's magic into your blade so that it was a) lasting, and b) strong enough to kill a high-level wraith.

My sequence started with *Lifeforce*, which shifters associated with the Moon herself. Then I went with *Strength/Power*, followed by *Heritage*, as a nod to our ancestors, the First Guardians. Then came the rune for *War/Victory*, and finally, the death knell—inverted *Strength/Power* and inverted *Lifeforce*.

"Cheater," I said without any heat. "I don't chant, by the way. I just whisper a prayer as I channel, and it hasn't failed me yet."

"Interesting," Aiden mused. "The Guardians' rune specialists chant. There's power in the combined voices, I think."

I shrugged. "*When* I become a Guardian, I won't be

handing over my blades to anyone else to bless. I like my way."

He was quiet for a moment, as aware as I was that my place in the program was no longer secure. "I don't *want* you to fail, Avery," he said softly, "but yesterday was hard to watch."

"It was even harder to experience, but I'm still here, Aiden. I haven't changed my mind."

"I didn't dare dream that you had."

I blew out a frustrated breath and rolled my shoulders. To business, then. "You're distracting me. Get ready to etch."

He chuckled, and I felt the sound low in my belly. "Yes, ma'am."

I closed my eyes and settled in, doing my best to ignore the heat of Aiden's body and the scent of heady leather and masculine spice. I rolled the wooden handle of my drypoint needle between my fingers, and then I reached for the current of bright magic flowing within me, both separate and apart from my beast, who was curled up for a nap. Under the Full Moon, the magical current roared.

I opened my eyes and began tracing the runes on my first sword, using my will to suffuse the blade with magic.

I began to pray, my voice low and soft:

"Goddess above,

Hear my plea.

Bathe my blade

In your glorious light.

May it shine through the dark

And be worthy of your gift

So that I may protect my kind

From the horrors of the night.

Bless this steel

With your strength and might

So I may honor your blessing
With courage and fight."

I repeated my prayer once more as I scratched over the runes on my second blade with my needle. Aiden worked next to me, engraving his blade with runes to match mine, his lips moving in a quiet prayer of his own.

As I released the current, my blades glowed with a soft white light, the runes themselves shining a molten silver for a few seconds.

Aiden finished his prayer, and his blade began to glow, his with a bluer hue. Different flavors of magic, I supposed.

"Wow," he said, a grin stretching across his handsome face. "It worked."

"Maybe I should be tutoring *you* in runes," I quipped.

He snorted. "Calm down. You're excellent with the few spells you use regularly, yes, but your grasp on theory is middling at best."

That particular gripe of his was getting old. "Theory doesn't protect us from soul death, Aiden."

"I would beg to differ."

He rolled to standing, nimble as always, then held out a hand. I grasped it, and he pulled me to my feet.

He didn't release my hand right away. His grip was warm and firm, his palm the rough and calloused one of a swordsman, not the smooth and soft one of a professor. Soft turquoise flames lit his eyes as his gaze dipped to my lips before skirting away.

"Thanks for letting me do this with you," he said. "It really is impressive that you're able to cast a strong and effective Moon blessing, especially as a shifter sharing magic with a beast soul."

It was useless continuing to play coy about the existence of my beast, so I didn't correct him, and I didn't really want to. His praise was like a stroke down my back, and I preened under it.

"Thanks, Aiden."

He smiled, and it was a little cocky. "Good night, Avery."

He released my hand and collected his stuff. I sat down on the bench next to my swords and watched him walk away.

Aiden, at his core, wasn't really the haughty, uptight professor he appeared to be. He was a talented, respectable male with a powerful, impressive beast. He was also a caring older brother and quadmate, a good teacher, and he was going to make an excellent Guardian.

His future bonded mate would be a lucky girl.

For the first time, I let myself admit, only for a moment, that I wished she could be me.

FOR THE NEXT FEW WEEKS, I THREW MYSELF INTO MY STUDIES and focused on rehabbing my shoulder. I prepared for midterms with my friends in the dorm study rooms most weeknights. I ran laps around the bleachers of the arena while the rest of the trainees did combat drills. I lifted weights and drank a lot of coffee.

I kept my hands and mouth to myself when I sat next to Elijah in our shared class. He seemed fine—cordial, easygoing, and studious as always. He didn't bring up Kace's attack on me, but I caught him staring at my shoulder sometimes, like he was contemplating violence.

It had become a constant struggle to ignore the way my body and my beast acted around him, not to mention the others in his quad, but all I could do was keep my eye on the prize—full health and being ready to go hard in training by the time we returned from our two-week-long spring break. The big "open" practice, where we'd have our last quad challenges, was scheduled for after school resumed.

Curfew came again, this time falling midweek. I took my freshly blessed blade, my brother, and George for another patrol around the campus perimeter the night of the New Moon, but all was quiet. A few screeches and shouts in the far-off distance, but no action near our walls.

Curfew expired, and the world outside became safe at night once again just in time for us all to prepare to head home for spring break.

Which was why I looked at Mallory like she was speaking Greek when she announced at breakfast on the last day of classes that most of the students wouldn't be heading home tonight.

"A party?" I asked, my forkful of waffle paused in front of my mouth. "On the lake? Tonight?"

"Yes, and you're going." She pointed her cream-cheese-covered knife at me. "You have no tests left to study for, no wraiths to kill, and no spells to cast under the Full Moon. And Dr. Lee cleared you for normal activity. You have no excuses not to be social."

"Except that half the campus thinks I'm an uppity female who deserves to be ripped apart."

Mal waved a dismissive hand. "It's more like a third. We don't care about them."

"*And* it may be our last big pre-spring break lake bash at this insane mansion," Allen added. "The Crimson Quad graduates this year, and it's Kellan Crimson's family's house."

I'd heard whispers about this quad. They were the next hottest thing on the market besides the Blackwell Quad, and they were in the senior Guardian training class. The seniors trained separately from the rest of us because, I assumed, they were out fighting real wraiths. Kellan Crimson was also a griffin shifter—a mythic, like Elijah, and one of only two in the school and probably the entire state of Georgia.

Chance nodded enthusiastically, his puka-shell necklaces clacking. "There's a two-tiered swimming pool, Avery."

"*And*," Mallory went on, an evil gleam entering her green eyes, "there are plenty of eligible males in this school, thirsting after our hot new sword-wielding female. The Blue Moon Ball is next month, friend, and we should start interviewing candidates for your date."

Ian had watched all of this with his chin propped in his hand, his blue eyes alight with glee.

"Shut up," I told him.

He sat back and put a scandalized hand to his chest. "*Moi*? I said nothing."

"You were thinking it."

He grinned. "Listen to our friends. They have sage advice. We're in *college* now. When are we ever going to get to attend a rager at a lake mansion? We're going, end of discussion."

I sighed. When in Rome, as they say, and I did hate to rain on my little brother's parade. "Fine. But *you* have to call Dad and tell him we won't be back home until some ungodly hour in the middle of the night."

He saluted me, and Mal clapped her hands in excitement. "Yes! Wear something sexy, Avery. Your swords do not count."

30

AVERY

"Uh, this is where the party is?" I craned my neck to stare at the monstrosity of a house through my car's windshield.

"You're surprised?" Ian asked from the passenger seat. "The elder Crimson Quad owns one of the most profitable techno-rune development companies in the entire country. That's six million dollars' worth of twenty-first century lunar magic right there."

"Six million?"

He shrugged. "I stalked the online real estate listing. The house is eleven thousand square feet."

I believed it. We'd been directed to park wherever we could find a spot on the vast lawn, it was there I learned that the two stories visible on approach were actually *five* stories on the backside slope down to the lake. At least four balconies jutted off the back of the house, overlooking an expansive two-level patio, and a winding external staircase led to the top of a tower that rose from the middle of the roof.

Brody parked his Jeep next to us. Ian jumped from the

car and threw himself into Brody's arms as if the forty-five minutes they'd been apart on this drive had been forty-five years. They both wore sweatshirts over swim trunks, their feet clad in flip-flops like we were sunning ourselves at the beach and not shivering in the mountains of Northern Georgia.

I cast a longing look at my duffel bag where it sat on the backseat. I'd packed my swords carefully away in there, but the itch to get them out and strap them to my back was strong. I was in a strange place, though with not-so-strange people, but the party atmosphere could bring out the violent side of some shifters. I didn't know what to expect.

After I slid from behind the wheel, I shrugged my fleece jacket over the flimsy little top I wore at Mallory's insistence. She did lose the battle over the tiny skirt she suggested I pair with the top. It was jeans or I wasn't going at all.

Rolling my shoulders, I took a deep breath and squinted up at the house again.

"For the love of the Moon, Aves, act like you've been to a party before."

I glared at Ian and waved a dramatic arm at the house. "We have never even *sniffed* at this kind of wealth, Ian. It's a lot to take in."

Brody chuckled, sliding his hand into Ian's. "Come on, you two. It's just hanging out with all the people we see every day—just with slightly less clothing than usual."

They set off up the winding sidewalk that led to the back patio, and I trudged along after them.

At least fifty people milled around both levels of the stone patio, and more were in the pool, which was indeed two-tiered. A hot tub connected via a stone waterfall to a large infinity pool overlooking the dark waters of the lake. Water cascaded from the pool into an only slightly smaller pool down below. Partygoers floated and splashed and drank from plastic cups with straws that lit up like glow sticks.

Brody and Ian fist-bumped a bunch of Support Squadron guys on the way into the house, and I managed a wave at a freshman girl I knew from Aiden's class. She was the serious, studious type, so I was not expecting to see her atop a float in a tiny bikini while a gregarious guy I knew to be a hyena shifter did body shots out of her bellybutton.

Inside were three different living rooms under two-story vaulted ceilings, a media room hosting an aggressive video game competition, and a professional DJ. Students spilled out of the huge kitchen, where there appeared to be a keg and at least two bartenders slinging drinks from a mountain of liquor bottles lined up on the counter.

Kind of ridiculous. Shifter blood burned through booze quickly, though if we went on a real bender, we could get a buzz for an hour or so. Alcohol at parties was more about the atmosphere.

"Where the hell are Mal and the rest of the group?" I shouted at the side of Ian's face.

He shrugged. "Around here somewhere. We'll find them."

Brody handed me a cup of something fruity for the journey. We wandered past a set of wide-open French doors, which led to a large side patio. Phoebe Atkins— beautiful, blonde, Heath's number-one fan—was on that patio, delicately sipping something *not* in a plastic cup. Her bright floral beach dress and coordinating bikini was the epitome of well-bred-Southern-girl resort chic. She was surrounded by several of her similarly dressed besties— mostly girls who'd already bonded to their Prime quad of choice. Some of those guys milled around the patio, too, their attention bouncing between their bros and their bonds.

Phoebe curled her perfect lip as I walked by, then she leaned in to whisper something to one of her friends. The girl glanced my way, rolled her eyes, and the two of them giggled together.

Neat.

Mal certainly wasn't on that patio, so we were moving on.

We hadn't gone ten more steps into a spacious room containing a bar, a shuffleboard table, and two pool tables when we ran into another bitch who did not like me.

"Ugh, no, this room is at capacity," Callista declared from her spot perched on the edge of one of the pool tables. "Find somewhere else to hang out, freak."

I looked at Ian. "Is she talking to you or me? I didn't know your proclivities had become public knowledge around campus."

"I sure hope so," he replied. His grin widened at Callista's rapidly flushing face. "I'd hate to think I was being out-freaked by my boring sister."

Callista slid from the table, her thick wedge sandals clomping loudly on the wood floor. She wore a strappy black swimsuit that covered less than a bikini would've on her voluptuous body, the succubus of a shifter boy's wet dreams. Her dark hair was in a sleek ponytail, her bold makeup still perfect and unsmudged by party activities.

Her crew gathered around her. Unlike Phoebe, she had a lot of unbonded friends, so the room was bursting with peacocking Prime males and scantily clad blue-blooded girls. It stank like posturing dominance and horny shifters in here.

"You think you're funny," Callista said, sneering at me.

"Keep it up. Hopefully the next person who pulls a Kace Mahoney will actually finish the job."

Was she still sore about me holding a sword to her throat in the hallway of the Magical Ed building? That was *ages* ago.

"The next person who pulls a Kace Mahoney is going to end up dead," I told her, and I meant it because I'd decided I was no longer taking beatings from my classmates. I let my beast peek through my eyes. "So hopefully no one in this room is thinking about it. We're not at school anymore."

Thick, cloying aggression seeped into the air around us. A few of the guys rumbled angry growls.

A stocky blond dude with a ponytail stepped forward, but Brody slid into his path. "Try it, Jenkins. Avery doesn't need swords or a beast to rip you apart. She'd love to do it, too, after I inform her how underhanded and shitty you were to your fellow trainees last year in your failed attempt at becoming a Guardian."

That was a bluff, because it'd be difficult for me to best a guy that big without blades or beast, but I appreciated Brody's confidence in me.

"Look," I said to the group, "we're just trying to find our friends. They're clearly not here, so we'll be on our way."

We did not need to get into a brawl in this room, especially because Ian and Brody, while scrappy, would be ordinary shifters facing Primes, and none of us had our weapons.

"There you are!"

A relieved sigh left my chest. "Hey, Mal."

She trotted into the room, wearing a bright green bikini and a crocheted sarong. Allen and Chance followed on her heels, both barefoot and shirtless, their lean muscles glistening with water droplets.

"Oh, ew, no," she said, surveying the room. "Why are you guys in here? Ash and some of the crew are on one of the upstairs balcony patios. Let's go."

"Yes, please get the stench of filthy female animal out of here," the stocky blond, Jenkins, growled. "The disgusting cat mixing with whatever the fuck Baxter is hiding is making my beer taste like shit."

An angry snarl ripped from Allen's throat, and golden fur rippled across his chest. He lunged for Jenkins, whose brown eyes had turned to molten honey, his nostrils flaring like a bull's.

Ian and Brody tackled Allen to the ground. He struggled under them, but his fur faded away as Brody expressed some rather impressive dominance, forcing Allen's wolf to settle.

Mallory, bless her, just rolled her eyes at her bonded mate's antics. "Yes, Avery and I are taking our stink upstairs. Have the night y'all deserve!"

She grabbed my hand and dragged me from the room, while Ian, Brody, and Chance shoved Allen out behind us.

I RESTED MY ELBOWS ON THE RAILING OF ONE OF THE FOURTH-floor balconies as I surveyed the pool deck below. The cascading waters were lit up in a vibrant aquamarine, and there were at least two dozen students floating and splashing around. Twice as many were scattered around the deck, half naked and trying valiantly to get a buzz from their drinks.

Ian and Brody had taken a dip and were now prancing around shirtless and damp, talking to people. Hungry gazes tracked their every move. It made me immensely thankful that Ian was so solidly *with* Brody, which meant I would not have to hunt him down later and drag him off whichever panting boy he decided to get naked and sweaty with when I wanted to leave.

Mal and the rest of the crew had taken over the patio furniture on the balcony. Chance was entertaining the group by reading tarot cards for a few bright-eyed freshmen girls who'd wandered by.

"Why aren't you down there?"

The voice startled me out of my lazy people-watching. A guy I recognized as one of Allen's peripheral friends leaned against the railing, his back toward the pool and his dark-blue eyes focused intently on me. He was at least five inches taller than me and had shaggy dark hair and an intense five o'clock shadow.

Julian, maybe? A black bear shifter, but his beast was closer to the size of a smaller black bear found in the wild, which made him ordinary rather than Prime. Bear shifters, unlike wolves, were more likely to be Primes, but smaller bears weren't that uncommon. This guy played on the school's club lacrosse team, if I recalled Allen's hasty intro-duction from weeks ago correctly. I'd learned that shifter-only schools did not participate in national collegiate athletics for obvious reasons, but they did have their own club leagues.

I shrugged and gave him a polite smile. "Didn't bring my suit. Should've expected a place like this to have a heated pool. Two, even."

Julian laughed under his breath. His wet swimsuit clung to strong, meaty thighs, and he'd thrown a jacket over his top half. On the jacket's left chest was the Proteus College logo, two lacrosse sticks bisecting it like crossbones. "Fair enough. I forget it's your first time at a Crimson party." He took a swig of the beer in his hand, and then he slanted an apologetic look my way. "First and last, I guess, since those rich fuckers are graduating."

"Surely another one of these power quads has a five-story lake house and will pick up the mantle," I said wryly.

He laughed again. "We can only hope. The big pre-break party is always a highlight. A chance to let loose. Maybe find an excuse to talk to a very interesting and very hot girl on the quiet corner of a balcony."

The tentative, hopeful smile he gave me just then might've fooled one of those bright-eyed freshmen, but this wasn't my first rodeo. Julian was smooth, and he was here to get laid. At his core, he was a predator, and he hadn't had the pleasure of seeing me skewer large violent beasts, both real and conjured, so I probably looked like tasty prey.

I didn't hate it. He was attractive, and Allen didn't let bigots and assholes into even his wider circle of friends.

But the intensity of that pretty blue gaze, which had politely never strayed from my face, didn't create sparks under my skin. There was no exciting flutter in my belly. My beast hadn't even rolled over and opened an eye at this guy.

It hit me that I'd stumbled over the "I'm fucked" line, after all.

"'Interesting' is the polite way of putting it," I replied with a self-depreciating chuckle. "More like controversial, wouldn't you say? A pot-stirrer? A drama queen?"

His gaze finally strayed down to my chest and then to the sliver of exposed stomach between my top and my jeans. He leaned in to whisper in my ear, his pine scent surging. My beast huffed irritably. "I like controversial. It's sexy. *Intriguing.* I want to know more—"

"Step away from her, Julian, before I rip out your spleen and throw it in the pool."

He stiffened, and I blew out a resigned breath. My beast's ears perked up, her pleased rumble echoing deep within me.

Definitely fucked.

Wyatt stood in the wide doorway, a lazy smile on his face that did not match the red sheen rolling over his eyes. He'd either just arrived or wasn't planning on partaking in water activities, because he wore his usual dark, distressed jeans, boots, and a white V-neck T-shirt that showed off the tattoos that decorated his neck and chest.

Julian shifted a bit, but he didn't abandon his spot next to me at the railing. "What's this, Gale?" he said, lifting his chin, his tone hostile. "Are you pissing a circle around the new girl? Since when does a *Prime* bear from a fancy quad have any interest in a shifting female?"

You know, with all the beatings I'd taken this semester because I refused to shift, it was tragically funny that everyone had declared me a shifting female anyway.

Wyatt's smile slipped. "Fuck off before I make you."

Julian tried valiantly to hold Wyatt's wild red glare, but it was no use. He dropped his stare to the floor and swore loudly. "See you around, Avery," he muttered, and then he slunk off.

I crossed my arms over my chest and reclined against the railing. I lifted a brow, inviting Wyatt to explain himself.

The red in his irises cooled to his usual bright green, and his lazy smirk returned. He held my stare with all the authority of one of the most powerful and desired males in school for a few long seconds, and then he finally spoke. "You and I have business, Wildcat."

My brow went higher. "Do we?"

He lunged for me and grabbed my hand, interlacing our

fingers together. He began to pull me back into the house. "Come here."

"Wyatt!"

"Just for a few minutes."

I tossed a pleading look over my shoulder at Mal, who smiled and raised her glass. She was draped across Allen's lap, and he could only shrug helplessly at me. No one on this balcony was going to tangle with Wyatt Gale, and Ian—who would have no such qualms—was inconveniently in the hot tub many stories below us.

Wyatt led me down a long hallway, home to what I presumed were a fraction of the twelve bedrooms in the mansion. All the doors were closed, and my enhanced hearing allowed me to pick up a hint of the activities going on behind those doors. Wyatt better not have been planning to invade any of these rooms because I didn't desire to accidentally glimpse a classmate's bare ass.

"Moondamn all these horny assholes," Wyatt muttered.

"Where are you taking me?" I demanded. "And where are the rest of your overbearing band of brothers?"

He tried a door handle and swore when he found it locked. "Aiden doesn't come to college parties anymore, babe. He and Heath went home to covertly chaperone another date Clara is being forced to go on tonight."

"Oh." My relief for Clara distracted me for a solid two seconds. "Good."

"And Elijah's around here somewhere. Last I saw, he was shooting the shit with the avians. The raptors are less afraid of him than most—ah, *jackpot*." He shoved through an unlocked door and yanked me inside.

"Wyatt—"

He flipped the light on. We were in a laundry room that was damn near the size of my whole dorm room. Pristine custom cabinets lined one wall alongside a sink and small refrigerator. On the opposite wall sat a large washer and dryer, a white granite countertop fitted across the top of both. A window overlooked the vast lawn that sloped down to the lake. A plush rug covered the cold tile floor.

Real home-improvement-channel porn right here.

"Can't believe no one's fucking in this room," I mused. "Look at all this *space*."

"Their loss is my gain." Wyatt grabbed me around the waist and hoisted me onto the countertop above the washer and dryer.

"Wyatt!" I yelped. "I am not going to fuck you. Obviously. Come on."

"I know that, Wildcat." He slotted his body between my legs and wrapped his big hands around my thighs.

I gripped the edge of the counter, frozen in place. Fire burned in my belly at his nearness. His eyes blazed—not red, but a bright, shimmery green—as he searched my face. A lock of his dark red hair had flopped onto his forehead, softening the dangerous predator between my legs into something a little bit boyish.

"But I've decided," he went on, "that I'm ready to collect on our bet."

"What?"

He tutted. "Nice try. I never got that kiss you owe me from when my bear bested you."

My stomach swooped. He was right.

Wyatt's nearness had my beast purring like a chainsaw, which drowned out all my common sense.

He lifted a hand to brush my hair away from my face. That sweet gesture morphed quickly into something *more* as he threaded his fingers through my hair and gripped it tightly. I couldn't turn away from him even if I'd wanted to.

"Say yes," he whispered, his eyes darkening.

"Has anyone ever told you no?" I whispered back.

A deep chuckle. "Not a heterosexual female."

Of course not.

"One kiss," I said. I meant to sound firm, but my words just came out all breathy and stupid.

Another chuckle. "Sure, Wildcat."

He cupped the back of my head possessively, and he pressed his lips to mine. I melted into his hold, the heat burning low in my belly, making my body soft and pliant for him. He growled his approval, and his tongue pressed against the seam of my lips, demanding and sure.

He consumed me then, and I let him. My arms found their way around his neck, and his hands wandered up under my shirt, rough fingertips skimming the skin over my ribs. He was leisurely with his kisses, exploring, probing, plundering. He took what he wanted, and I gave it willingly.

"Mmm, this is well worth all the holes you put in my bear when we sparred," he purred against my cheek.

I stifled what would've been an obscene moan as he began to trail his lips down my throat, nipping and then soothing with his kiss.

"*Wyatt*," I gasped as he yanked the straps of my top down my arms, taking the built-in bra with them and exposing my breasts to the cool air.

"Fucking perfect, Wildcat," he rumbled, kissing down my chest.

"This is not one kiss!"

He paused and looked at me, green eyes blazing as he cradled my tits in his hands. "Do you want me to stop?"

"I—"

The door clicked open. I let out a tiny squeal, and Wyatt pulled me against his body, concealing my naked chest from the intruder. He whipped a look over his shoulder, his expression murderous.

A split second later, he relaxed, his chest rumbling against me as he laughed.

"There you two are," Elijah said with a wicked grin. He wore one of his usual unbuttoned linen shirts, ratty jeans that molded to the taut muscles of his legs, and no shoes. He locked the door and leaned against it. "Dove, you look flushed and delicious."

Wyatt narrowed his eyes at Elijah. "Can you keep it together near her like this?"

Elijah's irises went molten gold, and his pupils narrowed. "Yes. I'll stay over here," vowed the sexy, terrifying monster, whose sole focus was now on me. "Is that okay, Dove?"

I swallowed roughly. "You want to... watch?"

He gifted me with a gorgeous, fangy smile. "Please."

The need within me was a blazing inferno now. "Okay," I whispered.

"Fuck yes," Wyatt said. He stole another blistering kiss, feeding me his tongue, and I moaned into his mouth.

He dipped his head and wrapped his lips around my nipple, sucking hard. He rubbed his thumb gently across the other nipple as he licked and sucked. I gasped, shutting my eyes and reveling in Wyatt's touch. His body was hot and hard between my legs, and he smelled like a crackling fire.

Wyatt switched breasts, groaning happily, and I opened my eyes, locking stares with Elijah. Those eerie, glowing yellow orbs drank in what Wyatt was doing to me like he needed every drop to survive.

"Gorgeous, Dove," he said, his words ragged. "I think Wyatt should make you come."

A growl ripped from Wyatt's throat. "*Fuck.*"

"I said *one kiss*," I moaned despondently. "Why can't I think straight around you four?"

Wyatt licked my nipple one more time before bringing his lips back to my face and kissing along my jaw. "All four of us, huh? That's convenient, baby."

No, it wasn't. It was so *inconvenient*, and it was starting to make me want things I couldn't have.

Wyatt's fingers went to the button of my jeans, and I had to decide if I was doing this.

Again.

I let out a tortured moan. "Wyatt—"

A loud knock sounded behind Elijah at the door. "Avery Baxter! I know you're in there with Gale!"

Wyatt's fingers froze. He heaved a frustrated sigh and dropped his forehead onto my shoulder.

Elijah, however, was unbothered. "I can send your brother on his way, Dove. I'll be nice."

"Avery! That bear better not be touching your bikini areas. I will go get my sword out of the car."

"Why is your brother such a cockblock?" Wyatt muttered into my shoulder.

"He is normally very supportive of me getting laid," I said. Elijah's sly smile slipped, and Wyatt's hand tightened where it was wrapped around my thigh. "But he thinks you guys are particularly bad news for me."

Wyatt pulled my shirt up over my chest and secured the straps on my shoulders. He smoothed the fabric almost reluctantly, and then he stepped away, officially releasing me from his clutches. He shot me an apologetic smile. "He's not wrong."

Lust fog—cleared. I returned his tight smile. "Right."

Another aggressive knock. "Aves!"

I hopped down from the counter and headed for the

door. Elijah watched me curiously, opening the door to allow me to slip past him.

"Have a good break, Dove. See you soon."

"Bye, Elijah."

As he shut the door behind me, I met my brother's accusing stare with my tired one. "Can we go home?"

His face softened immediately. "Yeah. Let's go home."

31

HEATH

Aiden and I watched in silence as two chrome Mercedes SUVs crawled up the long, canopied driveway of our parents' estate. The occupants would be met at the front door by our house manager.

"That looks like the Nelsons again," Aiden mused as he studied the cars from our perch—the large balcony off our shared quarters. "Do you think Dad's decided to force Clara on a second date with them?"

"Probably," I muttered. "Their parents are by far the richest of any of the families he's been dangling her in front of."

It'd been a long two-week break in the Blackwell household. Clara had gone on three more dates with shitty teenage Primes our parents had selected. Aiden and I made sure one of us was always in the house, keeping an eye on the situation, so that we could shadow any dates she was whisked away on.

Our dads—both Holden and Stephen—decided that Aiden and I had made enough trouble already, so they kept the details of these dates to themselves until the last possible minute. They also quit telling Mom anything because she'd proved susceptible to being sweet-talked out of information by her sons.

The cars parked at the top of the estate's circular driveway. The Nelson kids exited the first Mercedes and swaggered to the door in their best suits. They were a newly formed quad and all Prime felines, which was typical of Dad. The two Nelson sons were lion shifters, and their two best friends were a leopard and a jaguar.

The second SUV spat out the elder Nelson Quad and their bonded mate—a diminutive redheaded woman wearing a dark-green pantsuit.

Dread began to pool in my gut.

"I don't like this," I said to Aiden. "If their parents are here, that means Dad's trying to make a deal."

"You're right," he said, shoving off the stone railing.

I was already headed for the balcony doors. "We need to know what's going on."

He followed me back into our living room. Once we'd both graduated from prep school and formed our quad, Dad allowed us to move out of our childhood bedrooms and into a guest wing on the third floor of the house. We had a four-bedroom apartment to ourselves, but nothing would feel like *ours* as long as we were under the roof of Blackwell Manor.

We left our wing and snuck quietly down two flights of stairs. When we reached the landing overlooking the grand foyer, we were just in time to watch Mom and the Nelsons' mate lead a sullen Clara away, the older women exchanging performative niceties as they went.

Mom's two fat corgis scuttled along after them.

Holden and Stephen greeted the elder Nelson Quad

with handshakes, and then they all disappeared down the hallway leading to our dads' offices.

That left the younger Nelson Quad milling around in the foyer. They didn't look particularly excited to be here.

I was about to storm down the stairs and demand an explanation as to what exactly was going on when Aiden grabbed my arm and pulled me out of sight. We crouched low, peering through the slats in the imperial staircase that was the centerpiece of the manor's grand entrance.

"It's bullshit we're supposed to wait for the bonding to start fucking her." That was Anthony Nelson, oldest Nelson son and the leader. He had the look of an all-American high school quarterback. Tall, handsome, wavy brown mane, blinding white smile.

He was also about to be dead.

"Easy," Aiden warned.

His brother, James, snorted as he adjusted his tie. "What our parents know won't hurt them, man. You know these latent bitches—they're gagging for Prime cock."

Now I was the one to grab Aiden before he climbed the railing. "Settle down. We won't let them touch her."

"At least she's hot," one of the non-Nelsons drawled from where he slumped against the wall. "Your parents could've bought us an ugly central bond. This one's Prime feline blood and has a nice rack and a tight ass. Even if we have to wait a few months, it could be worse."

"I dunno, man," said the last guy. "We're going off to college in the fall, and she still has to finish high school. Are we really expected not to fuck all the willing pussy at Proteus just because they found us a bond this early? Get real."

Anthony shrugged a bulky shoulder. "If she has a problem with it, I'll just knock her around a bit. Dad says it's the job of the quad leader to keep the bitch in line. Centrals can get uppity."

That was it. I jumped to my feet and stalked down the stairs, Aiden hot on my heels.

My wolf was howling for blood. When I hit the bottom of the stairs and the little assholes saw me coming, their spines went ramrod straight.

Anthony pasted a bland, polite smile on his face and extended his hand. "Hey, Heath, how's it go—"

"Listen up, Nelson," I said, my voice low and full of murder. "If you touch my sister, ever, in any way whatsoever, I will kill you. This bonding is not happening."

His face turned haughty. "Well, that isn't really up to you, is it, bro?"

"Did my brother stutter?" Aiden said, his tone just as haughty. "Welcome to the real world of being a Prime shifter, Nelson. Go ahead and challenge him, beast to beast, and see what happens."

An amber sheen flashed over Anthony's brown eyes, a growl reverberating in his throat. He stepped toward me, and I let my wolf surge to the surface. I pressed, bending him to my will, and he snarled as his spine bowed instantly.

"Does anyone else have any smart comments?" Aiden asked.

"Boys!" Holden's voice boomed from the hallway.

Our dads strode into the foyer, the elder Nelsons in tow.

"What's going on out here?" Holden asked.

"Nothing," Anthony replied, straightening and wiping his brow.

Dad, perceptive as always, slid me an annoyed glare before returning to his polite business face. "I see. Well, we appreciate everyone stopping by to finalize things. Your mother should back shortly so you can say goodbye to Clara before you leave."

"Dad—" I began.

"Quiet, Heath," he snapped, his words a physical whip against my flesh.

My wolf clawed at the bars of his cage. I clenched my teeth and sucked in a calming breath.

Mom came trotting around the corner with Clara and the Nelsons' mate. "Oh, look, your fathers have finished up already," she gushed happily.

The moms air-kissed each other's cheeks obnoxiously before Mrs. Nelson rejoined her mates, pressing herself into the nearest man's side.

Mom gave Clara a light shove in the younger Nelsons' direction. "Say goodbye to your future bondmates, honey. Hopefully they can pop by on occasion to take you out between all their classes and activities at Apollo Prep." She winked at Anthony, who returned an oily smile.

Aiden snagged a flustered Clara before she was within touching distance of any of those shitheads, and then he wrapped an arm around her shoulders. "Yes, good luck with the rest of your semester," he said tonelessly to them. "Clara will let you know if she's interested in going out with you again."

One of the elder Nelsons let out a boisterous laugh. "Well, she better be! She'll be doing a lot more than that with our boys after they've bonded!"

Mom had the decency to wrinkle her nose at that inappropriate statement, but our dads didn't blink an eye.

"Um, yeah," Clara said with a half-hearted wave. "Bye, guys. Happy almost-graduation."

Anthony looked like he was about to rip Clara away

from Aiden, but he must've decided he didn't have a death wish. He forced a smile at her. "We'll be seeing you, doll."

He jerked his head at the front door, and his quad followed him out without another word.

Our dads and the rest of the Nelsons exchanged fake smiles and another round of hearty handshakes, and then the rest of our visitors finally left, the slam of the heavy front doors behind them booming like a cannon blast in the cavernous, cold foyer.

"What did you do?" I growled at Dad between clenched teeth.

"I've secured Clara's future and ours, Heath," he replied irritably. He swept his long mane of hair over his shoulder and folded his arms across his chest with a derisive sneer. "The Nelsons have offered to sell to our firm a controlling stake in one of the most profitable companies in their portfolio. We've been trying to get into magical pharmaceuticals for a while now, and now that our families are to be *joined*, as it were, they are offering to sell that slice of equity at an unbelievable price."

"That unbelievable price is *your daughter's body and soul*, Dad," I snapped. "How could you? What fucking year is this?"

Mom wrung her hands. "Oh, Heath, please don't talk to your father that way."

Stephen cut me a scathing glare. We used to be close, he and I, until my wolf surpassed his in dominance and power. "You don't make the decisions in this family, son. Arranged bondings are still alive and well in the highest echelons of our society. We are securing this family's legacy while you and your brother run off to play soldier."

"Clara likes the Nelson boys," Mom insisted. "Don't you, honey?"

My sister could only stare at the marble floor. "I've only really met them once, Mom."

Holden waved a dismissive hand at that. "You'll have plenty of time to get to know them. There is no higher calling for a shifter female, Clara. You honor the Moon by becoming a blessed vessel for a group of fine young Prime males."

"Right," she muttered.

"And it's okay with you, Dad, that I just overhead Anthony Nelson brag about his right to 'knock around' his mate if he feels like it?" I asked, seething. "You're still feeling good about selling your daughter into a life of abuse at the hands of her bonded?"

Clara gasped.

Mom looked anywhere but at me.

Dad's expression turned to ice. "I'm quite sure you're exaggerating, Heath. If Clara behaves as a good mate and spouse should, then no such thing should be necessary."

Aiden and I could only gape at him. To my knowledge, none of my fathers had ever put their hands on my mother in that way, but she'd never done anything but exactly what they'd asked of her since they'd bonded the year before Aiden was born.

Holden slanted a harsh glare at Aiden and then back at me. "That's enough out of you two. Do not interfere with this match, or I will make your lives hell. Clara will bond with her mates under the Full Moon after her seventeenth birthday, and that's the last we'll be discussing it."

"The fuck she will," I growled. My wolf rose. Fur ghosted down my arms and my chest. My vision sharpened, and a snarl tore from my chest.

Dad loomed, his lion emerging. The gray of his eyes pooled into molten silver, and his long hair thickened. His body seemed to grow larger, muscles swelling and veins popping.

His gaze snared mine, and I held on, my wolf pushing against the weight of his unspoken command to yield.

It was excruciating. Knives dug into my skull. My wolf trembled in my chest, snarling, growling, shaking his head wildly. I could shift, let him out, force my dad to fight me beast-to-beast, smear our blood all over these marble floors and hope I lived to fight another day.

I'd give him a better fight than I would've even a year ago, but the force of the power he could channel from his quad as a bonded Prime would be overwhelming—it was *now* as he battered ruthlessly at me, and his lion would be able to do the same.

I didn't think he would kill me, but I grew less sure of that by the day. If he had to choose me or the mountains of money to be made in magical pharma, he'd probably rip my throat out and mourn me later.

My vision went spotty, narrowing so that those glowing pools of silver were all I could see. My body swayed.

"Heath," Aiden said quietly. Urgently. "Let's go. We're not going to settle this tonight."

I dropped my gaze to the floor. The pressure relented instantly.

Dad let out a satisfied chuckle. "You are impressive, son. But you aren't me."

He snapped his fingers at Mom, and she hopped to, following him out of the room, her hands trembling and her eyes glassy. Stephen gave all three of us a disgusted look before stalking back down the hall that led to his office.

Aiden's hand landed on my shoulder. "You okay?"

"Yeah." I shook out my limbs. "We need to talk. All of us."

32

WYATT

Elijah picked me up on his way to Heath and Aiden's house, rescuing me from the two weeks of torture I'd endured at the hands of my four little sisters. Willow in particular had been a real problem, sneaking out of the house three different times in the middle of the moondamned night. I'd had to hunt her down and remove her from two college house parties and what had been basically a drunken orgy in a field.

I was too young for gray hair, for fuck's sake.

But I was reminded once again that dealing with Willow was nothing in comparison to what Heath and Aiden were facing when it came to Clara.

We'd arrived at Blackwell Manor half an hour ago, and we'd spent most of that time sitting in Heath and Aiden's living room, staring at one another like a bunch of morose fuckers after Heath explained that Clara's time was officially about to run out. We only had about six months until she turned seventeen.

"I can just kill them," Elijah suggested with all the seriousness of someone throwing out an idea for what to eat for dinner. Instead of taking a chair or section of the huge couch like a normal person, he was sitting on top of the dining table, his long legs swinging aimlessly. "The Nelson boys will be at Proteus in the fall. I'm certain one of those little cretins will manage to provoke my beast, and I can keep the reins extra loose." His expression hardened. "There won't be any more of our female family members harmed on my watch."

Heath rubbed the back of his neck, worry heavy on his face. "You know we can't let you do that, man. Not only will they expel you, but at some point, the Council may decide you're too dangerous to let live. We aren't Guardians until we graduate."

"I'll do it, then," I said with a shrug. "Bear rage is unpredictable. My dad will probably still let me into the Guardians, and I don't give a fuck about my degree."

Aiden rolled his eyes skyward. "As much as I share everyone's desire for murder, it doesn't solve the problem. Dad will just sell Clara to the next-highest bidder."

Clara sat on the couch cushion next to mine, hugging her knees into her chest, a blanket wrapped around her shoulders. She'd been staring at the wall in a daze the entire time we'd been here.

George, who Elijah had snuck into the house in a duffle bag, was curled up at her feet like a docile puppy. It appeared his joint combat adventure with the wildcat had extended the list of people he tolerated to include Clara.

"I'll just run away," Clara said tonelessly. "Maybe Avery's dads will take me in. I can be a city girl."

Heath frowned. Elijah suddenly found a rip in his jeans very interesting. Aiden pursed his lips.

Avery's flushed face, her moans, the taste of her skin, the feel of her tits in my hands—it all flashed through my brain.

She was a wet dream and my own personal fucking nightmare.

And now that her name had been spoken aloud, we were going to have to address that beautiful, infuriating elephant in the room.

"No, Clara," Heath said. "First of all, there's nowhere you could run that Dad and the power of the Council couldn't find you. Second, you deserve to be able to live your life free and happy. I'm going to get that for you. We all are."

He cast a look around at each of us, but he didn't have to. We all knew.

We had a job to do. One that hadn't exactly felt like a sacrifice until a few months ago.

"We'll bond before your birthday, and then I'll formally challenge Dad for custody of you," he told her.

She sucked in a surprised breath. Heath had promised his sister he'd protect her, but this was the first time he was admitting our plan to her.

"It's the only way, Clara," Heath continued. "There are strict rules set by the Council for intra-family disputes, and custody is one of them. But once I win, it's ironclad. *No one* —not our other dads, not Mom—can take you away from us unless they want to challenge me directly."

"You're going to bond so you can be more powerful," Clara said, eyes widening. "You should bond with Avery."

It was a brick landing in my gut, the feeling so visceral that bile rose in my mouth. My bear snarled.

"Avery has a beast," Aiden told her, his jaw so tense, his teeth might've cracked.

Clara shrugged. "I know. She told me."

What?

At our incredulous looks, she frowned. "Why are y'all looking at me like that? You just said she has a beast."

"She's never *admitted* it," Heath said slowly. "To us or anyone, as far as we know. Though it's obvious if you've seen her fight."

"Or her eyes go electric," I added wistfully.

"Or her intriguing aura," Elijah said, his irises shining yellow-gold before he snuffed them out.

"But she's been insisting on keeping up this charade that she's latent," Aiden said, "presumably because it's why the school let her in and gave her scholarship money. I can't believe she just told you outright."

Clara just shrugged again. "Well, she did it so I wouldn't be scared when Paul and Harrison were coming for me." She scrunched her brows, tapping her chin with a pink fingernail. "Do you think she's a Prime? Is that why she's so secretive about it?"

I barked a laugh. "Yeah, right."

"We did consider it," Heath told her. "Female Primes are exceedingly rare—as rare as mythics. But it wouldn't make sense for her to hide it if she was. She's been attacked multiple times by Prime males, and if shifting into her animal would've helped her win those fights and avoid injury, she would've done it by now."

"Not to mention the fact that her lack of Prime beast is the real hurdle to her becoming a Guardian, much more so than her being female," Aiden added. "And she wants that badly."

"For some unknown reason," Heath muttered, "she has a death wish. A reckless streak. An insufferable hero complex."

I patted Clara's knee. "She's probably a fox like her brother. Or maybe a wolf or cat. She can still be your hero, princess."

She narrowed her eyes at Heath. "But she can't be my

sister."

His face was an emotionless mask. "No."

Whatever these feelings were, they were slowly fucking poisoning me. The worst of them all was this miserable, nagging guilt I felt no matter which direction I turned.

I let the bear's rage seep in, and I'd keep doing it until I couldn't feel anything else.

Clara shrugged off her blanket and stood up. Her eyes glistened, but she sucked in a breath and blinked the tears away. "I wish I was strong enough to insist that you not do this for me, Heath." She looked around the room. "Any of you. But I'm not. I hope you find what you're looking for."

She padded out of the room, her bare feet silent on the wood floors as she went.

Elijah whistled. George uncoiled his thick body and slithered away, following her out.

None of us felt compelled to ask what George was up to. We had other shit to deal with.

After a long, tense silence, Heath rose from his chair and made his way to the French doors that led to the apartment's stone patio. The Moon was huge tonight, just a few days past full, its rays skimming the forest of trees below. He studied the scene through the glass like he was begging our deity for answers. "This thing with Avery has to stop," he said, his voice a pained rasp.

"It needed to stop a long time ago," Aiden muttered. "Why is this so fucking hard?"

I snorted a humorless laugh. "Because she's sexy. And wild. And fearless."

"Talented," Aiden added with a wistful sigh. "Smart."

"A gorgeous and intriguing soul." Elijah grinned wickedly. "And I could listen to her sweet moans all day."

"Fuck, that's enough," Heath groaned. "This is what I'm

talking about. We all lose our fucking heads every time she's even mentioned. But there is *zero* question she has a beast soul. Are we in agreement about that?"

We all grunted an affirmative noise.

"We need to cut this obsession out at the roots, unless we want to roll the dice with a weaker, unstable central bond." Heath banged a fist against the thick glass of the door. "And I can't do that." He sounded so crushed, and it only fanned the flames of my bear's rage. "I can't risk Clara. I have to take on my dad with every advantage I can muster."

Aiden watched his brother crumble, wearing his own heartbreak on his face. "That's it. Avery Baxter is nothing to us from now on." He swallowed roughly. "And we need to treat her as such."

Elijah's yellow stare pierced our jaguar. "No. She doesn't deserve that."

"Of course she doesn't," Aiden snapped. "But it's better if she hates us."

Dark-red fur rippled down my arms. I shook my head violently. "Fuck. This sucks."

"I won't do it," Elijah hissed. "I agreed to bond with whatever girl you three managed to agree on, but I won't hurt my dove."

Aiden shook his head. "You have to stop calling her that. She agitates your beast and threatens your control. Out of all of us, *you're* the one who should've steered clear of her a long time ago."

Elijah hissed at him, his grip tightening around the edge of the table. He sucked in a slow, deep breath. When he exhaled, all the fight drained right out of him. His shoulders slumped, and he went back to playing with the rip in his jeans.

"And it's going to hurt her anyway, Elijah," Heath added,

his voice a sad rasp. "Better for her to want nothing to do with us now before we're waltzing around school bonded to... Phoebe Atkins." He had trouble getting that name out, which was rich, considering she'd been among his top contenders only a few months ago. "Or whoever."

Aiden cleared his throat and slanted a chastising look my way. "And if Avery steers clear of us, the less likely one of us is to end up threatening guys who talk to her at parties with bodily harm and then groping her tits in a laundry room."

"Oh, fuck off, asshole," I spat. "Like you're the king of control, Mr. 'I held her while she came all over Heath's face.' At the fucking front gates of the school, I might add."

"Yes," Elijah said softly, the mention of our little tryst in the laundry room rousing him from his daze. He looked at Aiden like he was dinner, his pupils slitting dangerously. "Watch where you throw those stones, *Professor*."

"*Enough*," Heath barked. "This shitshow ends now. When we get back to campus, we are actively on the market for a bond. A Prime-blooded, latent female, preferably between our age and Aiden's. We will act like it."

"Which means we can't all be panting after the wildcat, or it sends the wrong message," I drawled. "Fine."

I could pant after other chicks. It was a particular talent of mine, but Avery's mere fucking existence would suck all the fun out of it.

I sank deeper into my bear.

We sat in silence for several long minutes. The tension slowly leeched from the room, and the jagged bite of anger and beastly dominance dissipated, leaving a colorless void of empty fucking nothingness.

Heath went back to staring at the Moon. "We all know what we have to do," he said finally.

I had so much fucking respect for Heath, as a leader and a brother. If it were my sister in trouble, he'd make the same hard decisions for me, without a doubt. My bear pressed against my skin, his fury a comforting blanket. "Yeah," I said darkly. "No more fucking around."

"Agreed," Aiden said. His expression would've been bored but for the turquoise rings glowing around his irises.

Elijah stared off into the distance, his eyes unfocused and his face placid, devoid of all his earlier agitation. "All good things must end, as they say."

Fuck that. We'd make them good again. Someday. Somehow.

We were the most powerful quad in our generation. We deserved to have the things we wanted in this finite fucking life—power, freedom, and the ability to keep our loved ones safe.

And we were going to get those things by whatever means necessary.

33

AVERY

Thirty seconds before I sat down in my Tuesday morning Folklore class, an email hit my phone.

From: Blackwell, Aiden

To: Baxter, Avery

Subject: Tutoring

Dear Miss Baxter,

I'm cancelling our tutoring session tonight and all sessions for the rest of the semester. You've demonstrated sufficient knowledge and skill with the Runes 101 curriculum and will receive an A.

- Professor Blackwell

I stared at it. Aiden hadn't said anything about this before the break, but he had seen me successfully perform a Moon blessing, so maybe I'd earned the rest of the semester off? I'd just have to get over the pinch of disappointment at losing that slice of time with Aiden when I got to be the sole object of his unwavering focus.

Still, something uncomfortable began to churn in my gut.

I'd had a blissful, relaxing spring break at home with my family. I felt good. My shoulder had healed, which I'd accelerated by spending some time as my beast, lounging around in the privacy of our house. Ian had even brushed out my fur, and I swore the extra endorphins had fixed me right up.

Or maybe it was the nightly TLC I'd given myself with thoughts of Wyatt's hot mouth on mine, Elijah's glowing yellow eyes, Aiden's rasp up against my neck, or Heath's demanding tongue between my thighs that'd done it.

As nice as it was to spend time at home, I'd been looking forward to returning to campus. I was ready to kick ass and earn back my place on the leaderboard, but if I was being honest with myself, I'd been looking forward to seeing each member of the Blackwell Quad again. An itch plagued me, like I was an addict jonesing for my next fix of... I didn't know what.

Heath's bossy care? Aiden's praise? Wyatt's panty-melting smile? Elijah's dangerous allure?

But when classes resumed yesterday, something hadn't felt right.

Wyatt and Heath had ignored me completely. It wasn't unusual for them to keep their distance from me during the school days. It wasn't as if I'd expected Wyatt to show up to school and announce we were *something* after our encounter at the lake any more than I'd have expected the same of Heath after what happened between us the night I'd helped Clara.

But I no longer felt the heaviness of their gazes on me when I wasn't looking.

The hyperawareness we had of each other.

The sizzling tension that I'd pretend was my imagination.

As of yesterday, all of it was gone. The difference was stark.

And now Aiden had summarily dismissed me from tutoring.

My beast bristled. *I don't know either.*

The class took a collective breath, which tore my attention from my phone, and Elijah strode into the room.

I braced myself, waiting for him to take his usual path up the center aisle stairs. He'd always pause, and those golden eyes would meet mine. He'd give me a sly, knowing smile, and then he'd make his way to the seat next to mine.

Not this time.

My stomach sank through my chair as he made his way to the far side of the room and offered a fist-bump to a couple of the avian shifters, and then he winked at the blushing girl sitting behind them. My beast hissed angrily within me.

He grabbed a seat, cracked open his backpack to grab his laptop, and settled in to listen to the lecture as he always did.

He didn't even *look* at me. The same guy who'd stared at me like I was the only thing on this planet while his quadmate lit me on fire was now acting like I didn't even exist.

I opened my own laptop. The pages of today's reading assignment blurred. I clenched my teeth tightly together, desperately trying to keep my lip from trembling.

NOTHING CHANGED IN THE WEEKS THAT FOLLOWED.

Heath, Wyatt, and Elijah melted into the crowd of elite students in the dining hall, in the classroom, even in training. They had flirty smiles for the girls who batted their lashes. They joked with and fist-bumped the same assholes who call me an abomination under their breath when we passed in the hallways. During one particularly grueling individual challenge against the SWIM, I took a gorilla-wraith fist to the head so hard, the impact with the arena floor left me with a mild-but-real concussion. Heath didn't even *notice*, much less drag me off to the infirmary to glare at Dr. Lee while he fixed me.

Aiden managed to never look my way in Lunar Magic class.

I hadn't even seen George, and I wondered forlornly if Elijah had convinced him to keep away from me.

At least classes had been busy and the homework heavy. I'd signed up for every individual combat opportunity that was offered to my training class, and I'd managed to gain some ground on the leaderboard, but I still needed to kill some major wraiths with a team if I had any hope of advancing to camp this summer.

And then the day finally arrived—the day the Guardian training program opened the arena to the rest of the school and the public so they could watch our power quads work. Today I would challenge the SWIM with a unit of four and finally earn back my rightful spot on the leaderboard.

I'd been paired with a moderately skilled trio of Primes who Brody assured me were *probably* not going to try to kill me. It would've been unfortunate to experience another simulated soul death, not just because it would be the end of my chance to become a Guardian, but also because the whole damn school was in the bleachers.

But my assigned partners had failed to show up.

Cash was ready to giddily throw me out of the arena and probably the program, but then Ward Gale stepped in.

And now, as I stood at the edge of the arena and warmed

up my shoulder with a few slashes of my sword, a heated conversation unfolded in front of me that made it clear that I hadn't been imagining things these past few weeks.

Something was very wrong.

I could only listen in stunned silence as Heath, Wyatt, and Aiden squared up to Ward and brutally and unapologetically attempted to destroy everything I'd been working for.

"No, Ward," Heath growled. "It doesn't matter that Elijah's not here. We do quad challenges with just the three of us all the time. We don't need a fourth, and we definitely don't need *her*."

"She's not a part of our quad and never will be," Aiden added, sounding as though the idea disgusted him.

That knife through my back hurt like hell. My beast flattened her ears against her head and hissed.

If Ward was surprised by their attitude, he didn't show it. "Overruled. I'm assigning Baxter to your team. Everyone else has a full four."

"We run our attack with full rotation of Prime beasts, Dad," Wyatt drawled. He looked like he didn't really give a shit about anything right now, least of all me. "She'll hinder us."

That was a fucking lie, and they all knew it.

Especially Ward, who raised a single bushy brow. "Oh? If Elijah was here, he'd be shifting?"

They just stared at him.

"That's what I thought. Shut your mouths and sit your asses down. You're up last as the grand finale."

As Ward stalked off, the guys didn't acknowledge my presence. Heath heaved an annoyed sigh then marched over to a nearby bench, and the others dutifully followed. The three of them sat down and spread out, leaving no room for me.

I could take a hint. Sliding my swords back into their sheaths, I walked to an empty bench ten yards further down the way. As I sat down, I kept my attention firmly on the first quad that'd taken the floor to enthusiastic applause.

There was no time or space for me to marinate in this hurt. I had to get on that floor and show that I had what it took to hang with the most talented men in the Guardian program. If I wanted to move back above the cut line, I needed a lot of kills, including several Giants.

Then, and only then, would I allow myself to feel... blindsided? Betrayed? Like an idiot for allowing myself for one second to fantasize about there being something real between me and them?

Because the Blackwell Quad now seemed determined to make it clear that there had been nothing at all.

I searched the crowd and found Ian across the way, seated in the front row and surrounded by his friends from the Support Squadron. Everyone around him was laughing and cheering as the quad on the floor plowed through the first swarmers, but not Ian.

His face was hard, and his blue eyes glowed dangerously as he stared in the direction of Heath's bench.

Couldn't get anything past my brother. Add one more item to my list of problems: keeping Ian from trying to stab any members of the most powerful quad on campus.

It was a long hour of simulated wraith battles as team after team took the floor. Three people "died." Four others ran out of bounds rather than take a death blow. Only one quad managed to kill a Giant without also taking a huge loss of points.

The crowd had somehow grown even larger and louder

over the course of the hour. I spotted a whole section of faculty and staff, and there were also family members scattered throughout the crowd.

I hadn't thought of inviting my dads up here to witness me killing wraiths that were complex magical illusions. They were about as impressed as Ian and I were with the fact that no one in the program went near a real wraith until senior year, but they were also pretty astounded by our description of the complexity and power of the magic produced by the SWIM.

Next year, I decided. I'd sit in the stands with them, like the other senior Guardian trainees were doing today, and we'd critique everyone's skills together.

Cash's obnoxious voice echoing through the speaker system knocked me back to earth. "And finally, the last team of the day will be our current leaders! Heath Blackwell, Aiden Blackwell, and Wyatt Gale of Blackwell Quad, with one substitute."

I didn't even merit a name.

The lights dimmed as they did before the start of every challenge, and I walked out onto the floor. Heath, Aiden, and Wyatt were already there, standing in a neat line, their weapons strapped to their backs.

Not one of them looked at me as I stepped up next to Heath.

The floor lit up with the soft glow of the magic as it conjured our first opponents.

"Care to tell me what your problem is?" I asked in a low voice.

Heath didn't reply as the usual opening salvo materialized on the floor—a dozen swarmers, this batch a mix of two-headed feline things and some bat-bodied spiders the size of a Rottweiler.

"Just follow my commands and don't ask fucking questions, Avery." He turned to say something to Wyatt, giving me his back.

Dismissed.

The wraiths formed their swarm. Adrenaline pulsed through my body, bringing my beast on high alert. I reached behind my head and pulled my swords from their sheaths. Heath, Wyatt, and Aiden ceased to exist as anything except the extra blades and brawn I needed by my side to slay every grotesque thing on this floor.

The wraiths charged, and I let the fight take me.

We were seamless. It was as if I was fighting alongside Ian and my dads. I didn't have to wonder who was going to be where or whether someone had the monster at my back while I dealt with the one at my front. Wyatt swung his ax. Heath and Aiden wielded their sabers. I carved with my swords. In concert, we tore through all dozen of the wraiths in record time.

When they flickered out, four Rippers appeared, spaced evenly around the edges of the arena. Huge horned beasts with glowing void eyes, clawed feet, and rotting flesh that would smell rancid if they'd been real.

Cash wasn't messing around. For the rest of the teams, the Rippers had been run two at a time, but he'd thrown all four at us at once.

Heath became his majestic golden wolf and Wyatt his sleek and powerful bear. Aiden twirled his sword expertly around his wrist, his Moon-blessing runes visible under the radiant magic of the arena. I dismissed with a furious shove the ache that punched me at sight of them.

We clawed and cut and stabbed and dodged in concert. Phantom talons raked my skin. Behind me, Wyatt's bear bellowed in pain and roared with rage. Heath's wolf snarled and tore out a wraith's throat, and I sliced through its neck. Wyatt did the same to another, and Aiden was there to take its head off with his blade.

We destroyed all four wraiths. The crowd was deafening around us.

The final two Giants flickered onto the floor. Humanoid, twelve feet tall, claws, antlers, spikes, and tails. One charged immediately at Aiden. He shifted smoothly into his jaguar, dodged, and jumped onto its back. He and Heath worked that one while Wyatt and I handled the other. Giant hands battered me. More pain as phantom fangs sank into my skin. A hit from a tail simulated a cracked rib.

Heath and Aiden downed their wraith. I dodged another swipe of the tail, sheathed my swords, and sprinted to Heath and Aiden's target. I picked up Wyatt's heavy ax and swung it with all my strength, removing the fallen wraith's head.

Heath and Aiden, still beasts, bolted for the remaining wraith. They joined Wyatt's bear, all three of them piling onto the monster as it screeched and clawed and bellowed in pain. They took it to the floor. I ran for it, heaving the ax again and bringing it down, cleaving the head from the body.

It flickered out. The crowd roared. The leaderboard flashed in blinding LED above us.

Thousands and thousands of points were awarded to each of us and to the Blackwell Quad. The words RECORD TIME flashed in red across the top of the board.

I leaned on Wyatt's ax, sucking in huge, panting breaths. I closed my eyes.

I did it. *We* did it.

Had I ever had so much fun in my life? At my core, I was a predator. Killing wraiths, even fake ones, made my beast soul fucking *sing*, and doing it alongside talented and powerful teammates was a high like none I'd ever experienced.

Opening my eyes, I found Ian in the crowd. He stood on top of his seat, wearing a huge smile and clapping wildly for me. Brody jumped up and down next to him. Mallory, Allen, Chance, and Ash were the stands somewhere too. If I listened hard enough, I was just able to make out Mal's exuberant shouting above the noise.

Heath, Wyatt, and Aiden had ducked into the shadows at the edge of the arena to shift back to human form and dress, and they returned to the floor to stand under the lights and bask in the cheers of their adoring fans.

Their expressions were blank, devoid of any joy or even pride at what we'd accomplished out here.

I wiped my brow, and then I went to hand Wyatt's ax back to him.

A strong hand wrapped around my bicep, stopping me in my tracks.

I met Heath's furious hazel glare, and I yanked my arm out of his grip like he'd burned me.

"Don't think this means anything, Avery," he growled. "It isn't happening again."

"What isn't?" I spat. "Us fighting as a unit? Or you fucking touching me?"

His nostrils flared, and golden starbursts ignited in his eyes. "Both."

Wyatt was on Heath's other side, sweaty and shirtless. He laughed, and it sounded mean. Reaching across Heath, he snatched his ax from my hands without a word.

Aiden stood behind them both, his gym bag slung lazily over his shoulder and his glasses back on his face. "Can we get a move on?" he asked irritably, like I wasn't even standing there. "I have papers to grade."

Tears welled in my eyes. Horrified, I blinked them away. It'd taken them a mere handful of words to eviscerate my high. To tear me down and make me feel so fucking small.

I needed to *go*.

Without a backwards glance, I hurried to my bench, grabbed my bag, and headed for the arena doors, wiping the stray tear from my cheek before anyone could see it.

34

AVERY

By the time the arena doors had slammed behind me, anger had overtaken hurt. I stalked down the hall that led past the trainee locker rooms, intent on meeting up with Ian and the rest of our friends outside and getting the hell out of here.

A man stepped into my path.

"Impressive," he said, but it did not sound like a compliment.

I took a step back and shifted my bag into my left hand, freeing up my dominant hand to grab a sword if necessary. I eyed the man warily.

He was tall and built like a Prime male—at least six foot three or four, broad shoulders, thick arms, and a long mane of dark hair that contained a few stray grays at the temple. He looked to be in his forties, but given how shifters aged, he was probably older. Menacing gray eyes took my measure, and his lip curled.

I didn't allow Prime males to menace me, but this one gave me serious pause. His hair was a dead giveaway that he was a lion shifter, and the beastly dominance he wore like a cloak said he was a very powerful one.

Instead of rising immediately to the challenge like she normally would've, my beast paced her cage, wary and guarded.

"Thank you," I replied tersely, moving to step around him. "If you'll excuse me—"

He shifted, blocking my path again. My beast hissed, her fur standing on end.

"You know," he said lightly, adjusting the cuff of his sleeve, "I'd heard about the female who'd shown up to this college and decided to make waves in the Guardians. I found it distasteful, certainly, but I'd assumed the males here wouldn't stand for it and that you'd be put right back in your place."

I shifted from foot to foot, debating whether reaching for my sword would escalate this too quickly. "They did try, sir. But maybe you'll all get lucky and a real live wraith will eat my soul in field training."

"Hmm." He pondered me again. "Perhaps. You won't luck into fighting alongside my sons again, that's for sure. Your future... unit will be less skilled."

Shit. This was Heath and Aiden's terrible dad. The one trying to sell Clara to his rich friends.

My beast growled a low warning in my chest.

"I'm told," he went on, "that you don't shift. Not even in the heat of battle or when injured." He leaned closer, his gray eyes turning silver. "What are you hiding?"

"Step away from me, Mr. Blackwell," I said through gritted teeth.

That made him smile. "Ah, so you've figured out who I am. You'll know, then, that I'm a member of the Southeastern Council. You will tell me who and what you are. Now."

"No, and it's against the law for you to even insinuate that I have to."

His silver eyes began to glow, and dark-brown fur crawled up his neck. He lashed out with the invisible force of his beast's dominance, hitting me with such a punch, I nearly stumbled backwards.

Pain flared and dug into my skull. He pushed his will onto me, to answer his question, to bow, to submit.

To *shift*.

My beast tore to the surface of my skin. I held her tightly, desperate to prevent the shift. She shoved with all her might, roaring as she broke the crucible Blackwell had put me in.

It was his turn to almost stumble as his hold snapped, and he snarled in surprise.

I took advantage of his momentary shock and bolted, skirting around him and sprinting for the doors at the end of the hall that led outside.

When I burst into the warm evening air, I didn't stop running until I was safely wrapped in Ian's snug embrace.

IT WAS DIFFICULT TO TELL, BETWEEN MY BROTHER AND ME, which of us was watching the other one harder.

Ian was as rattled by my confrontation with Councilor Blackwell as I'd been. I swore up and down that I hadn't shown my beast's true colors—no fur, no fangs, some glowing eyes at the worst—but there was no denying the man knew I had a beast and that she was powerful. A high-powered female beast was a rarity among us, sure, but it wasn't illegal, nor was it the main reason I was hiding her.

Dad assured me that the Council had no power over the Guardians, which was why it was more important than ever that I become one.

Ian was also acting like I was one mean look from Heath away from a nervous breakdown. I wasn't *really*, but I'd have been lying if I'd said the whiplash his quad had given me didn't hurt. My beast was pathetic and confused over it all, which made *me* feel pathetic and confused, and I hated it.

On the other hand, I was on Ian's ass constantly because I was worried he'd run off and try to stab a member of the Blackwell Quad, including the guy who was a professor and the one who was a terrifying mythical snake monster. Ian didn't discriminate, and he was going to end up severely injured or dead if he tried it. Brody and I kept watch on a rotation as best we could, but Ian just shrugged it off like he was amused by our antics. I knew better—that was how he lulled us into complacency.

"Okay," I said to my brother as we stood in the hallway in front of my Shifter History classroom. "You have walked me the thirty feet from Lunar Magic class to this one, and no one tried to kill me, nor did I collapse under the unbearable weight of my sorrows."

He pointed a finger in my face. "I'm getting tired of your attitude, Aves. Excuse *the fuck* out of me for caring about my sister."

I swatted his hand away and arched a brow. "I'll stop complaining about you smothering me if you stop plotting to murder any or all members of the Blackwell Quad."

He lifted his chin and sniffed. "No deal."

"Oh, good," I said as Mallory and Brody arrived, both just getting out of some useless upper-level magical theory class. "You guys can escort my brother to O-Chem." It was my turn to point a finger in Ian's face. "No. Throat. Slitting."

He winked. "Sure thing, Aves."

My beast gave a guttural growl within my chest, the only warning I received before Kace Mahoney sauntered around the corner, Drew the panther in tow.

Ian's eyes flashed electric blue. He reached behind his head where the hilt of his katana stuck out from along the side of his backpack, and he yanked his blade free.

Passing students gasped and hurried along.

I groaned. "Brody, help."

"Babe," he cooed at Ian, rubbing his knuckles lightly up and down my brother's side. "We're not allowed to spill blood in the hallways. Patience. We've got all summer to run into him in one of the local bars."

Ian cooled down, sheathing his blade with a disappointed sigh.

Kace sneered as he saw me and slowed his steps.

Great.

"Well, if it isn't the whore of the Guardians," he said. Drew snickered at his shoulder. "Heard Blackwell tossed your ass to the curb. Who're you spreading your legs for now in that joke of a program?"

Mallory linked her arm through mine and blinked owlishly at him. "Avery, is this the guy who didn't know a wraith from his own teammate? Maybe I should check him for a concussion."

"Shut up, you mangy fucking house cat," Drew snapped.

"Go away, both of you." My beast began to pace her cage, and I let her peek through my eyes as I leveled Kace with a glare. "Unless this is an official challenge?"

Kace stepped right into my face. Brody and Ian shouldered in front of me like a couple of reckless idiots, and they both winced as Kace's dominance hit them full force. I tugged Ian behind me, and Mallory yanked Brody over to the wall.

"Outside, Baxter," Kace growled, crowding me, his fetid breath wafting into my face. "Now that King Blackwell doesn't appear to care what happens to your ass, it's time someone showed you what happens to females who don't know their fucking place."

I shoved him in the chest with everything I had. He stumbled backward, his eyes widening like he was shocked at my strength. It was so ludicrous yet so fucking typical—the guy had seen me run and jump and swing a sword, but it still somehow came as a shock to him that I might actually be strong. "Back off, Mahoney. If you ever touch me again, I will kill you. Count on it."

"I said," he gritted out, "get the fuck outside. We're finishing this."

Before I could respond, Kace's huge body suddenly went flying sideways. He hit the wall so hard that he crashed through the sheetrock, bellowing expletives as he went.

Wyatt had arrived, apparently, and he gave Kace's plight a cursory glance, a lazy smirk on his face, like he hadn't been the one who'd just thrown him through a fucking wall.

Heath was with Wyatt, of course, since we all had this class together. He gave me an irritable look before pushing past us. "Stop causing so much fucking trouble, Avery. It's getting annoying."

I gaped at his back. "Excuse me?"

"You heard me," he said tersely, without turning around.

Ian lunged, reaching again for his blade, but I snagged him and handed him to Brody.

Wyatt moseyed along behind Heath. He paused to shoot me a taunting smile over his shoulder. "Sorry I took your kill, Wildcat. Probably should've let you get expelled. Would save all of us some headaches."

My beast snarled in my chest, then buried her nose in her paws. "Fuck off, Wyatt," I said, only managing to sound tired.

He chuckled and disappeared into the classroom.

I gave my frowning friends and very pissed-off brother a half-hearted smile. "It's fine. I'm used to... all of this."

Mallory shook her head sadly. "I'd just thought maybe Heath's quad was... different."

I wasn't sure if I'd thought that, too, or just wished for it like a deluded fool.

Shrugging, I shouldered my backpack and headed for the door. "We live and we learn, Mal. See you guys at lunch."

I steeled my spine, shoved every emotion threatening to spill out of me into the cage with my beast, and went to class.

35
_____

AVERY

"You look very nice," Brody told me in his most sincere tone. He sat on the counter in between my bathroom sink and Ian's, wearing dark suit pants and a half-buttoned white dress shirt. He was also watching me like I was a bomb that was about to go off. "I'm glad you decided to come tonight. Save me a dance?"

"Did Ian send you in here to butter me up?" I asked, slanting a stern look his way before returning to carefully applying my mascara. "I said I was going to this thing, and I'm obviously not backing out now that I have on a full face of makeup and a ballgown."

The gown was a rental, but I'd managed to find one that I didn't hate and fit great. It was an ice-blue number, form fitting with off-the-shoulder sleeves and a high slit up my right leg. The material was feather-light and stretchy enough to keep me in relative comfort for the duration of the Blue Moon Ball.

Two Full Moons would fall within the month of May, with the first one occurring tonight, and the second—the Blue Moon—falling on the last day of the month, after the semester ended. Blue Moon months were always a cause for celebration among shifters, and here at Proteus College, we celebrated by going to fucking prom.

"Look, Avery, I realize I've only known you for, like, four months now, but I don't need Ian to tell me that you're feeling down. Any sane person would be."

I capped my mascara, adjusted the sleeves of my dress, then turned to face him. "I'm going to make camp, Brody. I'm one step closer to doing what I came here to do. There's nothing to be down about."

There wasn't much chance for movement on the leaderboard at this point, since the rest of our training schedule would be drills and conditioning. There was only one more wraith combat challenge on the calendar, and it was with a partner of our choice. Ian and I were going to wreck shop.

I'd deal with the fact that I'd be at camp for most of the summer with the *rest* of the top of the Guardian class when I had to.

Brody gave me a dubious look. "I'm not worried about your ability to handle the Kace Mahoneys of the world, who think it's open season to harass you. You don't give a shit about them. You did, however, at one point in time, give a shit about the members of the Blackwell Quad, and the way they're treating you now is unacceptable. You'd have to be a robot for it not to hurt."

I would neither confirm nor deny ever giving a shit about Heath, Aiden, Wyatt, and Elijah, but being seen and cared about by someone other than a member of my family gave me a pleasantly warm feeling in my chest. For a moment, anyway.

"You're a keeper, Brody Dara," I said with a genuine smile. "If it doesn't work out with Ian, we can have a lavender marriage. I'll make you very happy."

He barked out a laugh and hopped down from the counter. "I don't doubt it," he said, squeezing me in a hug. After releasing me, he finished buttoning his shirt, hiding that toned, brown chest away. "It's not too late to find you a date, you know." He snagged his tie from the counter and looped it around his neck. "Do you want me just to pluck one out of the crowd tonight? Blond, brunet, canine, feline…. I will even *selflessly* volunteer to check cock size for you. Just text me a list of your preferences."

It was my turn to laugh. "Polite pass, but thank you."

I had no interest in that sort of male company right now. Maybe Ian and Brody would agree to accompany me on a quick trip to Colorado after the semester ended in a few weeks. I could hunt down Tad for a little rock-climbing lesson and a quick hookup. He was sweet, attractive, and human. Moon willing, he could scratch the itch the Blackwell Quad had ignited under my skin. I needed it gone before I clawed my own flesh off.

My beast gave an irritated huff.

Oh, suddenly you have an opinion about Tad?

She growled and flopped onto her back, ignoring me.

The bathroom door swung open, and Ian stuck his head inside. "Are you two ready? Allen and Mal have only been here for half an hour, and they've already drank half a bottle of my best tequila."

"All done, babe," Brody said, turning his blinding white smile on my brother. He finished with his tie and held out his arms.

Ian, dressed in a perfectly tailored gray suit, slinked into Brody's embrace and buried his face in his neck. "Ooh, you smell nice."

"All right." I waved a hand in front of my face. "Cool it, you two, or else I won't be able to get the stench of horny shifter out of my towels. I'll get my shoes, and then we can go get this night over with."

"That's the spirit, Aves," Ian said drolly. "I bet you'd be more enthusiastic about this if you'd just let me commit some light murder this week."

"Ian Baxter, your sword better be locked away in your closet."

He rolled his eyes. "Obviously. The polyester of my harness does not go with this suit."

Brody beamed at me guilelessly. "See? Best behavior for all of us. Let's go—the ball started an hour ago."

With one last look in the mirror, a quick adjustment of my boobs, and a final fluffing of my hair, I was ready.

Off to do a fun college thing like a real college student, and that was that.

When we entered the historic ballroom that was attached to the college's main building, even I had to admit I was impressed.

Thirty-foot ceilings towered above us. Intricate crown molding created recessed quadrants, breaking up the starkness of the white paint. Tall white columns held up the ceiling throughout the room. Old hardwood floors were covered with large mahogany-colored carpets. A wide staircase led to a second-floor balcony that encircled the entire room.

Soft blue fairy lights had been strung between the old crystal chandeliers, tiny stars twinkling overhead in the dim lighting. Tall black vases sat atop tables adorned with silver tablecloths, each one holding an arrangement of moonflowers. Several bars lined the walls, and one long table of finger foods had been set up nearby.

Students and faculty dressed in their finest stood around the space, talking, drinking, laughing. There was a dance floor in the large open space in the middle of the room, and the DJ already had what looked like a third of the student body out there, grinding on each other to a sultry beat.

"Oh, there's Ash and Chance!" Mal said. She waved excitedly, gripping Allen's arm as she hopped up and down on her monstrous heels.

Brody offered me the arm that was not occupied holding Ian's hand, and I placed my hand lightly in the crook of his elbow. He led us through throngs of people to a table where Chance and his date—one of those bright-eyed freshman girls he'd seduced with a tarot reading at the lake—waited for us. Ash was nearby, wearing a crisp black suit that fit her like a glove. Her date was... maybe the hottest girl I'd ever seen?

"Um, is that a teenage Jessica Rabbit?" Ian whispered, gaping at the voluptuous redhead. He untangled his fingers from Brody's. "I must meet her."

Brody cast me a pleading look. Biggest puppy-dog eyes ever attempted by a feline shifter, no doubt.

"Go meet the glamorous lady," I said, laughing as I shooed him away. "I'll go get us drinks."

"Take a buddy!" he hollered over his shoulder as he scurried after Ian.

No thank you. If I could patrol the streets of my neighborhood under a New Moon without a buddy, I could walk alone from this table to the bar and back just fine.

The trek to the far side of the ballroom was more arduous than it should've been because of the four-inch heels I'd decided to torture myself with tonight, but I had three cups of punch balanced in my hands in short order.

As I weaved my way back through the crowd, I nearly stumbled when I met the harsh, penetrating hazel gaze I'd been avoiding—and missing—for weeks.

Gold flared briefly in Heath's eyes as he looked me up and down, his expression morphing from boredom to fury in a blink. He wore a dark gray suit that fit him to perfection, his sculpted jaw freshly shaved and his sandy blond hair artfully styled. The perfect, polished Alpha.

On his arm was Phoebe, looking herself like the perfect, polished shifter princess in an ethereal pink ballgown. Diamonds dripped from her ears, throat, and wrists. Her blonde hair was twisted into an intricate updo, showcasing her elegant, long neck.

My beast snarled in rage. I tore my stare from Heath's and blinked away the headlights, willing the bile that threatened to rise in my throat to stay the hell down.

"Oh, goodness," Phoebe gasped with a tinkling laugh. "Avery, we almost ran right into you." She tightened her grip on Heath's arm possessively and gave me a patronizing little pout of her lip. "Aw, do you not have a date tonight? Bless your heart. It is hard to be a new student at your age, but of course—" She batted long dark lashes at me innocently. "—you're making it harder on yourself, aren't you?"

I pasted a look of confusion on my face, blinking right back at her with wide eyes. "What do you mean? I didn't even wear my swords tonight."

"Ugh, barbaric," she huffed, sticking her tiny nose in the air. "It appears even your Alpha lineage can't buy class. At least everyone has seen you for the uncouth city trash you are."

I had a feeling the "everyone" she spoke of was limited to

the man whose arm she had wrapped in a vice grip with her baby-pink claws.

The violence my beast was spinning within me won out. "I suppose you're right, Phoebe. It is so *uncouth* of me to aspire beyond getting on my back for a quad and letting them use me as a battery and breeder."

"Avery," Heath growled in warning.

"As if any notable quad in this school would want you," Phoebe spat, scandalized. "Everyone knows you're an affront to the Moon's will. A *cursed* female."

Lovely. Phoebe was an old-school bigot. I flicked a glare at Heath, letting my beast peek out through my eyes, just for fun. "Classy, Blackwell."

His wolf rose to the challenge. Golden fireworks erupted in his eyes, and a deep, dangerous rumble sounded in his chest. "Move along, Avery. Don't speak to me or my date for the rest of the night."

He tugged Phoebe away. She smirked triumphantly at me, though I had the sinking feeling nobody won in that exchange.

As I trudged back toward our table, still carrying my drinks, I passed the dance floor.

Out in the middle of it was Wyatt. Clinging to him like she was a stripper and he was the pole was Callista. Her wisp of a black dress revealed an almost-but-not-quite scandalous amount of ass and leg, and her dark hair was slicked into a long, perfect ponytail. She rolled her hips erotically as she straddled Wyatt's thick thigh, and he wasn't being shy about where he put his hands on her body.

The bile came up this time, and I swallowed it down with a silent scream of frustration.

My despair—or my beast's—was a siren call to Wyatt. His green-eyed gaze collided with mine, pinning me to the spot as I tried to sneak by, and he smirked lasciviously at me over Callista's shoulder.

Callista chose that moment to press her lips to his neck, and he grinned wider as he arched it for her, his focus never straying from me.

The beast reared her head one more time. My vision sharpened, and my teeth lengthened.

Wyatt's smirk faded, and a red sheen rolled over his green irises.

"Avery," a deep voice snapped.

I broke my torturous stare-off with Wyatt to find Aiden, dressed in a slim-fitting navy suit, his chocolate waves styled to perfection. From behind a pair of dark blue frames, he eyed me like I was an annoying, naughty child.

On his arm? The hot professor I'd seen fawning over him in the dining hall a time or seven.

"Control your animal," he said tersely. "This is a school function."

"Who is this, darling?" his date asked, wrinkling her nose. "I haven't had this one in class. I'd have remembered a female with such a... *loud* beast presence."

Aiden cast me one more harsh look, his jaw flexing and his nostrils flaring. "She's no one, Eleanor."

At this point, after *this* many hits in a row, I couldn't hold onto my composure. My face twisted into something that no doubt revealed how that statement had crushed me.

Aiden's irises lit up with his telltale turquoise rings, but I was finished with all of this.

I turned and fled, marching toward our table as fast as my heels could carry me. When I arrived, I slammed the drinks down in front of Ian, who was seated and deep in conversation with Chance's date.

Ian took one look at me and jumped to his feet. "Where? I will kill them."

I sat down and dragged him back into his chair. "I'm fine. I just need a minute."

He squeezed my hand, his anger shifting quickly to concern. "Do you want to leave?"

"Maybe." I took a sip of my punch and wished the vodka in it could dull my pain. "Why don't you and Brody dance a little bit. Have some fun, then we'll go."

This was embarrassing enough. I couldn't be spotted fleeing so soon.

It took me some coaxing, but Ian did eventually leave me to grab Brody and dance. I sat at the table, sipping my drink as I watched Allen spin Mallory around the dance floor like a tiny ballerina. I sent soothing thoughts to my beast.

She needed to get over this thing with the Blackwell Quad even more than I did.

That thought, of course, conjured its fourth and final member. Elijah breezed into the ballroom, an easy smile on his handsome face. Unlike the rest of his quad, he wasn't wearing a suit, but he was still dressed nicer than I'd ever seen him, in a pale yellow dress shirt, its collar open to the top of his chest, and dark slacks. The gold hoops he wore in each earlobe winked under the fairy lights, and his dark hair looked wet, like he was just out of the shower.

I hated the relief that rushed through me at the fact that he was alone.

He gave a few lazy waves and head nods to random students, but at some point, he caught the attention of the rest of his quad. I watched as Heath, Wyatt, and Aiden emerged from the crowd—without their dates—and followed Elijah up the stairs to the balcony level. They passed the clusters of students and faculty lingering up there without acknowledgement, and then they disappeared onto one of the small outdoor patios.

Fuck this. I was finished sitting around with my hurt feelings and confusion. I wasn't crazy, and I wouldn't be made to feel like I was. There had been something developing between me and every member of the Blackwell Quad before the break, and then a switch had flipped. They were now very intentionally treating me like dog shit, and I wanted to know why. I did still have a modicum of self-respect left.

They were alone now, all four of them, and I was going to get answers.

"... WAS ABLE TO FIND AN OLD CELL PHONE," ELIJAH WAS saying as I pressed my body against the wall. I peeked around the doorframe just enough to catch sight of the four of them huddled together and deep in conversation. "Horatio and I powered it up, and there was a call from a contact labeled 'Archprime' the day before she was killed. Then there was an outgoing call to the same number the night after it happened."

"Not a smoking gun," Aiden mused. "But the timing is suspicious. Worth following up on, for sure."

"We should have some time before camp starts for us to —" Heath cut off abruptly when I stepped out of my hiding place.

My heels clicked against the stone floor, tiny gunshots in the tense silence that had fallen over the group. They all turned to face me, four deadly, gorgeous assholes watching my approach with rigid shoulders and smoldering glares.

Wyatt recovered first. He slouched against the railing, affixing his lazy smirk to his face. He'd loosened his tie at some point in the past half hour, giving us all a tantalizing peek at the decorated pale skin of his neck and collarbone beneath his all-black suit. "Just can't stay away from us, can you, Wildcat?" he drawled.

Heath crossed his arms over his chest and put on his quad leader face. "This is a private conversation, Avery—"

I held up a hand. "Stop it. I've had enough of whatever this is. I'm finished being disrespected by all of you. Something happened over the break, and you all came back to school determined to be complete assholes to me. To ignore whatever it was going on between us before that. To pretend like every single one of you didn't put your hands on me—"

Wyatt chuckled. "We put our hands on a lot of girls, babe. It doesn't make you special."

"Nice try, Gale." I lifted my chin even as my beast let out a pained whine. "Low blow, but I'm still standing."

"The affairs of this quad are none of your business, Avery—" Aiden began, but I wasn't having it.

Not tonight.

"You're obviously trying to send me a message with the way you've been treating me," I said, meeting Aiden's glacial stare with all the power I could muster. "Use your big-boy words and tell me exactly what that is."

They were silent for a few moments. Heath and Aiden glared, Wyatt fidgeted with his tie like he was bored, and Elijah, who hadn't looked at me once, could only stare at his shoes, frowning, his hands tucked into his pockets.

I wanted to ask him if he had been talking about his mother before I interrupted. I wanted to tell him about mine —about how I wondered if their deaths were similar.

And I wanted to tell Heath and Aiden what a piece of

shit their dad was—that he'd more or less attacked me in the locker room hallway of the arena.

But I couldn't. Not after the way they'd treated me. They'd stomped to death any fragile seedling of trust that might've been developing between me and any one of them.

Heath shifted on his feet, a brief uneasiness flickering across his face before he wiped it away. "Fine. It isn't any of your business, but we've decided to pursue a bonding. You are a distraction we don't need."

The bile stirred again, but I held on for dear life. "Oh?" I asked lightly. "And I take it that, despite the clear chemistry between us, I'm not a candidate for your bond? Is that what all the asshole behavior has been trying to tell me?"

Aiden let out a weary sigh. "You know you aren't an option, Avery."

"Why not?" I took another step forward, bringing me within a few feet of Heath. In my heels, I was eye level with him. "Just say it. Say it out loud. Say that you think shifting females are lesser. Abominations. Beneath you."

Heath rumbled an angry growl. "That is not it. We can have respect for females with a beast and still believe they aren't the right choice for our bond."

I stepped even closer until we were nearly toe to toe. I met his golden-glazed smolder and held it because I had the power to do so. "And why do you believe a shifting female isn't the right choice for the bond of a powerful Prime quad?" I asked in a low, harsh voice. "Is it because you believe in the lie made up by our ancestors to malign a *hero* just because she was female? Admit you think that because I share my soul with a beast, just as you all do, that I'm somehow defective. That the Moon would never dare bless our bonding with the power you all must be desperately craving, simply because I'm your *equal*, not a latent conduit."

Heath blew out a breath and raked a hand through his thick hair. He looked away from me, agony marring his beautiful face.

Aiden, as furious as I'd ever seen him, stepped up next to his brother. "You think you have everything figured out," he spat. "You think you're the exception to the rules. You don't, and you're not. Drop it, Avery."

Wyatt had lost his cocky, devil-may-care smirk. A red sheen glinted in his eyes. "This is what you wanted, Wildcat. We told you the cold, hard truth. You aren't it for us."

"I wasn't under the illusion that I was," I replied softly, pretending I didn't feel like his bear had just clawed my guts out and strewn them all over the stone floor. After a deep breath, I dared a glance at the quietest member of the quad. "Elijah?"

He gripped the railing behind him with white knuckles. Slowly, his glowing yellow gaze met mine, his pupils the narrow slits of his beast.

Aiden moved to block my view of Elijah. "Don't. You agitate his beast. You know that."

"I'm sorry, Dove," Elijah rasped. Those were the first words he'd spoken to me since he'd let me out the laundry room door at the lake house all those weeks ago. After I'd let him watch what Wyatt did to me. "I really am."

"I don't believe you," I whispered.

"I don't blame you."

"Just go, Avery," Heath said, anger and frustration bleeding into his every word. "You got your answer."

I did. I did get my answer.

My beast had curled into a little ball. Pain fled. An empty, numbing feeling remained.

Without looking back, I turned and left.

36

AVERY

"It is *spooky* out here," Mallory said with a dramatic shiver. "I can't believe you do this during every curfew."

She walked next to me as close as she could get to my body without bumping into my swords where they stuck out on my back. It was a balmy 59 degrees on this May evening, so I wore a simple long-sleeved workout shirt under my harness. Mallory had on leggings and a Proteus sweatshirt that hit her mid-thigh.

Since Ian was still insisting I go nowhere unescorted, Mallory had volunteered to accompany me on my rounds at the campus perimeter under the New Moon. It was useless, but it was a compulsion I hadn't been able to shake.

"I'm just not used to sitting around during this part of the lunar cycle," I told her. "Just being out under the stars with my swords on my back helps me feel normal."

"I bet, you ridiculous badass," she replied, nudging me playfully. "I mean, I saw you in action against that quad that challenged you on the second day of school, but seeing you in the arena was something else. They'd be stupid not to

make you a Guardian. Who cares if you're a female and a...
cougar."

"Nope. Try again."

Mallory and Brody had taken to trying to trick me into revealing my animal. It wasn't that I didn't trust them, but the fewer people who knew the truth, the better.

Until I became a Guardian, at least.

"At least we're out of here in two days," she went on. "Summer vacation. Allen and I get to go to Palm Beach; you, Ian, and Brody get to go kill as many real live wraiths as your heart desires. We all come back next year tanned and refreshed."

I was ready to get the hell off this campus. Its one thousand acres was too small for me and the Blackwell Quad, and I was looking forward to a blissful month of vacation before we had to report to camp in mid-June.

Because I'd done it. Cash announced cuts earlier this week, and, much to his chagrin, I'd officially made camp as a Guardian. Even better—Ian and Brody coasted in at the top of the Support Squadron list, and Ian had convinced Ward to let him come to camp even though it was only for rising seniors, because he a) "had already killed a shit-ton of real wraiths," and b) "was going to sneak in anyway because none of these fuckers can be trusted to watch my sister's back."

No complaints from me.

In the few weeks that'd passed since the ball, I'd kept my head down, focused on finishing my assignments, taking end-of-year exams, and doing the bare minimum to keep my spot on the leaderboard. I'd stopped going to Aiden's class entirely and turned in my last few assignments by email.

He didn't object.

Or reply at all.

No member of the Blackwell Quad had shown up to training for the rest of the semester. At the top of the leaderboard by thousands of points, they got to slack off for two weeks without worrying about the cut.

I'd have been annoyed if I wasn't so relieved.

Horrible screeching sounded in the distance, beyond the walls. Male shouting echoed through the night.

Mallory shivered again. "That's so creepy."

"Ever seen a wraith?"

She nodded. "Back when we lived in Fulton City near you guys. My parents were able to afford to ward the house, but I saw a few smaller ones run down the street once or twice." She nudged me again. "I guess it was you guys that were out there making sure we were safe."

"Not when we were thirteen," I replied. "But after you moved away? Yeah. But it didn't really get bad out there until the past few years or so."

She sighed. "After I got my beast and we decided to move into the shifter territory, my parents were lucky to snag a house in one of the little towns right next to a Guardian post. Good wards around the city walls. Haven't seen a wraith since."

More screeching and monster bellows erupted. They sounded a lot closer this time.

Mallory tensed.

"I was told the Guardians sometimes run the wraiths up against the school's wards," I said in a low voice, "because they're so strong."

"Um, you might've mentioned that before I followed you out here," she hissed.

"I haven't seen it happen. Not the semester I've been

here," I told her. "But if you're uncomfortable, we can head back."

We'd walked all the way around to the front of campus. A mile of dense forest lay between us and the heart of the college.

I motioned in front of us. "A little ways ahead is the front gate, so we can just cut back down the entrance road—"

Another ear-splitting screech sounded, followed by the eerie chittering of swarmers.

It sounded like they were right on top of us.

I reached out and touched the brick wall next to me, seeking the comforting warm buzz of the wards' magic.

It was gone.

Alarm shuddered through my body, and my beast went on full alert. I yanked my swords from their sheaths.

"Shit, Mal—"

Mutant rat wraiths the size of border collies crawled over the brick wall twenty feet in front of us. Their dark grey fur had melted off their lean bodies in odd places, exposing ghostly bones. Long arms like monkeys had and three-inch claws helped them scale the wall easily, a half dozen of them hitting the dirt in concert.

Six sets of jarring violet eyes turned on us. Shock and horror sank into my body as reality struck. That wasn't the light blue glow of the magical constructs I'd been fighting for months—these were real fucking wraiths, *on our campus.*

The wards had failed.

"Oh, holy fuck," Mal gasped. "Avery, what the fuck? Shit, shit, *shit.*"

"Shift and fucking *run*, Mal," I barked. My beast shoved hers with the order.

In a blink, Mallory disappeared, her clothes falling to

the grass. An orange tabby cat bolted from the pile, shooting like a furry bullet into the darkness of the forest.

As I'd dared to hope, none of the wraiths peeled off to chase her. My beast and I were a much tastier prize.

An alarm blared in the distance, coming from the direction of the main campus. The breach of the wards must've set it off.

The swarmers charged. I ran straight for them, hurdled the first one that reached me, and sliced through the neck of the one behind it with ease. Adrenaline flooded me, and I whirled, swinging my swords, hacking off limbs to maim and slow. In the past, Ian would've been with me as we handled a swarm this size, but all the training alone against SWIM's opponents had served me well.

I severed heads.

I stabbed one that leapt at me through the heart, destroying the exposed organ enough for the kill.

I took minimal damage—claws tore through the leg of my pants, and I suffered one deep gouge on my arm.

The dead wraiths lay in the grass around me. As my training dictated, I waited, catching my breath as I watched the swarmers melt away. Unlike the wraiths we faced in in training, which disappeared in a flicker as the magic holding them together released, real wraiths oozed into the ground upon their deaths, their corrupted souls disintegrating into nothing.

I was only given ten seconds to confirm all six swarmer deaths before an ear-splitting cackle announced the arrival of another monster.

A Ripper launched itself off the wall and landed in the remnants of the swarmer goo. My heart jumped into my throat, and I tensed, sending a prayer up to the Moon that this one had traveled alone behind the throng of swarmers.

Glowing violet voids focused on me. It emitted another high-pitched cackle. This one looked like what might've been destined to be a hyena soul, with its round ears, long, thick neck, and whispers of darker spots dappled over its thick gray hide.

That was where the similarities ended.

Its maw was twice the size of a normal animal's, a grotesque clown mouth flashing rows of needle teeth as it advanced on me. Its body was cracked along the sternum, and the same eerie violet light that churned in its eye sockets leaked out through its ribs. Fish-hook claws as long as my hand sank into the dirt as it prowled closer, its rank stench finally reaching my nose.

And because it was a Ripper, it was as large as a powerful Prime shifter.

I spun my swords. "Let's go, you disgusting piece of shit."

It cackled again, and then it leapt for me.

I dropped, my knees hitting the ground as I arched my back. The wraith sailed over me, and I slashed both blades outward, severing rotting muscle and tendons in its hind legs. It hit the ground hard, roaring a brain-battering screech as it stumbled on broken legs. I flipped around and lunged to my feet, rank gray goo dripping from my swords.

Before the wraith could regain its footing enough to attack me again, I launched myself onto its back and drove both blades into its body. I skewered the heart with one blade and severed the spine with another.

It screeched and flailed, pitching me violently to the side as it staggered and fell to the ground. I crawled slowly to my feet, wincing as what was definitely a bruised hip made itself known.

The Ripper lay still. I'd stabbed it through the heart, but unlike a swarmer, where that could be sufficient for the kill, this one needed its head removed or the whole heart cleaved from its body.

I got started removing its head. Two strikes to its thick neck weren't enough. More roars and screeching sounded nearby. I had no idea how wide the break was in our wards, but I had a hunch there were now other monsters lurking in this forest.

I hacked away, panic rising with every stroke. I was a sitting fucking duck out here alone.

The moment I finally severed the spinal cord and the putrid gray flesh began to ooze away was the moment my luck ran out.

Another hyena Ripper burst through the trees with a horrifying shriek. Glowing void eyes zeroed in on me.

It flew ten feet in a single leap.

I hit the ground and rolled out of its path, dropping one of my swords as I went. I groped for it and was trying to scramble to my feet, when an enormous rust-red bear came barreling through the trees and tackled the wraith to the ground with a vicious snarl.

"Wyatt!" I gasped. "Watch out!"

The wraith sliced a deep gash into Wyatt's furry side as they wrestled. Dark blood seeped from it, matting his fur.

I ran for them, swords raised.

"There!" a deep voice bellowed.

Aiden, Heath, and Elijah sprinted into view. The runes on Aiden's Moon-blessed blade emitted a soft glow—he must've dug deep to recharge them in low magic before they ran out here.

"Avery, stay clear!" Heath barked. "Aiden's got it."

Normally I'd have ignored him, but the fight with the first Ripper had taken it out of me. I stopped in my tracks and sheathed my swords while I caught my breath.

Aiden ran for Wyatt and the wraith, his saber raised. Just as Wyatt tore the wraith's throat out with his teeth, Aiden was there to take its head off with one smooth, powerful strike.

Heath grabbed my arm and hit me with the full force of his Alpha stare. "Everyone is sheltering in the dining hall. Go back there and reinforce your brother and the other trainees. The faculty is warding the building until the Guardians can send in reinforcements, and the Council's specialists are on their way to repair the perimeter wards."

I shook my head. "No. I'm staying with you guys."

Beggars could not be choosers right now, and this was an emergency.

Gold flashed in Heath's hazel eyes. "Avery, for the love of the fucking Moon, do as you're told for once in your life. We have Aiden's blade, and my quad will hold the breach in the wall until help arrives. You're already tired and probably fucking injured, and I don't need one extra back to watch."

"Dove, please do what they say," Elijah said, his voice low. His pupils slitted and then bounced back to round in a blink. "We'll draw the wraiths away. They won't be able to resist us—especially not me."

I shook my head violently again, panic wrapping its claws around my throat. "No, you don't understand—"

"Avery, go," Aiden said, moving to Heath's side. "That's an order from your *professor*. Once the woods are clear and the wards are repaired by the Council's team, we'll come spring everyone from the dining hall."

"But—"

A roar sounded in the distance. Ear-splitting screeching followed.

Wyatt bumped my back with his big furry head, shoving me in the direction of the school with a soft snarl.

"Fuck." Heath tossed his sheathed saber to Aiden, who caught it in his free hand. Heath's body flowed seamlessly into his giant golden wolf. He and Wyatt the bear took off in the direction of the screeching.

Aiden secured Heath's sword to his waist and sheathed his on his back. He looked at Elijah. "You ready?"

Elijah nodded, his gaze distant as he stared into the trees.

"Aiden," I tried once more. "Please don't leave me out here alone."

He spared me a dismissive glance. "Shift into your animal if it will help you run faster. The wraiths will be drawn to the power of our beast souls."

"They'll be drawn to me—"

"Just *go*, Avery. For fuck's sake."

He sprinted away, chasing after Heath and Wyatt.

Elijah reached for me and gave my hand a perfunctory squeeze, saying nothing, and then he shot off after Aiden. Before he disappeared into the trees, I caught a glimpse of his body as it shuddered and grew, morphing violently into a huge serpent-shaped monster. He let out a screech that put the wraiths to shame as he faded from my view.

"Shit," I whispered.

And then I had no choice but to do what they said.

I turned and ran for the school.

I hurdled fallen limbs and dodged branches. I stumbled on a rock, caught myself, then leapt over a small ravine where there may have once been a creek.

I made it maybe a quarter of a mile before the trees began to shake in front of me. The ground vibrated under my feet, announcing the arrival of something really fucking big.

A Giant tore through the trees in front of me. *Tore*

through them like they were bamboo reeds and not decades-old maples with trunks I couldn't get my arms around.

It was at least twelve feet tall, bipedal, and humanoid like most Giant wraiths were. This one had what looked like a jackal head and a long, crocodile mouth full of teeth. A fucked-up Anubis on corrupted Moon magic steroids.

Clawed hands bigger than the rat swarmers I'd killed chucked a tree to the side. Hairless gray flesh was pulled tight over knotted muscle and gaunt ribs. Void eyes, glowing sickly violet, drank me in with deep and desperate hunger.

I ran.

It howled and snarled and gave chase.

I weaved through the trees, adrenaline coursing through my veins like white-water rapids. My beast surged to the front, pumping strength and speed into my limbs.

It was no use.

The wraith swiped at me from behind, its huge hand hitting me with the force of a bus. I flew twenty feet and hit a tree.

A barrage of pain racked my body. My shoulder had dislocated on impact. Tree bark raked my side as I slid to the ground.

I rolled, disoriented, groping for my swords.

The Giant attacked again, pinning me to the ground.

My beast took over.

37

AIDEN

With a wild swing of my saber, I removed the third Ripper's head. "That's the last one!" I shouted.

It was the hardest fight we'd ever had, and the first against real live wraiths. Fifteen L2 swarmers had preceded six L3 Rippers and an L4 Giant, and we'd run that gauntlet for ten minutes that felt like ten hours. Elijah's beast had been able to subdue the Giant, but it'd taken both my blade and Heath's teeth to separate its head from its body.

None of us were unscathed, either, but as I took stock of my brother's wolf, Wyatt's bear, and our basilisk, I was satisfied nothing appeared to be life threatening. Their lacerations, bruises, and broken bones would heal rapidly if they remained in animal form.

A guttural, terrifying roar sounded from deep in the forest.

Beast ears perked up immediately, and we all stared into the darkness of the trees.

"That sounded like a shifter," I said. "Not a wraith."

Heath's wolf bobbed his huge head.

Another ground-shaking roar sounded—this one the unnatural pitch of a wraith.

Heath snarled.

I swore. "That's another Giant. And it's coming from the direction that's closer to campus."

Why the fuck hadn't it come straight for us—a regular smorgasbord of powerful Prime shifter souls—like the rest of the infestation that'd made it over the walls?

My stomach bottomed out as a frigid jolt of fear hit me.

"Avery," I whispered.

Elijah took off, his powerful serpent body winding through the trees with the ease of a gazelle.

Wyatt and Heath bolted after him.

I set my sword down and stripped off my clothes. I'd move faster as my jaguar, and I could use even the short stint in beast form to heal the gouges I'd taken to the stomach when a Ripper had caught me with its claws. I also suspected I had several broken ribs.

My jaguar pressed to the surface, and the sharp pinch of the shift was over in a blink. My beast was bloodthirsty and ready to kill.

I clamped my jaws around my sheathed blade, and then I sprinted after my quad, my beast's powerful stride eating up the distance between us in no time at all.

We ran for half a mile, Elijah in the lead, Heath and I side by side behind him, and Wyatt bringing up the rear. We drew closer to the screeching and bellowing of the Giant, my beast brain growing excited with the anticipation of the fight.

My human brain was consumed by terror.

What if it went after her? What if she's hurt?

The four of us burst into a clearing—a clearing that

hadn't been here an hour ago. Trees had been torn out at their roots and tossed to the ground.

There, among the fallen logs and branches smeared with both the disgusting gray matter of wraith guts and the deep-red blood of a living, breathing beast, was a hideous jackal-headed wraith. A Giant even larger than the one we'd just put down.

Fighting valiantly against it with teeth and claws was the most beautiful beast I had ever seen.

A *silver* tiger.

Huge—as big as my jaguar and even more muscular.

Ethereal eyes, glowing electric blue as they brimmed with power.

Eyes I knew intimately.

A wave of euphoria broke through the terror.

Mate, my jaguar said.

I felt it with every fiber of my beastly soul. That tiger was my Moon-blessed mate.

My Fated.

The perfect bond I'd been so desperately searching for.

Heath's wolf howled, his eyes glowing gold. Wyatt met my gaze, and his bear eyes, usually tinged red with rage in a fight, were lit up the brightest emerald.

He roared. Heath howled again.

Elijah's beast was frozen, almost as if he was in shock—a thing I didn't know was possible for the basilisk.

They'd felt it too.

That was *our* mate.

But she was hurt.

Deep red gashes marred her perfect fur. Her muscle was exposed where there was a tear in her shoulder. She limped on a broken hind leg even as she expertly dodged a blow from the wraith's wicked curved claws.

The wraith limped, too, its movements slow and jerky. My mate had taken an enormous chunk out of its neck, but now she was doing the only thing she could by herself.

Wearing it down. Trying to survive.

We did this to her. *I* did this to her. I *left* her because I assumed the beast soul she'd so annoyingly kept hidden wouldn't compare to any one of ours—that we were enough to draw every wraith in the vicinity to us.

Instead, we left this majestic creature alone.

The tiger rolled sluggishly to her feet. She finally glanced our way, bright blue eyes weary, fading.

She froze.

No!

The wraith slashed at her, its claws aimed at her beautiful tiger face.

Elijah shot at the wraith like a sidewinding bullet. His basilisk was as tall as the Giant but had only half the body mass. It didn't matter. Elijah struck at the wraith, his terrifying jaws locked on the mass of neck the tiger hadn't taken, and then he wrapped his long body around it, constricting as he took it to the ground and rolling clear of our mate.

The tiger collapsed to the forest floor.

Heath shifted back into a man. "Aiden! We need your blade!"

My jaguar resisted. He wanted to go to his mate.

We have to kill the wraith so she can be safe.

He relented. Fur and claws retracted in an instant, and I was naked and human again. I grabbed my saber from where the jaguar had dropped it on the ground and sprinted for the wraith, which was still thrashing and screeching in Elijah's clutches.

Heath and Wyatt, both human now, ran for the tiger.

For *Avery*. Our fucking *Fated* bond.

Who we'd left alone in a wraith-infested forest when she should've been with us, fighting side by side the way she had during our last run against the SWIM. Despite Elijah's absence, nothing had ever felt so right as that.

And we'd taken that gift and tried to throw it away.

My jaguar yowled, his despair permeating every inch of me.

We had to get her back.

But first, we had to save her life.

38

ELIJAH

The jaguar hacked off the abomination's head. We wished we could torture the thing for hours. Kill it twenty more times for hurting our mate.

The jaguar ran back to her. We uncoiled and followed.

The wolf held the tiger's head in his lap as he stroked her pretty fur. "Killer, you did so well. We're going to stay right here with you while you heal up enough to shift back, and then we can take you to the infirmary."

Our mate's belly expanded and contracted in labored breaths.

The bear knelt at our mate's side. His face was terrible as he rubbed soft hands over the tiger's ribs and belly. "She's bleeding everywhere, and her hind leg is broken. Fuck, *fuck*. Why would she not tell us what she was? We wouldn't have left her!"

The jaguar fell to his knees at our mate's back. He ran a soft, reverent hand through her fur. "Look at her," he said in a low voice. "She's not white, but she's close enough. There are more than a handful of shifters who would see her and think she's the betrayer reborn. A walking curse." He looked at the wolf. "Can you imagine what Dad would do if he knew a powerful female Prime not-quite-white tiger was running around the college?"

"I don't want to imagine it," the wolf replied, a growl ripping from his chest. "She told me her mother was murdered. What if she was the same kind of animal? *This* is why she was hiding her beast. *This* is why she wants to be a Guardian. She'll be one of the best fighters they have, and she'd be protected. Just like we always wanted for Elijah."

Hearing the name of our human half jolted us out of our stupor. We'd been admiring our beautiful mate.

With an angry hiss, we nudged them all out of the way and curled protectively around our tiger.

The jaguar fell on his ass and threw his hands helplessly in the air. "Well, that's *that* mystery solved. She wasn't making Elijah's beast volatile. He's not a danger to her, nor is she to him, like we thought. The basilisk just wanted to be with his mate."

Yes. Our mate. So pretty. So perfect.

The jaguar slapped the ground in anger. "How could we have gotten everything so fucking *wrong*?"

The bear got to his feet and began to pace. "Our Fated. Moon-blessed. Handpicked for us by the deity. *Her*. The girl we all wanted but thought we couldn't have. The hottest, most lethal female we've ever met. We are the luckiest bastards." He let out a humorless laugh. "But we are *so* fucked."

The wolf sat next to his brother, misery on his face as he gazed at our tiger. "We made the best decision we could with the facts we had. She has to understand that."

We nuzzled our mate under her chin, sniffing her fur, tasting her essence. She was jasmine and lavender and tangy copper blood.

"I doubt it," the bear said, his voice grim. "She's going to punch each one of us in the dick and tell us to go fuck ourselves."

"It doesn't matter," the wolf snarled. "She's our *Fated*. She's ours, and we're hers. End of discussion. We'll figure it all out later. Right now, we just need her to heal."

We tuned them all out after that. Our mate's breathing had grown steady, and she was sleeping peacefully. If other monsters came for us—for *her*—we'd put them down, and then we'd curl around her again, where we belonged.

No one would ever take her from us.

Not unless they wanted to die with our fangs in their throat while we crushed their bones in our embrace.

39

AVERY

Awareness came and went. Rough but soft hands on my fur. Deep voices whispering to me, then arguing with one another. Cool, smooth scales wrapped around my beast body, holding me gently.

Mates, my tiger half said.

No, I told her. *They rejected us.*

She huffed, which turned into an audible whine as pain shot through my ribs.

"Hey," a deep voice cooed at me. "Lie still, baby. We've got you."

My beast eyes fluttered open. Heath sat a few feet away, naked, his worried gaze on me like I was a precious, breakable treasure.

The long, cool body curled around me tightened slightly, and an annoyed hiss sounded.

"Elijah." That was Aiden's voice. He sounded exasperated. "She's our mate too. You have to let us near her."

No. Not their mate. They didn't want me.

The tiger huffed again. She'd been hurt by them just as I

had, but the pull to their beasts would be harder for her to resist.

"Wildcat, can you shift?" Wyatt's voice came from somewhere at my back. "I'll be able to carry you to the infirmary once you do."

I growled.

"Easy, Killer." Heath crawled closer, and he reached to pet my nose. My tiger let him get one good stroke in before I took over and snapped my teeth at him. Heath chuckled, but it sounded forced. "None of that. We don't bite our mates."

I managed an angry snarl before the pain crescendoed, making me dizzy.

"Don't agitate her," Aiden barked at Heath.

"Just because she's pissed at us doesn't make it any less true," Heath barked back. "She's our Fated."

Just hearing the word brought back the echo of ecstasy marred by bone-deep hurt that had consumed me the moment my tiger had laid eyes on these men in their glorious beastly forms.

I couldn't deny it. Mallory had waxed poetic many times about how it felt when her cat and Allen's wolf realized they were Fated. I recognized it for what it was.

It was supposed to be the most joyous moment that an incredibly rare few of us would ever experience.

And yet mine had been tainted.

By all the cruel things these men had said to me to push me away.

By their buying into the bullshit smear campaign that'd been waged against females with a beast for millennia.

And by their abandonment in this forest when I'd needed them the most.

It was too little, too late.

I hate them, I thought at my tiger.

She whined again—mournful, angry, desperate.

Pain scorched my body, and everything went black once again.

To Be Continued

༄

Avery and the boys are back in Shifter Guardians Academy Book 2 - Edge of Steel.

Want to read a draft of Chapter 1? Sign up for my newsletter to receive all my bonus content.

ACKNOWLEDGMENTS

Oh nooo. What now?? Do not worry—Avery will be fine, but she will also be more than a little pissed off at these boys. Camp is going to be interesting. Will the boys be able to win Avery back? Or will Ian murder all of them before they have a chance?

Don't forget—you can read a preview of the draft of Chapter 1 of the next book (which features Avery's stint in the infirmary and yes, the return of her dads) by signing up for my newsletter. The welcome email contains a link to download the epub file containing all my bonus material. If you're already signed up for my newsletter, the link is in the release-day email!

Thank you first to you, reader, for picking up this book. I know you have an endless mountain of choices to wade through when looking for a book, and taking a chance on a new series or author is always a bit of a gamble. If you're new to me, welcome and thank you! If you're not, thank you for coming back for more!

To Morgan for reading as I write, being a sounding board, and assuring me that no, there was not too much Dr. Lee thirst in this book.

To David for helping me sort out the shifter legends and lore.

To Cherie for the beautiful cover. We did a little something different for us on this one, and I'm so thrilled with how it turned out.

To Kaitlin for the beta read and the thoughtful comments.

To McKinley and Jamee for the riotous time I always have going through their excellent edits and hilarious comments.

To Rahaf for the sage career and life advice.

To Rachel for holding my hand through my first signing events.

And to Eliana Lee, Kate Farlow, Jaymin Eve, Sinclair Kelly, Lola Rock, Amanda Richardson, Lucy Smoke, Grace McGinty, Merri Bright, Morgan B Lee, and Sarah Reynolds for being awesome and supportive colleagues and pals.

ALSO BY ELIZABETH DEAR

Shifter Guardians Academy

Paranormal/Modern Fantasy Why Choose

Clash of Claws

Edge of Steel (April 2026)

Rage of Beasts (TBA)

A Knight's Revenge

Dark Contemporary Academy Why Choose

Storm the Gates

Seize the Castle

Kill the King

Max & Frankie: A Knight's Revenge Novella *(M/M)*

A Knight's Revenge: The Complete Series

The Dylan St. James Omegaverse

Contemporary Why Choose A/B/O

Dylan St. James: Omega Concealed

Dylan St. James: Omega Revealed

Seraphina Bryce: Omega Unleashed

Daisy: TBA

Blackstone Academy

Paranormal Wolf Shifter Romances

Mave Fortune: A Rejected Mates Story *(M/F)*

Ben Fortune: A Shifter Love Story *(M/M)*

Knox: An Alpha's Redemption Story *(M/F)*

Asher's Story: A Blackstone Academy Novella *(M/M)*

Standalone Shorts

Haunted Games: A Masked Man Romance Novella *(M/F)*

ABOUT THE AUTHOR

Elizabeth is a corporate girl who recently discovered she's also a dreamer and storyteller. She's a military spouse, a mom, and a lover of genre fiction, especially romance and urban fantasy. Academy romances were her first love. When not writing or spending time with her family, her favorite pastime is going on a journey with a powerful heroine, her sexy, obsessed love interest(s), and a cast of characters she'll still think about days later.

While always a romance writer, Elizabeth tends to jump around the subgenres and romantic pairings. Her specialty is strong and uber-competent female leads with a backbone and a smart mouth. Elizabeth also discovered that readers love that her heroines tend to have supportive, loving families—particularly strong sibling relationships—so she tries to incorporate that into each of her series. She loves to write action, suspense, banter and steam.

For info and links to all the things, including my newsletter sign up, please visit my website at elizabethdearwrites.com.